Learning the Ropes

Also by T. J. Kline

The Cowboy and the Angel
Rodeo Queen

Learning the Ropes

T. J. KLINE

AVONIMPULSE

An Imprint of HarperCollinsPublishers

Excerpt from *Rodeo Queen* copyright © 2013 by Tina Klinesmith.

Excerpt from *The Cowboy and the Angel* copyright © 2014 by Tina Klinesmith.

Excerpt from *Finding Miss McFarland* copyright © 2014 by Vivienne Lorret.

Excerpt from *Take the Key and Lock Her Up* copyright © 2014 by Lena Diaz.

Excerpt from *Dylan's Redemption* copyright © 2014 by Jennifer Ryan.

Excerpt from *Sinful Rewards 1* copyright © 2014 by Cynthia Sax.

Excerpt from *Whatever It Takes* copyright © 2014 by Dixie Brown.

Excerpt from *Hard to Hold On To* copyright © 2014 by Laura Kaye.

Excerpt from *Kiss Me, Captain* copyright © 2014 by Gwen T. Weerheim-Jones.

EPub Edition SEPTEMBER 2014 ISBN: 9780062370082

Print Edition ISBN: 9780062370105

JV 10 9 8 7 6 5 4 3 2 1

For my non-cowboy, football-loving boys.
Thank you for always keeping me on my toes
and reminding me of the joy boys bring.

Chapter One

ALICIA KANANI SLAPPED the reins against her horse's rump as he stretched out, practically flying between the barrels down the length of the rodeo arena, dirt clods kicking up behind them as the paint gelding ate up the ground with his long stride. She glanced at the clock as she pulled him up, circling to slow him to a jog as a cowboy opened the back gate, allowing her to exit. 16.45. It was good enough for only second place right now. *Damn it!* If only she'd been able to cut the first barrel closer, it might have taken another tenth of a second off her time.

She walked her favorite gelding, Beast, back to the trailer and hooked the halter around his neck before loosening his cinch. The titter of female laughter floated on the breeze, and recognition dawned as the pair of women moved from behind her trailer. Alicia cringed.

"Look, Dallas, there's Miss Runner Up." Delilah jerked her chin at Alicia's trailer. "Came in second again, huh?" She flipped her long blond waves over her shoulder. "I guess you can't win them all . . . oh, wait," she giggled. "You don't seem to win any, do you? That would be me." The pair laughed as if it were the funniest joke ever.

"Isn't it hard to ride a broom *and* a horse at the same time, Delilah?" Alicia tipped her head to the side innocently as Delilah glared at her and stormed away, dragging Dallas with her.

Delilah had been a thorn in her side ever since high school when Alicia first arrived in West Hills. There'd never been a lack of competition between them but, years later, only one of them had matured at all.

Alicia snidely imitated Delilah's laugh to her horse as she pulled the saddle from his back and put it into the back of the trailer. "She thinks she's so funny. 'You haven't won, I have,'" she mimicked in a nasally voice. "What a bitch," she muttered as she rubbed the curry comb over Beast's neck and back.

"I sure hope you don't kiss your mother with that mouth."

"Chris!" Alicia spun to see Chris Thomas, her best friend Sydney's brother, walking toward her trailer. She hurried over and gave him a bear hug. "Did you rope already?"

"Later tonight, during the slack. Too many entries, so hopefully we finish before the barbecue starts."

She'd rodeoed with Chris and Sydney for years until Chris had gone pro with his team roping partner. For the last few years, they'd all been pursuing the same goal, the National Finals Rodeo in their events. So far their paths hadn't crossed since Sydney's wedding nearly two years ago. She'd suspected she might see him here since they were so close to home and this particular rodeo boasted a huge purse for team ropers. Her eyes did a quick survey of him, realizing the past couple of years had been very good to him. Unfortunately, he had always oozed self-confidence and she was sure he was aware of the fact.

"I see Delilah's still giving you a hard time."

She shrugged and gave him a half-smile. "She's still mad I beat her out for rodeo queen when Sydney gave up the title."

"That was a long time ago. You'd think she'd let it go." Chris stuffed one hand into his pockets and leaned against the side of her trailer, patting Beast's neck. "Maybe you should put Nair in her shampoo like she did to you."

Alicia cringed at the memory. "Ugh! It was a good thing I smelled it before I put it on my head. That could've been traumatic. But I got her back."

Chris laughed out loud. "Didn't you put liniment in her lip gloss?"

She pinched her lips together, trying to keep from laughing, at the reminder of the prank. They had some good times together in the past. She wondered how they'd managed to drift apart over the past few years. She missed his laugh and the way he always seemed to bring the playful side of her personality to the surface. One minute they were traveling together, the three of them inseparable, and the next they hadn't spoken more than a few words in years.

"So, how'd you do?" he asked.

"Second, so far. Again," she clarified.

Chris gave her a lop-sided grin and crossed his arms over his chest. She tried not to notice how his biceps bulged against the material of his Western shirt or how much he'd filled out since she'd last seen him. And in all the right places.

"Second's nothing to complain about."

"It's nothing to brag about either," she pointed out, tearing her eyes away from his broad chest and trying to focus on the horse in front of her. She went back to brushing Beast, feeling slightly uncomfortable at the way Chris continued to silently watch her, as if he wanted to say something but wasn't sure how to bring it up. She finally turned and faced him. "What?"

He grabbed the front of his straw cowboy hat with his palm and adjusted it nervously. "Are you going to the dance tonight?"

Alicia felt a sizzle begin in her stomach and spiral outward. She fumbled with the brush, nearly dropping it and prayed she'd misheard him. Like his sister, Chris had a heart of gold and would do anything for his friends but, unlike Sydney, he was a flirt. A player. The type of guy with a new girl on his arm at every rodeo and never serious about any of them. He always had been and, she suspected, always would be. But, in spite of the way she and Sydney teased him about his philandering ways unmercifully growing up, she'd always harbored a huge crush on him, even if he'd never seen her as anything more than another pesky sister.

She stared at Beast's back, her hands no longer moving, unsure how to answer him. Chris must have seen her discomfort—he'd always been able to read her too well—and pushed himself away from the trailer, curling his lip with distaste.

"It's not for me," he exclaimed. "That'd be so wrong." He reached over and pinched her ribs, causing her to squeal and scoot away from his fingers. "It's for . . . someone else."

Alicia forced out a shaky laugh. "Are we back in high school again? Did some guy send you over here to see if I *like* him?" She tossed the brush into the bucket in the tack compartment and slipped a flake of alfalfa into a hay net before hanging it on the side of the trailer for both of her geldings, grateful they were easygoing enough to share. She arched a brow and cocked her hip to the side. "If some guy wants me to go to the dance with him tonight, he better be brave enough to ask me himself."

Chris ran his hand over her gelding's neck and shook his head, laughing. "Damn, woman, no wonder you're still single. You're brutal on us guys." He slapped her butt as he walked by. "Maybe, I'll see you there tonight."

"Hey," she yelled after him. "That's mine, and unless you put a ring on this finger, keep your hands to yourself."

Chris shot her a quick wave but continued to laugh. She watched as he walked away, trying to drag her eyes away from admiring the way he filled out his jeans and to slow her racing heart. Then he looped his arm around the shoulders of a pretty redhead who didn't look like she'd ever touched a horse, let alone ridden one. *She might be looking for something to ride, but it isn't a horse.*

She rolled her eyes as she turned back to her animals,

trying to quell the flutter in her stomach. She couldn't believe Chris could still make her feel this way. It didn't even make sense. She would never act on her feelings for him. In fact, she'd never told anyone, not even Sydney. It was just a stupid, girlish crush. Chris was nothing more than a friend, not to mention one of the most eligible cowboys on the circuit. And she was just a girl from the poor side of the barn who never registered as anything more than a nuisance on his radar.

CHRIS SAT ASTRIDE his bay gelding, Jaeger, in the practice arena, one leg casually looped around his saddle horn, while he and David waited for their turn. There were at least thirty pairs of team ropers in the slack and, so far, it was taking forever to get through them. At this rate, they were never going to make it in time for the barbecue tonight. His stomach rumbled, reminding him he hadn't eaten all day.

"Who was the girl you were talking to earlier?"

He casually glanced at his partner, David Greenly. He raised his brows at his friend. "Why? Interested?"

David shot him a disdainful glare. "Hardly."

They'd been rodeoing together for the last five years and when David encouraged him to go pro, Chris jumped at the chance. The two of them shared a common goal—to win the National Finals so they could open a roping school together. However, it took time to build their reputation and Chris wasn't known for his patience. He needed to remember they were taking it one step at a time, one go-round at a time. In the meantime, he wanted to enjoy every spare moment, while David seemed content to be a workaholic.

At this point, they knew each other well enough to finish the other's sentences. If he didn't watch himself, David would realize Chris was setting him up. Chris was tired of watching David push himself day after day, striving to be the best without any thought to what he was giving up. If he heard it once, he'd heard David complain about wanting to settle down and have kids a thousand times. Neither was high on Chris's list of priorities, but that didn't mean he couldn't help his friend have what he wanted—the family he'd missed growing up with a single dad on the rodeo circuit. Besides, he was tired of David being his wingman and never having a woman of his own. It was beginning to make him feel guilty, like he was hoarding the ladies all for himself.

Not that. Chris had any intention of getting tied down like his sister had, regardless of his mother's begging for another grandchild. It wasn't that he had anything against the institution of marriage, he was just having too much fun enjoying his freedom.

He shot David a sly look. "I've talked to a lot of girls today. Which one are you talking about?"

"At the trailer. The barrel racer with the paint?" David absent-mindedly slapped the end of his rope against his thigh while his horse hung his head, bored and dozing. "She didn't look like one of your usual bunnies."

He was known to flirt with the women who lurked behind the chutes trying to find a cowboy to tame. Chris chuckled at the thought. Like he would ever be tamed. "Dark hair? Really pretty?"

"Yeah, she was pretty." David shrugged but didn't look away. "I suppose."

Chris could see he was interested but didn't want to appear overly so and laughed at him. "That's Alicia Kanani, Sydney's best friend. You don't remember her?"

He looked surprised. "The one who was rodeo queen a few years ago?"

"That's the one. Why? Want me to talk to her for you?"

David frowned and shook his head. "The last thing I need right now is a female distraction. You don't either," he pointed out. "Get your head in the game. We are sitting fourth in the standings and we need to be higher before the National Finals."

"Yes, sir." Chris snapped him a mock salute while David glared at him. "But if you think I'm going to act like a monk because you do, you're insane. With all these available females just vying for my attention? I mean, just look at them."

Chris nodded his head toward the fence where several women in miniskirts, cowboy boots, and half-shirts waved, trying to catch his attention. He winked at one of the women along the fence line and laughed as she started whispering to her friend. "You see? I'm just being friendly, the way my mama taught me."

"Sure you are." David shook his head and jerked his chin toward the chutes. "Quit fraternizing with the bunnies and pay attention. We're almost up."

The pair jogged their geldings to the gate and waited for their turn. As the steer was loaded into the chute, David walked his mount into the heeler box while Chris urged his into the opposite side and waited for the cowboy manning it to stretch the barrier rope across the front. He backed his horse into the corner of the box, feeling his haunches bunch under him, twitching with anticipation.

Chris settled the loop of his rope in his right hand, slipping his reins through his left until they were exactly the way he liked them. His gelding pawed his front foot, anticipating his opportunity to bolt forward. He inhaled deeply, practically tasting the damp earth. A slow smile spread over his lips. He loved this life.

Settling into the saddle, murmuring to his gelding, he let out the breath. He glanced over the chute at David and, seeing he was ready, nodded to the cowboy who released the steer from the chute. He nudged the gelding's sides, breaking from the box as the rope snapped, clearing him to make a clean run.

Swinging the loop over his head, he felt the rope slide deftly through his fingers until instinct told him it was exactly the size and position he wanted it to be. Reaching his arm forward, he tossed it perfectly over the steer's horns, flipping his hand over and catching the rope in his fingers as he simultaneously wound it around the saddle horn and turned his gelding. He directed the steer forward, the rope pressing against his thigh, as David aimed his loop downward to catch the steer's back feet. Watching over his shoulder, he heard the zip of the rope and saw David catch both feet. Chris spun his horse to face his partner, stretching their ropes taut as the official snapped his flag, signaling their time. 5.2. It was a great time; enough for first place, but they wouldn't know if they could hold their position until after tomorrow's performance.

The men rode toward one another causing the rope to loosen and slip from the steer's hind legs. David wound his rope as Chris followed the steer to the end of the arena where another cowboy removed his rope and a third opened the back gate for him to exit.

"Nice run, Chris."

He twisted in his saddle in time to see Alicia loading her horses into her trailer. "Thanks. You're leaving?" A curl of disappointment twisted through his gut, surprising him.

"Yeah, if I leave now, I can get home in time to help Dad feed the horses."

"Oh." He noticed David riding up behind him. "Hey, do you remember David Greenly?"

"Who wouldn't? You're practically rodeo royalty," she said, her pretty almond eyes turned toward David as she smiled up at him. "That was a great catch."

"Thanks," he muttered.

Chris looked from one to the other and frowned. David might be a man of few words but he'd never known him to be shy. He wondered at David's uncharacteristic surly frown. From the way his eyes slid over her curves, he was obviously attracted to her but you sure couldn't tell it by the look on his face. If he could get David to loosen up and find a nice woman to put up with his hypercompetitive, driven nature, they could start having fun roping again. Right now, David seemed intent on making it work.

He knew David's dad was putting him under a lot of pressure to make the Finals this year, and Chris could see it taking a toll. David needed to find a woman to loosen David up while keeping his eyes on the championship, and Chris was sure Alicia was perfect for him. Sweet and fun, she'd always been a smart girl with ambition and a knack for talking them both out of trouble. She was just as driven as either of them. To tell the truth, growing up he'd always wanted to hook up with her himself but didn't want the complication that would arise from dating his sister's best friend. If David let himself, Chris knew he would fall for her dark beauty immediately. That is, if he would quit frowning and actually talk to her.

Chris leaned on the horn of his saddle as Alicia locked the back gate of her trailer and leaned against it. "How is your dad? I haven't seen him since the rodeo last year."

"Good, still working at the Diamond Bar." She crossed her arms, leaning against her trailer and smiled up at him.

"He hasn't moved on yet?"

Alicia cocked her head. "As if he would ever leave. He's been working for them since before I was born."

"And your mom?"

Alicia glanced at David, sitting stick-straight in the saddle, his eyes sliding over her as if he was trying to gauge her worth. It wasn't hard to see he was uncomfortable and wanted to move on. Chris knew David was irritated with him, but Alicia was sure to think she was the cause and Chris wanted to warn him to dial back the attitude. Just because his family was rodeo champion stock didn't mean Alicia was going to let someone treat her like chopped liver.

"She's still working for them too, running their house. I'm sure she'd love for you to stop by to say hi before you head out of town."

"I'm sure we could do that." Chris sat up and glanced at David. "Matter of fact, we're finished. If you want to wait for us, we can load our rig and head over to the house to help your dad feed." He didn't wait for David to agree, avoiding the pointed look he shot at Chris.

David sighed and shook his head, clenching his jaw. He refrained from commenting but it didn't hide his irritation. Chris glared at him in warning. What did David have to complain about? Chris was setting him up with a beautiful woman—unless David didn't realize what Chris was doing and thought Chris was trying to hook up with her. The thought almost made him laugh out loud. David would know by now that Chris liked women without strings attached. No commitments, ever. Alicia was the opposite. She was the girl you built forever with and Chris had no interest in forever. But, David? He was a different story.

Chris wasn't worried that Alicia might not be interested in his partner. He was the type of guy every girl wanted to settle down with—sturdy, dependable, ambitious—and for some reason, women were drawn to his "Aw shucks" demeanor. Chris had enough of them ask him about his friend to know the air of dependable, quiet strength surrounding him was what women sought in marriage material. They weren't looking for a fun-loving, irresponsible husband. They wanted a guy they could count on and, of the two of them, that was definitely David.

Alicia glanced at David again cautiously. "I'm sure Mama and Daddy would love for you guys to come have dinner with us but I'm not sure David wants to."

Chris shot David a warning look and cocked his head, smiling at Alicia's forthright comment. "Who cares what this guy wants." Chris jerked a thumb at David. "I'd love a home cooked meal. I'm sick of his ironed grilled cheese and cold French fries." He grimaced and she laughed.

"It can't be that bad."

"It is," David agreed, barely cracking a smile. Chris wished his friend would just lighten up for a few minutes. "I guess I'll get started loading the horses then. Sounds like I'll see you in just a bit, Alicia." David spun the horse and headed past several large stock trailers on his way to the one he shared with Chris.

Alicia watched him leave, curiously, before raising her brows and turning to Chris. "Wow, he's kinda intense."

Chris stifled a chuckle, glad she wasn't judging him by their first encounter. "Yeah, but he's a good guy and I know he's got my back no matter what."

"You mean he'd bail you out of any kind of trouble you get yourself into," she said, jingling her keys, trying to hide the smile tugging at the corners of her lips.

"I mean, he has. Several times," he clarified before giving her a guilty smile. "Probably will again before this weekend is over." Chris glanced back in the direction David had gone. "I better go help him. If you want to head out, we'll just be a few minutes behind you. I think, after all these years, I can still remember the way," he said before winking at her and watching her pull out of the arena before nudging his gelding toward his trailer.

As he rode closer, he could see the fury in David's face and wondered at the wisdom of their dinner plans.

"What the hell was that?" David tossed the saddle blanket into the trailer. "I thought we were going to go to the barbecue before we headed out tonight. We were leaving remember?"

Chris shrugged off his friend's anger. "So? We have a change in plans. It's not a big deal." He loosened his gelding's cinch. "Since when do you complain about a meal you don't have to pay for?"

"I'm not complaining about the meal. I'm complaining about you being so obvious." He leaned over his gelding's back and crossed his wrists. "If I want a date, I'll get one myself. I don't need your help."

"Yeah, because it's happened so often over the past three months."

David shook his head and sighed as he brushed the horse. "Have you ever stopped to think that not everyone is like you? You have more notches on your bed than I have trophy buckles."

Chris laughed out loud. He wasn't offended by David's comment. He knew he had the reputation of being a playboy and he'd never tried to correct the rumors that he slept with the women he flirted with. He'd assumed they would get cleared up eventually. The truth was, when they were on the road, he gave most women a ride home only when they were too drunk to drive, and then he slept in his truck or a spare bedroom if they were generous. He'd seen the devastation drunk driving created after losing a friend on her way home from a rodeo. After that night, he vowed to do his best to see any woman home safely. He'd never thought it might make him look like a dog.

Then there were the women he took home because he was afraid if they were left to their own devices, they'd be taken advantage of by some of the less than gentlemanly cowboys who preyed on "buckle bunnies." Sure, he was a red-blooded man and there were nights he didn't go to bed alone, but not nearly as many as people suspected. But only Sydney knew the truth. These rumors following him were getting out of hand and he was going to need to clear all of it up before it bit him in the ass.

"Walk a mile in these boots, my friend, and you might find it's not all you think it is." He shook his head. "I'm sick of listening to women trying figure out how to get your attention. Alicia is a pretty, sweet woman who can cowboy with the best of them. I just thought you two have a lot in common and you're not the type of guy to love 'em and leave 'em so I know you won't hurt her. Besides, you'd better settle down and start having that family you talk about soon or you're gonna be too old to have kids."

"Whatever, Chris." David rolled his eyes and tossed the brush into the shelf on the door. "You've already roped me into this. It's not like I can back out now. It just would've been nice to have some warning."

"It's feeding some horses. We have to do the same with our own."

David untied his horse's lead rope and loaded him into the trailer. "Just do me a favor and ask first next time."

"Sure." Chris chuckled quietly, congratulating himself on a match well-made. Tonight they'd have dinner and, hopefully, he'd convince the pair to go to the dance. Tomorrow, they'd head out and, if all went according to plan, David would be so busy watching for Alicia at the next rodeo that Chris might get ten minutes all to himself.

Chapter Two

ALICIA PULLED THE truck into the circular drive, hoping there was enough room for both rigs to fit in front of her parents' tiny modular home. She was worried about Chris and David coming over. She wasn't blind. She knew Chris was trying to set her up with David, which was embarrassing enough, but she didn't really want him to see where she lived. Her parents worked hard but she wasn't exactly proud of the fact her mother was a glorified housekeeper and her father cleaned stalls for a living. She sighed, guilt sweeping over her. She hated feeling ashamed of her upbringing but the emotions wouldn't stay buried.

Face it, you're poor, she scolded herself. *That's not going to change anytime soon.*

She'd always been the poor kid growing up. When she was young, she'd worn clothes that smelled like moth balls and musty books, never owning anything new or firsthand. What she wouldn't have given for a trip to the mall, just once. Even when they'd moved into West Hills and she'd gone to high school, everything had been second hand. She'd been grateful for even the little she had, but it wasn't easy when she saw girls coming to school in every new fad, while she was wearing the same jeans she'd had for four years. She hadn't wanted anyone to know so she learned to sew, managing to refurbish thrift store deals into Western couture, and made all of her own riding shirts for rodeos. She'd even sold a few of her designs to other queen contestants to make ends meet and help her parents out. Chris knew because he'd seen it firsthand over the many years she and Sydney had been friends, but what would David Greenly think when he saw what little they had?

You saw the look on his face. He'll think you're not worth his time.

She sighed as her mother came onto the porch. Alicia had already called her from the rodeo grounds to let her know Chris and David were coming to dinner. Of course, her mother was thrilled. Both of her parents adored Chris since meeting him. Who could blame them? Everyone loved Chris. He was one of those people who excelled at everything with minimal effort. His easygoing nature drew others to him like a magnet and he never seemed to lack people vying for his attention, especially women. Not that he ever turned them away. In all the years she'd known him, she couldn't believe he'd never realized she had a crush on him, too. Maybe, like David, he didn't think she was worth his time and attention.

Alicia unloaded her horses and turned them loose into the small pasture beside their home. Both geldings took off at a run, kicking their hooves into the air as she hung the halters on the hook beside the gate.

"Where's Dad?" she called to her mother.

"He's out in the mare barn, feeding." Her mother looked toward the gate. "Where are Chris and his friend?"

"They're loading up and will be here in a few minutes. Does Dad need my help?"

Her mother waved her off. "The boys can help him. I'm going to head over to the house and get dinner on the table for Mrs. Langdon. I'll be back in a few minutes but can you take the lasagna out and put the garlic bread into the oven in ten minutes?"

"Sure, Mom." Alicia headed into the house, plugging her phone into the charger on the counter. "Anything else you need me to do?" She took a bottle of water from the refrigerator.

"Nope, Dad will be in after he checks on the yearlings."

Alicia sighed as she watched her mother walk down the pathway leading to the main house. She'd been the Langdons' housekeeper and cook throughout her pregnancy while Alicia's father ran the entire stable of champion cutting horses. For years, the Langdon family had been trying to get Alicia to work for them, showing their horses and training, but she couldn't give up on rodeo and settle for the same life her parents had. The Langdons were wonderful people who had taken care of both of her parents over the many years in their employ but Alicia refused to quit rodeo until she reached the pinnacle—the National Finals Rodeo. She had to prove to herself and everyone else that she wasn't just some poor kid the Langdons helped. Reaching her goal would also help her do the one thing she wanted most: help her father train his own horses instead of someone else's. Watching her mother head over to the Langdons when she should be having dinner with her family made Alicia realize that nothing short of the Finals would be enough.

She sighed, rising from the chair as the buzzer sounded, and reached for the oven mitts her mother left on the counter. This year she was closer than ever to making the Finals. She might not win every rodeo but the second place purses were adding up. If her luck and her geldings continued to hold out, she'd place in the top ten this season and be in Las Vegas competing this December. The mere thought caused flutters of nervousness in her stomach.

Her parents didn't have any idea what she was planning but she already had her eyes on a ranch on the outskirts of town. Nothing as large as the property the Langdons owned, but it was plenty of room for the three of them to build a house and enough space for her father to finally raise his own horses, the way he'd always talked about doing. Adding this season's winnings to what she'd already saved over the past two years should give her enough for a nice down payment. But she didn't want to get her parents' hopes up until she put an offer on the place. She couldn't bear to get their hopes up only to have it fall apart later.

DAVID PARKED THE truck behind Alicia's trailer and looked around at the tiny house. "Not much to the place, huh?"

"We can't all have parents who own cattle ranches or were world champions," Chris pointed out, wondering if David realized he sounded like a snob.

His friend arched a brow at him in indignation. "I wasn't criticizing, just stating a fact. Sensitive much?" David climbed from the driver's seat and Chris followed.

Maybe he was being a bit oversensitive but he knew how Alicia hated being judged for her parents' lack of money and he didn't want to see David get off on the wrong foot from the start. Noah Kanani had come from Hawaii and worked hard to earn the respect of Bradley Langdon, one of the largest cutting horse breeders in the nation. Jessenia was one of the sweetest women he'd ever known and he'd thought of her like a second mother when he was younger. As much as he hated to see how hard she worked as both housekeeper and cook for the Langdon family, he could only imagine how it troubled Alicia.

"Hey," Alicia called from the front porch. "You can either tie your horses to the trailer or turn them out in the pasture behind the house. We don't have any broodmares out there right now."

David glanced at Chris, letting him make the decision. "Pasture?"

"Might as well. You want me to do it and you can head inside?" Chris wagged his brows at his friend suggestively.

"Why don't I handle the horses?" David muttered, opening the back of the trailer.

"Chicken," Chris chuckled and shrugged. "Whatever. More food for me." He hurried up the porch steps and followed Alicia into the house, immediately hit with a whiff of Italian spices and garlic. His stomach rumbled loudly and Alicia glanced at him over her shoulder, laughing.

"Dinner is just about ready, if you want to wash up in the bathroom at the end of the hall. Towels are in the bottom cabinet."

"I remember," he said, winking at her. "David should be in shortly. Does your dad need any help?"

She bent over and checked the bread in the oven. "No, Mom just left for the main house but she'll be right back." She shot him a sideways glance and the corner of his mouth curved up. "I think she's pretty excited to see you."

"I've missed your mom. I know I should stop by more often when I'm home. But you know how it is." He shrugged by way of apology. "I'm on the road most of the time and when I do come back, Dad needs my help at the ranch. Time flies and I never realize it's gone."

"I know."

Chris narrowed his eyes, wondering if she really did know. She'd never travelled as much as he and David did, staying close to her parents and helping them whenever she could. Even at that, she was still sitting pretty in the standings.

He watched her adjust the tray of bread in the oven, trying not to notice the rounded curve of her rear, although parts of him were making the task extremely difficult. She'd always been a pretty girl but she was his sister's skinny best friend, smart enough to be a year ahead of him in school even though they were the same age. Back in high school he'd almost asked her to the prom but hadn't been brave enough. When she told him she was going to a rodeo instead, he insisted on driving her and was there to celebrate her first professional win. In the end, he never did ask her out, for fear of jeopardizing their friendship. Instead, he'd forced himself to back off, admiring Alicia from a distance. He arched a brow. He didn't remember her having these curves back then, or even at his sister's wedding.

The front door slammed and Chris tore his gaze, and wandering thoughts, from Alicia's backside, poking his head around the corner to see Jessenia come inside.

"Cristobel!" She hurried forward and enveloped him in a hug, squeezing him impressively for such a tiny woman.

"Jessie!" He laughed at the Spanish nickname she'd given him in high school, as he lifted her from the ground and swung her around once. He placed her back on the floor. "I'm sorry I haven't been by sooner."

She gave him a frown. "I should hope so. I don't even know how long it's been since I've seen you," she scolded in her thick Spanish accent.

Chris tried to look sheepish when he heard the clomping of boots on the steps of the front porch. The door opened as Noah came inside, making sure not to track dirt into Jessie's immaculate house. "I sure hope that cowboy putting horses in the back is with you, young man."

Chris laughed and thrust out a hand to Alicia's father. "He's my roping partner. It's good to see you again, sir."

"Alicia, why don't you go see if that young man outside needs anything else?" Jessie suggested.

Chris wondered if she wasn't already having the same thoughts as he was about the pair and looked over at Alicia, leaning against the side of the doorway, watching their interaction.

"Sure, Mom." Alicia sighed and pushed away from the wall, rolling her eyes as she moved past them to head outside.

"Don't mind her," Noah said as she closed the door. "She's just mad about quitting rodeo."

"I CAN'T BELIEVE I let him get me involved in this," David muttered as he threw two flakes of hay to the geldings.

It wasn't as if they didn't have plenty they needed to work on. What they really should have done was head to Chris's parents' ranch to practice before their second go-round tomorrow. If they didn't get some better times, there was no way they were going to stay in the top ten and get to Vegas. It pissed him off that Chris would rather spend precious practice time flirting with girls from his past, and trying to get him to do the same.

"You know, some people think talking to your horse is a sign of insanity."

The quiet laughter at the pasture gate made him clench

his jaw. She might be a great girl but he wasn't looking to get involved with anyone nor did he have time for a relationship, contrary to what Chris seemed to think.

"Yeah, well, that tends to happen anyway when Chris Thomas is your roping partner."

She leaned her arms over the fence, resting her chin on them. "He does have that effect on people," she laughed. "Need some help?" She pushed herself from the fence and opened the gate.

"I'm about finished, unless you want to grab a can of grain from the trailer?"

"Sure," she said, hurrying toward their trailer in front of the house.

David couldn't help but notice the way her full lips curved into a pretty smile making her dark eyes light up or the slight sway of her hips as she left. She was exactly the type of girl he was attracted to, a girl-next-door with natural beauty, even with her hair pulled back and no makeup. Chris knew it, too, damn him. But what he didn't realize was that it only made him more driven to focus on winning so he could earn enough money to be able to settle down and have the things he wanted in his future—a wife, kids, his own ranch—like his brother.

She returned with a coffee can of grain, shaking it. The horses jerked their heads up and whinnied their approval as she came near, drawing him out of his pointless daydreams, and she passed it to him over the fence.

"Nice looking boys," she commented, jerking her chin toward the animals. "You two are doing pretty well in the standings, at least for now."

David shrugged. "Not if I can't keep Chris's head in the game."

She gave him an understanding smile. "You guys have been roping together for almost five years, right? You know he'll manage to pull it out in the end. I have no idea how he always seems to do it but he does. I wish I had that talent."

He caught her frown from the corner of his eye as he poured the grain over the flakes of hay and locked the pasture gate. "Let's hope so," David grumbled. "Personally, I'm tired of almost making it to the Finals. I want to be there this year and I'm not letting him lose focus."

She cocked her head at him, as if she was trying to read his thoughts, and he wondered if he'd said more than he should've. He didn't normally let his mouth get ahead of his brain and good sense but for some reason this woman had him acting out of character, admitting things he wouldn't under normal circumstances.

"I mean ..." He closed his mouth, wishing he'd just kept it shut from the beginning, and wondered again how she was able to get him to let his guard down so quickly.

"I know what you mean," she cut him off. "It's hard to come so close over and over only to be disappointed, especially when it's not your fault." She glanced up at the back of the house. "I'm hoping to make it to Vegas, too. Even if other people do have a different opinion as to where I should be."

He stopped walking and stared at her, knowing there was far more she wasn't saying. He arched a brow. "Maybe we have more in common than either of us thought."

She smiled at him, and the sadness he'd seen in her eyes disappeared for a moment. "Maybe we do," she agreed.

"So, tell me," he began, looking around him at the various fenced pastures. "What's up with this place?"

"Dad's run the day to day operations for the Diamond Bar for the last twenty-five years and Mom works for them in the house. I guess you could say it's turned into a family affair." The frown was back, marring her brow. "They're nice people and they've been good to us."

"You're sure it's fine for the boys to be in the pasture?"

"What?" She glanced at the horses quietly eating. "Oh, they're fine. It's not like you guys are staying long. It's just dinner."

David felt a twinge of disappointment. She was different than he'd expected her to be. He'd assumed any woman Chris introduced him to would be shallow and, well, a floozy. Alicia wasn't like that at all. He found himself interested in her and wanted to spend more time with her. He needed to stay focused, and keep Chris focused, but they obviously weren't going to do any practicing tonight. Why not invite this pretty barrel racer to the dance tonight after all? If they weren't going to work, maybe one night of fun with an attractive woman wouldn't be such a horrible idea. If nothing else, it might get Chris to quit pestering him.

"THE PLACE LOOKS great, Jessie. I like the new counters in the kitchen," Chris said, reaching for another piece of garlic bread, wiping the excess butter from his hands on the paper towel beside his plate. "Did you have it professionally done?"

"No, I did it myself." Alicia shook her head as her mother blushed slightly at his compliment. "But, thank you."

Alicia caught Chris's eye. "I think you have a little something right there." She rubbed at the end of her nose. David choked back a laugh, covering his mouth with his napkin. Even her father laughed at the joke.

"You hush," her mother warned, playfully slapping at Alicia's arm with her fingertips. "He can compliment my taste any time he wants to if it means he'll come around more often."

Chris smirked at Alicia and turned toward her father. "Dad told me Bradley just sold one of his studs for $12,000. Was it the one you've been training?"

"He was a great horse before I ever got my hands on him. I was just lucky to work with such a talented stud."

Alicia watched her father shake his head, lowering his eyes in humility. She hated that he wouldn't take any credit for the work he did. He was an amazing trainer and was wasting time mucking stalls and grooming for someone else. He should be training and selling his own horses for that price. If only she was able to get the down payment for that property sooner . . . She looked down at her plate, suddenly losing her appetite.

"That's pretty impressive, Noah," Chris commented. "You still afraid of them, Jessie?"

Her mother laughed quietly. "Not afraid, just cautious. They're so big! Did Alicia tell you she will probably be working with Noah soon?"

"Really?" David asked as both cowboys turned to Alicia in surprise. He'd been quiet throughout the meal and Alicia glanced up at him.

She set her napkin on the table and cleared her throat, unsure how to answer the question. She had no intention of taking Bradley Langdon up on his offer to train and show his horses. She wasn't about to get trapped into the same life her parents had, working for a dream that wasn't her own, but she hadn't broken her decision to her parents yet. Until she could offer an alternative solution, or purchase the property she wanted, she'd been stalling.

"Her riding prowess hasn't gone unnoticed all these years and Bradley wants her to show his horses. Maybe even start training a few and giving lessons."

"That's a big accomplishment," David acknowledged, smiling at her.

Her father looked at her proudly and her heart ached. He saw it as such a compliment and she saw it as a prison sentence. How could she ever make him understand?

"I guess," she agreed, hoping they would assume her hesitancy was discomfort and change the subject. "I still have to finish out this rodeo season," she pointed out.

Why was it that no one seemed to care that she wanted nothing to do with helping anyone else earn money from her work? If she ever quit rodeo to train, it was going to be to train her own barrel horses and give lessons on her own ranch. Why did everyone assume she would jump at the chance to train for the Diamond Bar.

Chris frowned, his brows dipping low. "I think it's a waste of talent." Every set of eyes at the table spun to look at him. "I mean, Alicia is an amazing barrel racer, she always has been. Why quit to train cutting horses? Do you even *want* to show cutting horses?"

She glanced at her father, biting her lower lip nervously. He turned to her expectantly, waiting for her answer. She couldn't help but appreciate that Chris seemed to understand her desire to race, voicing her thoughts, but she could've kicked him when she saw the disappointment in her father's eyes. "I don't know. I never really thought about it before."

Chris sighed and rolled his eyes. "You've always talked about being a barrel racer and teaching other girls to run. I never once heard you say anything about showing." He wiped his mouth with his napkin and placed it in his plate. "In fact, I remember you laughing at the girls who went to horse shows."

She saw David's body jerk to the side and Chris shot a glare at David. Alicia silently thanked him for shutting Chris up, even if it was with a kick under the table. This was something she needed to talk about with her parents privately. She didn't need his help or, in this case, him instigating trouble.

CHRIS RUBBED AT the knot forming on his shin and glowered at David.

"Are you guys ready for dessert? Blackberry pie?" Jessie asked, looking at him pointedly. "If I remember right, that's your favorite, isn't it, Cristobel?"

He gave her a grin. "I love your blackberry pie but you've stuffed me with lasagna and garlic bread." He shot a sly look at David who was watching Alicia intently. "I guess I could have a small piece and then work it off dancing tonight."

"I thought you said you wanted to head out?" Chris didn't miss David's suspicious glance.

"We should go to the dance and have some fun." He nodded toward Alicia across the table. "I know how much this one likes to dance. Maybe she could teach you a thing or two. Your moves are pretty horrendous."

"I don't know," Alicia hemmed. "I have to be back down there early tomorrow for the next go-round." She stood and started to clear the table.

"You'll do fine, hon," Noah chuckled. "Beast knows the pattern in his sleep."

Alicia rolled her eyes as she hurried to the sink with the plates, not wanting her father to see her irritation. She needed to focus on tomorrow's run. If she came in first it would move her up in the standings, bump her above Delilah, and add a hefty chunk to her savings. She had to be at the top of her game, not exhausted from dancing with a couple of cowboys, no matter how ruggedly good looking they might be. Although, an ice cold beer and some loud music might curb the frustration building in her right now.

"Come on, Ali." Chris came up behind her with a stack of plates. "It'll be like old times." He cocked his head to the side and gave her the puppy dog eyes that used to get him his way with his sister.

She glanced up at David, who followed Chris into the kitchen, bearing more dishes. He shrugged and looked resigned to Chris getting his way again. She wanted to be angry and shake him. Maybe if people told him no once in a while, he'd understand responsibility and that life wasn't all about fun.

Instead, she looked back at his pleading blue eyes and sighed. Her heart thumped in her chest as he took a step closer before lowering his voice.

"Come on, Ali. You know you want to go."

She did and couldn't fight it when her heart did a flip in her chest. Alicia sighed. "Fine." How did he always manage to turn her brains to mush?

Chapter Three

ALICIA FOUND HERSELF squished between two cowboys in David's pickup truck on her way back to the rodeo grounds to attend a dance she hadn't wanted to be at in the first place. The entire truck reeked of men's cologne, and she wanted to beg Chris to open a window before she choked but kept silent, unsure which of them had taken a bath in the stuff. It practically made her eyes water. What in the world ever possessed her to agree to this?

She tapped her heel on the floorboard nervously, feeling herself on edge but not sure why. Both men were oozing with charm and neither was hard on the eyes, as her mother had pointed out several times before they left, but seated between the two of them, she couldn't help but feel awkward. Most women would kill to be in her position and she just wanted to get out of the truck and get back to her horses. She shifted nervously in the seat and

Chris glanced her way, nudging her with his elbow and jerking his chin in a "watch" gesture.

"First round is on David," he declared.

David turned his head toward them. "Why me?"

Chris smiled broadly and Alicia fought to keep a straight face. Something about him pushed the constant chatter of worry in her head aside and drew out her playful side. "You're the designated driver. It was my turn last time."

David rolled his eyes and looked out the windshield again. "Can't you just go out and have a few beers? Aren't we getting kinda old for this?"

"Okay," Chris laughed, deepening his voice to mock David. "It's time to grow up and be serious, right? Fine. Since you're so old and mature, you can be the designated driver at every rodeo." He shook his head but smiled at his friend. "Can't you loosen up and just have some fun?"

Alicia didn't want to be stuck in the middle of their banter, joking or not, and breathed a sigh of relief when David dropped the truck into park. She shoved Chris out of the passenger side door.

"Easy, woman! Where's the fire?" He moved to let her out.

"I'm trying to breathe some fresh air. I almost died from the lack of oxygen and cologne poisoning. Did you use the entire bottle?" she teased, inhaling deeply the sweet, clean scent of straw in the air as they headed for the entrance gate.

Alicia reached into her wallet to pull out the money for her entry when the girl at the table reached for her hand, connected a band around her wrist and stamped her hand. "Um, I need to pay."

"I've got it," David said, his voice husky and deep.

"Thank you."

Was this a date? Did he expect her to spend the entire evening with him or was he just the designated driver, as Chris said? She wasn't sure what sort of idea he had about tonight and the lack of certainty made her nervous. She glanced up in time to see Chris heading toward the bar at the other end of the makeshift dance floor.

"You know, you don't have to babysit me. You'll have your hands full keeping an eye on Chris."

David followed her gaze in time to see Chris throw an arm around a pretty brunette waiting in line behind him. He turned back to Alicia and chuckled jerking a thumb in Chris's direction. "That's the never-ending chore of a best friend, especially when it comes to that guy. However, I'd much rather hang with you. If you don't mind?" he clarified.

He *wanted* to be with her? This was David Greenly. His father and brother were both world champion rodeo cowboys. He could have his pick of any girl here, and there were several waiting in line from the glances being cast in their direction, and he wanted to be *her* date for the night? She rubbed her suddenly damp palms against the thighs of her well-worn jeans, the best she had in her closet. Maybe this was a pity date, something he promised Chris he'd do as a favor. She eyed him suspiciously. He didn't seem like the type of guy to be dishonest. Quiet and perhaps reserved, but not conniving. Could he be for real?

So far, she liked what she'd seen of David. He might not have Chris's easygoing nature but he seemed mature, responsible, and ambitious. She could appreciate those traits and most cowboys didn't seem inclined to cultivate them.

"You want to dance?" He glanced at the couples already rocking to a quick country two-step as the band played. The steady beat of the drums and bass guitar gradually grew louder as they picked up the pace.

She bit her lip. It had been a long time since she'd danced with anyone. These days, she headed straight home or back to her trailer instead of attending the extra rodeo events. Those she had attended with friends were meat-markets for the groupies who hung out behind the chutes all day waiting to rope their own cowboy. Most of the real cowgirls stayed near their trailers because once the sun went down and the music cued up, it was harder to tell the buckle bunnies from the real cowgirls. Especially once the cowboys had their beer-goggles on.

"I promise, I won't break your toes." The corners of David's mouth tipped up.

It was the first real smile she'd seen from him yet and it was disarming. His dark eyes gleamed with mischief and she had to admit, David Greenly was an enigma. One minute he was serious and the next, teasing. She wasn't sure what to make of him.

"Sure." He reached out for her hand, leading her to the dance floor. "But it's been a long time for me so I can't promise I won't break yours."

He gave her a grin. "I'm sure you can't do too much damage. You can't weigh more than the steer who stepped on my foot last week."

"Hey!" She slapped at his arm playfully as he spun her away from him before twirling her back into his arms and resting one hand at her waist.

"I'm kidding," he teased, his eyes glimmering from the lights surrounding the dance floor as they moved with the other dancers. "That was for the cologne comment."

Alicia rested her hand on his shoulder and looked up at him, apologetically. "I didn't think you heard that." Her eyes fell to the base of his throat and she watched him swallow. "And that was directed more at Chris than you."

"Uh huh."

He didn't sound convinced and she wondered if she'd injured his male ego. She looked back up at him, mesmerized by his dark eyes and the way there was just enough five o'clock shadow on his jaw to give him a natural sex appeal. She inhaled and the scent of laundry detergent and the muskiness of the outdoors filled her senses. So, he hadn't been the one wearing cologne after all. She liked the natural scent of him. His lips were close to hers as he spoke and she watched him form words but her brain wasn't connecting the sound with anything familiar. Finally, he smiled and his voice broke through the haze surrounding her brain.

"Do you want something to drink?"

"What? Oh, sure." She nodded slightly, bumping his chin with her forehead. "Oh, I'm sorry!" She pulled back from him as he chuckled.

"I guess my toes were the least of my worries." He rubbed his jaw. "You've got a hard head." He led her to the stacked bales of hay people were using for seating. "I'll be right back. Beer, water, or soda?"

"Whatever you can get is fine."

David nodded and headed toward the end of the long line for the beer tent. For someone with such a quiet demeanor, he had a mischievous side to his personality she found surprisingly endearing. Her mother always warned her not to judge a book by its cover. Perhaps David's subdued personality only seemed more so because of Chris's boisterous nature, but with his dark good looks, he was every bit as attractive. David wasn't quite as tall or muscular as Chris, a bit on the lean side, but if the muscles she'd felt under her hand were any indication, David was solid as a brick wall. Her eyes grazed over his form, still waiting in the slow-moving line and she bit her lip, wondering why she was even comparing David to Chris.

"Aw, isn't that cute, Dallas? Little Miss Second-Rate thinks she has a chance with David Greenly." Delilah moved toward Alicia, her cat eyes narrowing as she stalked closer. "I heard he was slumming tonight."

Alicia wasn't sure what drove Delilah to make her life hell but she wished she'd find a new hobby. Dealing with her was becoming exhausting. "Don't worry, Delilah, you still win that title. You're still the first choice when a guy wants to slum."

The corner of Delilah's eye twitched and Dallas gasped, covering her mouth in shock but not before Alicia saw the smile she tried to hide. Alicia hadn't expected her comment to hit its mark, especially after some of the other barbs she and Delilah exchanged in the past. Knowing it did only made her feel immature and uncomfortable. This wasn't a real date. David hadn't asked her; Chris had conned them both into coming. Provoking Delilah would only make her go searching for answers and that would surely backfire but Alicia wasn't sure how to backtrack and diffuse the situation.

Delilah glared at her and pointed a manicured finger in her face. "Look, we both know you're nothing but a fraud. Just because you got lucky with a horse that can run doesn't mean you can keep up with the big girls. Go home, clean houses or stalls, whatever it is your parents do, and leave it to the real cowgirls to get the job done."

"Delilah," Chris drawled, looping an arm over her shoulders. "Are you still mad because Ali beat you out for the rodeo queen title?" He clicked his tongue against his teeth, a sympathetic look on his face. "That's probably because even the judges could see she's one hundred percent woman and everything about you is fake." His eyes skipped from her blond extensions to her ample breasts.

Alicia's mouth dropped open in shock. Dallas looked like she wanted to run and hide while Delilah's face turned color, her lips parting in fury. "I . . . you . . . hmph!" She shoved Chris away from her and stormed away.

"Don't be too mad," he called after her. "It's not Ali's fault she's smarter, prettier, and can ride better."

Delilah looked back at him, her eyes narrowing in fury as she flashed her middle finger at him. Alicia couldn't stop the appalled laughter that bubbled up from her chest.

"I can't believe you said that!"

Chris shrugged and rolled his eyes, unapologetically. "She deserved it. I'm tired of watching her prance around every rodeo like she owns it. Just because her father spoils her doesn't give her a right to expect everyone to bow down to her." He looked around. "I can't believe David left you to deal with her alone."

"He's in line." She pointed him out. "And I was doing fine."

Chris snorted. "Yeah, looked like it."

Alicia pressed her hands together over her heart and gave him her best damsel-in-distress voice. "Thank you for the sarcasm, oh knight in shining armor." What made him think she needed his protection? "I've been dealing with Delilah since high school. I know it's hard to believe but, so far, I'm still breathing and my reputation is intact. I'd say I'm doing just fine. Without your help, I might add." Chris looked properly contrite so she dropped it.

He jerked his chin toward his friend. "So, what do you think of David?"

She grinned and shook her head as he changed the subject, blatantly trying to pump her for information. "You just don't give up, do you?"

Chris gave her a guilty grin. "Not until I get my way."

"And you called Delilah spoiled?" She shrugged her shoulders, unwilling to give in so easily or give him the answer he wanted. He was already too confident. "He's okay, I guess."

"What do you mean 'okay'? David's . . . oh, I see, you're screwing with me now." He frowned at her, his deep blue eyes narrowing.

"You're really not good at this matchmaking thing," Alicia pointed out, bumping his shoulder with her own "You're supposed to be subtle."

He sighed in resignation. "Yeah, not my strong suit. I'm usually the set up not the one doing the setting up." He sipped the amber liquid in his cup.

"Why the big push to get us together? I haven't even talked to you since your sister's wedding. For all you know, I have a boyfriend."

He shot her a look of disbelief, looking down his nose, and she hid the stab of pain in her chest. What made him so sure she didn't?

"Sydney would've told me." He shrugged. "And there's not really a hurry. I just hate to see him so serious all of the time. He's so focused on the prize at the end of the road he's forgetting to enjoy the ride." A blond with breasts spilling over the top of her peasant blouse walked by and winked at Chris, his eyes following her movement. "And the perks that go with it."

"Chris, you're a pig," Alicia scolded, crossing her arms over her chest and shaking her head with disapproval. "And I'm nobody's *perk*."

"That's not what I meant and I'm not a pig." He turned back to her, slightly offended." I just appreciate beauty when I see it. Like you." His gaze heated as it slid over her, making her stomach flip awkwardly. Chris finished his beer and tossed the cup into a nearby trash can. He reached for her hand. "Come dance with me. That's a swing I hear playing and you were always a great partner."

Alicia held her hands out. "Oh, no, you don't! It's been a long time and you only liked dancing with me because I was light enough for you to toss around like a rag doll."

"Exactly," he agreed, dragging her out to the dance floor, not giving her another chance to refuse.

The music was fast, a blaring rockabilly rhythm that had Chris twirling, twisting, and spinning her until she gave up trying to figure out which direction was up. A crowd began to surround them, giving them room to dance and cheering them on. She'd forgotten how much fun she had dancing with him. He was a strong lead and she never had to think with him. He was always in the right place at the right time to catch her, no matter where she ended up. When he spun her back against his chest and reached for her hands, her body responded without even thinking. Curling her hands into his, he slid one arm to her lower back and the other under her knees, flipping her into the air and backward over his arm, catching her effortlessly while the crowd cheered. As the strains of the music slowed, Chris spun her back against him and dipped her.

She stared up at him, her dark eyes locking with his deep blue, dizzy from the exertion and trying to regain her focus. Her heart thudded heavily against her ribs, feeling like it would burst. She expected him to lift her to standing again but he continued to stare down at her, his eyes going dark and languid. His fingers at her lower back were against her skin and she could feel the heat burning into her, scalding her and making shivers of delight course up her spine.

She was breathless but, suddenly, she wasn't sure if it was from the exertion or the way he was looking at her. She was the first to break the silence, unable to hold his smoldering gaze any longer without melting in his hands. "Um, Chris, just how long are we going to stay like this?"

The look in his eyes vanished as quickly as it appeared, replaced by his usual grin and impishness. He bent toward her and pressed a quick kiss to her lips, causing her heart to plummet to her toes, before lifting her upright and taking her back to where David waited for them as if nothing had happened.

WHAT IN THE hell was that?

Chris wasn't sure what had come over him. One minute he was flirting with some blond walking past him, the next he was kissing Ali on the dance floor. Of all the women he could kiss tonight, she was the last one he should even consider locking lips with. Here he was pressuring David to ask Ali out and then he kisses her, in front of everyone. What kind of friend was he? He wasn't even sure what had possessed him to do it. He had to get it together.

Damn it! Ali seemed awkward as well, pulling her hand away from his as he walked her back to David, and tucking it into her pocket. He had to do some damage control otherwise this was going to get messy. This was exactly why he'd avoided her for the last two years. He didn't want to ruin their friendship. What was he thinking? He caught the look of surprise on David's face as they headed toward him and quickly decided to play it off as a joke.

David eyed him curiously but refrained from commenting, turning his attention back to Ali and handing her one of the cups he held. "I see I missed all the fun."

"Thanks," she said, taking the drink. "I think I better sit down. I'm dizzy now."

David arched a brow and Chris could read the unspoken question in his eyes. He shook his head slightly, letting David know they could discuss it later. He wasn't about to try to explain his actions right now. Not when he wasn't even sure what to say or what had just come over him. He had to get away from them. Looking around and spotted one of the women he'd been flirting with earlier today standing near the band.

"Thank you for the dance, Ali, but I'm off to enjoy a few of those perks we talked about."

He knew the comment made him sound like a jerk but he didn't want her to get any wrong ideas about why he'd kissed her. Especially when he found himself wanting to do it again and was trying to keep himself from letting his mind stray out of the friend zone.

She laughed at him and his heart skipped. He wasn't sure if it was the sweetness of the sound or the relief that she wouldn't let his mistake affect their friendship. "You'd better be careful, Chris, or one of these days you're going to fall for one of those buckle bunnies and she'll break your heart." She poked a finger against his solid shoulder.

"Unless he catches some disease first," David muttered.

Chris ignored the insult and winked at Ali, giving her a cocky grin. "It'll never happen. It's not in my DNA to fall for anyone."

He realized the honesty of the statement after it slipped out and felt momentarily depressed by the truth of it. Chris saw a flash of sadness in her eyes but it was gone quickly and he almost convinced himself he'd imagined it. His words hung heavily in the air between the three of them, like a wet blanket, and he wasn't sure how to lighten the mood again until a busty brunette bumped into the back of him, knocking him forward and nearly spilling the three beers she carried. She apologized and giggled as she righted herself.

Chris laughed, relieved to have an interruption. "Duty calls." He turned to follow the brunette, grateful for the excuse to leave. "Hey, honey, need some help carrying those?" Chris asked as he disappeared into the crowd.

"I can't believe no woman's ever filed a paternity suit against him," David said as Chris hurried into the crowd after the brunette.

Chris moved far enough that he was out of earshot but could still see Alicia and David through the crowd of dancers. He tried to pretend to listen to the brunette, but he'd already forgotten her name, his eyes strayed to Ali as David took her hand and led her onto the dance floor. As the band struck up a slow country ballad, Chris watched them sway to the music, David's arm curled protectively around her minuscule waist. Ali looked up at him and smiled brightly, her brown eyes lighting up with delight at whatever he was saying. Chris could see it in her face, could tell David interested her, and they seemed to be having a great time together. So far, he'd even seen David loosen up and joke around with her, something he rarely saw, especially at rodeos where he was all business. This was exactly the effect he'd been hoping Ali would have on David. It was what he wanted, so why did he feel like slamming his fist into someone's face?

He saw David tighten his hold on Ali and she tucked her head into the curve of his shoulder, under his jaw, closing her eyes. Chris watched as her fingers trailed over the nape of David's neck and his heart dropped to his toes. He wasn't sure where this jealousy was coming from but he was going to get rid of it the only way he knew how—with a distraction, any distraction, and he needed it right now.

He'd been too busy watching Ali and David to notice the brunette had already moved on but Chris spotted two girls standing off to the left side of the stage, eyeing him like sugar addicts would a piece of candy. "Howdy, ladies," he drawled. "Would one of you like to dance?"

"Me!" A leggy blond shoved past her friend in an attempt to move closer to him. She slipped her hand into his and he led her to the dance floor.

Now this was the type of woman he was comfortable with. Nothing serious, no emotions, and no one got hurt. His eyes slid over several faces on the dance floor until he spotted Ali with David again and clenched his jaw, tripping over his own feet. Chris didn't want to think about Ali anymore. She conjured up too many images of marriage, kids and his future. Better to let her play house with someone who wanted the same things, someone more like David. He was a man she could count on.

Chapter Four

CHRIS SAT ON his gelding, Jaeger, nursing his hangover as the bright light of day pierced the dark sunglasses he wore. He cupped his forehead in his hand, rubbing his temples, trying to will the headache away. The next thing he knew, his head dropped forward with a jerk as he nodded off with the sound of the announcer beating against the sides of his throbbing brain. He cringed as his horse stamped a foot, jarring him, as he tried to remain as still as possible to keep the pounding to a minimum.

"Cool it, Jaeger," he muttered as if the beast could understand him.

"Yeah, Jaeger." David sidled his mount next to Chris's. "Your master is grouchy because he had far too much to drink last night and had to sleep in the backseat of the truck so he didn't embarrass himself."

"Shut up, David."

"I see you woke up on the wrong side of the truck this morning." He laughed at his own joke before stretching his arms toward the sky and yawning loudly. "Not like the bed in the extra bedroom. You were right. Dinner at Ali's house was a great idea after all."

Chris glared at his best friend before remembering he couldn't see the daggers he was shooting at him from behind the dark glasses. He didn't usually drink so much but when feminine distractions didn't work to take his mind off Ali and David, he turned to drink.

And when did David start calling her "Ali"? That had always been Chris's nickname for her. No one else called her that. How close did David and Ali actually get last night?

"You're a dick."

David chuckled quietly. "I know. Make sure you're ready. We're up in a few minutes. We need this win."

"Yeah, yeah. You just worry about your own loop, not mine." He wasn't in any mood to deal with David's redis-covered sense of humor. "What's got you in such a good mood this morning anyway?" He regretted the question as soon as it left his mouth.

David looked at his saddle and adjusted his reins, unable to hide the grin that spread across his face. "You mean, besides a comfortable bed, a filling breakfast, and a pretty girl giving me a kiss this morning for good luck?" He shrugged. "I guess nothing."

"I thought you didn't care about dating, that it was a waste of your precious time?"

"I'll admit it. Ali wasn't what I expected."

Chris took off his sunglasses and handed them to the cowboy opening the gate for them. "Then maybe you should be thanking me instead of giving me a hard time." He shot a sidelong glance at David, still grinning like a Cheshire cat. "Ali kissed you, huh?"

He looked over at David suspiciously. Maybe he was just screwing with him? Chris hadn't missed the funny look David gave him after seeing him on the dance floor with Ali; maybe this was his way at getting back at him. Or testing the waters to see if Chris was interested in Ali for himself? The thought struck him in the chest. He wasn't, was he?

Chris didn't want to even begin to think about why he felt a knot of dread forming in his gut any more than he wanted David to suspect his jealousy. It was irrational so he stuffed it deep within but it chewed at the edges of his mind. Ali wasn't the type of girl to kiss a guy right after meeting him. At least, she hadn't been before. Maybe she'd changed in the past two years since he'd spent any significant amount of time with her. People could change and not always for the better. Chris clenched his jaw, trying to focus on the task at hand. He didn't have time to be worrying about Ali.

Easing his horse into the chute, Chris turned Jaeger so he could back the gelding into the corner. He casually flipped the loop over his wrist and slid the eye of the rope forward until it felt right. Jaeger's hind end tucked under him as Chris adjusted his reins, shortening them. He looked over at David who waited, watching for Chris's nod, with his rope at his hip. Chris tipped his chin down at the chute operator just before the steer burst through the gate, jerking the barrier rope free as it passed. Jaeger came out of the gate quickly, eating up the ground with his long stride as Chris swung the rope over his head. He let it fly as he came alongside the steer and watched it hit the tip of a horn before slipping off and circling in front of his horse.

How could he have missed? He never missed.

The crowd's groan echoed across the arena. Chris quickly rewound the rope and set his loop again, swinging over his head as David kept the steer running straight. This time, it circled the steer's horns cleanly and he twisted the rope around the saddle horn, turning Jaeger sharply to the left. David was already in place and immediately caught both heels. He looked toward the clock as the announcer called out their time: 9.6.

This was definitely going to keep them out of the money and knock them down a few places in the overall standings. He braved a glance at David. His face was a dark mask of fury as he refused to look at Chris. Clenching his jaw so tightly it caused his teeth to hurt, Chris headed to the back of the arena with the steer as he watched David ride out.

Damn it!

Chris might act nonchalant, like he was coasting through life, but he knew this was a big loss and was going to cost them. He didn't want to face David right now, not when he was the reason they'd lost. What the hell was doing worrying about Ali kissing David when they needed this win? He'd never let himself get jealous over a woman before, why now? He'd better get his head on straight or David was going to kill him.

ALICIA WATCHED THE pair make their run and cringed when Chris missed. It never happened and she worried Chris would spend the rest of the rodeo beating himself up about it. She could see it in the way his shoulders slumped as he rode to the back of the arena and the way he ignored the other cowboys as he dropped his rope over his saddle horn. She knew he wasn't as carefree as he wanted people to believe, at least not when it came to his chosen profession. She wanted to say something, to console him the way she knew he would do with her, but he hurried out the gate before she could even say anything, not even noticing her waiting for him. She hurried to the trailer and found David dismounting. He threw his rope into the tack compartment of the trailer.

"Damn it!"

"You okay?" She was apprehensive. She didn't know David well enough yet to predict how he'd take the loss. She could predict Chris's reaction but David might be one of those guys who preferred to wallow in a loss alone.

He spun to face her, looking surprised to see her at his trailer. "Yeah." He tucked his glove into the seat, behind the saddle horn. "This just really messed us up and he knows it." He leaned against his saddle. "I just don't get it. He never misses."

"I have only a second before I have to go get Beast warmed up but I wanted to make sure you're okay." Alicia glanced over her shoulder, looking through the horses for Chris.

"It's fine. *I'm* fine," David clarified, waving her off, distracted. "Hey, good luck," he said as she started to walk back toward her trailer.

"Thanks, I think I'll need it."

"Hang on." He reached for her hand and pulled her toward him. His fingers found the back of her neck and he leaned forward, his lips meeting hers. He caught her gasp of surprise, taking advantage of the moment to pull her against his chest. Her heart skipped a beat before pounding almost painfully in her chest as her hands found his shoulders.

Even though she hadn't expected it, David's kiss wasn't unwelcome. Last night, he'd barely given her a chaste peck on the cheek after her mother insisted he and Chris take the spare room instead of heading back to the Thomas ranch, even though Chris was already passed out in the backseat of the truck. This morning, she'd barely been bold enough to kiss his cheek for good luck. She certainly hadn't expected this from him.

It had been a long time since a guy had kissed her like this, as if he was trying sear her, to mark her as his own, and she wasn't sure what to think. Last night's sweet gesture sent the butterflies residing in her stomach into flight. By comparison, this kiss should have been enough to melt the sunscreen she'd applied that morning but instead, she felt awkward and she wasn't sure why. When he took a step back, she rocked back on her heels and bit the corner of her lower lip, unsure what to say or if she should say anything.

"I just wanted to wish you luck properly."

She could easily read the desire in his dark eyes and wondered at her lukewarm reaction. It wasn't as if she felt nothing, but it wasn't the electric fireworks she wanted to feel when she found that guy who was meant for her. It might be a girlish fantasy but she couldn't shake the desire to find the guy whose kiss made her heart stop mid-beat. A guy who could send a sizzle of excitement to her toes with a mere glance.

She heard a quiet cough. "I'm not interrupting anything, am I?"

Alicia felt a slow burn creep up her neck and cover her face. "No, I . . . I mean, we . . ." she stammered, turning to see Chris smirking at them.

Her heart tripped up and was suddenly off to the races, beating faster than when David kissed her. The tension between them almost sparked and the heat curling in her belly worried her. *You're supposed to feel this with David. He's the emotionally available one.* But the knowledge didn't stop her heart from racing, or the heat from spreading through her limbs as Chris gazed down at her.

He didn't move to dismount and just stared at her from atop his horse. She wished she could read his eyes but he had those damn sunglasses on again. His grin and words implied he was joking but his tone said otherwise.

"I've . . . uh, gotta go," she said to David, jerking her thumb toward her trailer. "I'll see you in a bit?"

She knew she must sound like a babbling idiot but

she had to get away and get her head on straight. If she didn't gain at least a semblance of control over her body's reactions she was going to make a fool out of herself in front of both men. She needed to focus before her event or she was going to end up the same way they had—at the bottom of the pack and without a paycheck. She glanced back at Chris and David as she walked to her trailer. Chris was just dismounting and tying his gelding to the trailer when David approached him, looking furious. Things were about to get heated when David brought up their run and she didn't want to be there when that bomb went off.

"WHAT IN THE hell was that?" David was furious and barely restraining his anger. Chris had seen him like this before, usually after David spent time with his father, but he knew this time he deserved it. "If you can't sober up enough to do the job, maybe, just maybe, you shouldn't get shit-faced the night before, Chris."

"It had nothing to do with that," he grumbled, loosening the cinch on the saddle.

"Really?" David looked doubtful. "Because you threw like you were still drunk."

"I get it. I screwed up." He shook his head, knowing there was no excuse, prepared to take whatever punishment David saw fit to dole out.

What could he say? That his mind wasn't on the steer running down the arena? That he was too preoccupied thinking about the sexy brunette he'd just seen David kissing? That it had driven him nuts trying to figure out what the hell was wrong with him to even consider kissing Ali last night?

Seeing Ali with David had sucked the wind from him and made him want to punch his best friend. But he couldn't let either of them know how he was feeling. He didn't want to settle down and he certainly didn't want a relationship, not even with someone as great as Ali. Even the thought sounded boring—settling. The mere idea had him feeling like he was being strangled slowly, but the thought of her with anyone else . . . he clenched his fists at his sides and took a deep breath.

Why hadn't he thought this through before he set her up with David? Why didn't he set her up with anyone else, someone he wouldn't have to see her with at every rodeo? He'd spent so many years pretending his desire for her didn't exist that he'd forgotten how strong it was and convinced himself that a lie was truth. Now there was nothing he could do but cowboy up and ignore this jealousy until it faded again.

In the meantime, he owed it to David to bring their rank back up. Chris knew the pressure David was under to be a champion and, even if Chris wasn't faced daily with the same overwhelming burden, it was a big part of their future plans for a rodeo school. Without the title that came from winning the National Finals Rodeo at the end of the year, marketing would become a much more difficult prospect.

"We have a few days before our next rodeo. We can stay at Mom and Dad's this week and get some practice time in." He leaned against his saddle and looked at David over the gelding's back. "I promise, we'll do nothing but work."

David eyed him, dubious, arching a brow before tossing his Western shirt into the tack compartment and slipping a t-shirt over his head. "Nothing but work?"

Chris shrugged and laughed quietly. "Okay, mostly work. And I'll buy tonight." David knew him too well.

David glared at Chris. "I'll believe that when I see it." He crossed his arms over his chest and Chris could tell he was debating the proposition. "You're driving, too."

Chris slipped his horse's bridle off and hung it in the tack compartment, trying unsuccessfully to hide his victorious grin. "Deal."

He was getting off cheap with a couple of rounds considering he'd just put them out of the money today. It was the least he could do for David. "Does this mean you're scrapping your 'no women' policy?" He took the saddle David held out to him.

David took a deep breath and Chris could practically see the wheels turning, forming excuses. "Let's not get ahead of ourselves. I don't know. I really like Ali but . . ." David shrugged. Chris clenched his jaw hearing David call her Ali again and sighed. "I just don't know . . . what?" David asked, irritably.

"I didn't say anything." Chris slid the saddle onto the rack and held his hands facing his friend. He might not have said anything but it didn't stop him from getting frustrated with David. Couldn't he see what he had right in front of him?

"You didn't have to say anything. She's a distraction, Chris. All women are. You missing today just proves what happens when even one of us gets distracted. Neither of us can afford it, especially if we plan on moving forward with the school in the next year."

Chris glared at him. He didn't need any more reminders about how he let David down today. He wouldn't be forgetting any time soon. "I wouldn't expect her to wait for you. At this rate, by the time you get around to settling down, you'll be too old for any woman to want."

"You're one to talk." David rolled his eyes. "Look, I'm not trying to beat a dead horse, just stating the facts. We need to figure out what's most important and give that everything we've got."

"You sound like your dad," Chris muttered.

"Screw you, Chris." David started to walk away. As if thinking better of it, he spun on his heel and glared at Chris. "How many NFR buckles do you have? Just because the man acts like a jackass doesn't make him wrong. Maybe, you need to grow up."

He watched his friend storm off, leaving Chris to finish taking care of the horses. He should have kept his mouth shut. He knew David and his father had a complicated relationship. Any conversation about the man was bound to lead to trouble. As much as David hated the pressure his father put on both him and his brother to succeed, both sought the man's approval. As a past roping champion, he ran his sons ragged, pushing them to exhaustion, forcing them to uphold the family name in rodeo. It didn't leave much room for anything else, including the wife and kids Chris knew David wanted or the rodeo school they'd planned to open next year.

DAVID WATCHED FROM the stands as Alicia's horse pranced to the back gate of the arena. The crowd pulsated with excitement, eager for the ladies speed event. He knew how nerve-wracking it was to be the first in any go-round, especially with the crowd as loud as this one, but he could see the determination in her eyes as she focused on the first barrel. Alicia nodded and the cowboy shoved open the gate as her sorrel paint rocked back onto his hind legs, rearing slightly, before bursting into the arena in a flash of color, triggering the time clock. Heading to her right, she pulled the horse's head up as he wrapped his body around the barrel before pressing on toward the second turn.

He almost groaned out loud when he saw her horse drop his shoulder, slowing down as they curled around the barrel. He could hear her encouraging the gelding, yelling for speed as she headed for the final turn. She sat deep into her saddle as he slid toward the final barrel, hugging it closely without touching it. As they rounded the turn, Alicia leaned forward in her saddle, urging him for more speed. David was caught up with the crowd.

"Come on, come on," he muttered, ignoring the look Chris gave him. "Push him," he whispered, glancing at the clock. "You got this."

She was practically lying over the horse's neck, one with the animal as he stretched out, his massive rump rippling with muscles, his hooves pounding in the dirt as she crossed the finish line.

"Ladies and gentlemen, there you have it. The time to beat will be 15.43. That's gonna be tough to do no matter how easy this lovely lady makes it look."

David could see the smile curving her full lips. She was thrilled and wasn't even trying to hide it. It was an amazing ride. He started down the bleachers with Chris right behind when he saw his father across the stands, heading toward him. "Crap," he muttered.

Chris followed his gaze and frowned. "When did he get here?"

"I don't know." David didn't hold out much hope that his father had missed their event. While other people fawned over his father and his past rodeo fame, Chris had seen enough of Colt Greenly's drunken tirades to dread any appearances he made these days.

"Go congratulate Ali. I'll be there in a minute after I see what he wants."

Chris adjusted his straw cowboy hat and looked at David from under the brim. "You sure you don't want me to stay as a buffer?"

David shook his head. "No, I'll take care of him. I just hope he's not planning on hanging around."

He made his way toward his father, noticing the way he was stumbling through the crowded stands. Chances are he was already drunk, which was going to make him antagonistic. It was easier to go to him than to let him try to navigate the bleachers with his bad leg. David knew getting around the rodeos and the ranch was becoming more difficult as the old riding injury flared up more often. It also didn't help that his father looked like he'd gained about twenty pounds in the few months since David had gone back on the road. David talked with his brother about how they could get their dad to a doctor, but his father refused to listen, preferring to drink his pain away, which didn't help his tendency to be vocal in his criticism.

"Hey, Dad." He pretended to be happy to see him but he knew he'd never been good at hiding his feelings.

"You seem kinda cheery for a loser."

David clenched his jaw and inhaled slowly, reminding himself of the people surrounding them and why he couldn't say what he was thinking right now.

"We didn't lose, Dad. We just didn't place in the money." He started back toward the trailer. At least there wasn't an audience there.

His father looked down his nose at his much shorter son. "If you don't get paid, you lost." His father sighed loudly. "It wasn't even you that lost it. I don't understand why you and your brother can't just rope together. Why'd you go and pick this kid for your header?"

"Stop," David warned his father.

His father hadn't agreed with his decision to rope with Chris instead of his brother. Even though his brother suggested the arrangement—one of the only times they'd defied their father—before buying a cattle ranch and settling down with his high school sweetheart. His father still wasn't able to accept the decision. David wished he could put his foot down to his father the way his brother had; however, now that his brother retired from professional rodeo, their father was even more determined that David carry on the NFR torch.

David caught a glimpse of Alicia and Chris walking back toward the trailers, her reins held loosely in her hand as her gelding followed like a dog on a leash. He saw her head fall backward with laughter at something Chris said and jealousy churned in his belly. She was exactly the kind of woman he hoped to find someday and settle down with—kind, determined, ambitious, beautiful inside and out. He hadn't known her long enough to believe she was "the one" but he sure didn't want to miss the opportunity to find out if she might be.

Chris slid his arm around Alicia's slim shoulder and gave her a squeeze. It was a friendly gesture but there was something in the way Chris looked at her that troubled David. There was an eagerness in his friend's eyes he didn't like. He'd seen the same look in Chris's eyes last night on the dance floor. Chris couldn't be interested in Alicia. Why would he have set them up if he were?

"Are you even listening to me?" His father's gruff voice broke into his thoughts. He followed the direction of David's gaze. "Tell me you aren't getting distracted by some bunny."

"She's not a bunny, Dad, and no, I'm not losing focus. I know what I need to do and I'm doing it." He didn't want to throw Chris under his father's scrutiny any further by pointing out that he was the one who'd lost focus this morning. "Everyone is entitled to an off day."

"Not if you want to get to the Finals." His father frowned at Chris and Alicia. "And he needs to remember he's here to rope cattle not women, even if they do throw themselves at him."

"She is not throwing herself at him." David clenched his jaw. "They have been friends for years."

"Yeah," his father scoffed, "they look like *friends*."

David had had enough and spun on his father. "Was there a reason you came? Or do you just want to criticize?"

His father narrowed his eyes, ignoring David's question. "You're falling for some gold-digging barrel racer?"

Colt Greenly was far too observant for his son's liking but David wasn't going to give him the ammunition admitting the truth would offer. He quirked a brow at his father, waiting for him to say what he wanted so he could leave.

He chuckled. "You're a fool, boy. Leave the bunnies alone and stick to the job at hand." He moved down the last few metal steps of the stands. "I'm moving onto your brother's property. We're putting a trailer on the place and I'm selling the ranch."

"What? Why?" David couldn't hide the surprise in his voice. Their ranch had been passed down from father to son for several generations. His father loved the ranch, raised his boys on it. In fact, he'd been furious when David's brother had chosen to buy a ranch instead of running theirs. It might be a lot of work and, with his injury worsening, David knew it was difficult for his father to keep up, but he couldn't picture it being sold to a stranger. "What did Christian say?"

"He knows the ranch is just sucking money at this point. It needs repairs I can't afford. I'll just buy a modular and put it on his property. It will be easier for everyone." His father eyed him as if waiting for David to bite at the bait he offered.

What his father wasn't saying was that if he sold the place, he wouldn't have to work at all and could continue to drink his pain away in privacy. He wondered how much of that money would be used for liquor or gambling. David couldn't help his father if he wouldn't admit there was a problem and Colt had no desire to face his demons.

"I hate to see you sell the place, Dad. Is there something I can do to help?"

"Yeah, win." His father looked around to see if anyone was nearby and lowered his voice. "If you paid off the mortgage I took out on it, it could stay in the family. But you'd need to find someone to run it when you're gone. My leg . . ." He pressed his hand against his thigh, as if trying to remind David of the painful injury. Like the man ever let either of his sons forget what he'd sacrificed.

And when did his father take out a mortgage? The property had been paid in full for years. He had no idea his father had taken out a loan against it but he didn't have the funds to pay it off nor did he know anyone who could run a ranch of that size while he was driving across the country, rodeoing.

"Dad, I . . ." David shrugged. "I would if I could." He looked down at the ground, ashamed to turn his father down.

Colt sighed, his disgust obvious. "That's what I figured." He shook his head. "I thought I did better than this with you boys."

"Dad—"

"No," he interrupted David, holding up a hand. "I don't want to hear it. I'll let you know when the sale goes through. Maybe between now and then you can find some sort of miracle for your old man."

David didn't miss the caustic tone, just one more barb his father passed along to his boys. Wasn't it bad enough he'd antagonized their mother until she ran out, but now he seemed intent on pushing his sons away, too. David watched his father limp away, pasting on a smile when several younger cowboys stopped him, asking for his autograph. He was grateful for the sense of family loyalty his mother and brother instilled in him growing up but, right now, it was nothing more than another boulder on the mountainous pressure weighing him down. *So I'm supposed to carry on the family name and win the title while somehow saving the ranch?* David's hand curled into a fist and he wished he could find something to punch.

Chapter Five

ALICIA LEANED FORWARD on the fence, watching the last of the barrel racers making their runs. So far her time was holding strong; no one had even come near it, but she wasn't ready to celebrate yet. There were three more girls to go and one of those was Delilah and the $200,000 horse her father bought to help her win. Her stomach twisted and did a backflip when she heard Delilah's name called over the loudspeaker. Alicia watched her charge into the arena, leather quirt between her teeth. Determination was etched on her brow and Alicia felt sorry for the horse, knowing Delilah would be whipping it for more speed in the stretch.

As Delilah came around the first turn, Alicia found herself willing the barrel to topple and her heart leapt when she saw how closely Delilah cut the second barrel, certain it would fall. She cringed when she didn't even seem to touch it and her horse continued its furious pace toward the second and then third barrels before speeding home. Alicia glanced at the clock as Delilah's horse stretched out, running hard, and seconds ticked past. 15.39 . . . 15.40 . . . 15.41. The buzzer sounded, signaling a finish, and Alicia's head fell forward.

"Damn it," she whispered.

Chris and David flanked her on either side and she hated that they witnessed her disappointment, especially considering she was still in the money and they were going home empty-handed, but did she really have to come in second to Delilah again? Maybe Delilah was right and she was just out of her league.

"That sucks."

David's words summed up her feelings precisely. She'd hoped she'd be able to earn enough at her hometown rodeo to finally put an offer on the property. She was dying to tell her parents she'd bought them a house and to make her father's dream a reality but apparently it wasn't going to happen this weekend.

"Look at it this way, Ali," Chris said, circling his arm around her shoulders and giving a quick squeeze to cheer her up, "it took a horse that cost nearly a quarter million to beat you."

She rolled her eyes and frowned at him. "Thanks, that helps so much."

David chuckled at her sarcasm but she could read the sympathy in his dark eyes. She sighed. "I'm going to get the horses home."

Alicia made her way down the bleachers, hoping to be one of the first to the rodeo secretary to collect her check and avoid Delilah altogether.

David followed her. "Why don't you come out with us tonight and drown your sorrows in a beer at the Ole Corner," he offered.

Alicia turned and faced the two of them. "I should probably stay home. With Beast dropping his shoulder, I've got a lot of work ahead of me this week. I've got to make sure next week's run is just as good or better."

"Come on, Ali." Chris bumped her arm with his elbow, playfully. "You're the only one who won any money today. We'll let you buy us a round."

"Really, Chris? I can buy?" she feigned excitement, rolling her eyes skyward. "Such a gentleman." She covered her heart with both hands before fanning her face. "Be still my heart."

David arched a brow as she mocked Chris. "Nice to see every woman isn't immune to your charm."

"She wants me," Chris countered and gave her a wink.

Alicia glared at him. His remark hit a little too close to the truth for her liking. Even as she fought the urge to melt into a puddle at his feet, she wondered, when he looked at her like that, if he didn't suspect the truth. She might be able to joke with him and pretend she didn't feel anything more than a casual friendship but that didn't stop her from imagining what it would be like to be held by Chris again, or to kiss him, or have his hands . . .

Stop, she ordered her wayward thoughts. *No sense even fantasizing since it was never going to happen.* Chris had left a string of broken hearts behind him and she wasn't about to have hers tossed into the battered debris.

"Look out!" a voice called.

David yanked Alicia backward just as a big sorrel barreled past, nearly running her over. "Watch where you're going," David yelled after the rider.

Delilah circled the frantic animal and looked backward over her shoulder. "Oh, so sorry. I was just so excited about my win . . . my head must be in the clouds." Her voice was sickeningly sweet and made Alicia want to gag. Or throw something at her as she continued running her horse through the crowd.

"I really hate her," Alicia muttered. "Why did it have to be her?"

"That's exactly why you need to come out with us tonight," Chris urged. "We'll have so much fun, you'll forget about bleached blonds with sugar-daddy aspirations. Besides, at least you didn't lose."

"Just leave her alone, Chris. If she doesn't want to go, it's fine." David sounded enraged and she wondered at his intensity. "And we didn't lose."

Chris stopped and scowled at his partner. "I didn't mean us. Are you going to hold his over my head all night because I thought we talked about this already?"

"Yeah, well, it doesn't really change the fact that we're barely holding on to the top ten by our fingernails now, does it?"

Alicia was surprised by David's anger. He'd kept it under control when she was at the trailer but something had suddenly unleashed it and she wondered if this wasn't a sign she should beg off going tonight. David didn't seem like he was any mood to go out, regardless of Chris's assurance of a good time.

Chris shot him a warning look. "Cool it," he muttered through clenched teeth.

David threw his hands into the air. "That's right. I forgot. Everything has to be your way, doesn't it, Chris?" David pushed past him and headed to the trailer, leaving Alicia staring after him wondering what just happened.

She chewed at her lower lip. Alicia felt bad refusing but she just didn't want to deal with Delilah and her flunkies tonight. She just didn't have the patience for them tonight. Just the thought made her sick to her stomach. "I don't think I can deal with the crowds at Maverick's."

"Then let's go to the Ole Corner and play pool. It'll be nearly empty."

The Ole Corner was a favorite with locals who just wanted a quiet place to hang out, away from the fake cowboys and even more fake groupies. It had smaller dance floors and wasn't nearly as fancy as the bars where most of the out-of-town cowboys frequented. It also wasn't filled with the women trying to pick them up. Delilah was sure to be prowling for her next victim tonight and that meant looking for someone in the money. Alicia arched a brow at Chris.

"Come on, Ali," Chris prodded. "You know you don't have anything better to do. You're not going to ride either of those horses tonight. Besides, I promise, we'll have a good time. So good we'll all forget about today."

Damn him and those puppy dog eyes. Damn him for knowing exactly what she wanted to hear. It was as good a place as any to have a pity party and at least she'd have good company.

"Fine," she said, sighing. "But you're buying me dinner."

CHRIS GAVE A low whistle as Ali stepped onto the porch, glad he waited in the truck while David met her at the door instead of where someone would witness his reaction to her. She looked absolutely gorgeous. There was just something sexy about a girl who knew how to keep it simple and she'd certainly done that. Pairing her jeans with a short, flowing shirt held up by thin straps, she showed just a hint of her flat stomach behind her belt buckle. She'd never been one to wear much makeup but the little she did wear always seemed to accent her best features: her eyes and full lips. Chris felt the heat churning in his veins and settle below his belt. God, how he wanted to kiss those lips right now.

Down boy, she's not your girl.

He knew he was an idiot. Chris shook his head and forced himself to tear his gaze from Ali and focused on his hands, gripping the steering wheel of the truck. She was David's now; he'd stupidly made sure of that. They even looked like a couple, walking to the truck, hand in hand. Besides, he reminded himself he had absolutely no interest in relationships. Right?

Hell, he thought rubbing on hand against his temple, he had no interest past finding some sweet woman to dance with tonight at the Ole Corner.

Chris dared to glance up at Ali as David approached the truck and opened her door. *Who are you kidding?*

Jealousy gnawed at his gut, eating away at the lie that protected him for years. The realization hit him between the eyes. Suddenly, the thought of holding Ali, of kissing those lips every morning, of being able to bury himself into her made him want to rethink his priorities. David opened the door, interrupting Chris's ridiculous thoughts, and Ali slid inside, buckling herself into the seat between the two of them. The heat from her skin was almost palpable and he moved away from her.

"Hey, Chris. You look nice."

"You, too." Chris clamped his teeth together and stared out the windshield, refusing to look her way. It didn't stop him from seeing the way David laid his hand on her knee possessively from the corner of his eye. As if Chris needed the reminder of who she was with tonight; the uncomfortable ache in his groin reminded him Ali wasn't his. He shifted and forced himself to think about anything other than her firm thigh pressed against his, grateful that the Ole Corner was only a few miles away.

It took longer to find a parking spot at the bar than it did to drive there from Alicia's house. Chris dropped the pair off at the front door, glad to put some space between him and the woman brushing against his shoulder as she exited the truck. She smelled good enough to eat, like strawberries on a hot summer day—sweet and tempting. He bit back the groan that threatened when her hand landed against his knee and he quickly moved away. Alicia gave him a curious glance but didn't say anything.

Chris cleared his throat. "Okay, kids, you can have all the fun you want tonight. If I don't find you right away, just come find me when you're ready to leave. Otherwise, I'll find a parking spot and join you inside."

"You sure?" Ali asked, sweetly. "We can wait for you here."

David barely tore his gaze away from Ali long enough to look at Chris and when he did it was filled with pent up fury.

Chris clenched his jaw. He knew that look and prayed that tonight wouldn't end up with him backing David up in a fight. He looked at his partner pointedly "I promised David I'd make up for today, so go. Order me a beer and I'll be right there."

David's eyes cleared for a moment, acknowledging Chris's unspoken apology, before he helped Ali from the truck, curling his hand around hers as he pulled her toward the front door. Chris drove away before she could say anything else. He was beginning to think he should have come alone. Maybe he should just head over to Maverick's and pick David and Ali up later. He wasn't looking forward to watching David and Ali together all night. He was having a hard enough time ignoring the knot of pain in his chest as she took David's hand and walked inside. He climbed from the driver's seat, forcing himself not to slam the door. This was a stupid idea.

"Best way to forget one woman is to find a different one," he reminded himself. Oddly, the thought didn't bring him even a small measure of comfort. In fact, it made him feel pathetic and shallow.

Chris headed straight for the bar and ordered three beers, spotting David and Ali walking toward a single empty table in the back corner between the televisions and pool tables. There weren't many seats left and, if this place was full, he could only imagine how busy the more popular bars must be. Laughter and shouting came from the back room just before a loud cheer encouraged someone to "take another shot."

"Kinda busy in here tonight, Jeff." Chris recognized the bartender as one of his high school football teammates. "Did David order yet?"

"Nope, what can I get for you?"

"What's on the tap?" Jeff recited several brews and Chris ordered what he thought Ali might like. He turned as another shout came from the back room.

Jeff sighed. "I hate nights like this. It's good for business but bad for the bar." He'd no more than slid the frosty mugs onto the counter and finished wiping away moisture from the counter when the sound of shattering glass broke through the cheer of the crowd in the back. "See what I mean?" Jeff grabbed another towel, waving to a large bouncer partially hidden in the shadows across the room before hurrying to clean up the mess.

Chris maneuvered through the throng of bodies near the only television and moved past the makeshift dance floor near a beaten up jukebox blaring a Carrie Underwood song. He twisted his body to barely avoid being hit by a pool stick as he made his way to David and Ali through the crowd.

"Sorry!" the player apologized.

"No problem," Chris muttered. He slid the frosty glasses onto the table as foam spilled over the sides and, reaching for his own, raised it in a toast. Ali and David followed suit slowly, as if they didn't trust him. "Here's to coming in second, if at all."

Ali's hand lowered her glass back to the table and a deep frown creased her brow. "That's not funny."

David slammed his mug back on the table and glowered. Chris cursed himself for bringing up a sore subject and tipped his head to the side. "I'm only kidding, Ali." He set his drink down and nudged the hand curled around her mug. "Lighten up. It can't be that bad."

"Maybe not for you guys, but I'm tired of always coming in second. I had plans for that purse. I needed that money." Her fingers traced random patterns in the frost covering her glass and Chris wondered if she realized she'd drawn a cloverleaf pattern, just like the one she'd ridden today.

David frowned at Chris, shaking his head in disgust, before chugging the brew in his glass. Chris wasn't sure if the look was meant to remind him of how they'd lost today because of his throw or if David had something else on his mind. Okay, he messed up. It wasn't like moping about it tonight was going to change anything. Why couldn't he just get over it?

"Excuse me for a second." David rose and headed to the bar, leaving Ali and Chris to wonder about his sudden departure. Chris watched as David placed an order, chatting with Jeff behind the bar.

"What's with him?" Ali sounded hurt by David's quick departure.

"I think he's still pissed I missed that throw today." He watched David slam back a shot glass of amber liquid.

There was only one reason David ever touched hard liquor and it wasn't because of a loss. Chris sighed. "Nope, it's because he saw his dad today."

"His dad? Colt Greenly? He's a legend."

She looked confused but Chris kept his mouth shut. It wasn't his story to tell. "Tonight might not have been the best night for a second date," Chris warned as he watched David toss back a second shot. He didn't want to betray David's trust but he didn't want Ali to speculate about what happened either. "Let's just say, not everyone is a fan of Colt Greenly."

"Should we go?" She looked past Chris to where her date was drowning his sorrows in a third shot. David glanced over his shoulder at them and shook his head, heading back toward the table juggling three more beers.

Alicia frowned and Chris could see the uneasiness in her dark eyes. Chris swallowed the last of the beer in his glass. "I'm going to go see what he's doing. I'll be right back. Hang tight." He felt bad leaving her waiting at the table as he intercepted David near the dance floor.

"Feeling thirsty?"

"Chris, I'm not in the mood for your games tonight," David warned. "You can either take one of these or get out of the way."

"How many shots was that? Three?"

Chris glanced back at Ali as she bit her thumbnail, trying not to look anxious. If he were David, he wouldn't leave her at the table alone for long. She'd end up with one of these other cowboys trying to pick up on her. Women who looked like Ali did tonight deserved to be showered with attention. If David wasn't going to do it, there were at least ten guys in this bar, him included, who'd be happy to fill in.

For how long? How long would you be content with one woman?

Chris clenched his jaw, irritated at the direction of his thoughts, and turned on David. "Look, I get that you're pissed at your dad, but you're on a date. Act like it and quit ignoring her. Ali doesn't deserve this so sober up and show her a good time." He grabbed one of the drinks from David's fingers. "And I'm done for the night so those were a waste." He left David standing on the dance floor and took the glass to Ali. "I'm going to play a game of pool, want to join me?"

"I . . . uh . . ." She watched David approach. "Maybe later." Her voice was quiet, tentative. He could understand her discomfort. What he didn't understand was David's stupidity.

"Just let me know. I'll be over there." He pointed at the farthest pool table where a busty brunette in a tight tank top and skin-tight jeans was racking for a new game. "Giving her a few pointers on her game."

Alicia laughed quietly and shook her head and Chris felt the relief course through him. At least he'd made her laugh. "You never change, do you?"

He shrugged. "Why mess with perfection?" Chris saw her glance at David heading their direction. He didn't want to be a third wheel on their date. In reality, he wanted to whisk her away himself, but knew he'd only hurt her. Chris gave her a cocky grin.

Chris arched a brow and gave David a pointed glance. *Cowboy up.*

THIS DATE WAS turning into a train wreck and Alicia wasn't sure how to stop it from crashing at the end of the track. What should have been a good time, playing pool and having a few drinks with a guy she grew up with and a guy she was starting to like a lot, had quickly turned into an angsty pity party. David hadn't wanted to talk about his father; that was obvious when the mere mention of the man sent him ordering another round of shots. She glanced across the room where Chris sat glaring at them from the pool table and watching her like a hawk. She was ready for the night to be over. Of all the bad dates she'd had in the past, this one was easily topping the list.

"Thank you! Oh, you're so sweet!"

She heard Delilah's voice before she even caught sight of her sliding through the front doors and closed her eyes. Could this night get any worse?

She glanced across the table at David, frowning down at the numerous shot glasses of yellow liquid, lined up in front of him, like he was divining some sort of mystic spell from within them and realized she wasn't getting any help from him tonight. There was only one way she was going to be able to tolerate Delilah tonight—either with liquid courage or by forgetting her existence entirely; either way, it was impossible without one of the glasses David was hoarding. She reached for one, snagging a lemon wedge, and tossed it back, stuffing the citrus between her teeth, grimacing. The tequila burned her throat and she coughed, pounding a hand against her chest.

Delilah slid next to David. "What are you doing over here, cowboy? Come join us at the winners' table."

David blinked at her dumbly, as if he was having trouble focusing. With the number of empty shot glasses in front of him, Alicia was surprised he hadn't passed out yet. He squinted at Delilah, leaning close before backing away and looking at Alicia, confusion etched on his face.

"Buckle bunny?"

Alicia couldn't stop the laughter before it spilled out. She tried to cover her mouth but her reflexes seemed slower than usual. "Sometimes I wonder."

The words slipped from between her lips before she could stop them and she had to mentally count the number of drinks she'd had. She rarely drank more than one beer so the two empty mugs and shot of tequila, coupled with the fact that she hadn't eaten since lunch, was hitting her hard and fast.

Delilah glared at Alicia. "I'm not the one trying to sleep my way to the Finals." She stood with her fruity drink and pouted at David. "When you get tired of sitting at the losers' table, I'll be over there waiting for some big, strong guy to ask me to dance." She spun on the heel of her boot to storm away but immediately ran into Chris who came up behind her.

"Hey," she screeched as her drink toppled backward and spilled down her mountainous cleavage. "Chris Thomas, it's no wonder you lost today. You're such a klutz!" She flung the liquid from her hands toward the floor as David and Alicia laughed hysterically. "Oh!"

Delilah stormed away and Alicia covered her mouth with a hand, trying to hold back her laughter. Chris unbuttoned his dripping Western shirt.

"Apology accepted, Delilah," he yelled after her.

He draped his shirt over the back of the chair and plucked his t-shirt from his skin with his fingers, not paying attention to the liquid staining the front. Alicia tried to ignore the way the wet cotton material clung to his chest, hugging his waist and revealing just a shadow of the six pack below. She felt her smile falter as her chest constricted and she fought to breathe normally. She inhaled deeply, prepared to thank him for chasing Delilah away, when he turned his hot gaze on her. She couldn't remember him ever looking at her the way he was now and her muddled brain was having difficulty reconciling the desire she saw in his eyes with the guy she'd grown up with. The cowboy in front of her was all male, muscled flesh and raw sexuality. She clearly saw why girls fought over him like the last piece of chocolate on earth.

"Great," Chris complained. "Now I smell like coconut."

Longing hit her hard, grabbing her by the throat and making it impossible to breathe. She looked over at David, frowning into his shot glasses and then back at Chris, shooting her a flirty grin. As much as she missed her friendship with Chris, she realized it was becoming more difficult to be *just* friends.

"I've gotta get out of here." She brushed past Chris and ran past the pool tables, ignoring the snide comments she heard from Delilah and her friends.

Let everyone think she was drunk and going to throw up. She just might, but not because of the alcohol. She couldn't feel this way for Chris. No girl in her right mind would want a guy with his reputation for more than a one-night stand and, as wonderful as that one night might be, Alicia wasn't willing to throw away years of friendship for a moment of passion. She bent over, bracing her hands on her knees, gasping for air. She had to get control of her raging emotions before either of them came out looking for her. She doubted David could even walk at this point, but if Chris came out she wasn't sure she could keep her hands off him.

Chapter Six

"WHAT IN THE hell are you doing?" Chris grabbed David by the front of his shirt, pulling him from the tall stool. "You are screwing this up."

"Get your hands off me." David batted at Chris's hands, knocking himself backward into the chair. "Like you care. You think I don't see the way you look at her? If you wanted her so badly, why did you even bother setting us up?"

Chris clenched his jaw, refusing to let David know how close to the mark his suspicions were hitting. His friend wasn't wrong but Chris wasn't willing to give up his friendship with either of them in exchange for his de-sires. Any more than he would let David talk about her right now in his drunken state. He eyed the front door, hoping to see Ali come back inside so he wouldn't have to go after her. Watching her run out upset and letting her go had been one of the hardest things he'd ever done.

He recognized the longing in her eyes and, knowing that she returned his desire, even for a moment, made him want to forget everything else around them, including his friendship with David.

"You don't know what you're talking about?"

David took a long swig of the beer in front of him and waved his hand at Chris. "Sure I don't. I've seen those looks you keep giving her, that kiss at the dance. At first I thought you were just flirting, the way you do with every other woman, but this is different." He shook his head at Chris, laughing at him. "Don't you think if she wanted to sleep with you she would've done it by now?"

"Ali is just a good friend, which is more than I can say about you right now. You're drunk."

David snorted and drained the last of his mug. "Yes I am, and I'm about to get completely shitty. Why not? I'm nothing but a disappointment anyway."

"When are you going to quit listening to your old man?" Chris slipped the empty glass from David's hand. "Stop letting what *he* wants control your actions. Do what you want for a change."

David stood, pushing Chris out of his way. "Easy for you to say. Your dad worships the ground you walk on. Your old man doesn't expect miracles from you."

Chris grabbed David's arm as he tried to push past, spinning him back to face him. "You and your dad need to realize we can't win every time. I get it. I screwed up today. We lost."

"This isn't about you, Chris." David shoved him backward, forgetting Chris was bigger and heavier than he was until David stumbled backward. "The world doesn't always revolve around you." He stormed toward the back door as Chris chased after him.

"Where are you going? You can't just leave Ali here." He held up the keys, jingling them in front of David. "Besides, I drove remember."

David glared at him, looking ready to take a swing, and Chris wondered what Colt said to him to drive him to this point. He'd never seen David get this drunk or act this antagonistic. They'd had arguments and fights over the past few years—friends who lived in the close quarters rodeo required always did—but never like this.

"Look, go sit down. I'll get Ali, we'll take her home, and then you can sleep this off." Chris eyed the front door. He was getting worried Ali since he hadn't seen her return yet.

David glanced at the group of girls at the table closest to them. Chris saw Dallas and Delilah watching them intently, taking in every word they said. This wasn't the time or place for them to have an argument. He didn't want either woman to have any ammunition against Ali.

David moved closer to their side. "You girls want to drive a cowboy home and have some fun?"

Chris's eyes narrowed. Did David have any clue what he was saying? If Ali found out about this, he'd would lose any chance with her. "Come on, David, I'll drive you home."

"You don't get it, Chris. I've had about all the *help* from you I can stand for one day." David slid into one of the chairs at the table and slipped his arm around Dallas. "You should probably go find Alicia," David slurred as Delilah giggled, pressing her breasts against his arm.

Chris wasn't sure what to do and was torn between both of his friends. He wanted to go find Ali and make sure she was okay but David would become even more suspicious if he did. If he stayed with David, convincing him to leave these two harpies, Ali could end up God knows where.

It didn't take a brain surgeon to make a decision. David had put himself in this position. Sure, Chris had caused them to fall out of contention for the money today, but that wasn't what caused this downward spiral . This was Colt's doing and David allowed his father to do this to him. Ali didn't ask for this drama tonight. Chris had pushed her to come, convincing her when she'd declined. He owed her.

David might be drunk, might not even remember this tomorrow, but the consequences weren't going to disappear with his hangover tomorrow. Chris could forgive his cutting comments, chalking it up to the liquor, but Alicia might not be so charitable, especially if she saw him with his arm around Delilah, nuzzling her neck. He had to get her out of here before she saw David since he didn't seem inclined to leave bar now. Chris might be second-guessing setting Ali up with David right now but he didn't want to see her hurt.

"You know, David," Chris said, shaking his head, "sometimes you can be a real jackass."

"Hey, you okay?"

Alicia looked up in time to see Chris walking toward her and hung her head. Why couldn't it have been David?

Anyone but Chris? She cursed the way the sight of him sent her heart galloping ahead the way Beast did in the home stretch of a race. Why did he have to look so good in nothing but his jeans and a t-shirt? His blue eyes were filled with concern and she knew she had to answer him. He was just trying to be a friend and here she was, fantasizing what it would be like to have him kiss her again, even if it was right here in the parking lot of the Ole Corner.

You're an idiot.

"I'm fine. I just needed some fresh air," she lied. Alicia shrugged but her fingers gripped the edge of the pickup tailgate. She was embarrassed by her reaction to him in the bar but she didn't want him to know that was why she'd run out. He couldn't know how she felt because she was sure she'd mistaken about what she thought she saw in his eyes. "I guess I can't hold my liquor like I used to."

"Light weight." He stood in front of her and bumped her knee with the side of his fist, giving her a wink. "You want me to take you home?"

His hand rested over her knee and she felt the heat soaking through her jeans, into her skin and traveling up her leg, pooling at her core. Her breath caught and she bit her lip, glancing at the front of the small bar just to avoid his gaze. The sounds of country music and laughter floated across the parking lot and she tried to think about something, anything but the way his thumb rubbed the inside of her knee, sending need sizzling up her thigh and making her heart thud painfully against her ribs.

She wondered why David hadn't come out with Chris. "Don't you need to get David?"

"David wants to stay a bit longer. I think he's trying to drown himself tonight." Chris gave her a reassuring smile when she looked at him, surprised at his nonchalance. "Jeff will keep an eye out for him and drop him off at my parents' place after closing up. I already made sure."

"You're not really as irresponsible as people say you are."

"Is that what *people* are saying?" He moved to the side of her and leaned his hip against the tailgate. He moved his hand from her leg and she missed his heat. "Or what you think?"

"I don't know. I've heard a few things, I guess." She laughed quietly, thinking back to their antics before graduating. "And I remember what you were like in high school and when we rodeoed together."

Chris joined her laughter. "Yeah, I guess after that incident racing trucks through Mr. Wolworth's strawberry patch, my reputation isn't totally undeserved."

She leaned backward on her hands, tipping her head toward the night sky. "Oh, goodness, I'd forgotten about that! He was so mad."

"His reaction didn't hold a candle to what Mom had in store for me. I don't know what I was thinking." He shook his head. "I had to pull weeds for him for years to make up for that. Mom made sure of it."

The door of the bar opened and music spilled out again as several patrons stumbled into the parking lot.

Chris looked up nervously and moved away from the back of the truck, pulling the keys from his pocket. "We should probably get going."

She wondered at his sudden hurry to leave but slid from the tailgate as Chris moved to hold the truck door open for her. She paused. "You're sure David will be okay?"

Chris nodded and shut the door as she buckled herself into the seat, making his way around the truck to the driver's side. The light inside illuminated the frown on his face as he looked toward the front of the bar. "He's a big boy. Jake'll make sure he gets home."

Alicia looked back at the bar in time to see Delilah exit as someone inside held the door open for her. At least she wouldn't have to deal with that witch until the next rodeo.

"HANG TIGHT FOR one second."

Chris parked the truck and ran into the gas station. He wasn't about to let David's troubles with his father ruin what should've been a fun night out. He might not have placed but Alicia pulled second place overall, which was no easy feat. They needed to celebrate the accomplishment, even if it wasn't exactly what she'd hoped for, and he was going to make sure she did. He'd promised her a good time and, so far, he hadn't delivered. The clerk behind the counter watched him as he headed for the cooler in the back wondering what Alicia might like best. He hadn't paid much attention to what women drank but he remembered their escapades in high school had usually been birthed from cans of Coke and Jack Daniels pilfered from his parents' liquor cabinet.

He grabbed a cold six-pack of soda from the refrigerator with a smile. High school had been a frustrating time for him, trying to balance rodeo with schoolwork and girls. Even then, he'd known exactly what he wanted to do and just lacked the patience to see it to fruition, which caused him to get into more than his fair share of trouble. His sister had been the straight-laced one in their family, always worried about how Chris's wild side might get her into trouble. Rodeo queens were supposed to be models of society, like pageant princesses, but that hadn't stopped her from going along to "protect him" and be his personal Jiminy Cricket, a sound voice of reason. Alicia, on the other hand, had been right by his side, whether racing trucks in a muddy strawberry patch or stealing the rival football team's mascot. Almost every great memory he had as a teen included Alicia. The three of them had been inseparable until Sydney went to work for Findley Brothers. Without her there as a buffer between them, it was too easy to let himself feel something for Ali so he pulled away, knowing there was no room in his life right then for anything other than rodeo. In the past two years, he'd spent every weekend becoming the best roper but, now, with her here, he felt something missing. He'd missed Ali.

"Give me a bottle of Jack," he said as he stepped up to the counter and pulled out his wallet.

"ID?" Chris didn't recognize the clerk and dragged his driver's license out for him to inspect. He rang up the liquor and soda as Chris spotted a bag of licorice at the register.

"That, too." He reached for the bag, remembering how Alicia used to love the candy.

Chris scooped up the bag and went back to the truck. Ali gave him a quizzical look but refrained from commenting and he set the bag on the floorboard.

"No peeking," he ordered. They drove to her parents' house in companionable silence, with the radio the only sound in the cab. Chris pulled into her parents' driveway and reached for the bag. "Come on."

He rolled down the windows and climbed out of the truck, leaving the radio playing quietly. He dropped the tailgate and jumped into the bed of the truck as she came around to the back and looked at him.

"What are you doing?"

"Trust me," he said, holding a hand out to her.

Ali took his hand, allowing him to help her into the back of the truck before he pulled a can of soda from the bag and popped it open, taking a long drink before handing it to her. "Hold this."

She didn't say anything as he opened the whiskey and poured a copious amount into the can of soda, pushing it toward her before repeating it with his own. "Are you kidding me?"

"Nope." He winked. "Just like the old days. Oh, and I got you these." He pulled the candy from the bag.

She laughed and sat down in the back of the truck, leaning her back against the hard metal body of the cab and pulling a piece of licorice out. "This brings back memories. The only thing we're missing now is Sydney."

"And a muddy field."

"Or a squealing pig to paint," she added.

"We did cause more than our share of trouble," he agreed as he leaned back beside her. "Like the time we borrowed my dad's truck and headed to the river."

"You mean stole," she corrected.

He laughed. "He's still convinced he just didn't hear us ask to use the truck."

She sighed and looked up at the sky. "Life was so much easier back then."

Chris wondered at the sadness he heard in her voice and followed her gaze. The sky was clear and, away from any street lights, thousands of stars sparkled overhead like diamonds, the half-moon illuminating her upturned face.

"Can I ask you a serious question, Chris?"

"Sure," he agreed, watching her take a long swallow of her drink. "But I get to ask you one first."

Chris couldn't tear his eyes from the slim column of her throat as she raised the soda can. She was so beautiful. He could just make out the faint pulse in the side and felt the shudder of desire skitter through his gut as he thought about kissing the smooth skin, making him forget what he'd been about to ask. She brought the can down and looked at him, expectantly. When he didn't finish, she went ahead.

"Why'd you stop coming around?"

Chris knew he couldn't tell her the truth. He could hardly confess that, after his sister's wedding and seeing

Ali's face light up, it had become too difficult to be around her without pursuing her—hell, without touching her—and it had just been easier to go on the road. Traveling with David had given him plenty of time and space to figure out what he really wanted in life without those brown eyes he could drown in staring at him every day. He was free to really live and experience all the rodeo circuit had to offer. If he'd stayed, he'd have given in to his desire and lost her friendship completely.

He shrugged. "I don't know. I guess I just got so wrapped up in getting to the top I didn't have time for anything else."

She frowned, her fingers tracing patterns on the can. "Or anyone?"

"You weren't supposed to still be here." The words tumbled from his lips before he realized what he was saying and cleared his throat, forcing himself to look at the sky again. "I mean, when you were queen, you were planning on heading to vet school the next year."

"Yet here I am, still living with Mom and Dad."

"Yeah, why?" He looked over at her, his eyes sliding over her face as she stared up at the stars. "If I remember right, you had big plans, Ali."

She frowned again and stared into the can, making him feel guilty for causing the smile to slip from her perfect lips. "I got accepted to a program out of state and I was going to go but I couldn't afford it. I knew Mom and Dad couldn't pay for it." She shrugged and finished off the soda. "Sometimes the things we want just aren't meant to be, I guess."

He took the empty can and set it aside, offering her another. She popped it open and took a drink before pouring the whiskey in herself. Chris pulled the bottle away from her, wondering if she even realized how much she'd just put into the soda.

"Weren't there scholarships you could've gotten?"

"Maybe," she said and shrugged before dropping her head against his shoulder and crossing her ankles in front of her. "But I could tell Dad didn't really want me to go and they needed me here. Then I started to second-guess whether it was really what I wanted. I was winning barrel races, so here I am." She rose to her knees and grabbed his bicep, her voice suddenly excited as soda sloshed out of can and into the bed of the truck. "Did I tell you about the place I want to buy, just outside of town?"

He smiled down at her, humoring her. He could tell the liquor was starting to take effect because she was beginning to talk quickly, her words starting to slur a bit. Unlike David, her tipsiness made her affectionate and adorable. "No, you didn't." He set his drink aside, barely touched.

Ali nodded, her hair falling over her shoulders, surrounding her face like a dark cloud. "It's a big spread, a few hundred acres. Dad could finally train his own horses." She sighed and plopped back onto her butt awkwardly.

She wanted to buy a place for her parents? Ali laid her head back on his shoulder as she continued to dream out loud.

"There's enough room that I could train barrel horses and give riding lessons, maybe take in some boarders and Dad can use the rest of the property to breed and train cutting horses."

Chris slid his arm behind her, around her shoulders, and she curled herself against his side. He couldn't remember ever feeling this comfortable with a woman, content to just listen to her talk and share her innermost thoughts. Well, his brain was comfortable, his body itched to move, draw her into his arms, feel her curves against every inch of him, but he forced himself to hold the need under a tight rein.

"What about you?" Her voice was husky, sultry, and filled with genuine interest in his desires. It was nearly his undoing.

She tipped her head back to look at him, the heat from her skin warmed him where she curled against his chest, the can resting on top of his thigh, her hand just inches from his throbbing groin. He could barely string two coherent words together when she shifted and her breast brushed against his side. Her lips parted as she waited for his answer and, damn, if he didn't want to kiss her right now. She was so soft and sweet, gentle and kind, with just enough fire to keep life interesting and keep him on his toes.

You'll break her heart.

The thought hit him like a bucket of cold water. He was *not* the kind of guy Ali needed or deserved. She was telling him her dreams, dreams that included settling down and buying a ranch. Permanency, daily routine, and that was something he never wanted—a daily grind.

Down boy, he warned himself, almost forgetting the question she'd just asked. Chris cleared his throat, praying she didn't notice his erection or how he clenched his hand to keep from touching her.

"I'm not really at the ranch these days and, when I am, it's only long enough to help Dad with something specific until he hires a new manager for the ranch. David and I are working on getting enough together to start a rodeo school. Something where we have a ranch but travel, doing clinics."

"Don't steal my property," she teased, poking him in the chest. "I've saved almost enough for the down payment." Her face fell and her lip protruded slightly in a pout. "That's why I needed the win today."

Chris knew most of what she said was the alcohol loosening up her usual reservations. Normally, she'd keep her worries to herself and, with most women, he wouldn't want to know their deepest concerns. But with Ali, he couldn't help feeling protective. He wanted to comfort her and reassure her. It pained him to see her doubt herself.

"Have you even asked your dad if it's something he wants?" She looked up at him again, which caused her to slide farther down his chest. The alcohol was beginning to slow her reactions and he caught her. "Whoa, easy there."

Chris shifted so they could lie down, letting her use his bicep as a pillow while Chris lay on his side, facing her, his hand at her waist. His brain rang out with warning bells—move away, don't touch her, drive home, get himself out of this—but his body quit listening. His fingers burned where they lay against her skin but he didn't want to pull away. His gut twisted as need circled, spreading throughout him, taunting him, tormenting. It would be so easy to ignore his good sense right now, to bend his head and take those full pouting lips into a kiss that he was sure would be incredible, to watch her eyes darken with desire instead of worry. His fingers twitched against her satin skin and her fingers curled against his chest, clutching his t-shirt.

And then he saw the tears in her eyes. Concern filled him.

"Ali, what is it?" He forced himself to move his hand from her waist, from the glorious temptation offered him, to brush away a tear on her cheek. "Talk to me."

"I don't know if it's what he wants. He always said he did but what if he changes his mind. And he's getting older. I see the toll it's taken for him to run the Diamond Bar. He can't do it forever." She gulped air as the tears continued to fall unchecked. He'd never seen Ali cry in all the time he'd known her and it broke his heart to know she was this worried. "What will they do then? They won't have a place to stay if I can't get this ranch soon."

"Honey, your dad is still doing just fine. He's got a lot of years ahead of him. Bradley isn't going to let him go or kick him out." Chris chuckled softly and brushed another tear away with his thumb as she hiccuped. "You're getting worked up over things that are a long way off."

"But they aren't." She shook her head in denial. "Do you know how long it's taken to save this money up to get this place? If I don't get it now . . ."

"There are other places, other ranches," he reassured her. "Relax. Everything will work out. I promise."

Her eyes met his. "You can't promise that. You've got everything, Chris. The property, the money backing you, the family, the security. There's nothing you want that you can't have."

Was that how she saw him? A spoiled, rich kid who didn't know what it was to want something and not get it? She had no idea how badly he wanted her but was denying himself because he couldn't sacrifice what they'd built over the years.

"You might be surprised," he muttered, staring into her eyes. She looked up at him and he could read her confusion.

He couldn't help himself. He couldn't hold back any longer. With her staring up at him, so trusting, so open, and so damn beautiful, how was he supposed to resist her? Chris dipped his head, barely touching his lips to hers. He shouldn't have done it. He should hate himself for taking advantage of the fact that she'd been drinking and wouldn't even remember the kiss, let alone most of this night, but he couldn't stop himself. He didn't want to.

He'd wanted to kiss her this way for as long as he could remember and he wasn't disappointed. Her lips were soft and, when his lips brushed hers in a light caress, she gasped slightly. He knew he should pull away, send her inside, and pretend this never happened. That's what a friend would do. Instead he tasted her, tentatively plucking at her lower lip with his mouth, breathing her in. Dear God, help him. Other than her surprise, she was open beneath him, her fingers curling against the hard wall of his chest, as his hands found her waist again, desperate to touch the skin exposed by her shirt.

He had to stop this now. She was his friend, his sister's *best* friend, not some groupie he could leave behind in the morning. Hating their circumstances, he drew back with painstaking slowness, need throbbing in him, centering in his loins. "Ali, I'm sorry, I—"

He didn't get a chance to finish his thought as her hands found his jaw and pulled him back to her, curling her fingers around the nape of his neck, her tongue sneaking past the barrier of his lips. The touch sent white hot flames of desire licking at his resolve, destroying it with the simple touch. His hand slid up the back of her shirt, gliding over her smooth flesh, his thumb brushing the lace along the side of her bra as his tongue plunged into her mouth.

Ali was unlike anyone else, like candy with a kick. Even the taste of her was sweet. Soda and whiskey. Sweet and sultry. And it wrecked him completely. One kiss would never be enough. He dragged her closer to him, groaning as she arched against his chest, his thumb brushing the curve of her breast. His heart stopped beating as she sighed against his lips, her head dropping backward, exposing her neck to him. He couldn't remember any of the reasons he should stop as he accepted all she offered, letting his lips find the sensitive curve at the hollow of her throat before nuzzling the soft shell of her ear. Her curves fit against him like a part of him he hadn't even realized was missing.

"Ali," he growled, his hand moving to cover her breast, his thumb brushing over the tight peak through the thin material. She arched against him, her fingers digging into the corded muscles of his back, her nipple pressing against his palm through the lace, shocking his senses.

What in the hell are you doing?

This was Ali and she was as far from sober as he'd ever seen her. One of them had to keep their wits and, thanks to his stop at the liquor store, he'd made sure it wasn't Ali. He couldn't betray her trust and take advantage of her this way, even if it caused him physical pain to stop kissing her perfect mouth. Chris eased away from her slowly, brushing back a strand of her hair that fell between them. The ache in him grew to gargantuan proportions as he separated himself from her with a hand on her upper arm. She whimpered softly against him, pressing her lips to his jaw. He was going to have to think fast if he wanted to repair the damage he'd done to their friendship, praying she was too far gone to remember anything come morning.

Chris smiled down at her, giving her his most rakish grin, and arched a brow. "Well, that was something we've never tried before."

Chapter Seven

ALICIA BLINKED, TRYING to focus and let her fuzzy brain catch up with her body, still vibrating with pleasure. She wasn't sure if she was more shocked by the fact that Chris had just kissed her or her reaction to it. It sobered her quickly. She'd never known a kiss that felt like this—like the world had just tilted on its axis while explosions went off inside her, melting her every bone. Her entire body felt like it was made of Jell-O, quivering as his fingers trailed over her ribs back to her waist. She fought the urge to beg him to kiss her again, to touch her again. Heat rose over her cheeks as she realized what she'd just done, what she'd allowed. She wasn't sure what to say now to his nonchalance.

Of course he's nonchalant. This is what he does.

Alicia willed her body to move but with the weight of him over her hip and his hand at the waistband of her pants, she was stuck until he shifted. Alicia cleared her throat and forced a quiet laugh. "I guess I can cross this off my bucket list."

She saw the relief flicker in his eyes at her words and felt her heart break a little knowing she was just a stand-in for him. Any woman would do as long as she was warm and willing. She was no better than the buckle bunnies he took home after every rodeo. Just one of hundreds, nothing special, even if he *had* known her for years. What made her think this might be different, that she might be something special?

As much as she wanted to be angry at him, she was far more disappointed in herself. She knew his reputation and Chris never claimed to be something he wasn't. He hadn't pretended this was anything more and she was a fool for believing, even for a moment, that the kiss meant anything to him. Chris was a one-night-stand kind of guy and, for some reason, she'd forgotten that fact. She couldn't let him think it meant anything to her.

"Not bad but I don't see what all the fuss is about." She attempted to give him a cocky grin, which was hard to do while she was still lying in his arms. If he thought she was too tipsy to remember, she could pretend none of it ever happened. Maybe then she could pretend he wasn't actually taking a sliver of her heart with him, the way she'd managed to pretend for years that he was nothing more than Sydney's brother.

"Ouch!" He clapped a hand over his heart, arching a brow but laughing. "It's a good thing I'm confident in my kissing abilities," he teased, his eyes dropping to her mouth as his lips spread in a sexy grin. "Unless you want to try again?"

She hoped he was kidding, even as she prayed he wasn't. There was no way she could kiss him again and keep her body under control. She bit her bottom lip hard to keep from asking him to repeat the kiss.

Chris groaned and rolled off her, lying on his back and tucking his right arm under his head, letting her continue to rest her head on the other. He laughed quietly as he looked sideways at her. "How is it that you don't have guys lined up for miles?"

"What?"

"You've got to realize what you do to a guy when you look at him that way, with those big brown eyes, and bite your lip?"

She sat up, bracing a hand against his chest, and looked down at him. "When I what?" He couldn't possibly think she was leading him on, teasing him.

"If you want me to kiss you again, Ali, all you have to do is ask. I'm happy to oblige."

She pushed herself to her knees, using his chest for leverage as dizziness overtook her. "I think once was enough. I think I'd rather kiss Beast." She crawled out of the truck bed and stumbled, surprised when he caught her arm, righting her.

Her eyes skirted past him to the two empty soda cans in the back of the truck beside the bottle of whiskey with nearly a third of the bottle gone. She hadn't really drunk that much, had she? She swayed unsteadily.

"Easy, cowgirl. Better let me help you inside."

She shoved his chest, frustrated when he didn't budge. "Don't try to give me that knight-in-shining-armor crap you pull. I'm not one of your bunnies. I can do it myself."

"Sure you can."

He was patronizing her and it was pissing her off. She jerked her arm from his grasp, falling against the tailgate of the truck. "Let go, Chris."

She fell backward and he caught her before her rear hit the ground, pulling her up against him. She twisted, trying to break his grip on her, and her elbow contacted with something hard and solid.

"Ow! Will you stop fighting me and let me help you?" He curled one arm around her waist, pulling her up against his chest, and rubbed his eye with his free hand.

"I think you've helped enough," she whispered, staring at his throat, not wanting to meet those blue eyes. She had no doubt he'd see the hurt she was trying to hide.

Before she could protest, he scooped her into his arms and carried her toward the house as if she didn't weigh anything, not stopping until he reached the door. Dizziness overtook her but she wasn't sure whether it was being in his arms, curled against his chest, or the alcohol. She closed her eyes and laid her head on his shoulder, cursing herself for her folly.

"I sure hope it's unlocked," he muttered.

"Hmm, Dad never locks it when I go out," she murmured against the expanse of skin just above the neckline of his t-shirt. He still smelled like the coconut drink Delilah had spilled on him but there was a musky scent that was all Chris and she inhaled. "Oh, everything is spinning."

"Been a while since you drank this much, huh?"

She nodded, the movement causing another wave of nausea, and she buried her hand into her hair, against her temple. "I think I'm going to be sick."

"Let's get you to the couch." Chris settled her on the worn sofa before he disappeared into the kitchen. She could hear him rummaging through the cupboard before the faucet turned on.

"Here." He pressed a cool glass of water into her hand, set a large mixing bowl on the floor beside her, and pressed her shoulder back so she lay propped up against the cushions. He laid a damp washcloth against her forehead and dropped two aspirin in her other hand. "Take these and finish that glass of water. It should help with the hangover you're bound to have tomorrow."

She did as he ordered as he sat beside her on the edge of the cushion. "I'm sorry I let you drink this much. I didn't mean for you to get sick. When you finish that, I'll get you to your room."

"No," she said, waving a hand at him. "I'll sleep here. If I move again, I *will* throw up."

How was she supposed to stay mad at him when he was being so sweet to her? She took another sip of the water, avoiding looking at him. Chris brushed her hair back from her forehead and adjusted the washcloth.

"Still dizzy?"

"A little," she admitted.

"Try putting one foot on the floor." He reached for the

blanket draped over the back of the couch and spread it over her. "Finish the water," he instructed. "The sooner you get to sleep, the less sick you'll feel."

She drank the last of the water and closed her eyes, willing the nausea to subside. "Done this a few times?"

He chuckled. "Just a few. Go to sleep, Ali. I'll see you in the morning." The last thing Alicia remembered as she drifted off were his hands gently removing her boots and belt before the calloused pad of his thumb caressed her cheek.

CHRIS WOKE THE next morning to the sizzle of frying bacon, the scrape of a spoon in a pan, and a monstrous crick in his neck. He rolled his head forward, stretching the stiff muscles and running his hand over the back of his neck, massaging the knot at the base of his skull. He stretched his long legs out in front of him and arched his back, glancing beside him at Alicia sleeping peacefully on the couch.

Common sense had told him to leave once she'd fallen asleep, to get as far away from this situation as quickly as he possibly could. Instead, he'd removed her boots, massaging her tiny feet. When she sighed softly, he felt every part of his body jerk to attention. He rose when she whispered his name, touching her face with his fingertips, fighting the urge to kiss her one more time. What could it hurt? She wouldn't remember it. But in the end, he'd only pressed his lips to her forehead before sitting beside her, ready to help if she woke and got sick.

He looked over at her, curled into a fetal position. Her mussed hair was tousled over the throw pillow and her mascara from last night was smudged under her eyes. In spite of it all, she was still gorgeous. Women paid top dollar to look as good made up as Ali naturally did. She had no idea how rare she was, but that unique quality was one of the things Chris adored about her, and what scared him most.

He brushed her hair back from her face but she didn't even stir. At least she'd made it through the night without getting sick. He picked up the empty bowl and her water glass and took them into the kitchen.

"Morning, Cristobel."

Jessie was far too cheerful for this early hour of the morning, especially considering there was a man sleeping on the couch next to her daughter, even platonically. He saw Noah sitting at the table reading the paper.

"Sorry about keeping Ali out so late last night," he apologized.

"And bringing her home drunk," Noah added.

"That, too," he agreed, having the decency to be ashamed. "Although that didn't happen until after we got here."

Noah gave him a reproving glance over the paper. "The two of you always did cause trouble when you got together."

"Sir, I can promise you, we weren't getting into any trouble. In fact, I brought her back early to avoid it."

"Cristobel, don't you worry about this sour puss. Sit and eat." Jessie patted his shoulder and slid a plate of scrambled eggs, bacon, and toast in front of her husband.

"Don't go to any trouble for me, Jessie, but I will get myself a cup of coffee, if you don't mind."

"Of course, but don't be ridiculous. You sit and eat. There's plenty." She reached for a coffee cup and poured the steaming brew, setting the mug in front of him. "Is she still sleeping?"

Chris nodded and sipped the coffee, grateful for the anticipated jolt of caffeine to his groggy brain. He thanked Jessie for the food as she slid a heaping plate in front of him. He'd just taken a bite of the salty bacon when he heard a knock at the door.

Noah looked up from the paper again, rising to look out the kitchen window. Chris could just make out a Mercedes pulling away from the end of the driveway, speeding off. He knew only a few people frivolous enough to drive a car like that to a horse ranch. If David had Delilah drive him to Ali's house, he was going to pummel him before David could get off the front porch.

"Would you excuse me for a second?" Jessie was about to protest when Chris hurried to the front door, opening it just as David was about to knock again.

He stepped outside, shutting the door behind him. "You've got some brass ones."

"Why doesn't it surprise me to find you here this early?" Chris could see David's mood hadn't improved.

"Someone had to bring Ali home last night."

"And stay?" David wasn't going to be deterred. "What happened to your eye?"

"What's wrong with my eye?" Chris moved down the steps toward his truck and twisted the mirror so he could look at it. A deep purple bruise surrounded his eye. He touched the swelling at his brow bone and remembered Ali flailing when she almost fell. "It was an accident."

"Sure it was." David cocked his head to the side. "Are you sure she didn't pop you for trying to put a few moves on her?"

"Things aren't like that between me and Ali." Chris didn't want to talk about how he got the black eye, or what happened after he'd brought Ali home last night. "Who was that dropping you off? Or do I even want to ask?" Chris shook his head as David ran a hand over his unshaven face.

"Look, I came to apologize to Ali. I don't owe you an explanation." David turned back toward the house.

"You think?" Chris grabbed the truck keys from his pocket and slapped them into David's hand. He just wanted to get David to leave before Ali woke. She didn't need to deal with this along with a hangover. "Go to my parents' place. I'll be out there later today. Ali can give me a ride."

"What's going on? I thought you were going to Chris's house last night."

Chris sighed when he heard Ali's voice from the front porch. He hadn't even heard her come outside and wondered how much of their conversation she'd overheard. He saw David look at him suspiciously before turning to Ali.

"Ali, I want to apologize for last night. I had an argument with my dad before we went out and I just . . . I guess it bothered me more than I thought it did."

Chris clenched his jaw at David's contrite apology. David certainly wasn't offering the information about who he left the bar with or how Delilah dropped him off this morning. David sure didn't seem like he was in a hurry to correct Ali's assumption about where he stayed last night. Chris watched Ali, curious to see if she was buying David's apology as he leaned against the side of the truck casually. David made his way up the porch steps to where she watched him, wide-eyed.

"Can you forgive me?" He reached for her hand.

"It's fine, David. I think last night we were all a bit out of sorts."

She shook her head and slid her hand from his grasp, waving him off as she looked past David and met Chris's gaze. His brows shot up his forehead in surprise. She *did* remember last night, and from the look on her face, she regretted every bit of it. Disappointment coursed through him, even as he reminded himself that it was for the best. Nothing could ever last between him and Ali. It was better to walk away now, before anyone got hurt.

"Did I do that to your eye?" She brushed past David and moved to Chris's side, carefully touching the side of his bruised eye.

He reached for her hand. The touch was enough to ignite sparks of desire in his belly, and below. He dropped her hand but not before David saw his reaction and narrowed his eyes.

"I'd say it makes us even." He didn't want to hurt her but he also didn't want her thinking there was more to last night than a kiss. An amazing kiss that, even now, had him needing a cold shower, but it couldn't be anything more than a memory.

She took a step back, as if slipping back into the friendship zone they knew so well, leaving last night in the past as a drunken mistake. "Mom sent me to get you both inside for breakfast. Yours is getting cold and she's dishing you up a plate, too, David."

She might be acting like Ali but there was something in her eyes that wasn't right. As many stupid antics as he'd pulled, as much trouble as he'd caused over the years, Chris had never seen her look at him with disappointment. It made him wonder if he hadn't just made the biggest mistake of his life.

ALICIA'S RAPID PULSE still hadn't slowed. She felt like she'd just finished a barrel race and tried to hide the shaking of her hands as she opened the front door. With as much whiskey as she had last night, she shouldn't remember what happened clearly enough to be embarrassed, but seeing Chris's black eye brought the memories flooding back with amazing clarity. Her head throbbed like a herd of horses was running through it but she wasn't sure if it was from her hangover or the blood rushing through her veins when she saw Chris and David together.

She'd never felt so torn.

She couldn't help her feelings for Chris. She'd been

trying to manage them since she was a teenager but she wasn't stupid enough to assume he felt the same way. In nearly a decade, she'd seen at least twenty women he called girlfriends come and go in his life, most within a couple of weeks. Since high school, he hadn't had a relationship last more than a few dates, at least, not according to Sydney. Chris was a free spirit who refused to be tied down by romance or relationships. He was a self-proclaimed bachelor and planned on staying that way. He'd made that abundantly clear. Things between them weren't romantic and she was never going to be more than a bit of fun for him.

But David was a different story. She hadn't known him long but he seemed to be the more level-headed, respectable choice. David Greenly was always on the radar of several cowgirls around the circuit. He was heart-stopping with his dark good looks but, until now, he'd never paid any attention to any women trying to catch his eye. He'd always been completely focused on being a champion, like his father and brother. She could appreciate that quiet determination to succeed but there was an underlying broodiness that she couldn't put her finger on. She wasn't sure she wanted to if his actions last night were an indication of his underlying issues. She wasn't sure she wanted to get anywhere near that hornet's nest. He and Chris were polar opposites.

David might not cause the frenzy of butterflies to take flight in her stomach when he reached for her hand but could she *learn* to feel that way with David, if she gave him a chance. In time, couldn't David show her that her feelings for Chris weren't real? Couldn't his attention cause the same inferno of desire to pool in her belly when she knew him better? Wouldn't she learn to crave his touch the way she did with Chris?

David reached for her arm, gently grasping her wrist as she reached for the door handle. "I really am sorry for last night. I was stupid and drank way too much." His voice was so rueful and sincere her heart softened.

She glanced over her shoulder at Chris, still leaning against the truck. Chris didn't want her and she had to let him go.

"It wasn't all your fault, David. We all made mistakes last night."

Chapter Eight

ALICIA FINISHED GROOMING Beast and led him to his stall. She was just heading to the mare barn to find her father when the ringtone sounded from the phone in her pocket, signaling a call. She ignored it, silently praying it wasn't David again. Breakfast yesterday had been awkward enough with David and Chris eyeing one another suspiciously, her mother watching all three of them and her father pretending to be oblivious to it all. Both of her parents noticed the palpable tension between the men and tried to keep the conversation going. It wasn't long before both of them headed for the Thomas ranch, leaving her to speculate where they would go from here, if either chose to speak to her again at all.

"Hey, Ali'i," her father greeted. She smiled, recognizing the Hawaiian word for royalty, her father's nickname for her since she was old enough to toddle to his knee. "Coming to help with Mama Bear?"

Alicia laughed, knowing no one ever volunteered to help with the cantankerous mare. "Not if I can help it."

Her father chuckled. "I guess I can't blame you."

He leaned against the wall of the stall he was cleaning. He looked a bit tired and she wondered again how much longer he'd be able to keep this pace. Managing all of these horses was a physical job and he didn't move as quickly as he used to, although he still looked far younger than his fifty-five years. She knew he'd been in to see his doctor about the arthritis wracking his hands with pain. Guilt flooded her heart as she watched him flex them stiffly, trying to alleviate the pain causing the joints to ache miserably. Ali wanted to help him lighten his workload but the only way she could do that was for them to have their own place, to work for themselves.

"Why don't you finish these last three stalls and drop some alfalfa into the feeders while I take care of Mama Bear?"

"Well played, Dad." She narrowed her eyes at him playfully and wagged a finger. "I think you just want to get out of cleaning these last few stalls," she teased.

Her father shook his head and moved to the stall next to her, housing the temperamental chestnut horse. "You know Bradley asked about you again this morning."

Alicia sighed as he went into the stall, murmuring nonsense to the grouchy mare. Her father was still hoping she'd take the job on the ranch. After runs like her last one, she knew without a shadow of a doubt, barrel racing was what she wanted to do until she couldn't sit in a saddle any longer. Sure, the thought of constantly scrambling to try to stay in the money made her wish for something with a steady paycheck but it wasn't worth sacrificing her freedom. The job at the Diamond Bar might be a sure thing and she knew Bradley would let them stay in the house as long as one of them was working the horses for him but it was only a temporary solution. If she took the job working for Bradley, she wouldn't have time to rodeo and would find herself, and her parents, stuck in the same position they were in now—tied down to a ranch, working all hours, for something that wasn't theirs.

"I don't know, Dad," she called from the stall. "I just . . ." Her phone buzzed in her pocket, signaling a text message. She pulled it out and glanced at the screen.

Sorry for Friday. Dinner, Sat. on the way home?
I want to make it up to you.

Alicia saw David's number flash on her screen as a missed call. She was surprised by his persistence. It didn't seem like him to pursue any woman, especially one who wasn't returning the attention. After last weekend, she wasn't sure she wanted to be around Chris or David right now. It might be safer to just lie low and let her heart gain some perspective, maybe a little clarity. When they left after breakfast, David had barely spoken except to ask if he could call her. By Sunday, he'd already texted her at least a dozen times to ask her to dinner and his tenacious pursuit seemed out of character. She couldn't keep putting him off but she just wasn't sure what to say or what she really wanted right now.

In the quiet of the barn, her ringtone sounded again and she saw David was calling her again. Mama Bear kicked the wall between them with a loud crack.

"Easy, girl," her father murmured. "Apparently, she's not a country music fan. Why don't you take that outside," he suggested. "She's acting extra crabby this morning."

"I'll just text him back."

Her fingers tapped over the keyboard.

Can't talk now. Will call back later.

"He's a good guy, you know. I don't think he'd ever do anything to deliberately hurt you."

"Who?"

"Chris. Who else would I mean?" He poked his head out the door of the Mama Bear's stall as Alicia moved toward where he worked with the mare. "I always hoped you and he might become more than just friends."

"Dad, I was texting David." She hoped her voice didn't sound as disappointed to his ears as it did to hers. "He wants me to have dinner with him this weekend after the rodeo."

He ducked back into the stall. "You should."

She laughed and leaned against the door of the stall. "You just finished telling me you wanted to see me end up with Chris and now you're telling me to go out on a date with David?"

Her father finished with the mare and closed the stall door behind him as Alicia leaned on the handle of the rake. "Honey, I know you're serious about getting to the

Finals. Your mother and I have both seen how hard you work to get there but there is more to life than competition. I don't want to see you so focused on winning that you forget to enjoy the journey or to find someone to enjoy it with."

She paused and inhaled the scent of the fresh pine shavings. Shame overflowed in her chest as she looked at her father. She'd been so worried about getting a place for her parents, trying to help him achieve his dream, that she hadn't bothered to notice how concerned he was for her happiness.

"Dad," she began but he cut her off.

"I know what you're going to say. You love rodeo, but I also know how much you love kids and teaching them to ride. I've seen you when you fill in for Bradley giving lessons here. You're good at it."

Alicia shook her head and laughed at her father. "Dad, what does teaching kids to ride have to do with dating Chris or David?"

"Well, I'm hoping that someday you'll be teaching my grandkids to ride." Her father ducked back into the stall she was supposed to be cleaning. "And you're not getting any younger, you know."

"Did you just call me old?" Alicia wadded the empty plastic from the shavings into a ball and tossed it into a garbage barrel outside the stall door. "Dad, I'm not in any hurry to find a husband or have kids. I've got enough to worry about taking care of you," she teased.

Ali pictured Chris and David in her mind. Even if she were looking, she wasn't sure either one was husband material. One was so afraid of commitment he practically ran in the other direction when he saw anything remotely close to a relationship and the other can't decide who he'd rather please, himself or his father.

"THERE IT IS." David walked toward Chris, carrying his saddle over one shoulder. "Where'd you find my phone? I've been looking for it everywhere."

Chris slyly cleared the text message thread from the phone and held it out to David. "It was sitting in the tack room. You must've set it down and forgotten it."

David's brows dropped forward in a frown. "I don't remember taking it out of my pocket."

Chris shrugged. "I don't know. Maybe you dropped it and Dad picked it up so it didn't get broken."

"Huh," David took the phone and touched the screen. "Is this a call to Ali?"

Crap! Chris had forgotten to clear the call log. He watched David press the button to return her call. It'd be better to admit now that he'd been calling her, pretending to be David before David made a fool of himself.

"Wait a second." David waved him off. "David, hang up," Chris instructed.

David hung up the phone and set the saddle down. "What?"

Chris shifted his baseball cap back on his head, nervously. "I asked Ali out to dinner after the next rodeo."

"What? I thought you said . . ."

"No," Chris clarified, "I called her, pretending to be you."

David crossed his arms over his chest and clenched his jaw tightly. "I don't need you meddling, Chris. I can ask her out myself if and when I want to."

Chris tipped his head at David, dubious. "Really? Because you were doing so well before I introduced the two of you." What the hell? Like his mother said, if he was in for a penny, he was in for a pound. "And I've been texting her since Sunday," he confessed.

"Damn it, Chris! Contrary to what you think, there are other things in life besides screwing women and having fun. Some of us actually want to make something of our rodeo career."

"That's priceless coming from a guy who went home with one of the easiest women on the circuit the other night."

"I told you, nothing happened."

"I'm supposed to believe you when you say it, but when I say the same thing, you call me a liar. Look, you like Ali, right?" Chris saw the look in David's eyes change from frustration to what almost looked like concession. "You have fun together, so what's the harm in going out to dinner?"

David's mouth scrunched up and he frowned, shaking his head. "Well, for one, she's got this really annoying guy friend. Says he's known her since high school and he's always around. To be honest, he's kind of a pain in my ass."

Chris laughed, relieved that David wasn't mad. He still wasn't sure why he was trying so hard to get them together. But he wanted to see her happy and if Ali was dating David, this desire for her would go away again. He didn't date taken women, especially not his best friend's, so life would get back to normal, with him dating a new woman at every rodeo and thoughts of white picket fences be damned

"Yeah, well, rumor has it, that pain in your ass isn't going to be there. He's got to get back and help his dad pick up a new bull so he'll have his own truck."

"You will?"

Chris nodded. "That means you have Ali all to yourself. Now, go call her and let her know where and what time."

David grinned and reached for the saddle, dialing Ali with his thumb as he headed for the tack room.

"You're welcome," Chris yelled after him.

"THERE YOU ARE." David looked up in time to see his father heading his way. "You should be out warming up."

David turned back toward the tack compartment of his trailer. "I'm fine, Dad. Chris and I have been working him out all week, the horse is warmed up. We're ready." He saw Alicia riding by on Beast and waved. "We're still on after your run, right?"

She turned her gelding and stopped at his trailer. "Yes, unless you want to change your mind."

David smiled up at her. He wasn't sure what was stopping Chris from keeping her all to himself but he wasn't about to question his friend's lapse in judgment. Chris's noncommittal nature was working to his benefit for a change.

"Not a chance." He saw her eyes flick to his father before widening a bit in recognition. "Alicia, this is my father, Colt Greenly. Dad, this is Alicia Kanani."

His father tipped his straw cowboy hat back and stepped forward, reaching up to shake her hand. "Nice to meet you."

"I've heard your name since I was little, Mr. Greenly. You're quite a legend."

His father tucked his thumbs in the front pockets of his pants and shrugged modestly. David clenched his jaw. He hated when his dad pulled this humble cowboy bullshit. This wasn't the man his sons saw. This was the act he put on for fans. They never saw the hard, demanding man who pushed his boys to win, no matter what the cost. Part of that cost had been their mother who'd left when they were only seven because she couldn't deal with her husband and his heavy-handed ways.

He watched as Alicia talked briefly with his father, impressed that she didn't fawn over him the way most people did although she remained quietly respectful. She asked him insightful questions as he became animated at her attention, offering suggestions. It didn't take long for her to wind him around her finger easily, he thought.

"I'd better go. I have to warm up my other horse," she apologized. "It was really nice to meet you, Mr. Greenly."

"Colt," he corrected, amiably, smiling up at her.

"Colt," she agreed before turning to David. "I'll see you tonight."

David smiled up at her, looking forward to spending some one-on-one time with her tonight. For the first time, it would be just the two of them. No crowds and no Chris. Oddly, he wouldn't have minded the crowds. It was Chris he was glad to have gone. Whether Chris wanted to admit it or not, David wasn't blind. He could see there was more between them than a long-standing friendship. The more time David could spend with Ali alone, the more he might be able to endear himself and solidify his relationship with her, without the shadow of Chris. For the first time, in a very long time, he thought about a future after rodeo, one where he could settle down and have a family. A real family, not like the one he grew up in.

He watched Ali ride toward her trailer where her buckskin gelding was tied.

"Frickin' trashy bunnies," his father muttered under his breath.

David took a deep breath, willing himself to control his temper as he clenched his hands into fists at his sides. He turned to face his father. "She's not a bunny, Dad. Her father's a trainer. She's in the top ten standings right now."

His father shook his head and gave him a disdainful sneer. "They're all trainers, son." He pointed toward Ali's trailer. "You need to stay away from that girl. I guarantee, she's looking for some cowboy to take care of her, help her pop out a few babies and sit on her butt getting fat."

Like he was going to take advice about women from a man who couldn't even keep the only one willing to stay through his abuse. David stepped into the trailer, wanting to get away from his father's prying eyes and jerked his Western shirt from the hanger, slipping his arms inside. His father followed him, standing at the doorway.

"Trust me. It's exactly what your mother did."

"This isn't about you and Mom." He sighed, forcing back the angry words he wanted to throw at his dad about how his mother had tried to make it work with him, tried to get him help with his drinking and gambling, had lied about all of her black eyes and stitches, until he finally threw her out. "Look, I've got a run in about ten minutes. Any other words of wisdom you'd like to impart before I go out there?"

His father narrowed his eyes and his voice grew serious with a warning tone David remembered from his youth. "Don't get smart with me, boy. I'm only looking out for you. Look what happened to your brother."

David wanted to argue that his brother was deliriously happy, married to a wonderful woman, and expecting their first son. His brother was running a successful cattle ranch and training rope horses with several championship buckles under his belt.

He kept his mouth shut because it wouldn't do any good. His father only saw that he wasn't roping any more, wasn't winning any more buckles, and wasn't keeping the family name in the top standings any longer. It didn't matter that he was content with the life he created for himself because it didn't serve Colt Greenly's vision. David brushed by his father and checked his cinch before slipping a foot into the stirrup, ignoring the older man.

"David, I mean it. Focus on the National Finals and leave the bunnies for these guys going nowhere."

David refused to answer his dad and jerked his rope loose from the tie on his saddle as he headed into the practice arena. Setting his loop, he took a few practice swings on a nearby roping dummy as his father's words continued to echo in his mind.

What if Alicia was just looking for a husband? Weren't most women? But she wasn't pursuing him, it had been the other way around. Besides, they weren't anywhere close to that point in their relationship. He wondered if he could he marry someone like her, from a background like hers? It made him feel like a snob but he wanted to find a like-minded woman, someone just as driven as he was. He knew her mother had immigrated to this country before she married Ali's father. They obviously understood hard work but as nice as they were, they seemed content to work for someone else, helping build someone else's fortune rather than their own. David didn't understand that mindset. He sought freedom, in his rodeo career and from his father's overbearing demands.

He looked back at his father, waiting on the other side of the chain link fencing, watching his every move with a critical eye. What would Alicia say if she saw what his father was really like? He knew his father couldn't keep up this performance forever. He might be able to fool people for a few minutes but anyone who spent longer than that with him got the full effect of his bitterness.

"Hey, you ready?" Chris rode up, interrupting David's spinning thoughts. "What'd your dad want now?" He jerked his chin toward the fence line.

David shook his head. "Just the usual." He looked out

into the arena, picturing their perfect run in his head the way he did before every go-round. "Just do me a favor. Don't miss today, okay?"

"Wouldn't think of it." Chris laughed. "Last week was a fluke. I've got this," he said confidently, nodding as the cowboy at the back gate let them into the arena.

Chris looked relaxed as he settled himself into the header's box and it showed in the way his gelding settled in, calm but alert. Contrary to the way David's horse pranced into the box, pawing at the ground nervously. David circled him to settle him. He knew the horse was picking up on his frustration from his latest conversation with his father. He should have walked away far sooner than he had. David took a deep breath and forced himself to focus on the task at hand.

The more he tried to forget the argument about Ali, the more it seemed to demand his attention. He tugged his reins backward, trying to get his gelding to sit back into the corner but instead, he lifted onto his hind legs, rearing slightly. David knew he had to settle the gelding or they'd never make it out of the box. He circled him around again, taking another deep breath, trying to calm his own tension. Chris shot him a concerned look. David knew if this went on much longer, Chris was going to have to let his horse move. It didn't bode well for their run.

"Come on," he growled under his breath, backing his gelding up again. He took another deep breath and adjusted his rope. His mount's muscles twitched under him but he remained in the corner of the box. David knew this was the best they were going to get and nodded to Chris.

Chris gave the cowboy manning the gate a nod and the chute opened, allowing the steer to burst from within. The horses jolted forward as the barrier rope snapped, signaling a clear run. Chris was quick to throw his loop, snapping up the slack in the rope and dallying it around his saddle horn, making a sharp left turn, giving David a clear shot at both hind legs.

David tried to focus on the way the steer's feet were landing in the soft dirt and timed his swing. He knew as soon as he tossed his rope he'd twisted his hand too much, dropping the tip of the rope. It slapped the side of the steer's feet instead of landing in front. David jerked backward but he knew he'd missed and quickly rebuilt his loop. Chris circled the steer but David knew far too much time had ticked by to put them into the money. He tossed his loop, catching only one hind leg and pulled the rope taut. The announcer called their time, including the penalty for missing one hind leg, and David dropped his head forward as he headed to the back gate. He glanced up at his father in the stands and knew by the way his shoulders were thrown back as he stormed down the stairs and his exaggerated limp, David wouldn't be talking to him until the next rodeo. He'd let his father down again, he'd let Chris down, and now he was supposed to face Alicia and pretend to have a pleasant dinner. He couldn't do this.

David hurried back to the trailer, not even waiting for Chris to join him, and unsaddled the gelding. He wanted to sneak away but he knew Chris would come by to talk. It was the last thing he wanted to do right now, especially considering how much grief he'd given Chris for missing last week.

"David," Chris called, walking his gelding to the trailer. "Hey man, don't worry about it. We're just having a couple of off weeks. It's fine."

David paused with his hands gripping the cinch. "It's not *fine*. We needed to win, Chris." He couldn't help but think about his father losing their home and how he'd come to David, for the first time, to help save the ranch. His father actually asked him for help and he wasn't man enough to provide it.

"Calm down, it happens."

David spun on him. "Not to me, it doesn't. I've been working toward this my entire life and I can't let myself get distracted now."

"Fine," Chris agreed. He sighed, slapping David's shoulder. "I know you, and next week we'll win first like this never happened. In the meantime, go to dinner with Ali and have a good time tonight. I'll see you Monday at my parents' place to practice."

"You're not listening." David brushed Chris's hand away. "I said I can't afford distractions—*we* can't afford them. That includes dinner tonight. My dad's right. I have to remember what's most important and not throw this all away now. The last thing I need to do is complicate everything with a relationship."

"David, you can't stand Ali up. She's about to go out and do her run."

"I'll call her on my way home and come up with some excuse. I'll just tell her I'm feeling sick." It wouldn't be a lie.

David glanced toward Alicia's trailer. He liked her, he really did, and he knew they could have had something special. She was the kind of girl that made a guy want to settle down but if he did that now, he might never have this chance to make it to the Finals again.

Chapter Nine

ALICIA PULLED INTO the diner David texted her about and looked for a safe place to park her trailer. She wanted to find a place safe enough to drop the trailer windows for the horses but still keep an eye on them. She spotted Chris's truck and trailer along the side of the parking lot and pulled behind him. She stopped the truck and got out, checking on the horses before heading toward the diner.

"Hey, over here." She glanced at the outdoor dining area and saw Chris leaning back in a chair, his feet propped up on another. He waved her over and took a long gulp of iced tea.

Alicia wandered into the eating area. "What are you doing here?"

"Having dinner with my favorite girl." He gave her a broad grin and motioned to one of the empty chairs. Her heart picked up its pace, feeling like a thousand horses pounding through her chest.

Stop it, she warned herself. *He's a player and you don't have time for his games.*

"I've been waiting for you."

Okay, he was playing dirty. That was just unfair.

She looked down at the table, noticing only two place settings, and looked back at him, confused. "Where's David?"

Chris shifted in his chair, sitting up, letting his boots hit the concrete floor. "About that . . . he couldn't make it."

She crossed her arms at him and arched a brow in disbelief, waiting for him to elaborate. When he didn't say anything more she threw her hands up, letting them slap against her thighs. "Again?" She turned to walk away.

Chris rose and dragged her back to the table. "Come on, Ali. This time it wasn't his fault. He got sick."

She allowed Chris to push her into a chair. "Really?"

"Didn't you see our run today? It was a mess." Chris sat down across from her. "He wasn't doing too well when I left."

She wanted to believe him, but his eyes said something different. He was hiding something and she could see it in the depths of those blue eyes. She was betting it had more to do with David's father than missing a loop. Bits and pieces of his conversation with David had carried. Alicia heard his accusations, about her being after David's fame, and they infuriated her. She'd worked hard to achieve every bit of her success she had and for someone who didn't know her to think she was trying to ride David's coattails was insulting.

"I didn't see it but I didn't do much better." The waitress stopped by their table, interrupting the conversation as Chris ordered them both bacon cheeseburgers, with no pickles, and onion rings. "You still eat them the same way," she laughed.

"Pickles are disgusting," he answered, wrinkling his nose in distaste. "If you even think of touching one, I will not be kissing you goodnight."

His voice said he was teasing but the look in his eyes didn't hold even a touch of humor. She bit her lip absently, unsure of how to respond and then remembered his comment about her biting her lip to tease men. She didn't want him to think she was encouraging him. Her heart couldn't take it but if she said nothing, he'd guess her feelings and that was even more dangerous. She wasn't sure what to say or what not to say and it made her uncomfortable with him, a feeling she'd never had before.

She smiled, arching a brow, waiting until their waitress left, promising to return with the iced tea they ordered and lowered her voice, trying for the same nonchalant tone he had. "You should be so lucky. At least Delilah didn't win this time."

"You two have quite the rivalry." He grinned at her and leaned back in his chair, hooking his elbow over the back.

She didn't think he'd let her comment pass without a remark but followed his lead. "She's always been like this with me, even in high school, don't you remember? I guess it's just what happens when you're from a small town."

"I suppose." Chris shrugged but stared at her intently as the waitress set the glasses on the table. "You really don't realize how jealous she is of you, do you?" he asked when they were alone again.

"Jealous?" Alicia nearly choked on her tea at the thought. Delilah had the very best life had to offer. She never wanted for anything. She had no idea what it was like to scrimp and save or how to work for anything. Even at twenty-four, her father provided everything she so much as looked at. "She's not jealous, she's a bitch. There's a difference," she pointed out.

Chris laughed out loud. "Well, from personal experience, I'd have to agree with you. But she is absolutely jealous. You have more talent in your finger than she does in her entire body. The only reason she wins is because she can hang on while that million dollar horse runs the patterns."

Alicia smiled at him. It was good to know someone could recognize the work she put in. "Personal experience?" she teased.

Chris shook his head and rolled his eyes, not meeting her gaze. "Yes," he admitted, looking embarrassed. "A few years ago I actually went out with her." He adjusted his hat on his head. "I'm sorry to say it wasn't only once either."

"Had a Barbie phase, huh?" She couldn't picture him with someone like Delilah. Then again, she couldn't really picture Chris with anyone. The only thing consistent about his type was that it was female.

"Something like that. But you don't have any room to

talk." He leaned forward on the table and pointed at her. "Remember Billy Maxwell."

"Oh, don't even go there," she laughed. "I can't believe I ever went out with that guy."

"Jock phase," he proclaimed.

"At least my stupidity was in high school. What's your excuse?"

"And then there was that long-haired guy you went out with right after graduation," he reminded her.

"Skid, oh my goodness!" she laughed as she remembered his name, blushing. "That was during my rocker phase."

"I had one of those. Dated a girl with about sixteen piercings, most of them on her face."

"Really? I can't even picture that."

Chris arched a brow and gave her a wicked grin. "Don't judge. You'd be amazed at how sexy piercings and tattoos can be."

A blush burned on her cheeks. She wasn't about to tell him about the tattoo she'd gotten after Sydney's wedding on a dare. An intricate tribal horse's head high on her hipbone. His mouth dropped open in disbelief.

"You have one?" She shrugged, refusing to answer him. "Please, tell me you have one or the other."

"Maybe."

"Where?" He looked intrigued and his blue eyes burned into hers. "Please, tell me it's somewhere good."

"Do you have any?"

"Yes, ma'am, I do. I have a couple tattoos. But no one sees them unless I'm naked." His eyes glinted mischievously. She could only imagine how many women had seen his tattoos. The thought was enough to keep her thoughts from straying to images of his nude body. "Show me yours and I'll show you mine," he promised.

"I'm not showing you anything," she insisted, breathlessly. She was grateful when the waitress brought their food, ending the conversation. She took a bite of the food and moaned softly. "This is amazing. Either that or I was starving."

She looked up in time to see his eyes focused on her mouth. His gaze was slumberous with desire and she fought back a shiver at the longing she could read in them. He quickly looked away, leaning forward in his chair to take a bite of his own burger.

"So, where are you off to now?"

She shrugged. "I didn't want to leave Mom alone this weekend since Dad is heading to a show with Bradley, so I'm staying at home. What about you guys?"

"We were talking about hitting up a few rodeos up north but after our last two runs, I'm thinking we should keep our entry money in our pockets. Looks like we have a few kinks to work out first so we'll probably camp out at Mom and Dad's to get some extra practice in. How's the house hunting going?"

"Coming in third didn't help much." She shook her head, hoping she didn't sound as disappointed as she felt. "I keep thinking 'I'll have enough this week to make an offer' then something happens and I'm just this much short." She pinched her fingers together.

Chris took a sip of his drink and looked at her

thoughtfully. "What about your parents? Couldn't they pitch in, too?"

Her parents had worked their entire lives with just enough to make ends meet. There had never been anything left over. She shook her head and twisted her mouth to the side. "They don't have anything saved. At least, not that I know of."

"Have you asked them if they even want to move?" She glared at him. "Okay, I get it." He held up his hands. "I'll mind my own business."

She swirled one of her onion rings in ketchup and took a bite. She felt guilty whining about her money woes to Chris. He was only trying to offer advice. "I'm sorry, it's just so frustrating."

"You know what we need?"

"What?" she asked, humoring him.

"Remember that swimming hole off the highway, near Jackson Ranch Road?"

She laughed and nodded. "I haven't been there in years. We used to go every weekend."

"We need to go now."

We? Was he asking her out? Or was this just a friendly outing, reliving old memories?

"You wouldn't be trying to get me into a bathing suit just to see my tattoo, would you?"

Chris gave her a mischievous grin that made her stomach do a backflip. "So it's something a suit won't cover?"

She regretted saying anything and didn't answer his question. "I could use a break and with Dad leaving this week for the show, there won't be much to do that the grooms can't handle," she said, changing the subject.

"We can make a day of it. Take lunch and just hang out, like old times. I have to help Dad tomorrow. What about Tuesday?"

She nodded and heard the sound of a hoof hitting metal. "Do you think that's yours or mine getting impatient?" She glanced at the trailers and saw Beast with his head hanging out the window. "Looks like it's mine. I'd better get going." She reached into her purse to grab her wallet.

"I've got it."

He slipped his credit card to the waitress, signing for the meal and rising to walk out with her. His hand slid to her lower back and her skin tingled at his touch, lightning shooting from his fingers directly into her belly and down her limbs. She knew better than to make more of his simple gesture than it was but couldn't help the pace of her heart. As she approached the trailer, she stepped onto the side rail to close the windows.

"Get your head in there, Beast. We're going home."

Chris moved behind her, with a hand on either side of her, and closed the window. She spun and found herself eye to eye with him, her breath catching in her throat as he stared at her lips.

"Um, thanks," she whispered, surprised she could get any sound out at all. She laid her hands on his shoulders, prepared to step down when he moved.

Instead of moving backward, Chris's hands found her waist and he lifted her from the side of the trailer and set her on the ground. She couldn't get her bearings with his hands on her ribcage and her fingers slid down the muscles of his biceps to grip his forearms. His eyes were dark with longing and she realized what he intended only moments before his mouth met hers in a scorching kiss.

They moved backward until she was pressed against the side of her truck, with every inch of him heating her flesh, his hands buried in her hair. His lips tasted her, teasing, branding her, demanding a response. She couldn't help herself as her fingers trailed up around his neck, drawing him down to her, closer. His lips moved from her mouth to her ear and down the side of her neck sending shivers of pleasure down her spine. His fingers trailed over her spine as she whispered his name, near frantic with yearning.

He growled and stepped away from her abruptly, leaving her trembling with longing. "Ali, what are we doing?"

She wasn't sure what he expected her to say. Her mind was still spinning with the dizzy exhilaration of his touch. When her eyes met his, she could see regret. She wasn't sorry he'd kissed her in the slightest. In fact, she wanted him to do it again, but she could see the guilt rising over him, drowning him with shame. Without another word, he turned and walked to his truck, climbing inside, leaving her standing beside hers with her hand over her kiss-swollen lips, wondering what just happened and how she was going to make it right.

CHRIS HADN'T TALKED to Ali since he'd walked away, leaving her standing beside her truck two days ago. They were supposed to meet at the swimming hole this afternoon but he wasn't sure it was a good idea. Just the thought of her in a bathing suit was enough to send every part of his body into high alert. His fingers itched with the memory of her silken skin, the softness of her long hair. Blood surged through him and he felt himself grow hard at the thought of her response to him. He couldn't recall ever wanting a woman as desperately as he wanted Ali, the one woman he couldn't have. He didn't want to hurt her, or betray David, but damn, if it didn't feel right when she was in his arms, fit against his body, her every curve soft against his solidity.

He tossed the bale of hay against the growing stack against the wall of the barn, ignoring the way the chaff stuck to the sweat covering his chest and back. As much as he wanted to have lunch with her, he knew it was a bad idea. The thought of her wet, in a skimpy bathing suit, coming out of the water, had him adjusting his jeans again.

"Damn it," he muttered, jamming the hay hooks into another bale of alfalfa, wondering why he was tormenting himself with thoughts of her near-naked body. This wasn't like him. He'd never wanted someone he couldn't have.

"Problems?" Chris looked up as David came into the barn. "Want some help?"

Guilt slammed into his chest, choking him with betrayal and deception. How could he do this to his best friend? Chris tossed the last bale off the back of the truck and settled it against the wall as a solution to his problem walked into the breezeway.

"Yes, I do. We're going to go have lunch."

"Okay," David agreed, drawing out the word suspiciously. It was obvious he didn't trust Chris but he sat on the tailgate, waiting to hear the details. "What are you getting me into now?"

"Nothing you won't thank me for later." Chris reached into the cup holder in the truck and pulled out his cell phone. He frowned as he looked at David. "You need a suit."

"A suit? What kind of suit? What for?"

Chris texted Ali to meet him at the swimming hole in an hour, reminding her that he'd bring lunch. "A bathing suit. We're going to the swimming hole." Pushing buttons quickly, he smiled at the response he received on the screen. "Okay, all set." He jumped into the truck and started the engine while David climbed inside. "Just trust me."

"The last time I trusted you, I had my eyebrows shaved off, remember?"

Chris laughed, recalling the prank he and two other ropers had pulled on David while they shared a room at last year's National Finals. "I promise, you can keep your eyebrows for this one."

Although, if Ali looks half as amazing as I imagine, she might just sizzle both of our eyebrows off.

Chris headed toward David's house to get his suit before heading to the deli to pick up lunch. "You'll owe me for this one."

Unfortunately, Chris would never let David know what it was costing him to force himself to take a step back from Alicia and insisting David explore what he and Ali might have together. The pain in his groin was only a minor inconvenience compared to the pain in his chest.

ALICIA SAT ON a rock at the edge of the water with her feet dangling down, her toes barely touching the cool water below. It was a still a little chilly to go swimming, but she had such fond memories of this place that she couldn't turn Chris down when he'd asked her to join him. That and she couldn't help but secretly hope they might repeat the kiss from the diner, even as she hated herself for wanting him. She heard a truck pulling into the parking lot above where she waited and rose, slipping on her sandals, heading back up the walkway to see if he needed help carrying anything. She'd just crested the top of the hill when she heard a giggle of a female voice and David's deep laughter.

Her heart dropped and she realized she'd been set up. Again. Damn Chris!

"Hey, Ali," David said, turning to see her.

She tried to hide her disappointment as Chris got out of the truck and draped his arm around Melissa Smart. Alicia didn't know her well since she was a little younger but she'd seen her working in the trendy coffee shop in town. She knew better than to hope Melissa was dating David. She was sure she was Chris's new girl today and tomorrow's old one.

Alicia pasted a smile on her face, not wanting any of them to see the chunk he was taking from her heart. "Hey, you finally made it."

"We come bearing fried chicken and dessert," Chris said, holding up the bag of food. He refused to meet her eyes.

Good, he should feel ashamed for toying with my feelings.

If Chris wanted to act like they hadn't kissed, she would do the same. She was tired of this game with him. Tired of being nothing more than someone to scratch his momentary itch. If Melissa wanted him, she could have him. Alicia ignored Chris and walked up to David, curling an arm around his waist as if the kiss with Chris had never happened, almost grateful he'd helped her make a decision.

"Feeling better?" She looked up at him as he slipped his arm around her shoulder.

"I do now."

From the corner of her eye, she saw Chris roll his eyes dramatically and wondered at his reaction.

"Well, I'm starving," Melissa announced, heading for the picnic table chained to a nearby tree. "I didn't even think anyone came down here anymore."

Chris eyed the lined trash can. "Looks like the park rangers are still taking care of it for now." He pulled out two buckets of chicken and a thermos of tea, handing each of them a plastic cup.

His fingers brushed against Alicia's as she took the cup and he looked up, meeting her eyes for the first time. She could see yearning there as he clenched his jaw tightly, pulling his hand back quickly. Her heart skipped, making it hard to catch her breath.

"Thank you," she whispered, barely able to tear her gaze from his.

"No problem," he replied, his voice tight, and she wondered what she'd done.

Chris completely ignored her during lunch, barely saying anything unless he was making polite conversation. He acted like they'd only just met instead of knowing each other for almost ten years. She tried to avoid watching him with Melissa while they ate. Or when she ran her fingers around his bicep, tracing the tribal band tattoo, or when she snatched the last strawberry from his hand, instigating him to chase her down to the water. Ali rolled her eyes and sighed.

"They're sort of ridiculous, aren't they?" David murmured, leaning toward her from their position lying on a blanket spread over the sparse grass and wildflowers along the bank of the river.

She rolled from her back onto her side, not even pretending she didn't know who he meant. "You'd think they were sixteen instead of twenty-four."

David laughed and reached for her hand, playing with her fingers before twining his fingers between hers. "I'm sorry about last weekend."

She met his serious gaze. "You know, I keep hearing that from you, David. I'm beginning to think you only want a friend." She met his gaze. "I'm okay with that."

His lips twisted to the side and she could tell he was thinking about her statement. "I don't know." He looked back at Chris and Melissa splashing each other at the edge of the water. "I don't want that." He jerked his chin at the pair. "I like you, Ali, I really do, but there are just a lot of things vying for my attention right now. I'm not sure how much I have left over to offer."

She appreciated his honesty. Respected that he would tell her the truth. "The Finals."

"Yeah," he nodded. "And a few other things," he added cryptically.

She turned toward him. "Your dad?" He looked at her intently. "I heard some of what he said at the rodeo."

David sighed. "You have to understand, my dad has this idea in his head about every accomplishment he expects me to achieve and a timeline for it. Nothing else is even a priority in his eyes."

He brushed his finger over her cheek and her stomach did a little flip at the tenderness of his touch. Maybe she *could* feel more than friendship for David with time. At least he wasn't toying with her heart.

"I'm sorry if what he said hurt you."

"What is it *you* want, David? Don't you want a say in your own life?"

He looked sad, as if her words had woken a buried need within him. He lay back on the blanket and looked up at the sky. "You'd think so but sometimes loyalty makes the decision for you."

She realized they were a lot alike. He wanted to please his father; she was trying to achieve her father's dream for him. It wasn't so different. "It might surprise you to know I understand exactly what you mean."

David turned toward her and braced himself on an elbow, just staring down at her. She tried to read his

thoughts. He was such an enigma with his quiet determination but below the surface, she could see a desire for
more. He curved his hand around her cheek, his thumb
brushing over the hollow, and leaned forward, meeting
her lips with a soft brush of his. There was a sweetness to
his kiss that touched her, reaching to the part of her that
was tired of being rejected, the part that was never quite
good enough to be the first and only. When his tongue
swept against hers, she met it with an eagerness she hadn't
expected. It wasn't the desire she felt with Chris, the physical longing he could stir in her, but it was sweet and innocent. She wasn't sure whether it was the knowledge that
David understood her need for more in life or knowing he
saw her as worthy of his attention, unlike Chris.

"Eh-hem," Chris cleared his throat. "I hate to break
up this lovely moment but I thought we were going to go
swimming."

David broke their kiss and shook his head. "You see
what I mean? It's like babysitting a two-year-old." He
smiled against her lips before turning to squint up at
Chris, who took a moment to shake water on them. "If
you don't mind. Why don't you go have fun your way,
and let us have ours?"

"Come on, you guys," Melissa called from the water.
"It's not cold."

Alicia turned to David and smiled. "I don't think
either of them is going to let us get out of here without
going in."

David sighed and sat up to pull off his boots. Alicia
couldn't help but watch appreciatively as he pulled the

collar of his t-shirt over his head before standing to remove his pants. He was taut and lean, with muscles chiseled from his shoulders to his calves from hard work and riding. She was surprised at how muscular he was, with ridges of muscle covering his back and chest, tapering to a narrow waist. She stood, forcing herself to ignore Chris as he headed back toward the water, and kicked off her sandals on the blanket. Alicia slid her cut-off denim shorts down her legs and pulled her t-shirt over her head, feeling a little exposed in her red and black bikini.

David's arm snaked out and wound around her waist, pulling her against him. He pressed a quick kiss against her surprised mouth. "You're making me rethink some of those decisions."

Before she could answer, he grasped her hand and dragged her down to the water with him, making her wonder if there wasn't far more to David Greenly than what she'd seen so far.

Chapter Ten

"You're bringing Ali this weekend, right? Sydney will kill me if she's not there."

David unbuckled the cinch of his saddle before looking at Chris over his shoulder. "I was planning on it, why?"

Chris shrugged and pulled the saddle from his gelding's back. "Just wondering."

David knew better than to believe his overly simple explanation. "Are you bringing Melissa?"

Chris scrunched his face and shook his head. "No. That was just a one-time thing." He walked past David and dropped the saddle on one of the racks in the tack room. "She's nice but a little too clingy for my taste."

"Why? Did she ask for a second date? Expect you to hold her hand?" David shook his head. "Just what is your taste, Chris?"

"Self-sufficient and sexy."

"Good luck finding both in one package." He wasn't about to mention Chris had ignored both in Ali, even though Chris had practically ignored her at the river.

"And now you understand why the search continues." Chris commented, with a self-deprecating laugh. "And you're one to talk. I practically had to force you to date Ali."

"You didn't have to *force* me. I just have a lot of other responsibilities that I prioritized above dating." He pulled the saddle off and stood it, upended, on the ground.

"Please," Chris teased. "Face it, you were too shy to ask anyone out and you needed a little help. There's no shame in that, man." He leaned over his horse's sweaty back. "Even the best of us needs a wingman from time to time."

"As usual, you have no clue what you're talking about." David hadn't meant for his voice to come out as harsh as it did but he'd been putting off telling Chris about his father's request and it was beginning to weigh on him. It wasn't going to go over well when he told Chris they weren't going to be able to fund the school after all. He just wasn't sure how to bring it up.

"I was only kidding, David." Chris dropped the brushes into the grooming bucket and walked to the front of David's horse, eyeing him. "What's going on? You're not telling me something."

David wondered how to begin confessing his dad's downfall to his best friend. They'd been planning this rodeo school for almost four years. Now that he had to try to bail his dad out, if he could even come up with the rest of the money, their dream was going to fall to the wayside. It was one or the other—the rodeo school or the ranch for his dad.

"If I can't come up with the money to save the ranch from the bank, they're going to foreclose on Dad and sell the place." David turned to face his friend. "It means everything I've saved for the school has to go toward saving the ranch."

Chris sighed and David could see the disappointment in his eyes. They'd both been looking forward to winning the Finals this year and starting their rodeo school next year, on the heels of their big win, banking on the windfall of marketing it would provide. Now, seeing that dream crumbling at his father's hands, he felt like a loser.

"That explains last weekend."

"You mean the fact that I choked." David narrowed his eyes at Chris, ready to remind him of his own miss the weekend before.

"You didn't 'choke,' you had a lot on your mind." Chris slapped his hand against David's shoulder good-naturedly. "Contrary to what you might think, David, you are *not* perfect."

"Says you." He grinned, grateful for Chris's understanding and his ability to lessen the tension in what could have been a difficult conversation.

"We'll figure something out. I'm not going to give up on anything that easily."

David shook his head. "Okay, but clue me in when you get it all figured out because I'm at a loss."

"If I can find someone to put up with your moping and complaining and still date your mug, I can figure a way out of this, too." Chris grabbed David's saddle and headed for his truck near the back gate. "Trust me, getting a woman to date you was a much more difficult prospect." Chris ducked as the curry comb flew past his shoulder and into the pasture outside the barn. "That explains so much! Your aim is off. No wonder you missed that throw last weekend," he teased, ducking behind the barn when the brush followed the curry comb and bounced off the side of the door.

CHRIS WATCHED AS David opened the truck door for Ali, taking the fruit salad from her hands. She looked sweet and feminine with her floral sundress and cowboy boots. She'd left her hair loose, hanging down her bare back, and her skin showed a pretty olive glow from the time she spent in the sun at the rodeos. He felt his body betray him, reacting to the mere sight of her, and turned away from the window, hating the desire coursing through him.

Damn it! What he needed was to find a woman who could help him forget the sweet scent of her hair and the taste of her lips. He should have brought a date but he hadn't wanted his mother to get the wrong idea.

Chris headed out to the backyard, intent on helping his father start the hamburgers on the grill. Anything that might distract him. Instead, he found his dad dancing to the country music playing from the speakers of the radio he'd recently installed.

"Dad, you need any—" He stopped short seeing his dad's ample rear swaying to the music. "Please don't do that in front of company."

Bill Thomas chuckled. "What? You could probably learn a move or two from your old man."

"Those moves should never see the light of day again," he teased.

"Chris, you leave your father alone. His moves are just fine." Chris looked over his shoulder as his mother came through the back door, followed by Alicia and David.

A commotion sounded as the dogs bolted for the front yard and he heard the scrape of the gate over the gravel driveway. "Sounds like Sydney's here."

A few moments later, his sister Sydney, her husband Scott, and their daughter Kassie came out to join the fun. "We finally made it," she announced wearily. "Ali!"

Scott and Chris rolled their eyes as the two women rushed to hug each other, talking in gibberish, gushing over hair, outfits, and figures. Scott made his way over to David and Chris as Bill passed him a cold beer.

"Are they always like this?" David asked.

"Yes," Scott warned, "and it never gets any quieter."

"I heard that," Sydney commented, arching a brow. "If you keep that up, I won't let you tell them the good news."

"What good news?" Julia Thomas looked at her daughter expectantly as Scott made his way to her, placing a hand on her shoulder.

"That you're going to be a grandma again," he proclaimed. The women yelped in delight and began hugging each other again. Scott winked at his wife. "Ha, told her anyway."

Chris clapped his brother-in-law on the shoulder as he returned to their small gathering by the grill. "Congratulations, again. So, think you'll give me a nephew this time?"

"I hope not!" Scott looked mortified. "I know what cowboys are like. I'd rather be able to chase them off. It'd be almost impossible to break the cowboy mentality we're raised with."

"Cowboy up," Chris cheered, holding up his bottle in a mock toast.

"Here, here!" David answered, clinking the top of his bottle to Chris's.

Scott and Bill laughed. "Have fun now boys, because that mentality will be out the window as soon as you get married," Chris's father assured them before leaving to get a platter for the burgers.

"Really?" David asked, glancing toward Ali.

"Don't worry," Scott laughed, placing a hand on the younger man's shoulder. "There are plenty of other benefits that more than make up for it."

Chris tipped his bottle at Scott. "You are saying that only because my sister is looking this way."

Sydney came over and planted a kiss on her husband's cheek. "Damn right," he answered. "You've seen her mad. Why would I ever do that on purpose?"

"We're riding today, right?" Sydney asked.

"You're not roping," Scott insisted, curling his arm around her waist as Chris scooped up his niece and she pressed a kiss to his cheek.

"Rope, Daddy!" Kassie spun in Chris's arms and reached for her father. "Peas?" Scott laughed and took his daughter into his arms as she squished his cheeks together before planting a kiss on his lips. "Peas, Daddy?"

Everyone laughed at her antics and Chris knew the

little girl would get her way yet again, or, at least, her version of it. "Fine, you can ride Mocha if your mother says it's okay."

"Come on, little girl, let's go see if Ali and Grandma need any help in the kitchen." Sydney grasped Kassie's hand and led her inside.

Chris watched his sister and smiled, seeing the look of pleasure that radiated between her and Scott. Not so long ago, he'd almost gotten into a fight with his brother-in-law to protect her honor, and now they were both blissfully happy with a second baby on the way.

"You know, your mom keeps bugging your sister to find you a nice girl to settle down with." Scott gave Chris a sympathetic smile.

"I know," he groaned. Images of Ali floated through his mind and he quickly pushed them aside. "She's going to have to settle for you and Syd having the babies because I have no intentions of becoming a boring old man any time soon."

Scott took a long draw from his beer and nudged David with his shoulder. "A lifetime bachelor ... that's what I thought, too. Look at me now. And, trust me, married life is *far* from boring."

"I don't know," David interrupted. "I think I have a better chance of getting married and having kids than he does."

"I just don't see the draw in marriage."

The words sounded hollow and sad. As soon as they were out of his mouth, Chris knew he was lying. Watching his parents and his sister and Scott, he could definitely see the happiness that radiated from both couples. He was growing weary of being a lone wolf, of never having the easy companionship he saw with his parents. He wanted to find someone who understood him and complemented him, who he could fulfill in return. But, so far, there wasn't anyone who he could tolerate for more than a few dates before he'd had enough. Chris suddenly realized it wasn't marriage he was afraid of, but rather monotony.

Scott laughed. "When the right woman comes along, you'll understand the *draw*."

Chris looked up as Ali carried out an enormous bowl of potato salad and smiled at him. His eyes locked on hers and he couldn't look away. She was so damn gorgeous with her dark eyes sparkling with excitement. How could something as simple as a barbecue with his family make her face light up with joy? She set the bowl down on the table and made her way to their small group, laying one hand on David's shoulder and another on Chris's. His flesh burned under the soft cotton material where she touched him. He shoved the hand not holding his beer into his pocket to avoid reaching for her as he inhaled the sweet, fruity scent of her hair. His jaw clenched with the effort.

"Dinner is ready if you guys want to take a seat."

"Thanks, Ali." Scott said, giving Chris a quizzical look as Ali headed back into the house. "Maybe you do understand the draw but you don't want to admit it."

David looked from Scott to Chris and frowned.

Damn it, the last thing he needed right now was David thinking he saw Ali as marriage material. Of course she was; he'd known that for years. It was part of the reason he'd avoided her. She was a temptation he couldn't trust himself to turn down. The solution was to drown the need with a variety of women who wanted nothing more than a few dances and a couple stolen kisses. They took the edge off and made him feel less lonely, even if it was only for a night, even if the relief didn't last and the feelings weren't real. But now he was beginning to wonder if it had ever been enough.

Chris finished off the beer in his hand and tossed the bottle into the garbage bin. "Marriage is for suckers, like you," he said, nudging Scott. "Who wants another beer?"

"HOLY CRAP!" BILL yelled from his position manning the chute gate when Alicia tossed the rope effortlessly over the steer's horns and dallied the rope.

"Dad, little ears," Sydney warned.

Alicia had barely turned to her left when David roped both back feet. Alicia felt her chest swell with pride at Bill's exclamation as she jogged the horse to the end of the arena where Sydney took the rope off.

"You've got some competition here, Chris," she yelled to her brother as he settled into the header's box.

David rode alongside her. "That was incredible. Why didn't you tell me you could rope like that?"

Alicia felt the blush rising over her neck and cheeks as she shrugged. "I don't know. I don't really get to do it often."

"You should do it more." She could hear the surprised awe in David's voice. "You're pretty amazing. I might have to partner up with you for some roping events. We should hit up some jackpots."

His eyes darkened with desire as they slid over her and she felt her stomach do a nervous flip. The crash of the gate bursting open drew both of their attention as they watched Chris and Scott rope a steer, although not nearly as quickly as they had.

"Chris, no offense but I think I'm going to keep Ali as my header for the next rodeo," David teased.

Alicia saw the dark frown crease Chris's brow as he rode to where Sydney waited. He brooded silently and Alicia wondered at his sudden moodiness.

"Ready to go again?" David asked, nudging his horse into a jog, and headed for the box. She glanced back at Chris and wondered if she shouldn't call it quits right now. He didn't look too pleased that she was out-roping him.

CHRIS SAT ON the lounge chair with Kassie curled in his lap, quiet but not yet asleep. He loved cuddling with the toddler and pressed a kiss to the top of her head as she snuggled closer. He looked across the fire pit to where his sister was smiling at him, her head tucked against Scott's shoulder, with her feet curled under her. David and Ali sat on the wicker loveseat, holding hands.

"You're such a good uncle, Chris," his mother said from the porch behind them. "You need a little one of your own."

Chris heard his father chuckle quietly. "Leave him alone, Julia. He needs to find a woman first."

Sydney gave him a sympathetic eye roll as their parents headed into the house and Chris shook his head. Why was everyone so concerned with finding him a wife these days? It wasn't like he had a biological clock ticking out of control. He was twenty-four, not forty-four. He still had plenty of time to have fun before starting a family.

His eyes drifted to where David and Ali whispered to one another. He saw her eyes flash in the dying sunset, flickering from the light of the flames as she laughed quietly at something David said. He felt the knot of jealousy balling up in the pit of his stomach, roiling and twisting, trying to find a foothold. He took a deep breath and let it out slowly.

"Looks like Uncle Chris put her right to sleep." Sydney's voice broke through his inner turmoil and he looked up to see her standing beside his chair. "Why don't you carry her inside and help me tuck her into bed?"

Chris rose from the chair, careful not to wake the sleeping girl. She barely moved and he wondered if anything short of a bomb would wake her. Sydney opened the back door for him and he carried Kassie into one of the guest bedrooms, where his mother had installed a new toddler bed. Sydney pulled back the covers and watched as Chris carefully lowered his niece into the bed before starting to back out of the room. Sydney grabbed his wrist, even as she leaned forward and kissed her daughter's forehead gently.

"Sleep tight, baby girl."

He felt his heart clench at the tender moment but tried to ignore the aching emptiness that filled him tonight.

Who was he kidding? It had been there for a long time but, until recently, he'd been able to shove it into the back of his mind, too busy wasting time with worthless pursuits to allow the ache to surface. But tonight, watching them all pair off, sharing quiet moments of tenderness, he felt like an outsider and the longing for more bubbled to the surface.

Sydney tucked her arm into his elbow and walked out of the room with him. "So, have you told her yet?"

"Told who what?" He stopped in the hallway and looked down at her.

"Ali." She couldn't hide the smile tugging at the corner of her lips.

Chris arched a brow. "What am I supposed to be telling her?" He had a feeling where this was going and he was tired of discussing his relationship status. They'd talked him into a corner and he was done feeling lonely today. He knew he was missing out. He didn't need anyone else pointing it out again.

"That you're in love with her. That you've always been in love with her."

Chris tugged his arm from his sister's grasp. "You're crazy. I'm not in love with anyone."

"You're a liar, Christopher Thomas, and every person out there can see it, including Ali if she'd open her eyes." Her voice was quiet but firm, scolding him for his denial.

He froze for a moment with his back to her before turning to face her. "What do you want me to do, Syd?

She's dating my best friend. I set them up and they are happy."

"You're an idiot, Chris." Her voice reprimanded him gently. "She doesn't love him. It's always been you. Ever since we were kids. I was just hoping, someday, one of you would finally wake up and see the other felt the same way. Haven't you ever noticed the way she looks at you?" When he didn't answer, Sydney shoved his shoulder. "Seriously? You've never noticed?"

"Do you think I would have set her up with David if I had?"

"Yes, because you have this idea that you can't be with one woman."

He looked over his shoulder when he heard the back door open and saw his mother come into the kitchen. Chris lowered his voice. "There's nothing I can do about it now."

"You have to tell her, Chris. At least give her the opportunity to make the choice. She deserves to make a decision knowing all the facts."

Chris's heart pounded against his ribs. He didn't think he could do it. If she chose him, he didn't know if David would forgive him. But she could just as easily choose David. Could he live with seeing her in love with his best friend?

Chapter Eleven

"Hey, cowboy, congrats on the win today." Alicia laughed as David spun around, surprised to see her. "I didn't mean to startle you."

"You didn't," he said, holding out his hand to pull her close to him. He circled his arms around her waist and pressed a quick kiss to her nose. "I was just off in my own head, I guess. Maybe thinking about our conversation last night."

She brushed her hands over the front of his shirt. "You mean about . . ."

"You, going to Texas next week with me." He smiled down at her.

She couldn't meet his gaze. She knew a lot of women on the circuit didn't think twice about traveling with guys, whether it meant sleeping in their beds or not, but it wasn't something she was comfortable with. He sounded excited to spend the time just the two of them but she wasn't ready to rush into anything. They'd had a wonderful time together at the barbecue but she just wasn't ready to jump to this next step. She didn't feel like they were *there* yet, there was something still missing. Some spark that wasn't igniting when she was with him.

"I don't think so, David." She saw his smile falter. "I just . . ."

"Ali, I want you to go with me but I *have* to go either way. I need the points and the money from the bigger purses. Plus, I can jump in on a few smaller jackpot ropings down there."

She looked up at him, surprised. Why did he need money? He was the son of Colt Greenly, four time calf roping champion with more sponsorships than she could count. His brother owned a big spread south of town and his father had a ranch somewhere nearby, although he'd always been secretive about its actual location. Maybe he was just trying to earn his own way, instead of riding the coattails of his family's reputation.

She fumbled with the snap on the pocket of his shirt. "I just don't think it a good idea for us to travel together yet. I like you and we have fun together but I'm not sure I'm ready for that leap."

He slid his hand up her arms and cupped her jaw in his palms. "I'm not sure where you see this going but I'm not playing games with you, Ali. I like you, a lot."

He bent and met her lips in a gentle kiss. She barely felt a twinge of desire and cursed herself for it. What was wrong with her? Here was a gorgeous man who was kind, gentle, and caring, thinking of her every need, wanting to spend time with her and she couldn't muster up even a little excitement at his kiss? There was no electricity when his hand slid down her spine and settled at her lower back, pulling her body against his. Where were the butterflies? The jolt of need? She wanted to feel *something*.

"There you are." They both jumped, turning to see Colt Greenly heading toward them, his limp slowed him while fury colored his face bright red. "What were you doing out there?"

David's jaw clenched and he stepped away from Alicia, moving her behind him as if he were shielding her from his father's wrath.

Or hiding you, the snide voice in her mind, the one that sounded like Delilah's, sneered.

"What are you talking about?" David threw his hands in the air and she could hear the exasperation in his voice. "We won."

"By three hundredths of a second." Colt shoved his finger into David's shoulder, pushing against him as if daring him to say more. "You were damn lucky and you know it."

"Whatever, Dad." David shook his head and sighed. "I just can't win with you, can I?" He turned and laid a hand on Alicia's back.

"Not when the only thing I'm looking forward to right now is living in a trailer."

David spun on his father, stepping up until their chests almost touched. "That wasn't my doing, now was it? But you expect me to make it right."

As if remembering they had an audience, David stepped backward. "I'm doing the best I can as quickly as possible. That's going to have to be good enough for you." He reached for her hand, leading her away from the trailer.

Colt chuckled. "If I'd known having a woman around would help you grow a pair, I'd have brought someone around a long time ago."

David dropped her hand and, as quick as lightning, pushed his father against the aluminum trailer. "This has nothing to do with her," he spit through gritted teeth. "Don't ever talk about her again."

"David," Alicia pulled at his shoulder, noticing several people taking an abnormal interest in them. "David, stop."

David moved away from his father and Colt stood, dusting his hands on his thighs. "You should listen to your bunny. She has more good sense than you do."

Shame flooded her, burning her cheeks, and she fought the tears filling her eyes. She turned away, refusing to let anyone see her cry, and willed the tears away. She'd been bullied most of her life. If Colt Greenly thought she cared about his opinion, he was about to find out how wrong he was. She had more class in her pinkie finger than he did in his entire body. People began to slow at the trailer, trying to watch the argument surreptitiously.

"It's a real shame, Mr. Greenly, that these kids need to see their hero acting like such a jerk. You might not think I'm good enough for your son, but neither are you."

She turned on the heel of her boots, trying to ignore his comment to David as she walked away.

"That girl has some spunk. She might be a bunny but that bunny's got claws."

"ALI, ARE YOU okay?" Chris wasn't sure what happened but she seemed frazzled as she saddled Beast. "You need some help?"

She glanced back at him and he instantly saw the tears welling in her eyes. "Hey, come here." He made his way toward her and tucked her into his arms, running his hand over the back of her hair as she started sobbing against his shirt. He moved her toward the back of the truck where she could cry without anyone noticing. "What happened? You never cry."

"Oh, I'm just so mad." He could hear the frustration in her voice. "That man is an ass."

"Who?" He looked over his shoulder for David.

"Colt Greenly."

"Ah. I have to agree with you on that one. What happened?" He stepped back, forcing some distance between them, as his body reacted to her nearness all the way to his loins. He took a deep breath and sat on the bumper of the truck and clenched his hands beside his thighs. He didn't want her to see the fury he was barely containing. The fact that Colt made Ali cry only made Chris hate him more. "He has a tendency to speak without thinking."

"He called me a bunny."

Chris laughed out loud, pinching his lips together and cutting off the sound when she glared at him. "You're really upset about *that*?" He tucked his fingers into his pockets to keep from reaching for her hands. "You're a woman in rodeo. A lot of those older cowboys see every woman as a bunny." He bumped the toe of her boots gently with his. "Especially the ones who could outride them."

She cocked her head at him. "It's not just him. I'm tired of trying to prove I'm not just the poor kid, the one who can't quite measure up. I'm sick of people thinking I'm second best."

"Then stop trying."

She swiped at her cheeks and crossed her arms, staring at the ground. "Because it's just that easy."

He slid off the back of the truck and moved toward her, tipping her chin up. Damn, she was adorable when she looked at him all trusting and innocent. He hated himself for the need that pulsed through his veins, making him want to pull her against him and kiss that worry out of her eyes.

"Ali, you're the only one who sees it that way. Every other person out here sees you as the competition, the one to beat."

She looked at his chest, embarrassed. "That's not what Colt told David. He thinks I'm not good enough for him. And there's always Dallas and Delilah."

"Screw Colt and those two Barbies. Why would anything they think matter to you? You need to consider the source." Chris tipped her chin up with a finger. "You are an amazing woman, Alicia Kanani, and anyone who doesn't see that is either stupid or jealous."

Now was the perfect opportunity for him to say something. He had her full attention and he knew his heart was in his eyes. Could she read it, see it exposed and vulnerable? Was Sydney right about the way she felt? He saw her lips part slightly and wanted to kiss her, to taste her sweet innocence. How could she ever see herself as less worthy than someone else? He wiped away a tear glinting just below her lashes.

"Ali, I—"

"Ali, are you okay?" David hurried to where she stood with Chris by her trailer and reached for her hand. "I can't believe my dad would say anything like that. I'm so sorry."

She took a step away from Chris and he felt a vacuum where her presence had been only moments before, as if the sun had clouded over unexpectedly. The moment to say something was gone but instead of feeling like David had saved him from disaster, he felt like he would regret this moment for the rest of his life.

"It's not your fault, David." She moved to finish saddling Beast.

"I don't care what he says, Ali." David stepped up behind her, placing his hands at her waist as Chris watched him whisper something in her ear.

Jealousy ate at him. Never in his life had he wanted to punch someone more than he did David right now. Seeing him touch Ali made him want to pummel him. He clenched his fists at his sides, wishing he'd never come over here. He didn't want to see David comfort her, putting his arms around her. Chris was supposed to be the one she turned to.

She turned around and kissed David's cheek, wrapping her arms around his neck. "Thank you," she whispered.

Chris felt the muscle in his temple tick as his jaw tightened until it felt like it would break. He was supposed to be the one to console her, to make her smile that way. What had he been thinking introducing her to David? Of course they hit it off. Who wouldn't want someone as special as Ali?

Ali's eyes met his over David's shoulder and she frowned, pulling away from David. "I have to get Beast ready. Wait for me after?"

"We'll go to dinner," he promised. "Wherever you want to go."

Chris removed his hat and scratched his head awkwardly. He should just walk away. Anything was better than watching the two of them make plans on how to spend tonight. Images of her in his arms, lost in passion, burned in his mind. He slapped his hat back onto his head as she mounted Beast, looking over at him.

"Are you coming tonight, too, Chris?"

He shrugged. "We'll see."

Chris forced a lopsided, cocky grin to his lips. He didn't want her to see the hurt he was feeling. Sydney was wrong. Chris could never let her know how he felt. It was better for her to think he didn't care, to let her find happiness with David. "You never know what girl I might go home with tonight."

Ali shook her head. "Once a dog, always a dog." Her tone was teasing but it didn't match the sadness he saw in her eyes as she rode toward the practice arena.

"You're too late."

Chris watched David approach where he stood at the back of her trailer as Ali rode away. "For what?"

"You had your chance with her."

Chris faced his friend and shook his head, trying to cover what he was sure was obvious in his face. "I already told you, it's not like that with me and Ali."

"I know what you *said* and I believed you for a while." David shook his head and arched a brow in disbelief. "Why didn't you just say something? I would've backed off a long time ago but now . . ." David threw his hands in the air. "Now, I can't."

"I don't know what you're talking about." Chris started to walk away when David grabbed his arm. Chris stared down at the hand gripping his bicep. "Let go of me, David."

David dropped his hand. "Don't lie to me. I know you too well. I've never seen you look at another woman the way you do her. It took me a while to figure it out. Are you in love with her?"

"You're crazy."

"You're sure?"

Chris tried to ignore the pain gripping his lungs, the burning threatening to steal his ability to speak. "I'm positive."

"Good, then back off. You're like a brother to me, Chris, but you opened this door and I'm walking through it. Ali's too special for me not to."

Chris didn't answer. He couldn't deny David's accusation so he did what he did best—walked away.

ALICIA UNTIED BEAST and loaded him into the trailer, eyeing the table where the rodeo secretary would be handing out checks for the winners. Finally, fate was smiling down on her. Her first place win put her over the amount she needed to place an offer on the property she wanted. Not to mention, she was meeting a great guy who was willing to fight for her honor for dinner tonight.

Just the thought of David was enough for shame to steal its way into her thoughts. She could see he wanted their relationship to move forward. It was evident in the way he reached for her hand, the appreciative looks he cast her way, but she wasn't ready to move forward and she hated herself for holding back. She wanted to feel about him the way he did for her. She wanted to feel those electric jolts when his hand settled at her lower back, or to shiver with tingles of pleasure when he kissed her. But so far, no matter how much she wanted to, she wasn't feeling the same way about him. She wondered if she'd ever feel that way about anyone.

Her eyes instinctively slid to where Chris leaned against the fence, flirting with two women in short, frilly skirts and half-shirts. Okay, she might feel that way about someone but why did it have to be Chris? She pressed her lips into a thin line, slamming the back gate of the trailer harder than she planned. Out of the corner of her eye, she saw Chris look her way but she refused to watch him slobber over two bimbos. What was wrong with him? Was he really that much of a player that he had no standards and any female was game?

She checked her brake lights before climbing into the driver's seat and caught sight of Chris heading toward her truck in the side mirror and sighed.

"Hang on, Ali," he called, jogging to the driver's window.

She blew out an exasperated breath, making her hair ruffle. "What, Chris?"

"Are you pissed at me?" He looked confused and she wanted to throttle him for being so obtuse. What did she have to do, throw herself at his feet naked? She wasn't the one sending mixed signals.

How was she supposed to explain her frustration to him without looking like an idiot? Chris had never led her on, or offered any commitment. He never claimed to be anything more than the player his reputation proclaimed him to be. She was the one stupid enough to let her heart run ahead of her good sense.

"No, I'm just going to be later for dinner." She busied herself with her phone. "And I'm waiting for them to hurry up and get the checks ready so I can head out."

"Congrats on the win today. Looks like we both came in the money." He pushed his straw cowboy hat back on his head and looked at her curiously as she tapped out a text message. "You sure you're not mad because you don't usually ignore me."

She turned her face toward him and rolled her eyes. "Contrary to what you think, Chris, you're not God's gift to rodeo and women. I'm a little preoccupied sending a message, if that's okay with you?"

"I see." He took a step back and she could see the hurt in his eyes before anger set in. "I was joking, Ali, but I can see I'm intruding on . . . something, so I'll just find someone more interested in my company."

Great, now she felt like a jerk.

"Wait, Chris." She climbed out of the truck as he started to leave and reached for his arm. "I just . . . I can't do this." Alicia threw her hands in the air.

"What's this?" He frowned and took a step closer to her. She backed up until her back was against the truck just to keep some space between them. Whenever he got close like this, the air thinned and breathing became a chore. She could feel the tension between them igniting, like a crack of lightning about to spark.

"This." She waved her hand between them, unable to vocalize what she was feeling. How could she explain that she wanted him to kiss her, that she hadn't stopped comparing every kiss from David to those from Chris and found David lacking? "Whatever *this* is," she tried to clarify.

Chris moved forward, his arm curling behind her, leaning into her as the door handle pressed against her back. "You mean this?" he whispered, his voice hoarse.

Every inch of her body became ultra-sensitive. Alicia felt his warm breath against her cheek as his fingers trailed over her bare arm to the strap of her tank top and over her collarbone making her practically sizzle with longing as warmth spread across her chest and limbs. Her breath caught in her throat when his eyes met hers, his gaze hot with desire. She wanted to arch against him, beg him to touch her, to plead with him to stop torment-ing her. Her limbs turned liquid and she grasped at his shoulders to hold herself upright, grateful for the solidity of the truck behind her.

"Chris," she whispered, unable to form any other coherent words as he bent forward, his lips finding the edge of her ear and trailing down to her jaw.

"Ali, you make me forget what I'm supposed to do." His words fell against her skin, so quietly she barely heard the tortured recrimination in his voice. "I only think about what I want to do to you."

She didn't know what to say, didn't think her lips could form words anyway. Her mind was too lost in the sensation of his lips against the hollow behind her ear, sending delicious shivers of delight down her spine. His tongue grazed the curve of her ear and she bit back a soft moan of delight, trying to remain upright when her legs wanted to go liquid. He pressed against her, every part of his body fitted against hers as his hands found her waist, his thumbs grazing the side of her ribs. She couldn't fight her body as it arched into him and she could feel his arousal.

"I can't do this." He pressed his face into the curve of her neck, knocking his hat backward to the ground, unnoticed. "I can't," he repeated.

It was like he threw a bucket of ice water onto her. She felt her heart splinter again, the way it did each time he pulled her close only to push her away. She pressed her hands against the solid wall of his chest, resisting the urge to slide them over the hard muscles, and pushed him back a step.

"Then don't. Don't do this to me. It isn't fair." She didn't need to pour her heart out to him. He had to see the need in her eyes, the love she'd been trying to hide for years. "If you're my friend, then stop playing this game with me."

Still shaking, Alicia slipped from his arms, leaving him by the truck and hurried to the rodeo secretary, intent on collecting her check, now. The sooner she had her money, the sooner she could get her priorities and her heart back on the right track. She didn't need a man who would toss her away without a second thought.

Chapter Twelve

"I HOPE YOU haven't been waiting too long." David leaned over and kissed her cheek, sliding into the booth beside her. She'd gone ahead and gotten them a table while he waited at the rodeo grounds for his brother to meet up with them. "It took longer than I expected."

"It's fine." She smiled at him but he could see something in her eyes. There was a hesitation that wasn't usually there and a sadness that hadn't been there earlier.

"Are you okay?" He narrowed his eyes. Something was wrong but he couldn't put his finger on it.

"Yeah," she said, a little too quickly. "I'm just tired. It's been a long weekend."

"This is where you bring us for dinner?" Colt slid into the booth across from Alicia as his brother sat beside him. His father reeked of stale beer. "You'd think you could afford something a bit nicer after that win."

"Stop, Dad. This place has great steaks so just figure

out what you want." David's brother leaned closer to Colt's ear. "Behave," he ordered.

David shot his brother a rueful glance before turning toward Alicia. "Ali, this is my brother, Christian." His brother stood and leaned over the table to shake her hand.

"I've heard a lot about you. That was a great run today."

"Thanks. It's nice to meet you," she said quietly.

She bit her lower lip and studied her menu. This wasn't like her but David didn't want to question her in front of his dad. Maybe she was just uncomfortable around his father. God knows, she had every reason to be after what he'd said earlier. He slid his hand to her thigh and lightly squeezed. He saw the flicker of humor in her eyes as she shifted and reached her hand down to meet his, twining her fingers between his to stop him from squeezing the ticklish spot near her knee.

It was a glimpse of her usual fun-loving personality and calmed his worries, but only slightly. The waitress appeared to take their orders and David ordered grilled steaks for him and Alicia while his brother ordered an Angus burger. His father slapped the menu on the table irritably.

"I don't even know what to order. Nothing looks good."

David shot the waitress an apologetic glance and she smiled down at him sympathetically. "Dad, just try the steak."

"No," he argued, waving his hand. "It's too expensive."

First his father complained that the restaurant wasn't

expensive and ritzy enough and now he was complaining about the prices of the food? There was no pleasing the man. David clenched his jaw. "It's fine, Dad. Order whatever you want."

Colt shoved at Christian's shoulder. "Oh, look at him. One win and money's no concern but he doesn't have anything to save the ranch."

"Dad," David muttered. "Not now. We'll talk about this later."

"It's always later with you."

"Sir," the waitress apologized, "why don't I just give you a few more minutes?"

David shot his brother a glance, pleading with him to help shut their father up, and glanced over at Alicia. She looked uncomfortable as Colt leaned toward her, narrowing his eyes.

"Maybe you're the reason he can't afford to keep the ranch that's been in our family for three generations. You realize he's as close to broke as they come, right?"

The color drained from her face and she looked around as if trying to find something to explain Colt's attack. "Excuse me?"

"You heard me." Colt planted both hands on the table and leaned closer. "I've been around rodeo longer than you've been alive. I know how you bunnies try to worm your way into our wallets." He jerked his thumb toward David. "Well, this one's got nothing."

"That's enough, Dad," Christian said, reaching for his dad's arm, pulling him back toward the seat. "You don't even know her."

"I don't have to."

Alicia's eyes flashed with fury as she cocked a brow on her forehead and laughed at Colt, surprising them all. "You're a sad, pathetic excuse for a cowboy."

"You can't talk to me like that." David watched his father's face redden with fury. "I'm Colt Greenly."

"You are a washed up, worthless ex-champion who expects his sons to put up with petty complaints at every turn. If you're so amazing, why aren't you still on the circuit? If you'll excuse me, David. I refuse to sit and listen to this abuse." She scooted out of the booth, past David, and hurried for the door, leaving all three men staring after her, speechless.

Christian was the first to speak. "Uh, David, you should probably go after her."

"Don't you dare!" His father bellowed, rising and slamming a hand on the table. "Let her go. She's trash and making you lose focus. You need to keep your eye on the Finals and leave the whores for someone else."

David jumped to his feet and leaned over the table, into his father's face. "If you ever talk about her that way again—"

"What?" Colt sat back down and leaned back in the booth. "What are you going to do?"

"Go find her, David," his brother muttered.

David watched Ali hurry from the restaurant, wondering how everything had changed so quickly. He'd gone from being ready to tell her he was falling in love with her to trying to subdue one of his father's tirades in a matter of minutes.

"Ali!" Alicia turned to see David running toward her. "Wait."

"David, I don't think we can do this." She shook her head and continued toward her truck. After her confrontation with Chris, she couldn't take any more today.

"Do what?"

"Us, this." She dug through her purse looking for her keys. "Your father hates me, and it's just making things harder on you. I've heard him, David. He thinks I'm nothing more than a bunny, trash, just after you for your money."

"What money? I don't have any." He reached for her hand and drew her against his chest. "He wants me to save the ranch from foreclosure. Other than giving the family yet another NFR title, that's all he wants me for."

"I get that he thinks he's looking out for your best interest." She'd been so intent on getting out what she wanted to say she'd barely heard him admit the pain his father was inflicting on him. Her eyes registered her shock.

David ran his hand through his hair, his face revealing his frustration. "I'm nothing more than a meal ticket to him. My brother, too. He wants us to be like him so we can provide for him." The words spilled from gritted teeth as if he couldn't bear to say them. "He's got a gambling problem. Not to mention that he can barely stay sober most days. Even when he is, he's popping pain pills for his leg."

David sighed, his shoulders slumping. "I've never told anyone about all his issues, not even Chris. This isn't about you, Ali. This is who he is. He ran our mother off years ago, practically chased her from the ranch. He's a mean son-of-a-bitch but he doesn't have anyone left but the two of us."

She laid a hand on his chest. "He's your father but you have to understand why I can't subject myself to his insults and bigotry." She turned back toward the truck.

"Ali, what do you want me to do? He needs me. Don't ask me to choose between you."

She paused, taking a deep breath, with her hands on the door handle before returning to him. "I'm not asking you to but I *am* going to make this easy on you." She laid her fingers against his jaw. "I like you but this isn't going to work, David."

She climbed into her truck and pulled out of the parking lot, trying not to look in the mirror to see David standing alone, staring at his hands as if they had the answers to what had just happened. As much as she regretted hurting David, she didn't regret the decision. She wouldn't subject herself to Colt Greenly and, unfortunately, he was part of the package that a relationship with David offered.

CHRIS BANGED HIS fist against the door, jarring it with his intensity.

"Cristobel?" Jessie answered the door, wiping her hand over her sleepy eyes. "What's wrong? Is it your sister?"

"I need to talk to Ali." His words came out slightly slurred, as if his mouth was full of cotton.

"What?" Jessie rubbed at her forehead as if she hadn't understood him.

"Ali. I need to talk to her."

"Are you—"

"He's drunk, Mom." Ali appeared at her mother's shoulder. "And, apparently, he wants to wake up Dad so that he can come out with his gun. Go ahead and go back to bed. I'll take care of this."

"I am not," he protested, but leaned back against the porch railing to keep his balance as the world continued to shift off kilter.

Ali brushed past her mother and stepped onto the porch, closing the door behind her with a soft click. "What do you want, Chris?"

She looked so sweet with her hands tucked into the front pocket of a hoodie, with her flannel pajama bottoms on, her pink toenails peeking out from underneath. The sight of her painted toenails was so utterly feminine it stole his breath away and scattered his thoughts. Her hair was mussed, as if she'd climbed out of her warm bed because of him and it didn't take much for him to imagine her there, his body pressing her into the soft mattress as he made love to her.

He took a quick step forward and cupped her jaw with his hands, seizing her mouth in a kiss meant to brand her. His lips teased her, stealing any reluctance on her part as they caressed hers in a primal dance. He slid his fingers into her hair, holding her against him, her soft curves cradling him as his other hand slid to her waist, pulling her against him, his arousal evident against her.

Her fingers curled in the front of his shirt but, instead of pushing him away, she pulled him closer, her hand sliding up the back of his neck to cup his nape as she opened her mouth to him, willingly giving him all he wanted to take. Chris swept his tongue against hers and heard her gasp of surprise.

He wanted her, every inch of her, writhing beneath him. He wanted to taste her skin, to feel her fingers trailing over his flesh. He wanted to hear her cry out his name, to bury himself into her, to see her arch her back as he brought her pleasure. He wanted to hear her say she loved him.

The realization hit him like he'd been kicked in the gut by a steer. This wasn't him being drunk. This wasn't jealousy. He didn't want to date Ali. He wanted her to be entirely his, to make sure no one else ever touched her again. He wanted her with him in the morning, to fall asleep holding her in his arms, to watch her bear their children. He wanted the entire fairytale—happily ever after. He was in love with Ali and he was finally ready to admit it.

He broke off their kiss slowly, his fingers trailing over her cheeks, letting his gaze travel over her sleepy eyes and kiss-swollen lips. He rubbed his thumb over her lower lip. "Ali, we have to talk."

She sighed and laid her forehead against his chin. He kissed the smooth skin of her brow. "I don't want to talk, Chris. All we ever do is talk. I'm tired of talking."

Chris tipped her chin up, leaning down and sipping from her lower lip. "Have something better in mind?"

"That depends," she whispered, her voice husky as his mouth found the curve of her throat at her jaw. She gasped as his hand slipped up the back of her sweatshirt and tripped along the skin at the top of her thin camisole shirt.

She shivered against him and he felt the blood pooling in his loins, aching for release, and he groaned against her throat. His hand moved over her ribs as his thumb brushed the soft cotton covering her breast, causing her nipple to pucker. She arched against his hand, filling his palm with her, and cried out softly. His fingers sought the hem of her shirt, slipping below, intent on the prize of her heated skin beneath.

"Ali, you drive me crazy, you always have." His need burned in him, making every part of his flesh tingle with icy fire. He wanted to confess the thoughts flitting through his mind like kids playing tag but his desire had hijacked his brain, making it impossible to think about anything but how good she felt in his arms. "I've waited for this for a long time."

"For what?" she whispered hesitantly.

Chris let his hands fall to the curve of her rear and pressed her against him. "I need you, Ali. I can't get you out of my head." His fingers found her waist as he squeezed her slightly. "It seems like I've wanted you forever."

CHRIS'S WORDS PENETRATED the fog of her desire. "What?" She pressed her hands against his chest as he tried to cover her mouth with his.

It didn't seem to deter him as he pressed his lips to her jaw, nibbling at the tender skin of her neck. She fought against the shiver of delight that raced down her spine, twirling magically in her belly before curling through her limbs. Her fingers twitched, itching to slip under his shirt, to feel the expanse of muscled flesh she knew was underneath. Her mind and body warred with one another until her heart was able to be heard above the deafening pulse racing through her ears.

You deserve to be loved, not just wanted.

Alicia didn't want to be Chris's flavor-of-the-week, especially when the smoky scent of whiskey still clung to him. She couldn't allow her desire to rule her. No matter how badly she wanted to give in to her needs, no matter how much her heart wanted to believe he cared for her, he only wanted her body. He'd as much as admitted his need for her was purely physical. Allowing this to go further would only make her exactly what Colt Greenly had accused her of being—a buckle bunny.

"Stop, Chris. I don't want this." She shoved against his chest and he stumbled backward, looking dazed. "I'm not some itch you can scratch."

He frowned at her. "I didn't say—"

"You didn't have to." She ran her fingers through her hair, ashamed of the way she'd let him touch her. What was she thinking? "Did you think I'd just jump into the back of your truck with you?"

She moved out of his reach as he tried to grasp her hand and pull her closer. She couldn't risk losing herself to the longing again. To do that would be the end of all her resolve. She saw the muscle in his jaw tick as he fisted his hands at his sides.

"I didn't think that. I came here because—"

"Oh, please explain," she interrupted. "Because it seems to me that you showed up at my home at two o'clock in the morning, drunk, pounding on the door, waking everyone, hoping for a quick booty call."

Alicia turned her back on him, unable to reconcile her assumptions with the hurt in his blue eyes.

His hands circled her waist and pulled her back against his chest, his hands clasping over her stomach. His breath against her ear was as hot as his hands burning her through the material of her camisole. She wanted to throw caution to the wind and press herself into his palms but she gripped her self-control with a tight rein.

"Ali." Her name was a prayer on his lips, a husky whisper of sound against her hair, and she ached at the longing she could hear in the one word. "That's not why I came." Chris spun her to face him and his fingers found her cheek. "Did you break up with David?"

"Why do you even care?" She avoided meeting his gaze. "You aren't my keeper, or my protector." She bit the corner of her lip, regretting the hastily spoken words as soon as they spilled out.

He tipped her chin up, a playboy grin slipping over his lips. "I don't want to be your keeper, Ali. I want to be far more than that, but I don't want to steal my best friend's woman."

She narrowed her eyes at him and shoved him away

from her and reached for the front door. "Why can't you be serious about anything? Is everything a joke to you?"

"Ali, I love you."

Alicia's heart stopped in her chest as she turned slowly, her hand on the door handle, unable to believe she'd heard him correctly. In all the years she'd known him, she couldn't remember him ever saying those words to anyone but his mother or sister. He couldn't possibly mean them and she knew from the way he swayed on his feet, he certainly wouldn't remember saying them in the morning.

I want to believe him . . . why can't I just pretend he meant it?

Tears burned in her eyes as her stomach twisted and turned before knotting. "Give me your keys and go sleep in the barn." She sighed, holding her hand out, feeling defeated and worn out from the emotional turmoil of the past eight hours. Chris dropped the keys into her hand and grasped her wrist, pulling her against his chest.

"Ali, say something."

She twisted her wrist, loosening it from his fingers, and stared into his eyes. Everything in her wanted to stay with him, to let him convince her, but it would all be a lie.

"You want me to believe you? Say it sober."

CHRIS WOKE WITH his head throbbing painfully. "I've got to stop mixing my alcohol," he groaned, pressing the heel of his hand to his eyes as the morning sun greeted him painfully through the doorway.

The soft whicker of the horses alerted him to someone

in the barn and he sat up, dropping his head in his palms with his elbows braced on his knees. He looked up to see Ali standing in the doorway, holding a cup of steaming coffee. She was a breath of fresh air in her hot pink t-shirt and jeans with her hair pulled back in a ponytail. Memories of last night came rushing back at him—kissing her, nearly losing control, practically assaulting her on the front porch before telling her he loved her. Chris sighed against his palms and peeked at her again through his fingers.

She came closer and smiled down at him. "Don't worry, Chris, I won't hold you to anything you said last night." She held the mug out to him. "You weren't exactly yourself."

He could either pretend he didn't remember any of last night or he could cowboy up and tell her the truth. His fingers slid over hers as he took the coffee and he pulled her down to the worn couch beside him. Chris rubbed a hand over the stubble on his jaw, wondering how to best voice his feelings without looking like an even bigger fool than he already did.

"Here, take these, too." She dropped two aspirin into his hand. "I guess this makes us even for the way you took care of me."

Chris tossed them into his mouth and washed them down with the brew, grimacing as his head and stomach revolted. "Ali, about last night," he began.

She laughed quietly. "Don't worry about it. What kind of friend would I be if I couldn't forgive a little drunken rambling?"

Rambling? Was he remembering what happened, or

what he'd wanted to happen? Had he been so drunk she hadn't understood him? His memories couldn't be that far off, could they? He didn't think so, but then again, he'd had a lot to drink before David called him, accusing him of sabotaging his budding relationship with Ali. He wasn't about to wait for them to make up and miss another chance so he'd rushed over to her house. It was a stupid thing to do in his condition, something he'd sworn he'd never do, and he was lucky Ali hadn't let him drive home.

"What exactly happened last night?" He sipped the coffee, watching her fidget on the couch beside him. "Because what I remember isn't lining up with what you're saying," he admitted.

She shrugged and started to stand but he laid his hand on her thigh and she froze. Chris set the mug on the floor. "I remember your mom answering the door." He turned and stared at her mouth. "I kissed you."

She bit her lip as if she didn't trust herself to say anything but her chest rose and fell like she was trying to catch her breath. He felt his erection throb to life and he forced himself to remain still. She wouldn't meet his gaze and it was driving him crazy.

"You kissed me back." Her eyes flicked up to meet his gaze and his pulse throbbed through his veins when she didn't deny it.

"I told you I love you." Chris could see the fear shadow her beautiful brown eyes and reached for her hand. He swallowed his pride and pressed on. "I meant it last night and I mean it now."

"Don't," she whispered, slipping her hand from his grasp and holding it up to ward him off. "Please, just don't."

He reached for the hand she held out and pressed a kiss to her palm. "Don't what?" He pulled her toward him, his lips finding the racing pulse at her wrist. "Don't kiss you?" His hand slid to her waist, his finger trailing up her ribcage. "Don't touch you this way?"

Chris pulled her against him, practically into his lap, and found the curve of her jaw with his lips. "Don't love you?" He touched his finger to her chin, forcing her to look him in the eye. "Ali, I can't help that. I've never been able to help that."

Chapter Thirteen

ALICIA COULDN'T BREATHE. She was too afraid that any movement might wake her from this dream. When she got up this morning, she convinced herself Chris's declaration had been the liquor talking. As much as his lips and hands could drive her insane with desire she had to keep a distance between them that would be safe for her heart. If she didn't, she was certain to end up with nothing more than broken shards. If the flutter against her ribcage was any indication, she was already a goner.

Finding him sitting on the couch, his face in his hands, looking despaired, jarred her. She'd never seen him look lost before, or so pained, and her heart went out to him. His eyes seemed to delve into the depths of her soul, reaching for the truth she'd buried there, hidden from everyone. Or so she'd thought. Over the past two weeks, every moment she'd spent near him seemed to unearth her feelings a bit more until she sat with him now, completely exposed and vulnerable. His hand cupped her jaw, his thumb brushing gently over the skin, sending ripples of burning desire down her spine to her core, settling in and creating a swirling need like she'd never known. Her love for this man was bound to consume but she didn't have the will to turn him away again. She'd already fought it for too long. They'd already come too far to go back now.

"Tell me what you don't want me to do because I honestly don't think I can stop myself from doing any of those things."

Chris didn't give her a chance to respond before his mouth was on hers, giving as much as he was taking. She wanted to push him away, remind him of every reason why they shouldn't be together, but she couldn't seem to conjure up even one. Nothing seemed to matter right now as her heart pounded in her ears, her eyes seeing only Chris. She needed this man, like the day needed the sun, and she couldn't deny herself this moment any longer.

Chris shifted, leaning over her, his hands searing her though the sides of the thin cotton t-shirt. His mouth met hers and she matched him perfectly, taking all he offered. Her fingers buried into his short hair, drawing him closer. She wanted to feel herself pressed against every inch of him. Hearing the words from him had released the dam of emotion she'd been trying to hold back far too long and they threatened to drown her. Alicia's fingers slid under the back of his shirt, desperate to feel his heated flesh under her palms.

Chris groaned against her mouth, his tongue delving inside as her hands slid over the hard ridges of muscle, her fingertips trailing over his spine. She felt the goose-flesh rise over the skin of his back. Desire surged through her as he laid her back on the couch, his entire frame hot where it touched her. Chris's hand slid up the side of her shirt and his thumb brushed the taut nipple, the minimal covering her bra provided only heightened his touch and she arched against him, unable to stop the agonized cry that left her lips as his fingers curved around her breast.

Alicia clung to him, her hands memorizing the curves and valleys of muscle, her hands caressed his chest before playing over the ripples of his abdomen. He growled, barely tearing himself from his assault on her mouth to reach one hand behind him, and yank the shirt over his head, throwing it aside. Chris looked down at her, pulling the hair band from her hair, letting it fall like a dark curtain through his fingers. It hung loose over the arm of the couch. Her eyes fell to the tattoo on his bicep.

"You're right." She let her fingers trail over the dark lines. "It's incredibly sexy." She smiled up at him, expecting to see victory in his gaze.

Instead, she saw hunger in his gaze, the smoldering lust she knew was reflected in her own and trepidation. "Ali, if you want me to stop, now would be the time. I know this is all sudden and . . ."

Alicia cupped his jaw for a moment before wiggling out from under him. She walked toward the doorway of the tack room and slid the door shut. Leaning back against the door, her hands tucked behind her at her lower back, and sought answers in his eyes. His blue eyes were filled with every bit of the hunger she felt but there was more in the depths, darkening them into seas of tender adoration. It chased away her fear and reservations. She had barely said anything to him, remaining quiet even after his declaration, still uncertain of his sincerity, but seeing the anguish in his eyes was enough to overrule her logic. With his heart laid bare, she could read everything in his eyes she needed to make a decision.

Alicia grasped the hem of her t-shirt and pulled it over her head, dropping it on the ground, and covered the three steps between them. She straddled his lap and cupped his beard-roughened face in her hands.

"Chris, I'm still not sure this is a good idea but I've never wanted anything more." She lowered her face until her lips were a breath from his. "I don't want you to stop."

Alicia sucked his lower lip between hers and he allowed her to take control, his hands running up her spine and curving over her shoulders. She ran her hands over the muscles of his chest, loving the way the sinew tensed under her caress. Her eyes slid over him, appreciating the sheer masculine perfection of his physique, chiseled from years of physical labor and riding. She lifted her eyes back to his and could see his barely restrained yearning.

"Ali, you're killing me." He gave her a lopsided grin and slid his hands up into her hair, drawing her to him and burying his face against the soft flesh between her breasts. The rasp of his jaw scratched against the sensitive skin deliciously and she gasped at the pleasure.

Chris pressed a gentle kiss on the upper curve of her breast, sending spirals of eager longing to her core. She arched into his hands as he cupped her breast, his thumb brushing the peak until she moaned deep in her throat. His fingers brushed the strap of her bra from her shoulder and his head bent to taste her. He nipped and kissed her collarbone, making her shiver against him.

Deftly, Chris twisted his fingers at the back of her bra and looked surprised when nothing happened. She laughed quietly, leaning backward, using his hands at her back to brace her, and could feel his erection straining against the denim of his pants.

"I thought you were supposed to be good at this," she teased and he froze.

As soon as the words left her mouth, she regretted them. They only served to remind her of just how many women Chris had actually been with. She was just one of several. The smile died on her lips and she stiffened in his hands.

As if reading her thoughts, Chris tipped her chin up and looked deep into her eyes. "Ali, look at me. It's only us now. I have never wanted another woman this much. And I have never, ever, told a woman I love her." He gently kissed her. "I love you," he whispered against her lips.

She wanted to say the words back to him, to tell him how she'd felt for years, but she held that piece of her heart back. When he changed his mind, when he decided this was too much, too serious for him, she didn't want him to know he was taking her broken heart with him. A sad smile curved her lips as she leaned back again and reached for the clasp between her breasts. She might not be able to hold him but this stolen moment would be enough. It had to be.

She unclasped her bra, letting her breasts fall into his hands, her gasp caught by his mouth on hers. Nothing in her life had ever felt this good. She wasn't inexperienced but no man had ever scattered her senses or made her shake with need the way Chris did. He dipped his head to taste her, his hands curling around her shoulders as she grasped his biceps, holding on as if he was her lifeline.

White-hot pleasure shot from his lips throughout her body, making her throb, and she squeezed her thighs around his hips. He growled, drawing her close, his tongue flicking against the hard peak before taking her into his mouth sucking, biting, laving the delicious pain away.

"Chris, I've already waited too long for you." Her fingers fumbled with the button of his jeans and he laughed against her flesh, standing and turning so she was seated on the couch.

He unbuttoned his pants and slid them over his thighs, just as muscular as the rest of him from life in the saddle. He knelt in front of her, dragging a finger between her breasts over her flat stomach, and unbuttoned her jeans, lifting her hips to pull them down her slim thighs before slipping her boots off. She could see his arousal as his eyes caressed her, sliding from her eyes to her breasts and down to the cotton underwear that matched her cast aside bra. His finger toyed with the lace at the edge and gave her a wicked grin, arching his brow.

"What?" Her voice was husky with desire and she felt the blush begin to rise over her cheeks.

"Just wishing I'd told you sooner." His fingers curled around the edge and slid it over her thighs, his fingertips caressing the flesh of her calf. "You're magnificent." His hands stroked her inner thigh.

"Don't tease," she pleaded, a blush covering her face as he savored the sight of her.

Chris smiled at her. "Honey, I have no intention of it."

His fingers found the already moist seam of her womanhood and slid his finger down the length. His other hand curled around her breast, his fingers plucking at the nipple. Her head dropped against the back of the couch as he tormented her. Alicia bucked against him, wanting to ask him for more but at a loss for words.

"Oh, Chris," she pleaded, gripping his shoulders.

His thumb stroked the nub of her pleasure and she cried out. She felt her orgasm building already, her body trembling against him.

"Chris, I can't wait."

"Don't, honey." He dipped his finger into her, his thumb massaging her, his mouth finding her breast and drawing a moan from deep in her throat. "You don't have to wait for me," he said, nibbling along the curve of her breast before taking the other mound into his mouth.

He circled the center of her pleasure as the coil of heat built within her, spiraling out of control, lifting her, carrying her as he continued to taste her. She couldn't hold back any longer and arched off the couch. Chris held her to him as her orgasm broke over her in waves of pleasure, shattering her, leaving her fragmented in his arms.

CHRIS HAD NEVER been a selfish lover but he'd never wanted to bring a woman pleasure as much as he did with Ali. Watching her fall to pieces at his touch was exhilarating, making him feel like he could fly if he wanted to. He rose and slid his boxers down his thighs as she tried to catch her breath. He saw her open one eye and look at him, a shadow of a smile playing at the corners of her lips.

"Like what you see?" He grinned back, confidently.

"Don't get cocky, cowboy."

He loved how, even in the middle of love-making, she didn't back down from him. She might look sweet and innocent, not to mention sexy as hell lying naked in front of him, but his Ali was a spitfire, all soft kitten with playful claws.

He glanced down, his arousal for her boldly evident. "Too late." He grabbed a condom from his wallet and slid it over the length of him.

Chris stalked toward her, lifting her and groaning as she circled her legs around his waist until he sat on the couch, letting her straddled him once again. She smiled as he laid his palm against her cheek, staring deeply into her dark eyes, growing serious.

"Ali, I won't hurt you."

"I know you won't."

Chris easily read the lie in her eyes and knew her distrust was his own fault. He'd cultivated this love 'em and leave 'em reputation. Ali wasn't stupid enough to fall for words. He was going to have to prove himself to her. He vowed to do exactly that, no matter what it might take.

He was going to show her that she was different, that she made *him* different.

His hands found her waist as she bent her head, brushing her lips over his, her tongue darting between his lips and driving him over the edge. He wanted to go slow but she was making it near impossible. He slid into her heat, growling deep in his chest.

She was incredible, pure heaven, and he was ready to explode. Her eyes widened, her body surrounding his, clasping at him, and she dropped her head backward, sucking in a gasp that pressed her breasts toward him. He wasn't strong enough to ignore the temptation. Chris slid his hand up and cupped her breasts, taking one into his mouth as Ali rose and slid down the length of him. He could feel the shudders in her as her body clutched at him, relishing the exquisite torture of trying to hold back his release.

"Chris," she whispered. His name was a prayer on her lips as she fell forward, her forehead against his shoulder.

Chris knew she was close, her entire body trembled around him and he couldn't wait any longer. Holding her waist as he drove into her, letting her ride him as each thrust brought him closer to the edge until she shuddered against him, her voice calling out his name in a hoarse plea. With one hand curled at the back of her head, he plunged his tongue into her mouth, needing to feel her surrounding every part of him, her sweet scent filling him, enveloping him with her pleasure. Chris held her hips, his fingers pressing into the rounded curve of her buttocks, her breasts pressed against his chest, her nipples grazing over his skin, and he couldn't hold back any longer. He poured himself into her, the seal of secrecy broken, releasing every bit of the love he'd been hiding for years.

Spent, his head dropped onto the back of the couch while she collapsed against his chest, her head curling into the curve of his neck and shoulder while her long hair tickled his arm, trailing over his ribs. He ran his fingers down her spine and felt her shiver against him. His body reacted, instantly coming back to life, surprising both of them.

He felt her lips curve into a playful smile against the crook of his neck. "Now I see why you have the reputation you do," she said with a husky laugh.

As much as he wanted to relax in the aftermath of what they'd just done, her words jerked him back to the reality of the situation. He'd just made love to his sister's best friend, a woman who might still be dating his best friend as far as he knew. He'd told her he loved her, and meant it, but was he really ready for a relationship that should follow that proclamation? And what would she expect from him? This was such foreign territory; he wasn't even sure what to say or where to begin.

He hated that she was already trying to lump herself in with the group of women he'd been with. She was nothing like them. Nor was any part of his reputation grounded in truth but rather silence that had grown to wild tales he'd never denied. He wished now he'd corrected them.

"Ali, you shouldn't believe everything you hear." He

brushed her hair back from her cheek and pressed his lips to her forehead. "So, what happens now?"

He felt her stiffen and wondered what he said wrong. She sat up, her hands cupping his neck and smiled at him, her breasts just under his chin, tantalizing him and making it difficult to concentrate on anything she was saying. "I need to get these horses fed and take both of my boys out for a ride to try to work out a few kinks before the rodeo this week."

He moved himself against her suggestively. "Done."

He didn't like the sadness he could see in her eyes, regardless of how she was trying to hide it and wanted to make her laugh, to regain the lighthearted fun they had together. His fingertips slid up her side, brushing the outer curve of her breast, and he reveled at the way her eyes softened with slumberous desire. He'd take her passion over fun any day. "I mean, what happens with us, honey."

She put her hands on his shoulders and climbed off his lap, reaching for her clothes. Chris couldn't help but admire the curve of her rear as she bent to retrieve her jeans.

"I don't know, Chris." She looked at him over her shoulder and he nearly groaned at the sexy picture she made. "This wasn't exactly planned." She slipped her arms into her bra and pulled her shirt over her head. "I'm not expecting you to get down on one knee, if that's what you're worried about." She reached up and ran her fingers through her hair, pulling it back into a ponytail, searching for the band to hold it.

Chris reached for his pants and slid them on before walking toward her, holding out the hair tie. This wasn't going the way he wanted. She was too dispassionate for what they'd just shared. He didn't like the cynical note in her voice, as if she was already regretting what they'd done. She plucked it from his fingers, wrapping it around her hair, before he reached for her hand, dragging her back into his arms. He dipped his head, taking her lips in a scorching kiss. She sighed and melted against him, his hands splayed at her lower back while hers held onto the sides of his arms.

When he broke the kiss he was gasping for breath, barely able to speak. He placed a light kiss on her nose. "Ali, I lo—"

She stopped him with a finger. "Chris, don't feel like you have to say something you don't mean." She slipped out of his arms and hurried out the barn door. "Do me a favor and throw a flake of alfalfa to each of the horses. Your keys are in the kitchen."

She practically ran out of the barn, heading back toward the house without letting him say anything else. She knew he couldn't go after her without his clothes. Chris wasn't letting her get away that easily.

"You said you'd believe me if I told you sober," he yelled after her. She didn't even acknowledge his declaration. After what just happened, how could she still doubt it. "Damn it!" he cursed as he kicked the grain bucket outside a stall as several horses grunted in their stalls. Frustration coursed through him as he jerked his shirt over his head. How was he ever going to make this right?

Chapter Fourteen

ALICIA HAD TO get out of the barn and away from Chris before she broke down into tears. His words were chipping away at the flimsy wall she'd erected around her heart. It had taken every ounce of self-control to not confess her feelings to him. She'd known Chris too long to believe he could ever be serious about anyone for more than a few dates. He might have feelings for her now but those wouldn't last and he would do what Chris did to every woman—leave town, heading for the next rodeo and another woman to warm him. Just because she'd never heard him say he loved anyone didn't mean he hadn't said it, or that it wasn't just a line to get him what he wanted. She couldn't let him to see how desperate she was to believe his words. She was stupid to have given in to him, regardless of what she thought she saw in his eyes, of what he said. Just because his actions led her to momentarily believe him, she couldn't afford to let it happen again. Even if Chris meant it, her heart couldn't take it when he changed his mind.

Chris was never going to change, never going to give himself to anyone completely. She was nothing more than an itch Chris needed to scratch and she hated that, in spite of knowing it, she hadn't been strong enough to push him away again. If he pushed her away again, the shards of her heart would tinkle as they fell in her ribcage. It was better to put on an air of nonchalance, like making love to him was something she did every day. She channeled her inner Chris—pretending it was nothing more than sex. While the act might have fooled him, it didn't fool her own heart, which throbbed with misery.

"You said you'd believe me if I told you sober."

She heard him yell from the doorway of the barn, echoing over the pasture. Her heart hammered in her chest painfully and she almost missed a step. Every part of her heart begged her to turn around, go back to where he waited and confess to him that she loved him, always had. If she stopped now he would know it was all been a ruse. She could run back into his arms and never leave. But doing that would doom her heart.

"Damn it!" The sound of Chris's curse and clattering metal carried to her and she wondered if he'd just kicked the grain buckets, wishing for a moment she'd thought to do it herself.

Her vision clouded as tears filled her eyes. She didn't want to go into the house because Chris would be coming in soon for his keys, and she didn't want to run into her mother who would demand an explanation for her tears.

Her cell phone vibrated in her pocket and she pulled it out, grateful for the distraction, until she saw David's face on the screen. Guilt and shame poured over her, weighing her down. If he found out about what she and Chris had done . . .

It shouldn't matter, they weren't dating any longer, but she knew it would. If David found out, it would crush him.

The voice in her head assaulted her with painful taunts, reminding her of how his father saw her as nothing more than trash, intent on using his son for money. He called her a bunny, a rodeo groupie who slept around to get what she wanted. Her stomach churned as she realized her rendezvous with Chris in the barn wouldn't make her look any better. She thought about sending the call to voice mail but it wasn't David's fault she'd already reached her mistake quota for one day within a few hours after rising. He probably wanted to apologize again for last night, not that it was going to change her mind.

"Hey, David." She cleared her throat, hoping he couldn't hear the regret in her voice or the bitter tears threatening to choke her.

"Ali, meet me for breakfast. We need to talk."

Alicia found herself wandering toward the stallion barn, passing the paddocks where several champion cutting horse stallions grazed in individual pastures. "It's not a good time."

"Then lunch. Please, Ali? I can't just leave things the way they were last night."

"David, I really don't think there's anything left to say." She could hear the desperation in his voice and wondered if she recognized it only because she felt the same way about her relationship with Chris.

"Ali, please. I understand why you feel the way you do. But," she heard him sigh into the phone. "You realize I don't really care what my dad says, right? That I don't feel the same way?"

Maybe it was because she understood how much it hurt to care deeply for someone and know the feeling would never be reciprocated, but it felt wrong to cast him aside without explanation. She sighed. "I have to be somewhere this afternoon at one. Maybe we can meet for coffee after?"

"Absolutely." His voice suddenly sounded rushed. "Look, I have to go but just call me when you get into town and I'll meet you wherever you want."

"Okay," she agreed.

"Bye, Ali." She heard him fumbling with the phone just before Colt's voice could be heard yelling in the background.

"How many times do I have to tell you to quit wasting time with that bunny? Is she really that good in the sack?"

"For the last time, do *not* talk about her. I'm a grown man and I've about had it with your meddling." She could hear the fury in David's voice. "For someone who wants an awful lot of money from me, you're sure pushing my buttons. I should walk away now and let you rot in that trailer."

"Why don't you just find a rich girl like your brother did? At least you'd be of some use since it doesn't look like you're doing anything to help us keep the ranch."

Alicia heard a scuffle in the background and couldn't help but wonder what in the world was happening with David and his father. She thought about hurrying back to the barn to send Chris to make sure they were both all right.

"Don't ever raise a hand to me again, Dad." David sounded breathless. "Or the next time you land on your ass it won't be because you tripped."

David's voice came through the phone again, startling her. "Hello? Hello? Ali, are you there?"

She stared at her phone, holding her breath. She didn't want him to know she'd heard any of what had just occurred. The line disconnected and she felt the icy dread creeping over her limbs. David's relationship with his father had crossed a line but she wasn't sure who it posed more danger for—him or his father.

CHRIS PULLED INTO his parents' driveway as his dog, Bueller, came running out to greet him. He'd been a gift from a girlfriend just a few years ago. He rubbed the dog's fuzzy golden head. The girlfriend had been around less time than it took to house train the puppy, but at least he'd gained a trusty friend from the short-lived relationship.

"Maybe you can offer me some sound advice because I think I'm really screwing things up." The dog plopped his furry butt on the ground and his tail thumped against the gravel driveway. "Thanks a lot," Chris muttered.

All of his relationships seemed to turn out this way and

he knew he was to blame. He never wanted to look past the surface of any of the women he dated and, even if he had, it didn't take a brain surgeon to see he was deliberately choosing women who weren't looking for attachments. So, what was it about Ali that had him ready to jump, headfirst? He'd told her he loved her. He knew what happened when you said that to a woman. They immediately started looking at white dresses and picking dates for a wedding. But not Ali. No, instead, she'd ignored him and, when she couldn't ignore it, she ran the other direction like a scared jackrabbit. He'd never known Ali to be afraid of anything.

Chris looked up as he heard an engine slowing in front of the house and recognized David's truck. He rolled his eyes at the dog. "Great, I must have hit the crap-jackpot." Chris stuffed his hands into the pockets of his jeans as Bueller rubbed against his thigh, trying to gain his master's attention again.

David parked the truck behind his and got out. Chris didn't miss the intent in his eyes; David was pissed and there was only one reason for him to show up here this mad first thing in the morning. Somehow, he'd found out about Ali.

"What the hell are you trying to pull?" David stormed toward him. "I call Ali's house this morning and her mother tells me you showed up last night, drunk? Was that after I called you?" David shoved him backward, ignoring the low growl of the dog.

Chris wanted to defend himself, to remind David that he'd known Ali far longer, had loved her for years, but he had no right. He'd introduced them, worked to convince

David to date her, and then moved in as soon as they had a bump in their relationship. He was a jerk and he didn't deserve David as a friend, but he couldn't lie to him.

"Bueller, get to the porch," he ordered, turning back to David. "Yeah, I went over there and I told her how I feel."

"What? Horny?" It was a low blow but Chris knew he deserved it.

David shoved him against the side of the truck, taking him by surprise. Chris knew he could take his friend in a fight. He easily outweighed David by twenty pounds of sheer muscle but he wouldn't. Right now, after what he'd done, he deserved any sort of punishment David felt inclined to give.

"You've never wanted her until now. I was right last night; you *are* trying to sabotage our relationship."

"No, I wasn't . . . I'm not," he corrected. "But are you sure you actually have one? She broke up with you. You said so yourself."

"We're meeting this afternoon."

Chris felt like he'd just had the wind knocked out of him. He wanted to break something, to pummel David for lying, but he could see the truth in his friend's eyes. Why was Ali meeting with him after what they'd shared that morning? He refused to believe he meant nothing to her. She wasn't the type of girl to sleep with a man she didn't care about. At least, the Ali he knew before wasn't. But did he really know her anymore? Maybe David was full of shit, maybe it was planned before he showed up at Ali's. Excuses floated through his mind, he wanted to believe anything but the thought that he'd been a pawn.

David eyed Chris, suspiciously. "Are you just getting home?"

Chris saw the frown marring David's brow as his face reddened. "I slept in the barn. I was too drunk to drive so Ali took my keys away. I don't know how I didn't kill myself getting there in the first place."

"Leave her alone, Chris."

He could hear the pleading note in David's voice and wondered at the reason for it. Didn't David realize he was the better man? It was one of the reasons he'd even introduced him to Ali—David was a good man who deserved a good woman to love. Maybe he should leave Ali alone. He was sure to cause her nothing but sorrow.

As if reading his thoughts, David pressed on. "She deserves better than the few nights you'll offer her until you've decided you're bored."

Chris adjusted his hat and met David's serious gaze but didn't say anything. He wanted to deny the accusation but his past spoke for itself and he wasn't entirely sure he wouldn't hurt her.

"Leave her alone, Chris. You can't give her what she needs. She needs someone who won't break her heart, someone who knows making love is more than a quick roll in the hay."

"Someone like you?"

"Someone *not* like you."

IF TIM BROOKS hadn't been the only real estate agent, Alicia would've felt better about using him. This was a small town, and small town people knew everyone's business, and she wanted this to remain under wraps until she chose to reveal it. She didn't want everyone finding out she was putting an offer on the ranch she'd spotted, and she certainly didn't want any counter-offers. She hoped she could trust him to keep his mouth shut.

"Well, Alicia, everything seems to be in order; however, there is one small issue."

Her excitement faded for a moment. Of course, something would go wrong. That was exactly her luck.

No, things are going to work out the way I want for a change.

"Tim, I thought everything was ready once I had the down payment."

He twisted his mouth sideways and frowned, apologetically. "Well, I've been trying to get you pre-approved for a loan but, so far, I'm not having much luck."

"What can I do to make it easier?" She'd do whatever she had to in order to make this a reality for her parents.

"Get a job."

"A job?" Alicia narrowed her eyes, hoping Tim was joking.

He shrugged. "Apparently, underwriters don't like seeing prize money as your source of income, even with your tax returns."

"What do you mean? It's what I do. I'm a barrel racer and it's how I've supported myself and my parents for the past seven years." Alicia couldn't believe what she was hearing. The bank wouldn't give her a loan because they didn't recognize what she did for a living? When

Tim didn't say anything else, she realized he was serious. "What kind of a job am I supposed to have?"

"They want to see a steady income, with regular paychecks. It makes you look dependable."

"I've saved nearly one hundred thousand dollars toward the down payment in less than two years. If that doesn't prove I can pay the bills, I don't know what does." She rose and began to pace his office.

"I know, Alicia. But your debt to income ratio is still borderline and, with the issue of your income, they aren't budging. There are really only two options. One is to take a steady paying job and the other would be to put twenty percent of the loan amount as a down payment."

Her eyes widened in shock. "Another ten percent? It's taken nearly two years to come up with this. You're asking me to do the impossible." Ali started to rise to leave.

He moved around his desk and pressed her shoulders, urging her back into the chair. "And that's why I suggested you take a steady job." Tim moved back behind his desk. "Depending on the job, you could still race on weekends but hold down the job during the week."

"And when am I supposed to work my horses? Or travel?"

"I'm just giving you the facts, Alicia." Tim shrugged. "But, whatever you decide to do, you need to do it quickly because it looks like the property is going into foreclosure proceedings and, if we don't act soon, at least put in an offer and get the ball rolling, it's going to auction."

She dropped her face into her palms and groaned. There was no way to continue to barrel race if she took a job, at least, not on a national scale. But she couldn't think of any job she was qualified for that would pay her what she was earning in rodeo. Without her winnings, she wouldn't be able to pay the mortgage on the property, anyway. This morning just continued to get worse. She should have stayed in bed.

ALICIA PULLED THE truck into the parking lot of The Queen Bean, the local coffee shop, and dropped her forehead against her hands on the steering wheel.

"Now what?" she whispered in the quiet of the truck.

She was still too far off from the Finals to even think about counting on a win to get her the rest of the down payment. A few wins at some of the bigger purse Texas rodeos might get her closer but it still wouldn't make up the $50,000 she needed, and not in the short amount of time she had left before the property went into foreclosure. And the likelihood of finding a job that would work around her rodeo schedule was almost nonexistent. She could see her dream slipping away.

Her phone rang and she reached for it, tapping the button to answer before looking at the screen. She'd already texted David, so she assumed he was returning her message.

"Hello?" Alicia didn't even bother to hide the disappointment from her voice. The last thing she wanted right now was to rehash Colt Greenly's insults with his son.

"Alicia? It's Bradley." She instantly recognized the voice of the man who'd employed her father for so many years. "I was hoping we might sit down and talk about my job offer."

"Job offer?" Her mind spun at the prospect. She'd been putting him off for so long, she didn't think he'd still be seriously considering her and, even if he was, she wasn't sure she wanted to be locked into someone else's schedule. But, if she took this job, it might be an answer to her prayers. At least, temporarily.

He laughed in the phone. "Yes, didn't your dad tell you? We're going to start showing more and we need someone who can travel with the horses. I'd also like to start giving lessons here at the ranch. You'd be great with kids."

"I . . . I'm flattered, Mr. Langdon, I really am but—"

"Why don't you meet with me at the house, say four o'clock? We can discuss numbers but I promise you won't be disappointed."

She had no doubt the salary would be more than what she was looking for but how much time would she be sacrificing? There would be no time for rodeo if she was showing horses every weekend for the Diamond Bar. "I'm meeting with someone right now, but I should be able to be back to the house by four thirty."

"Good!" He sounded as if she'd already agreed. "I'll be waiting for you!"

Alicia hung up just as she saw David pull into the parking lot, a deep frown marring his brow. He seemed to wear a permanent scowl these days and she realized she could sympathize with him. It seemed like nothing was going right for either of them. She sighed and exited the truck, locking it behind her and meeting him at the front bumper.

David quickly pasted a smile on his face when he saw her. "Hey, Ali." He leaned in and gave her an awkward hug.

"You look mad."

He opened the door for her and placed his hand at the small of her back. Nothing . . . no tingles, no butterflies, no sizzle of attraction. After spending the morning with Chris's hands on her, sending fire through her veins, she knew she'd made the right decision breaking things off with David. She cared about him but his touch felt almost brotherly. There was no electricity between them and she just couldn't pretend anymore. Sleeping with Chris might have been a mistake but trying to force feelings for David would be even worse and it wasn't fair to him.

"Not mad," he answered, eyeing her cautiously. "Just worried. About you," he clarified.

"Me?"

He nodded and placed his order for a coffee, waiting for her to place hers before he paid for both. "Your mom told me Chris showed up drunk last night and woke everyone up."

She didn't meet his gaze and prayed he wouldn't notice the blush creeping over her cheeks. The barista handed them their order and he followed her to a table near the back. Alicia wished he would change the subject.

I sure hope Mom didn't tell him Chris spent the night.

"He's got his head up his ass these days." Apparently, David was just getting warmed up.

She leaned back in the chair. "David, it's fine. I know how Chris is, so do my parents. He's impulsive and doesn't think a lot of the time. But my mother loves him, she always has."

David hooked an arm over the back of his chair and arched a brow. "Is she the only one?"

Alicia paused mid-sip and looked at him over the rim of her paper cup. "What's that supposed to mean?"

He let out a slow exhale and put his cup on the table before folding his hands. He studied her for a moment before speaking. "It means there's no need for us to have any sort of a conversation about giving me another chance, is there?" His eyes grew sad and he shook his head. "You're in love with Chris, aren't you?"

She was surprised by his point-blank question and wasn't prepared for it. She stared down at the cup in her hands as if she might find the answer in the latte foam.

"He's going to break your heart. You realize that?"

She pinched her lips together, still unable to meet his gaze, and nodded slightly.

"Ali, look at me." She lifted her eyes to his and was met with sympathy. He reached for her hand and squeezed it. "I care about you and I want to see you happy. I just hoped it would be with me." He kissed the back of her hand. "For the record, I love him like a brother but he only knows how to make Chris happy. I don't think Chris can make you happy."

She slipped her hand from his. "Can we talk about something else?"

David sat back. "Sure." The corner of his mouth curved up in a half-smile and his dark eyes glimmered mischievously. "Now that I've been friend-zoned, what've you been up to when you're not being yelled at by crazy ex-rodeo stars or assaulted by drunken cowboys in the middle of the night?"

She couldn't help but laugh at the humor in his voice. She really did like David and was grateful for his understanding. He was a good friend to have. "Well, there's this one cowboy who seems intent on stalking me and forcing me to have coffee with him."

"Huh, you don't say?" He tipped his cup toward her and winked. "You're a lucky woman."

Chapter Fifteen

IT WAS RIDICULOUS for him to sit here, wondering what David and Ali were talking about. If he wanted to know, he should just go into town and join them for coffee. They were all adults, not to mention friends, and should be able to sit down and talk this through. The problem was, he wasn't sure what *this* was. Were he and Ali dating? The way she'd acted this morning, it was nothing more than a casual romp but it hadn't felt that way for him. Then again, all of this was entirely foreign territory for him.

He had never wanted to be with someone for any extended period before but when he was with Ali, he found himself getting tongue-tied and twisted like he was sixteen again. Not to mention that his body seemed intent on losing all self-control as soon as she walked into the room. He might not be a randy teenager anymore but, so far, since this morning, all he'd thought about was the sweet scent of her skin as he pressed his face between her breasts. The taste of her clung to his lips and his fingers itched to glide over her skin again.

He slammed the side of his fist against the wall of the barn in frustration. He'd come out here to fix the broken stall door but he wasn't accomplishing anything but fantasizing about Ali. Ali, who was alone with David right now. After their conversation this morning, he could only imagine what David was telling her. He tried to convince himself that David didn't play dirty, that he would never try to steal her from him. But wasn't that what Chris had done? They'd never been in competition for a woman before.

Do you really think she'd choose you when she could have him?

It was the final straw. He wasn't about to sit around when he could lose Ali, not after he'd finally realized how much he wanted her. Chris threw his tools back into the tack room and left the job half-finished. He walked into the kitchen, ignoring his mother's worried frown and reached for his truck keys.

"Heading out for a while?"

He jingled his keys knowing his mother was trying to ask him why without voicing the question. "Just into town. Need anything while I'm there?"

She laid down her pen and crossed her hands over the bills on the counter. "You've been gone a lot lately. I know you're a grown man and—"

"Mom, I'm just running into town for a few things for the barn."

She arched a slim brow at him and cocked her head. "So, this has nothing to do with Ali?"

He could tell it was a rhetorical question. She had no doubt about being right. He leaned against the door frame, crossing his arms. "What did Sydney tell you?"

She laughed, her blue eyes glimmering with delight. "A blind man could see you're attracted to her. I didn't need your sister to tell me anything." Chris clenched his jaw, refusing to say anything, waiting for his mother to get to the point. She held up her hands. "Fine, I'll mind my own business."

"Good."

"But remember, son, Ali is like family. Your father and I love her. We don't want to see anyone get hurt."

"I'm not going to hurt her," he muttered. "Why does everyone keep saying that?" Chris started for the front door.

"I never said she was the one who would get hurt."

Chris shut the door before he heard any more. His stomach was twisted in as many knots as his thoughts. This was why he avoided relationships like the plague.

CHRIS PULLED INTO town and parked his truck in front of the hardware store and immediately spotted Ali's truck in front of The Queen Bean. He could see her through the front window, seated with her back toward him. He couldn't see anyone with her but it didn't mean she was alone. David's truck was parked beside hers so Chris knew he was in there with her.

"So what," he muttered to himself. Ali didn't have to clear her afternoon plans with him.

Her head tipped backward as she laughed at something her companion said. All thoughts of the hardware store vanished as his feet carried him across the street and toward the coffee shop. As he neared the entrance, he saw David clearly through the window, his hand over hers. Anger bubbled just below the surface as he watched him rise and put a hand on her shoulder before leaning down toward her.

Chris couldn't see Ali with David's body blocking her but it was clear that David was leaning forward for a kiss. His hands fisted at his sides, his jaw tightening to the point it was painful. David straightened, spotting him through the front windows and gave him a cocky grin. Ali turned in her seat and the color drained from her face. That look told him all he needed to know. He turned on a heel and headed back across the street, jerking his keys from his pocket.

"Chris, wait!"

He wasn't going to wait and hear her confess how she'd rather be with someone like David than him, how this morning didn't mean anything, how they could still be friends. He'd heard it all before but it was usually him giving the spiel. It sucked being on the receiving end of the speech.

He jerked open the door of the truck, surprised as she slammed it shut before he could get in. "Will you stop for a second?"

"Why, Ali? I think I get it."

"I don't think you do. We were just talking."

"Talking?" He cocked his head, looking down at her. "That didn't look like talking."

She narrowed her eyes at him. "You're jealous of David? Well, isn't that rich coming from the guy who's dated every woman within a twenty mile radius."

He ignored the tightness in his chest, hating the feeling more than he'd ever thought possible, hating the vulnerability he knew she could clearly see. Hating that her words stung. This wasn't who he was, this needy, jealous guy, crying over a broken heart. Screw this.

Cowboy up, asshole. Chris pulled the truck door open and climbed inside. "I don't have time for this crap. I have to get the barn fixed. Tell David I'll see him this weekend."

"HEY, LADY, WHEN are you coming back out this way?" Sydney's voice and the commotion she could hear in the background of the phone was a welcome reprive from the drama she'd caused herself lately.

"I wish I could. I could use someone to talk to," she confided.

"Then why haven't you called sooner? Spill it and don't leave out any juicy details." Ali smiled at her friend's scolding.

"I don't know if you have enough time for it all at once."

"Kassie just went down for a nap and Scott is in the barn since Derek just came back from a rodeo in Idaho. So, I've got all the time you need," she promised.

"I don't even know where to start." She sighed. "I'm really confused."

"You could start with telling me how things are going with David. You two seemed pretty cozy at Mom's house."

"Yeah, well," she hemmed, "that's over."

"Over? Chris didn't tell me that. When did that happen? Are you okay? Do I need to have Scott, Clay, and Derek kick his ass the next time we see him?"

"Slow down," Alicia laughed at her friend's rapid-fire questions. "The other night, I'm fine and no ass-kicking is necessary. I broke up with him."

"Why? You two looked so happy together."

"His father didn't seem to care." She lay back on her bed, the phone tucked between her shoulder and ear. "And had plenty to say about it when I went out to dinner with David, his brother, and Colt."

"I've met Colt Greenly once and he was an obnoxious jerk but I've never known you to let what anyone says bother you. If you can handle Delilah, he's a piece of cake."

"It tends to make a relationship hard when the family thinks you're after his money." She put the phone on speaker and tossed it onto the bed, rising to pace. "And Colt is much harder to take than Delilah. But I don't think it was going to work out with David anyway. He's really nice but, let's be honest, he's too good for me."

"What are you talking about?" Sydney yelled. "Did you fall off Beast onto your head? I thought you were going to say because of Chris. *That* I could understand but to think you're not good enough? That's just—"

"Wait a minute, what do you mean 'because of Chris?'" Alicia's heart stopped. *He wouldn't have told Sydney what happened, would he?*

"Alicia, everyone knows you guys have always had a thing for each other."

"Everyone who?" She reached for the phone on the bed. If other people could see she had this stupid girlish crush on Chris then he had to have known as well.

Sydney laughed. "Are the two of you blind? *Everyone*. Neither of you is any good at hiding anything. We've all just been waiting for you both to see it. Why do you think Delilah hates you?"

"Because of Chris?"

"Because Chris turned her down for the junior prom so he could go watch you barrel race with me."

Alicia thought back to the night. It was her junior year of high school and she was bummed because no one had asked her. It didn't help that they were graduating and Alicia was planning on leaving home far behind her, so she'd decided to forget about prom and get an early start barrel racing professionally. She'd promised to compete in the rodeo queen competition that year with Sydney but barrel racing was where her heart resided. She'd won her first go-round as a pro and Chris had been waiting to congratulate her at the trailer with a bear hug. She remembered practically melting into his arms as he swung her around before taking her out for ice cream to celebrate. It was the night she'd stopped looking at him as Sydney's brother.

"Don't you remember?" Sydney's voice broke into her thoughts, jerking her back from the memory.

"Yeah," Alicia whispered. "I do. I just . . ."

"You really didn't know how he felt?" Alicia could

hear male voices in the background of the phone. "Well, now that you know, what are you going to do about it?"

Alicia bit down on her lip, hard, trying to keep her angry tears at bay. All this time, Chris had feelings for her? Why hadn't he ever said something? And if he cared, why gallivant all over the state sleeping with a different woman every night of the week? Unless Sydney was wrong. Wanting and loving were two entirely different sentiments.

"Nothing."

Alicia stared out the window and it was suddenly clear what she needed to do. She couldn't put herself through the torment of seeing Chris at the rodeos, constantly flirting with new women while her heart was being shredded. By taking the job with Bradley, she would be able to get the loan from the bank, purchase the property, and help her father achieve his dream of training his own horses. Maybe it wasn't exactly the way she'd hoped to achieve her dream of teaching kids to ride barrels but there was more than one way to get there. This path would save the friendship between David and Chris and would be far kinder to her heart. This was better for everyone in the long run.

"You can't do *nothing!*" Alicia heard Kassie's voice demanding her mother's attention. "Hold on a second, baby. Mama will come out and watch you rope with Daddy after I get off the phone with Auntie Ali, okay?"

Ali smiled sadly as she heard Kassie's sleepy voice begging for the phone, to say hello. "Go have fun with Kassie and Scott. I'll come see you guys soon."

"What? I thought you had . . . Ali, you're not even making any sense."

"I'll call you in a few days when I get all the details situated." She didn't wait for an argument from Sydney before disconnecting the call and heading toward the main house to meet with Bradley.

CHRIS STOOD IN the doorway of the barn feeling sick to his stomach. He'd been trying to figure out a way to apologize to Ali, to explain his overreaction to seeing David kiss her cheek, but every line he'd rehearsed on the drive over here vanished when he saw her brushing down Beast, the light coming from the other end of the open barn highlighting her enticing curves. How could any woman look that sexy in a tank top and jeans?

He smiled and leaned against the wall, watching her as she held a one-sided conversation with the animal, telling him how handsome he was.

"Don't believe her, Beast. She says that to all the guys."

Ali gasped and spun, nearly dropping the brush. "Oh, my . . . are you trying to scare the life out of me?" She held one hand over her heart and his eyes followed. He flicked them back to hers and knew she could probably read his thoughts as he imagined her without the tank top.

She turned back to Beast, breaking the spell, but he could see that she hadn't quite caught her breath. As she brushed his back, the horse turned his head to look at the pair. Chris eased closer and put his hands on either side of her waist, leaning close to her ear.

"You've been avoiding my calls," he murmured, his lips brushing against the outer shell of her ear. "I wanted to say I was sorry."

She refused to look at him but her hand stilled on Beast's back, her chest heaving. It gave him the confidence to press on. She wasn't nearly as unaffected by him as she wanted him to believe and, if the discomfort of his pants was any indication, she could drive him crazy without even looking his direction. He wanted her again, right now, but he knew she was unsure. He promised himself he would take it slow and prove to her she could trust him with her heart. He'd prove he wasn't the guy his reputation had led her to believe he was.

"There's no need to apologize," she said, still refusing to look at him.

Chris smiled at her continued evasiveness. "Yes, there is. I want you to trust me."

"I do." Her voice was breathless as his lips found the hollow just behind her ear and he heard her gasp. His tongue licked the spot where her pulse raced and her head fell back toward his shoulder. He smiled against her flesh. Challenge accepted.

"Chris," she whispered. "We . . . we just can't."

"We seem to be doing just fine so far." He turned her toward him and took her mouth hostage, walking her backward toward the stall door.

Pressing against her, he explored her every curve, her denial forgotten as her fingers twined around his neck, pulling him closer. One hand splayed in her hair as his other slid down, cupping the curve of her rear, lifting her against his arousal. He sought her mouth, his tongue swirling with hers in a dance of yearning, his fingers digging into the soft curve of her hip as he fought to maintain control, even as he thought about carrying her to the tack room couch again. What was it about this woman that made him lose all semblance of restraint? Need exploded through his body, beating against his will to slow down, as she clutched at his shoulders. He forced his desire to the wayside, wanting to tease her yearning for him into an uncontrollable inferno of longing.

Chris plucked at her lower lip, nibbling at her before licking away the sweet torment. Ali let out a sexy little moan of frustration as he pulled back, settling her back onto her feet.

"I'm beginning to think something about this barn turns you on," he teased, his fingers trailing along the neckline of her shirt. Her eyes went soft and liquid, her body shifting toward him instinctively. He brushed a stray lock of hair back from her cheek, tucking it behind her ear. Anything to be able to touch her. His fingers curled around the back of her neck, while his thumb traced a path over the side of her neck.

She swallowed and bit her lower lip, making his lower half stand at full attention. "You have no idea how beautiful you are, do you?" She bowed her head, looking defeated. "Okay, that wasn't the reaction I expected." He took a step back and she covered her face with her hands, rubbing at her eyes before running her hands through her loose hair.

"What more do you want from me, Chris?"

"I don't want anything *from* you. I want you." He grasped her chin between his thumb and finger. "Why is that so hard for you to believe?"

She cocked her head at him and looked at him, perplexed. "Gee, I wonder."

He reached for her waist and drew her close again, wrapping his arms around her. "My reputation isn't real, you know. It's a lie."

She looked doubtful. "Sure it is."

He brushed the back of his fingers over her cheek. "Ali, it's fake. I'm not saying I'm completely innocent but most of the time, nothing happens. Most of the time, I take them home and sleep in my truck."

A bitter laugh slipped past her. "You expect me to believe that? I've known you for almost ten years, Chris. I know how you were in high school. I was there, too, remember?"

He wasn't sure how to convince her but he knew he had to make her see she wasn't just another conquest to him. This wasn't who he was. He was the tease, not the one who kept his head in every situation. He'd never been the dependable guy who thought past tomorrow. But Ali had him knocked off balance, spinning in a whirlwind of hunger, dazed enough that he was thinking about a future with her. She filled his thoughts every waking moment and his body craved her when she wasn't near. How could he have ever convinced himself he didn't need her? That he could ever get over her?

He'd always understood that she was a forever kind of girl, the one you brought home to meet the parents when you were ready to settle down, but there was nothing settling about Ali or boring about what she did to him. Or the things he fantasized about doing with her.

Beast whinnied and Chris felt Alicia jump backward, startled. "Party pooper," he murmured against her lips. He pressed his forehead against hers and stared into her eyes. "I'm not the same guy, Ali. Come with me to Nevada this weekend. Let me show you."

"I can't." She scooted away from him and unsnapped Beast from the cross-ties, clipping his lead rope to his halter. "I'm working."

"What do you mean working? Working where?" Chris followed her.

"Bradley Langdon offered me a job and I took it. I have my first show this weekend."

"You *what?* You're a barrel racer, Ali. You always have been. You're telling me that you're going to quit rodeo to show cutting horses?"

"I don't really have a choice, Chris. I need a steady job in order for the underwriters to approve my loan for the property." She glared at him as she looked back, over her shoulder. "Barrel racers don't get to pay small entries and still make big money like ropers."

"How much do you need?"

"It doesn't even matter, Chris. I either have to show steady income or double my down payment. Something's got to give or I'm going to lose out on the property."

"Are you sure this is what your parents want?"

She turned Beast loose into his pasture. "It's what I

want. So, to get it, I need to give up rodeo right now and start showing cutting horses."

Chris reached for her shoulders and turned her toward him. She looked up at him with her dark eyes, despair swirling in their depths. "How much do you need to get the property?"

"I have the job . . ."

She tried to look away but he tipped her chin toward him. "Stop being so stubborn. How much?"

"One hundred thousand dollars."

Chris inhaled deeply. It was a lot of money and would take most of what he'd saved toward the rodeo school but now that David couldn't partner with him in it, perhaps he and Ali could work out an arrangement. Maybe she could allow him to use part of the property for a rodeo school or they could be partners. It would certainly show her he was in this relationship for the long term.

"Done."

"I can't take that much from you! Are you insane?"

"A little." The corner of his mouth curved upward in a cocky grin. "You realize this would make us partners, right?"

She narrowed her eyes at him suspiciously. "Why would you want to do that?"

He cupped her face between his palms and stared down at her anxious brown eyes. "Because I don't think you're doing this for your dad. I think you want to train horses as much as he does. David and I were supposed to be using the money to start a rodeo school. If you can give lessons for the Diamond Bar, you can give barrel lessons for our school, yours and mine." He leaned forward, his lips barely brushing against hers. "Partners?"

"This is a bad idea," she pointed out. His heart dropped to his stomach as he waited for her answer.

"Is that a yes?"

She took a deep breath and held it for a moment. He could tell she was contemplating the consequences of a partnership with him. The only thing he was thinking about right now was how much he was looking forward to working with her every single day, to spending each night with her.

"Only until I can win enough to pay you back."

"With interest," he added. She gasped in outrage and he took full advantage of the moment, going in for a kiss meant to leave her bones liquid and her wanting more. Lightning seemed to shoot through him as they connected. This was exactly what he wanted and he couldn't have planned it any better.

Chapter Sixteen

ALI STARED ACROSS the table at Chris wondering if she'd just made the best decision or the biggest mistake ever. Unless she walked away this year with an NFR win, it would take her at least another two years to pay Chris back the money. In the meantime, they'd formed a business partnership in order to procure the loan from the bank. She had everything she wanted now, thanks in part to Chris, but she couldn't help but wonder if the cost would prove too high. Was this worth the broken heart she was sure she would have at the end?

She took a deep breath and held it as she signed her name to the bottom of the loan documents. Funny how it didn't bother her each time she initialed but actually signing her name made it seem so much more real, cemented in stone.

Tim looked over the documents one last time before glancing at Ali warily. "You're both sure this is what you want to do? It's a bit unusual."

Chris glanced her way, as if expecting her to back out. This was her last opportunity. She knew Chris expected this to be more than a business relationship but she was determined to make it clear—they were business partners only. Her stomach did a flip as she thought about the kiss he'd given her to seal the agreement when he offered her the money.

"We're sure." Her voice sounded more confident than she felt. Chris's hand fell on her knee under the table and she jumped, his touch sending waves of desire through her limbs, pooling in her core.

"Okay, then." Tim tapped the stack of signed paperwork against the top of his desk. "I'll turn this in today and we should hear back fairly quickly, especially with this down payment."

She had to admit that Chris was far more ready to start a business than she was. He'd already done his research and acquired all of the necessary documentation and permits. Then again, she hadn't been thinking about starting a business, she'd thought only about how to make life better for her parents. She looked at him from under her lashes as he shook Tim's hand. He wasn't nearly as carefree and irresponsible as he led people to believe. When it came time to talk about business, he became serious and intimidating. Chris knew exactly what he wanted and wasn't wasting any time getting it.

She'd never seen this side of him, the confident businessman, and she had to admit, she was impressed by the maturity she saw. At the same time, this man was so unlike the Chris she knew, he frightened her a bit. A small, wary voice in the back of her mind wondered if she shouldn't have contacted a lawyer to look at the proposal he'd offered before signing it. He swore it was the same agreement he and David had drawn up but modified with her name and she'd trusted him without looking too closely.

Of course, she'd been just a little distracted as he bent over her shoulder, leaning close to her ear, his warm breath on her neck making every part of her throb with yearning. When his arm came around her to point out something in the documentation, she'd found herself wanting to press her body into his hands. She had to get a grip on her emotions or she was going to lose her mind working in close proximity with him on a daily basis, especially if she meant to keep this nothing more than a business arrangement—no touching. When she'd said as much to him, Chris agreed with a chuckle, although she didn't find any humor in this predicament.

Tim turned to Chris. "I'll put in this offer on the property but I think they'll be pretty happy with it. Have you seen the place yet?"

Ali felt his eyes perusing her leisurely, as if they were hanging out at the swimming hole and not in the middle of a conference room buying a million dollar ranch. She shifted in her chair, nervous under his scrutiny.

"Not yet, but I trust Ali. She's knows me well enough to know exactly what I need."

She nearly choked on his innuendo, a furious blush turning her cheeks bright red. Tim jumped from behind his desk to offer her a paper cup of water from the nearby cooler and Chris patted her back, laughing quietly.

"Are you okay?"

"Knock it off," she muttered under her breath, reaching for the cup Tim held out to her. "Thank you."

"We could take a ride out to the property if you like. If you're going to plunk this kind of money down, you should probably see what you're getting."

"I'd love to see it." Chris rose from the chair.

As she rose to leave the office, Chris reached down and twined his fingers with hers, immediately breaking her no-touching policy, and led her toward his truck as Tim locked up.

"Want to ride me?"

"Excuse me?" Alicia spun at his question, her mouth falling open in shock as she tried to get her brain to function enough to come up with a scathing response.

"Do you want to ride with me?" His brows furrowed and he paused at the front bumper of the truck. "Are you feeling okay?"

"I'm fine," she answered, too quickly.

"Because you seem a bit," he searched for the right word, "tightly wound."

"I'm fine," she assured him again, jerking her hand from his grasp.

"Okay," he answered sarcastically. "As long as you're *fine*." Chris shut the truck door behind her and slid into the driver's seat, slipping the key into the ignition. "Because if not, we don't have to do this."

She glared at him. "It's not like I have another option."

"Wow, you sure know how to make a guy feel special, Ali." He twisted the key and gave her a sideways glance. "You could always show cutting horses."

She knew she wasn't really mad at Chris. She should be grateful for what he was doing for her. Chris was offering her the opportunity to follow her dreams, helping her buy the property she had her heart set on, allowing her to continue to barrel race in an attempt to reach the National Finals while still getting her parents out from under their commitment to Bradley Langdon. Yet, she was snapping at him like he'd been the one to force her into this situation. She should want to shower him with gratitude but her problem was that her mind, and body, couldn't get past the thought of showering *with* him. How in the world was she ever going to do this for a year? She heaved a dramatic sigh.

"I'm sorry, I'm just a little . . ."

"Tightly wound," he supplied, grinning as he pulled behind Tim's car.

This was the Chris she knew, the teasing smart aleck who didn't take anything seriously. Unfortunately, this was also the same man who sent her pulse racing and heat coursing through her entire being. She watched him concentrate on the road, fighting the urge to press a kiss to the light stubble on his unshaved jaw.

Get it together, girl. If you don't, this year is going to destroy you.

She'd managed to be friends with him for years while hiding her feelings. She could manage for one year. At least, she hoped she could.

"How far away is this place?"

"Just outside of town, off the highway. That was one of the things I liked about it. It's easy to find."

They'd barely started out and he was having a difficult time keeping his eyes on the road. Ali's eyes swept over him slowly, like a caress, and he could see the smoldering desire. The slightest tinder would cause it to rage but he found himself holding back, worried about stoking the fire too much too soon. He knew from experience that wildfires raged hot but they burned out nearly as quickly as they started. This was one fire he wanted to burn for a long time.

He marveled at the change in himself. A few weeks ago, he'd been a self-professed bachelor, doubtful he'd ever consider having a serious relationship. Now, when he finally found a woman who held his attention, one he wanted to spend every waking moment with, she rejected the notion. Not with everyone, just with him, and he knew it was his own fault. He was going to need to work hard to make her see he'd changed, that she'd made him want to change.

He followed Tim as they turned off the highway and recognition hit him. Warning bells started sounding in his mind. David's father lived out this way. He'd been out to the Greenly spread only a few times, since his dad had with a better set up than Colt did. Chris tried to remember what the house looked like. Large, sprawling ranch style with small guest quarters. Two barns, several fenced corrals. He felt the knot in his stomach tightening as his memories ticked off each description of the property Tim mentioned.

As they turned down the driveway and pulled up to the gate, Chris saw the familiar emblem on the wrought iron. He'd seen it for years on the buckle David's father had custom-made for each of his boys. His gut twisted and he shook his head as Tim opened the gate for them.

"What's wrong?" Ali didn't miss the tension bunching his shoulders.

"Nothing."

Chris chewed at the inside of his cheek. He couldn't tell her the truth, that they'd snatched this property out from under David and his father. How was he going to tell David that he was the reason they were being kicked out? Cringing as they pulled up to the house, Chris tried to ignore the worried glances Ali continued to cast his direction. He thanked whatever fates were smiling down on him that neither David nor Colt's trucks were anywhere in sight.

"It's pretty nice, huh?" Tim waved his arms out to his sides as they parked the vehicles. "Nothing too fancy but I think it will fit exactly what you both wanted."

Ali walked around the truck toward him and he could see the excitement in her eyes. Every glance from her was filled with ideas about how best to bring out the property's untapped potential. Chris looked around and could see where David's dad had let several repairs slide. They were going to need to put in a lot of work to fix up the place—if David didn't kill him first.

"What do you think?" Her eyes were alight with enthusiasm, her smile widening. His heart thudded in his chest. He hadn't seen her look this happy—well, ever.

Chris nodded and looked around, pretending he'd never been here before. "Definitely has potential. It's going to need a lot of elbow grease to fix it up before we can give lessons." Her face fell and he hated himself for pissing on her high hopes. Chris made his way over to her and laid his hand at the small of her back and leaned down to whisper in her ear. "It's perfect, Ali. Almost as perfect as you are."

The blush that colored her cheeks made up for his previous insensitive comment. She didn't need to know about the shit-storm on the horizon just yet. Once David found out who was buying his father's ranch, she'd hear about it.

"The guy who owns the place has already moved out but his son, who lives in the guest house out back, is still living there when he's home. At least until the sale goes through."

And he shoots his best friend, Chris mentally supplied.

Chris knew David wasn't ready to let the ranch go yet and was desperately trying to gather the funds to save it from being sold, or buy it outright himself. How was he ever going to break it to him that he'd just purchased it? And that he'd done it in partnership with the woman who'd just broken his heart?

CHRIS REACHED OVER the center console of his truck and took her hand in his. He was breaking her "no-touching" policy but right now, she needed his strength enough to overlook it. Alicia felt the familiar curl of desire dancing in her belly complete with the butterflies taking flight as she stared at the porch of her home, trying to prepare how she wanted to break the news to her parents.

"Are you ready?"

She rolled her eyes and turned toward him. "Is it that easy to tell I'm not?"

"You look a bit panicked," he teased. "Relax, Ali. You're giving your father his dream. How many people can say that?" He squeezed her hand, gently. "Come on, I'll be right beside you."

Alicia took a deep breath and opened the door. She wanted to treasure this moment, relishing each and every emotion, even the nervousness. She'd been looking forward to it for so long, waiting for this "someday" to happen, and now that it was here, she was worried. Her mother greeted them at the door, just like she used to when they were young.

"Hola, kids! Come on in." She shut the door behind them, "I just made cookies. Your favorite, Cristobel." She handed both of them warm peanut butter cookies as if they were sixteen again. Oh, to feel that carefree, even for a moment.

"Mom, I need to talk with you and Dad." Alicia heard the tremor in her voice. She needed to calm down.

"He's in the mare barn right now." Chris squeezed her hand again, a gesture her mother didn't miss. "What's going on, baby?"

Alicia realized her mother thought this was about

Chris. "Nothing's wrong . . ." Her words trailed off. She really wanted to talk to both of her parents together. Chris nudged her arm and pointed at the front window where she could see her father heading down the fence line toward the main house. "Hang on, Mom."

Alicia hurried to catch her father at the door. "Dad, I need you to come here for a second."

"Ali'i," he called, using his pet name for her. "I need to go see Bradley."

"It's important, Dad." She saw the change in his demeanor as he came back to the house. "Let's go sit in the living room."

Her parents looked at one another nervously and she caught the shadow of a smile on her mother's lips as her eyes turned toward Chris. She reached out and pinched his cheek playfully. "Oh, you!"

Poor Chris. He looked confused and Alicia realized both of her parents had the wrong idea. "Mom, this isn't about Chris. Well, sort of, I guess," she clarified. "But it's about all of us."

She sat on the couch, her parents taking the seat across from her while Chris leaned back against the cushions on her right and circled his arm behind her shoulder.

"We bought a ranch," she blurted.

Her father's brow furrowed with anger and his face turned red as he rose, leaning toward them. Alicia was grateful for the table between them. "You're moving in together? No, I won't allow it."

Chris shook his head and glanced at Alicia to clear up her misconstrued comment. "No, sir. Not like that." He held up his hands in surrender. "Ali and I have become business partners."

"Temporarily," she corrected, ignoring Chris's disapproving frown. "We bought several hundred acres just outside of town and we're starting a rodeo school. Dad, you can quit the Diamond Bar to start training and showing your own horses."

Her father looked shocked and dropped back onto the couch. He flexed his hands several times, making Alicia even more confident in her decision.

"But, I don't want to leave the Diamond Bar." His voice was so quiet she almost missed what he said.

"You've always talked about wanting to raise and train your own horses, your way. Mom wouldn't have to wait on anyone else. Chris is going to train rope horses and give clinics while I train barrel horses. We've been talking about having a few small modular homes put on the property for guests to rent out." She looked to Chris for back-up. "We're already planning on setting up some sort of summer camps next year." She knew she was rambling but they had to see what a great idea this was, how this would get them away from the burden of working for someone else.

"Baby," her mother began, folding her hands in her lap as if needing time to compose her thoughts. "Your father and I like what we do. I know that we complain sometimes, but who doesn't?"

"Bradley has been more than generous to us for over twenty-five years. We can't just up and leave him now." Her father shook his head and stared down at his work-calloused hands. She could see the rough skin and blisters, the swelling, arthritic knuckles no man his age should endure unless it was for himself. "I thought you just accepted a job with him?"

"This is what you've always said you wanted."

Her mother looked at her sympathetically, and Ali could see her future crashing down around her. "Dreams, baby. They were just talk, wishes, and what-ifs, from two people far too old to start over."

Alicia felt the tears burning in her eyes. "But it doesn't have to be a dream. Don't you see that? This can be a reality, for all of us."

Her father stood up and pressed a kiss to her cheek. "Ali'i, it is so sweet of you to want to give me *my* dream, but you need to chase yours." He stood and nodded at Chris before heading out the front door without another word.

Alicia stared at her mother, dumbfounded. Was he really going to throw this away? He couldn't. She'd bought this property for her parents, not herself. Everything she'd done, from saving the down payment to chasing the National Finals title was all to give them their dream. This was never supposed to be about her.

"Thank you, baby, for what you were trying to do for us. I understand, I really do." She rose and squeezed Alicia's hand as she passed before patting Chris's cheek gently. "Now, you two use this opportunity to grasp the things you want." Her mother stared at Chris. "The things that have been out of reach until now."

She watched her mother leave the room and her heart sank. Bile burned in her throat and she thought she might throw up. How could this have happened? "This was all for nothing?"

"Ali, look at me."

She turned toward him, expecting an "I told you so." Instead, she saw empathy and quiet strength. He'd told her repeatedly to talk to her parents, to make sure they wanted this before running ahead, but she hadn't listened. But even now, he offered her support.

"This isn't their dream but I know it's still yours. You want to ride barrels and teach kids to love it as much as you do. Maybe your parents aren't ready to take this leap of faith right now. That doesn't mean it isn't a great idea. This is our future." He lifted his hand and brushed her cheekbone with his thumb and tingles tripped over her, centering in her lower body. "You said so yourself."

She covered his hand with hers and, ignoring the desire to press a kiss to his palm, curled her fingers around his and moved it from her cheek, hardening her heart and feeling the aching loss to her core. "This is nothing more than a business partnership, Chris, and only until I can pay you back." She arched a brow at his cocky grin. "I *will* pay you back after the NFR."

His eyes flashed with innuendo and he ignored the stern tone of her voice. "Whatever you need to tell yourself to get to sleep at night, Ali."

Chapter Seventeen

"IT LOOKS ... NICE." Ali tilted her head to the side and inspected the back of his trailer. "Who did the logo?"

Chris eyed the large, bold scripted letter A with a C hanging from the cross bar with the silhouette of a rearing horse in the background. She didn't seem thrilled about it. "I did. Why? You don't like it?"

"I do, actually." She turned toward him and smiled. "It's different but classy."

It was the first time she'd looked happy all week. Most of the time, she was stressed. Between working her geldings and checking her phone for a message from Tim every fifteen minutes, her entire demeanor exuded tension. Chris had already decided to surprise her with the logo before they left this weekend for a rodeo in Reno, if he could convince her to go with him.

So far, she'd been digging in her heels, reminding him daily that this was a business relationship and nothing more. If she mentioned paying him back one more time, he was going to go caveman on her and toss her over his shoulder. He knew she needed time to realize she could trust him, trust what he was telling her was true, trust his feelings for her, but damn if she wasn't the most stubborn woman he'd ever known. She'd kept her distance from him all week, avoiding any chance for them to be alone. It was killing him to spend time making business plans with her, watching her work, without touching her. Every time he walked into the barn, he relived their morning in the tack room. Every fiber of his body would come alive, waiting for any chance to repeat the glorious moment. Unfortunately, Ali continued to shut him down at every turn, finding reasons to escape whenever he came around. He was at a loss to remedy the situation and hoped getting her away this weekend would convince her of the absurdity of the notion and put their relationship back on the right track, the track where she was in his arms again.

"I figured we might as well advertise when we head to Reno."

She tucked her hands into her pockets and sighed. "About that."

He cocked his head toward her. "Don't say it, Ali. You can't skip out. Reno has a big purse."

"I know it does, but . . ." She tried to interrupt but he wasn't about to let her get started.

He tucked his index fingers into her belt loops and pulled her toward him. He had to be careful how intimate he was with her these days. Too much and she'd bolt like a scared rabbit. "How are we ever supposed to see if this partnership works if you keep avoiding me?"

She placed her hands against the wall of his chest, refusing to let him pull her any closer. "Maybe if I thought our *partnership* was the reason you wanted me to go, I would think about it."

Chris curled his hands around her hips but let her keep her distance. Her hands against his chest sent warmth coursing through every inch of him, desire curling and twisting in him. "I swear." He held up three fingers. "Scout's honor."

She reached up, tucking one finger back into his fist and gave him a disapproving look. "It doesn't count if you were never a Scout, cowboy. It's two fingers."

Chris sighed at her continued stalling. "Come here," he ordered, grasping her hand and pulling her toward the living quarters of the trailer. "See, two beds, plenty of closet space, a kitchen, and a bathroom. That means you don't have to stop at any hotels or board your horses. I have the panels we can set up and we'll stop by Syd's on the way."

She dropped her head back and groaned. Chris knew he was swaying her. "I just don't think it's a good . . ."

He stepped behind her and circled her waist with his hands and leaned down to whisper in her ear. "I promise I'll be on my best behavior, *if* that's what you want."

She glared at him over her shoulder but he could see the humor in her eyes. He didn't miss the desire darkening them. "Sure you will." She shook her head. "You have to take the top bunk." Chris couldn't help the smirk that curved over his lips. "And, if we hear back from Tim about the property before we leave, I'm staying here."

"Deal." She scooted out of his arms and held out her hand to him.

Chris wasn't about to miss this chance. Grasping her hand, he pulled her toward him, catching her in his arms and planting a kiss on her unsuspecting lips. He caught her soft sigh and swept his tongue against hers, nibbling on her lower lip. She melted against him, soft and warm, her lips pliable under his. She might be trying to ignore the desire between them, to pretend that there was nothing more than a friendship between them, but her body responded differently as her hands fisted in the front of his shirt. Chris's hands splayed around her waist, drawing her closer. He felt his erection straining against his jeans and knew if he didn't stop now, he would lose control completely. That was something he refused to do. He wanted her to admit her longing for him, not be forced into it. That was going to take time and patience, but he would coax it from her if it was the last thing he did.

Chris drew back from her and saw the regret color her eyes. "That's not behaving yourself," she pointed out.

"Don't let those wheels start turning," he warned. "It was a harmless kiss." It didn't feel harmless, it was exciting and stimulating and he wanted to do it again but he wasn't about to tell her that. He exited the trailer and held a hand out to help her down. "If you go back on your word now, I might have to doubt you as a partner." She frowned at him and he winked playfully.

"Have you told David yet?"

Chris had been avoiding David because he wasn't sure what to say or how to broach the subject. He settled back against the well of the trailer and pulled Ali between his thighs. Her hands rested against his abdomen and he felt himself stir again.

Down boy. He took a deep breath, trying to control his body, but it only made him inhale the scent of strawberries. *Well, that backfired.*

"You mean, about us being partners?" She nodded. "No," he admitted. "And since you keep lying to yourself that this is a *business* relationship only, there's really nothing to tell him, is there?" He didn't mean to sound irritable but, damn it, how long was she going to keep fighting him?

David probably wouldn't even be surprised to find out about their relationship. He'd already accused Chris of having feelings for her but David had no idea the two of them moved forward with plans for the rodeo school without him or that they'd put in an offer on his father's ranch. It wasn't intentional but the longer he kept it a secret, the more it would look like they were hiding the information from him. David was going to be hurt enough when he found out about Ali; the news about the ranch would devastate him.

"I meant about starting the school and you know it." She shoved against his shoulder. "And, I don't think anything more than a *business* relationship is a good idea. I'd like us to be able to stay friends when this is over."

She kept telling him it wasn't a good idea for them to be together but he noticed she didn't move out of his arms. He wondered if she knew what she really wanted, what her eyes and body told him she wanted. He doubted it. He definitely didn't like her confidence when she talked about them being "over." Chris didn't see an end and he was bound to make sure she didn't either.

He wanted her to see exactly what he felt for her, to make it visible in his eyes, to chase away any doubts she had at that moment, and leaned closer to her, nudging her jaw with his lips. "Ali, we could be friends and lovers," he countered, whispering against her neck.

She pulled away and he berated himself for pushing her too far. When he saw the blush color her cheeks, he grinned wickedly, knowing he wasn't the only one thinking about the last time they were together. Chris wondered how many times he could make her blush this weekend. If he had his way, he would see that blush cover her entire body.

"It's about time you got here!" Sydney hurried down the porch steps as Chris parked the truck by the corral. Before Alicia could even shut the door, her friend enveloped her in a bear hug. "It seems like it's been forever instead of a couple weeks."

"Long enough that you're starting to show." Alicia put her hand on the slight baby bump Sydney was sporting. "How are you feeling?"

Sydney waved off her concern. "I'm fine. I don't know why so many people make a big deal about pregnancy."

She pointedly looked at her husband as he came out of the barn.

He circled his wife's shoulder with an arm and pressed a kiss to her temple. "Sue me for wanting to keep my wife safe and off these animals while she's carrying my child."

Sydney shook her head. "Not going to happen."

Alicia laughed as Chris made his way around the trailer. "Has she always been this stubborn?" Scott asked.

"Yes," Chris assured him as he gave his sister a hug before jerking a thumb at Alicia. "But I think this one has her beat. She keeps turning me down and breaking my heart."

Alicia's eyes grew wide as Sydney and Scott both looked at her expectantly. She tried to recover her composure and rolled her eyes at him dramatically. "Please, he's just looking for one more warm body in his harem."

She shoved past Chris but not before they all saw the blush burning her cheeks, turning her face crimson. She went to unlock the back of the trailer, hoping to avoid any more embarrassment.

"What's this?" Scott asked, pointing at the newly painted logo.

"Our rodeo school."

"Our?" Sydney picked up on the term quickly and eyed Alicia, suspiciously.

"Yep," Chris jumped into the back of the trailer and led Beast out, handing the lead rope to Alicia and returning for his gelding. "Ali and I are the proud founders of AC Rodeo School, specializing in roping and barrel racing."

"Really?" Her head pivoted from Chris to Alicia, like she was watching a tennis match. "When did that happen?"

He grinned at his sister before his eyes touched on Ali standing beside her. "Fairly recently." Chris winked at Alicia and handed his sister Jaeger's lead rope.

"Just this past week," Alicia clarified, seeing that he was being deliberately subtle, making it look like there was more to their situation than a business partnership. "We are still waiting to hear if our offer was accepted on a piece of property."

"Wait a minute!" Sydney laughed and shook her head. "Let me get this straight. You two bought a piece of property *and* you're in business together?" She looked from Alicia to Chris in elated surprise. "So, you're going to live together?"

Alicia's eyes shifted to Chris. They hadn't even discussed the living arrangements, especially considering that when they made the offer, they both expected Alicia's parents to move into the house with her. Now that wasn't going to happen and it looked like they had a few arrangements still to discuss.

Alicia had been too upset after finding out her parents didn't want any part of the new venture to contemplate the details. Chris was wonderful, trying his best to cheer her up, which had led to his suggestion that they leave early and spend a few days with Sydney before heading down to Reno for the rodeo. He'd even offered to go with her to talk to Bradley to tell him she'd changed her mind about the job offer but she'd insisted on going alone. If she was going to be a business owner, she had to face uncomfortable situations head-on, without Chris holding her hand for every one of them.

By the time she'd returned, Chris arrived with the trailer and began packing her gear inside. Bradley Langdon hadn't been too happy about her change of heart so she hadn't been in any frame of mind to talk about their living arrangements. Luckily, Chris kept her talking about various people they knew from high school and rodeos, keeping light conversation about who was married, who was winning and losing, and who had up and moved. In all of their conversation during the trip to the Sydney's, living arrangements had never come up and just the thought was enough to send her spiraling into a tailspin of panic.

Chris laughed at her expression. "Thanks, Sis, as if her brain isn't already working overtime."

He led her buckskin gelding from the trailer and walked with them toward the corral, turning all three horses into the pen, watching them stretch their legs as they ran around the corral.

He nudged Ali's arm. "I know we haven't talked about it but there's a guest house on the property, so quit worrying."

Alicia's shoulders immediately relaxed. He was right. There were several options if they got the ranch. "I'm not worrying," she lied.

"Sure, you're not." He laughed. "Besides, the house is plenty big enough for both of us. Since it's likely we'll be having guests staying in the house until we can get cabins up, you should probably get used to having other people around."

Chris laughed at her, his hands settling on her shoulders. "Besides, Ali. If I'm going to take advantage of you, it's gonna be this weekend when I have you alone to myself."

Alicia's stomach swirled in a storm of yearning mixed with fear. Sydney's mouth fell open and she stared at her brother as he headed back for the trailer and his last horse.

"Did he just say what I think he did?" Sydney asked. Alicia couldn't help the blush that burned her cheeks again as she refused to look at her friend. "Are you two—"

"No!" Alicia's voice was tenser than she meant and she sighed. "I mean, not really."

Sydney grabbed at her upper arm. "What do you mean, 'not really'? Either you are or you aren't, and it sounds like you are. Why didn't you call me?"

Alicia saw Chris grinning like an overconfident, cocksure ass as he walked his gelding toward them, and she knew he'd deliberately done this. Sydney was over-the-moon excited. How was she supposed to explain why this couldn't happen?

"We'll talk later," she muttered.

Sydney frowned, obviously unhappy with being put off, but would have to wait, albeit impatiently. "Fine." She sighed dramatically. "Then come inside and get some lunch. Silvie's been in that kitchen all day cooking up everything she thinks you might like. I don't think we'll ever eat all that food."

ALICIA SAT ON the porch with Sydney watching Scott and Derek working with a four-year-old gelding in the round pen. Scott had mentioned a few horses were ready to sell and when Chris realized they were from Valentino, Sydney's stud who'd been killed a few years earlier, he wanted to see if they might be right for their new business. Kassie was curled against Ali's chest with her thumb tucked into her mouth, dozing slightly.

"Think you might make *me* an aunt soon?" Sydney laughed as Alicia's mouth dropped open. "Oh, don't you give me that shocked face. From the looks of things—"

Alicia shook her head. "Don't be fooled by the way things *look*, Sydney. I'm not."

"Well, I don't know what you did to change his mind so quickly from being a confirmed bachelor to marriage material but my hat's off to you."

"I didn't *do* anything." Sydney snorted skeptically. "Don't kid yourself. Chris is just being the same flirt he always is."

Sydney reached for her glass of iced tea and tipped it toward Alicia. "Who's kidding themselves now? I know my brother and this isn't him flirting." She took a long sip and Alicia wondered if it was to see what she might say. As the silence stretched between them, Sydney finally spoke again. "He's got it bad for you, Ali, and you have it bad for him, or you wouldn't have joined him in this *partnership*." She held her fingers up for air quotes.

Alicia watched the men in the round pen. Chris rode the gelding, taking him through each gait, swinging a rope from the animal's back. The late afternoon sun began its descent behind him, shadowing his lean frame so that she couldn't see his face. But he could've been surrounded by cowboys and she knew she could've picked him from the crowd. She knew his every movement, mannerism, and quirk. The way he rested his reins on his thigh when he was thinking. The slim hips that never seemed to move in the saddle, as if he and the horse were two parts of a cohesive unit. The way his square jaw tipped when he was trying to figure out a problem. She could watch him forever and never become bored.

It wasn't just a physical attraction. Chris was confident with just enough cockiness to make him stand out. He'd been a shrewd businessman while negotiating with Tim for the property and protective when he found out Colt had insulted her, but this stereotypical cowboy persona was only a part of him. She was coming to realize his reputation was more a role he played and less the real man. When he thought no one was looking, he was kind, with a soft spot for kids, tender and genuine. It was no surprise that everyone loved him, or fell in love with him. A curl of desire snuck through her limbs, warming her as she recalled the way he'd held her, his hands and mouth bringing her to the heights of pleasure.

"You're in love with him, aren't you?" Sydney's voice was soft, sympathetic.

"I don't want to be," Alicia admitted, tearing her eyes from the subject of their discussion and meeting her friend's gaze.

Sydney laughed quietly. "Love's sort of unpredictable that way. Have you met my husband? Don't you remember what a jerk he was when I met him? You always seem to fall for the one guy you think you shouldn't." She glanced back at the corral where her brother was dismounting. "He's been in love with you for years, Ali. He just wasn't ready."

"What makes you think he's ready now?"

"I saw him at that barbecue when you were with David. He was ready to kill someone. I've never seen him so miserable. His eyes never left the two of you." She shrugged. "Maybe it just took him seeing you with someone else to wake him up so he'd see what he was losing by running wild."

Alicia shifted Kassie in her arms and looked down at the little girl. "Syd, how do I know I'm not just another of his one-night stands?"

"Um, maybe because it's been longer than one night?" She looked at Alicia like she was crazy. "You do realize he hasn't had that many, don't you?"

Alicia laughed. "Who are you trying to fool? He leaves with a different woman at almost every rodeo. I've heard people talking, even when I haven't seen it myself." She wasn't judging him for his past, but she didn't want to be just another notch on his belt.

"Ali, just because he leaves with them ..." Sydney paused as if wondering how to get her point across. "It's usually with one of the drunkest women in the room, right?" Alicia furrowed her brow, not understanding what Sydney was trying to get at. "He stays sober and drives them home in his truck. That way they aren't driving themselves. He's done that ever since that year when Susan Miller was killed. Most of the time he just sleeps in his truck. You didn't know that?"

Chris had tried to tell her she shouldn't believe the rumors about him and she'd completely disregarded him and practically called him a liar. She looked back at Chris unsaddling the horses. How many other things had he tried to tell her she'd ignored or brushed off as a line?

"I'm not saying he didn't sleep with *any* of them but he's not the player everyone thinks he is. He's just a nice guy with a bad-boy reputation. But until now, it's never mattered."

"Hey, ladies, what are the two of you talking about over here?" Scott climbed the porch steps and slid his hands onto Sydney's shoulders, massaging the muscles. He glanced at Kassie, sleeping on Ali. "Guess it was too much excitement having Aunt Ali come to teach her how to ride barrels."

Ali laughed, thinking about how excited Kassie was to be led around the barrels on her pony, pretending to ride as fast as her aunt did. Delight curled in her chest as she thought about Kassie staying at the ranch with her, or the other kids who she would be able to instruct through clinics and camps.

"Want me to take our little cowgirl inside and tuck her in?" he offered, interrupting her thoughts.

"Why don't we both take her and leave Ali to help Chris put everything away in the barn?" Sydney rose and scooped her daughter from Alicia's arms, giving her a quick wink. "Go," she ordered. "Talk to him."

CHRIS TOSSED THE saddle onto the rack and dropped the brushes into the grooming bin. Crossing the aisle of the barn, he grabbed several flakes of alfalfa and walked out to the corral to toss them over the fence before heading back inside to get the grain. He barely scooped a can of grain when he heard footsteps behind him. Glancing over his shoulder, he saw Ali standing in the doorway smiling at him.

Damn, if she wasn't gorgeous when she relaxed and let her guard down. He knew bringing her to visit Sydney was exactly what she needed. She'd been so worried about the loan and property, then devastated when her parents refused to move, he hadn't known how else to comfort her. But seeing her smile now, looking so calm and at ease, made his heart swell, knowing he'd provided her with what she needed most: time and a little perspective.

"Hey there, beautiful. I thought you were up at the house with Sydney."

"I was. They went to put Kassie to bed."

She continued to stare at him, her eyes soft and liquid. She looked like she wanted to say something but wasn't sure where to begin. His eyes swept over her, from the soft cotton t-shirt hugging her curves to the way her jeans accentuated her rounded hips and thighs. She was awfully curvy for someone so tiny. He almost groaned when she bit her lower lip.

"I'll take care of the horses if you want to go inside, too," he offered. "I know it was a long drive."

"You always do that." She edged closer, standing in the doorway of the stall that had been converted to a feed room. "Why?"

He stood up and furrowed his brow. "Do what?" He covered the few steps separating them.

"You take care of me." She reached up and brushed alfalfa leaves from his shoulder. He noticed she kept her hand against his chest. "You took care of me the night I drank too much, too."

Her hand slid over the muscles of his chest and she curled her fingers into the belt loop at the side of his waist. Her thumbs grazed against his sides and he felt longing settle into his gut, preparing to travel downward if this continued.

"You took care of me when Colt and Delilah insulted me." She didn't meet his gaze, staring instead at his throat, and he suddenly understood her hesitation.

He lifted her chin with a finger, wanting her to look into his eyes as he spoke, to see the depths of his love for her. "I've already told you why, Ali." His voice was thick. He was barely keeping himself from burying his hands into her hair and kissing her senseless. "I may not have always realized it, but I've loved you for a long time."

"Why didn't you ever say anything?" she whispered. Her voice wavered with uncertainty.

He set the can of grain aside. "I don't know, stupidity?" he answered honestly. He cupped his hands around the sides of her neck, his thumb tracing her jaw. "But when I saw you with David, something snapped inside me." She took a step back and he pulled her back to him. He could almost read her thoughts. "It wasn't because I wanted what I couldn't have. It took seeing you with someone to realize what I wanted. Until then, I didn't know what I was missing. When I told you and you ran away—"

"I didn't believe you." She bit her lip again.

The sleepy yearning he'd been feeling for the past week came awake, demanding satisfaction. How could that one small gesture shred his self-control? He ran his thumb over her lip.

"I get why you wouldn't believe me but I meant it when I said I've never spoken those words to anyone else before."

She smiled up at him. "Yeah, you *do* sort of have this reputation for being quite the ladies' man." Her voice was teasing but he could hear the skepticism she was trying to hide.

He pinched his lips together, hating that he'd let the stories about him get so out of hand. Chris sighed. "Ali, don't believe everything you've heard about me. Most of it has been grossly exaggerated."

"Sydney told me."

He wasn't sure whether he should be disappointed or grateful. He was glad she knew the truth about him but he'd wanted her to have faith in him. Being told wasn't the same.

"Why didn't *you* tell me?"

"I tried to but you ran out, remember? I thought you'd eventually believe me. Believe *in* me."

Her smile spread over her lips, soft, tugging at his heart with tenderness. "I might not have believed here," she said, pointing at her head. "But I believed here." She pointed at her heart. "Or I never would have—"

Chris didn't give her a chance to finish her thought. His mouth crashed against hers, desperate for her to comprehend the depth of his feelings for her. It wasn't just his physical need for her. She touched something inside him, made him want to become more, to prove himself, to be more than a man—to be a man she could be proud to love and be loved by. Chris pressed his body into hers, the wall braced against her back, and she circled her legs around his waist, her arms around him.

His lips found her jaw as she tipped her head backward, clutching at his shoulders. "What is it with us and barns?" he teased.

"Maybe I just love you in your natural element." Her eyes were lit from within, bright with want and need, sparkling with sassy humor.

"I love you au natural, but this time we aren't staying in the barn." Chris grasped her hand, leaving the grain behind, and hurried toward the house.

"I thought you were staying in your trailer?"

"Screw the trailer. I want to be able to see every inch of you stretched out on my bed, not cramped in that tiny space."

Chapter Eighteen

CHRIS PULLED HER through the doorway into the guest bedroom, locking the door behind him as he pressed her up against it. "Do you realize what kind of torture this past week has been? Wanting to touch you but trying to give you space."

Alicia tugged at his shirt, pulling it over his head, her fingers digging into the muscles along his spine as his lips trailed over her throat sending shivers of yearning to her core. "Almost as difficult as it was for me when you brought Melissa to the swimming hole."

He pulled back and held her chin between his fingers, looking down into her eyes. "You have no idea how sorry I am about that. It killed me to watch you and David together. You guys kept getting closer and I was hoping someone else could distract me."

"Did it work?" She didn't mean to ask, wasn't sure she wanted to hear his answer, but the words slipped out anyway.

His voice was husky. "Not a bit." Chris gave her a lopsided grin. "When I saw you in that bikini, and that horse tattoo on your hip . . ." His hand slid to the side of her waist, his fingers trailing over the spot. "I forgot she was even there." His fingers slid along the bottom of her t-shirt, finding the smooth skin of her waist and belly. "It seems like I've spent years trying to get you out of my mind."

"You have no idea what you do to me." He popped the hook on her buckle from her belt and reached for the button on her pants, his thumb circling her bellybutton.

Icy fire raced up her spine and she slid her hands over his chest to his arms. "You know, you could've had me at any time. I've always been yours for the taking, but I thought you never saw me as anything more than Sydney's friend. You've always had your pick of girls."

His hands stilled. "Ali, don't sell yourself short. You are the pick of them." He brushed the back of his fingers over her cheek. "I don't deserve you." He ran his fingertips down her arm, smiling at the goose bumps that rose on her flesh.

She looked into his eyes, unable to understand why he would believe that. "I think you have all of this backward." Chris shook his head in denial.

Didn't he realize she was the one who didn't deserve him? He was the rodeo star and she was nothing more than the poor kid who'd followed him and his sister around the circuit, trying to be like them. Sure, she might be in the top standings now, but inside she was still afraid someone would call her out for being a fraud—the poor kid from the wrong side of the barn—and Chris would get away as fast and far as he could. He'd find someone who had more to offer him. Until that day, in spite of the heartbreak it would cause her if he rode off and left her behind, she was going to make the most of every second. She wasn't going to let her own insecurities, or those planted there by people like Delilah and Colt Greenly, ruin what Chris offered.

She'd lived her life for others for too long. She'd saved every dime she won in order to help her dad reach a dream he really didn't have, to help her mother achieve more than it ever occurred to her to want, and to reach a status in the eyes of people like Delilah who didn't matter. For once, she wanted to grasp what was offered to her, what she desperately wanted, with both hands. She loved Chris and he said he loved her. For the first time, she was going to accept this moment, and the future outcome and consequences be damned. She smiled up at him and arched against him.

"Look, cowboy, I didn't let you drag me in here to waste time fighting over who is less deserving of the other. I came in here to throw you on that bed." She put her hands on his chest and walked him backward toward the bed until his knees hit the mattress before reaching for his belt buckle. "Then to take these off."

She slid the belt from his jeans and pressed her hand against his chest again, this time forcing him backward. Chris braced himself on his elbows and watched her as she pulled his boots off, barely catching herself as she stumbled backward. He had a grin on his face as he humored her and allowed her to slide his pants down his thighs, grunting with the effort.

"I thought girls wore their pants tight," she said, tugging at the denim material. She glanced up at him on the bed. "This isn't turning out nearly as sexy as it did in my head."

Chris laughed and sat up, slipping the jeans down his thighs easily before reaching for her shoulders and rolling over her on the bed. "Honey, you are the sexiest thing I've ever seen, and watching you trying to get my pants off . . ." Chris gave her that wicked smile that melted her insides. "If you need any proof, just look down."

She didn't need to look down. She could feel his arousal through his boxers against her thigh. Chris took her wrists in his hands and lifted them over her head but instead of releasing her, he held her hands together with one of his while his other hand slipped under her shirt. His touch was feather-light, sending jolts of electricity wherever his hand grazed over her heated flesh. She could feel the need coiling between her thighs as his hand would come close to her breast, barely brushing the curve before moving away quickly. She arched against him as his lips found hers, his tongue darting, flicking, and toying with her. When he tore his mouth from hers to find the sensitive hollow below her ear, he licked her skin and she cried out twisting against the exquisite torment.

She was dying for him to touch her. Instead, his hands released her wrists only long enough to pull her shirt over her head, exposing her to an onslaught of his lips against her breasts. His breath heated her skin as his mouth trailed over her shoulders and down to her cotton bra, caressing every inch of her. She shifted, wanting to ask him to take her into his mouth but unable to find the words as her thoughts scattered as quickly as his lips changed course.

"Chris, please," she whimpered. She groaned in agony as he avoided her breast, chuckling quietly against her skin.

"Please what, Ali?" His fingers reached back and twisted the clasp of the bra. He slid it up her arms to her wrists, freeing her to his reverent gaze. His fingers cupped her breast as he leaned closer, his breath caressing the taut point.

Alicia struggled against the hand holding her wrists, wanting to bury her fingers into his hair, to touch him and return the caresses driving her over the edge of sanity. His fingers tugged at the button of her pants and she wiggled against him. He growled deep in his chest and she knew his restraint was held by a thread as thin as her own. She heard the zipper release and felt his fingers slip just along the inside of her underwear, hesitating as he stroked the skin above her pelvic bone sending sparks of want to her core, igniting her. She instinctively squeezed her thighs around his hips. His hand moved to cup her rear and he pulled her against him.

She could see the adoration in his eyes and her heart lurched against her chest. She couldn't hide the truth any longer, she didn't want to keep it buried. She wanted to yell it from the rooftops, let everyone know that she loved Chris, that she had loved him for years.

There was no turning back and it might leave her broken but not telling him would leave her just as fragmented. She tugged at her hands and this time he released them. She cupped his face and stared into his blue eyes, shimmering with longing and devotion. She was certain her eyes were already showing him the truth her heart was screaming.

"I love you, Chris. I always have. It's always been only you."

Chris closed his eyes, laying his cheek against her heated flesh, his sigh whispering over the skin, igniting the fire within her. She curled her fingers into his hair, touched by how it affected him to hear the words from her. His lips pressed against the soft curve of her stomach. Rising, he slid his boxers down his thighs before removing her jeans, his hands caressing her calves, behind her knees, the inside of her thigh, and the soft swell of her hips. He followed the path with his mouth and hesitated as his lips touched the tattoo on her hip, his fingers curling around the seam of material covering the heated core of her desire.

"Sexy as hell," he said, smiling against her skin.

She tensed, her hands at his shoulders. "Wait, Chris—" A shiver of fear colored her words.

"Let me love you, Ali." His thumb traced the folds of her heat, over her panties. He slid the slip of material down her thighs and his mouth hovered over her.

She clutched the comforter as his warm breath stoked the fire within, igniting a raging inferno. His finger traced the outline of her and her body shuddered, trembling with need barely held back. When his tongue darted out, gently at first, then more insistent, she quivered with ecstasy. He stroked her, touching, laving, and lashing her with expertise born of worship. Alicia quaked against him, unable to hold her release back. When his finger touched the center of her pleasure, she exploded in peaks of light, like fireworks on the Fourth of July.

Lying on her back, near comatose, she felt Chris's weight leave her for only a moment before he returned, sliding up the length of her, his mouth on her breast, his hand fondling the other as his arousal nudged her. She tipped her hips toward him, silently demanding all of him, and gasped as he entered her slowly, filling her.

Chris drew back and hissed in self-restraint before his lips found her arched throat. She fought the need to cry out in delirium from the onslaught of pleasure. With each achingly slow thrust, Chris sent her farther over the edge until she lost control of her senses. Every part of her seemed to ignite at once, her entire body clutching at him, wanting all of him. Chris growled in answering passion and gave himself over to his release.

Alicia caressed his spine with her nails, pressing a kiss to his collarbone as the tremors in her body subsided. Lifting his head from the curve of her neck, Chris sipped at her lips, nibbling on them in sated bliss, surrounding her with contentment and making her feel treasured as his hands lazily swept over her body as if trying to memorize ever curve and valley.

He drew back, lifting his weight from her, and she held his shoulders, not letting him move too far. Alicia pressed a kiss to his chin and smiled up at him. "Well, I suppose the fact that we actually made it to the bed is progress."

She felt him stir, coming to life again within her, and he laughed quietly. "Maybe this time we can make it past the side of the bed."

"This time?" Her body clutched at him, greedy with desire, and she moaned softly as he inched forward.

"Honey, you didn't think you'd actually be sleeping tonight, did you?"

CHRIS HEARD ALI's cell phone ring and slipped out of the bed, retrieving it from her jeans on the floor and pulling his pants on. He recognized Tim's number and stepped into the hallway to answer it without disturbing her.

"Chris?" Tim sounded momentarily confused. "I just heard back from the lender. The offer was accepted. In the coming weeks, you and Ali are going to be the proud owners of a ranch."

"Already?" Chris thought they'd have more time for him to break the news to David. "I thought you said it would take them a while to get back to us."

"I guess the seller is highly motivated. He wants to close the deal as soon as possible. Even asked for a faster escrow but I wanted to check with you both before I said yes. I know Alicia wanted to move in quickly but—"

"That's fine," Chris interrupted, hearing Ali stirring in the room. "Tell them we'll move as quickly as they need. We're heading to Reno today to a rodeo. I'll have her call you on Monday when we get back."

He disconnected the call. Of course, Colt wanted a fast closing. He was notorious for his gambling habit, even though David and his brother thought they'd been able to hide it. He had to tell David this weekend and he had to explain the situation to Ali. She needed to understand what sort of predicament they were in before David blindsided her.

Out of the corner of his eye, he saw his niece watching him from her doorway, her head tipped to the side. He squatted down on his haunches and held open his arms. "Come tell me good morning."

She hurried into his arms, throwing her little arms around his neck and squeezing as tightly as she could. "Oh, that's a big hug," he teased, standing with her. "Do I get a big kiss?" She pressed her pursed lips against his cheek roughly in a loud smooch.

Chris sensed Ali behind him without turning. Her warmth seemed to radiate from the doorway. "And what about the pretty lady behind me? Isn't she going to give me a good morning kiss?" Chris asked, turning to find her eyes soft and liquid as she watched him with Kassie.

Her dark eyes practically sparkled with delight as she mimicked Kassie and pressed her lips against his other cheek.

"Mwah," she voiced, giggling with the little girl. "Good morning."

Chris didn't want to ruin the touching moment with the discussion he knew he was going to have to have with her so he slipped her phone into his pocket. He tipped his finger under her chin and kissed her gently. "Right back at you, beautiful."

It thrilled him to see her blush at his compliment. As much as she tried to put on a show of bravery, he loved her vulnerability. It made her trust that much more valuable.

"Break it up," Scott exited the room at the end of the hall, shutting the door quietly. He came and scooped Kassie from Chris's arms. "You two are going to warp my child," he teased as he headed down the hall with his daughter in his arms. "Come on, princess. Let's go feed the horses and make your mother some toast."

Ali snuck her arms around Chris's waist, looking up at him with a contented smile. She was so pretty with her hair mussed and smudges of eye makeup under her eyes from their love-making throughout the night. He felt his body harden and warm in response to the memory of her under his hands, his mouth tasting every inch of her. He bent his head, intent on tasting her again when she stopped him with a hand on his chest.

"What's wrong?"

"Nothing." He didn't want to do this now.

She narrowed her eyes, squaring her shoulders in preparation to fight for the truth. "You're not telling me something. I can see it in your eyes."

He loved that she knew him well enough to see beyond the surface, even as the trickle of dread crept down his spine. He kissed her quickly. "Nothing is *wrong* but can we talk about it on the way to Reno?"

She didn't look happy with his answer but sighed in

resignation. "Fine, but I need coffee before we head out."
She slipped from his grasp and headed down the stairs
leaving him to contemplate the best way to break the
news that her dream was going to be overshadowed with
ruining their friendship with David. Chris rubbed his
temple feeling the start of a migraine already. This might
prove to be a long day.

Chapter Nineteen

CHRIS WAVED TO his sister and Scott as he headed for the driveway. "See you in a few days," he promised.

"You'd better bring home a buckle," Scott teased.

They'd no more pulled onto the highway again when Ali turned to him. "Well?"

He gave her a sideways glance and grinned. "You've just been waiting, haven't you?"

She sighed and frowned. "Maybe." She took a sip of the coffee in her travel mug. "So?"

"We got the property." He grinned as her eyes widened in surprised delight.

"We did? Already? So AC Rodeo School is really going to happen?" He could hear the tremor of frightened excitement in her voice.

"I didn't have the logo made up on a whim," he teased. Chris paused and took a deep breath. "I think we should add David as a business partner. He and I were supposed to start this school but he had to pull out at the last minute."

She looked across the cab of the truck at him. "Then why would he want in now?"

"He only pulled out to loan his dad the money to save their ranch."

"He told me. Isn't he still loaning his dad the money?"

"His father's ranch was sold and it's going to be a rodeo school." He waited for her to realize the full implication of what he wasn't saying. Chris knew when he saw her shoulders slump and she looked skyward.

"Why didn't you say something when we went out there?" He heard the defeat in her voice.

"What was I supposed to say, Ali? I didn't know until after we'd already put in the offer and we went out to the property."

Ali covered her eyes with her hands, rubbing her temples. "And the guest house is David's? The son who lives there when he's in town," she repeated Tim's words.

Chris nodded at her. "I haven't told David about our partnership yet which would be bad enough but I can't tell him we're the reason he's homeless. I can't do that, Ali." It pained him to even think about telling David. He was like a brother.

"How did I not see this?" She turned toward the window.

Chris prayed she would be understanding, that she and David had stayed on good enough terms after their breakup, that she would realize how much it meant to him to be able to do this with the man who'd been his rodeo partner and best friend for the last five years.

"Ali, say something."

"I don't know if I can do this, Chris."

He never wanted to delve into the details behind her breakup with David. He'd rather not know if she still had feelings for David, but hearing her hesitation made him second-guess her feelings for him.

"Why?"

She turned to him. "I care about him. Have you stopped to consider what it might be like for him to see us together? This partnership was supposed to last only a year." She covered her eyes with her hand. "Maybe this is all a mistake," she muttered under her breath.

His heart stopped in his chest. Was she still thinking of them in terms of their business partnership? Or did she still expect him to skip out on her? He wasn't letting her get away. Not now or a year from now. She was his but the suggestion that she might still want out of their arrangement next year was like a fist squeezing his lungs.

DAVID SAW CHRIS pull into the participant area of the arena and park his truck. He walked past a group of barrel racers when he heard a familiar voice. "Hey there, cowboy. Remember me?"

He turned to find Delilah strutting toward him in a thin camisole, her breasts nearly falling out of the shirt. She had so much makeup on he wondered if he applied it with a trowel. She sidled up to him, winding her arms around his waist and pressing a kiss to his cheek.

He wiped at it, his hand coming away a bright red he assumed now streaked his face.

"Hi, Delilah. I didn't expect to see you down this far north."

He had never been the kind of guy to be deliberately rude to anyone but the way she treated Ali bothered him. He couldn't wait to get away from her clutches. How had he ever managed to end up in her house? He thanked whatever fate had been on his side that night that he'd passed out on her couch before she ever managed to get him to her bed. His reputation might take a hit but it was better than the alternative—that he might have shared her bed.

She laughed loudly, grating on his nerves. "I'm sure some of these barrel racers were hoping the same thing." She looked directly at Alicia exiting Chris's truck. "Like your girlfriend."

"Ali's not my girlfriend," David corrected, feeling a tug of jealousy. "At least, not anymore."

"Oh, that's too bad. You poor thing," Delilah gushed, running her hands up his chest provocatively. "And she dumped you for your best friend." She pursed her lips at David. "Then they went and formed a rodeo school. I thought you and Chris were going to do that?"

David slipped out of her grasp. "They did what?" He arched a brow, wishing his curiosity could be ignored.

"You didn't know?" She pouted, her hand sliding over his shoulder, and he brushed it away. She was trying to get him riled up and he knew it.

"See? Look at the back and side of the trailer. AC Rodeo School." She pointed at Chris's trailer as Ali retrieved the horses from the back. "I don't see a D in that name. I thought everyone knew about it? My girlfriend Dallas is dating a real estate agent and said Ali's been looking at some property outside town for a while."

A knot began to form in the pit of his stomach as he thought about how much of his father's troubles he'd shared with Chris. He knew about his father's money troubles, his gambling, and the fact that it was likely his father would be forced to sell the ranch.

In fact, he'd received a call just after arriving at the grounds this morning from his dad telling him he'd accepted an offer on the property since David hadn't been able to come up with the funds to buy out the loan. He said it was better to sell it than let it get foreclosed on, reminding David how he'd let them all down yet again. His father hadn't held anything back, making him feel like a loser, a disgrace to his family name. Dread crept into his chest, curling around his lungs. It couldn't be coincidence that Ali and Chris decided to form a rodeo school and purchase a ranch.

"I have to go," he spun on his heel and hurried in the opposite direction.

"Oh, okay, but you should hang out with us tonight after the rodeo. We're going to have our own little party at my trailer."

"Maybe." David eyed Chris as he unloaded Ali's geldings, tying them to the side of the trailer while he pulled out the temporary corral panels and began to set them up. He suddenly felt like a worthless third wheel that had been effortlessly cast aside.

CHRIS LOOKED UP from latching the panels in time to see David walking away from Delilah. What in the world was he doing talking to her again? As much as he wanted to wait to tell him, he knew it would make it only worse. "Ali," he said, coming around the trailer to where she tied Beast. "I have to go talk to him."

"Do you want me to go with you?"

"No, I need to do this alone." He turned two of the horses into the corral. "I'll be right back to set up the other corral," he promised.

He hurried in the direction he'd seen David disappear but didn't see any sign of him.

"Hey, Chris. Slumming, I see."

He stopped in his tracks and spun to face the voice. If she'd been a man, he'd have knocked her on her ass before the words finished leaving her ruby red lips. Delilah smirked and narrowed her eyes.

"Or is she just your charity work for the month. I know how you cowboys like hopeless causes."

Chris figured out Delilah's vulnerable spot years ago. "If that was the case, Delilah, someone would have already added you to their 'Save the Whore' campaign."

She pursed her overly made up lips and glared at him, ignoring the titter of several other barrel racers trying to hide their laughter. "You're such a stupid bastard, piece of—"

"Smart enough to stay away from your ass since you gave Craig O'Brian the clap in high school. I sure hope you've managed to get that cleared up?"

"I wouldn't have touched you with a ten foot pole." She turned her nose up and started to walk away.

"Who are you kidding? You've tried to touch everything male in this circuit." He started toward the beer and food booths being set up at the other end of the arena, hoping David was nearby. A hoof pick just missed the back of his head and he turned back to see Delilah breathing heavily, her eyes flashing with fury.

"Aw, you missed. You can't ride or throw." He winked and walked away, spotting David near the food booth.

"Hey, wait up," he called. He caught up to David and, seeing the plastic cup in his hand, frowned. "Starting early today, I see."

"Is that a problem?" David asked, shortly.

Chris stuck out his lip and shook his head, not wanting to start off their conversation with a fight, not when he had to bring up the delicate subject of the property. He was hoping David would listen long enough for him to ask him to join in the rodeo school as a partner. "Not as long as you're sober for our first go tonight."

"You sure you don't want to partner with Ali? Wait," he drew the word out. "That's right, you already did, didn't you? Had to one up me by stealing the girl *and* starting a business with her, too?"

Chris clenched his jaw, wondering how long David could've been drinking since he seemed to already have quite a bit of liquid courage. "I didn't steal her and the business is why I came over here to talk to you."

David chugged the rest of the amber liquid in the cup. "I don't accept your apology."

"I'm not apologizing," Chris clarified.

"Then I don't want to hear anything you have to say."

"Will you shut up for ten minutes and listen?" Chris asked, reaching for David's arm as he started to leave. Without warning, David spun, swinging his right fist at Chris. He dodged it easily and raised his hands. "What in the hell are you doing? I came over here to see if you wanted to join us in the business now that your father sold the ranch."

David stopped his assault as if he'd been slapped. "You know about that?"

"It's a long story," Chris assured him.

David narrowed his eyes. Chris could read the accusation in them loud and clear. "There's only one way you'd know about that, Chris. I didn't even know about that until a few hours ago when he called me."

"It wasn't deliberate, but maybe it was luck. Let's just say, if you still want to put your share into the business, it'll be going toward the ranch."

"You?" He looked toward the trailer where Ali would be waiting for Chris's return. "And Ali? You bought my dad's place?" He tossed the beer to the side and shoved the middle of Chris's chest. "What the hell? You son-of-a-bitch! You know what that place means to me, to my family."

He shoved David back. "Yeah, it meant so much that your dad hocked it in a game of dice, or cards, or whatever he was gambling on this week. We are trying to offer you a chance to stay on the ranch, as a part owner. You can stay in the guest house. It's yours."

"Oh, well, isn't that generous of you? And I suppose you and Ali will shack up in the main house?" Chris wasn't about to dignify David's comment with an answer. "Did you plan this all along? Introduce her to me and see how far the two of you could take this? Maybe my dad was right about her, maybe she was just after the money and you helped her get it, didn't you?"

"You're insane. Are you even listening to yourself? Why would I do that?" Chris turned his back on David. "We were on our way to the National Finals and starting our school next year. I had no idea it was your dad's ranch until after the offer was already made."

He spun on David again. "Maybe you should be taking this up with your dad, confront him about his problem instead of trying to fix it for him. Either way, Ali and I are offering you a way to stay, to keep the only thing I know that's ever mattered to you—the rodeo school." The fire seemed to go out of David and he looked ashamed. "David, you're my best friend, my brother. Why would you ever think I would hurt you?"

David looked over Chris's shoulder. He turned, seeing Ali staring after them, fear in her eyes. "Because you've done it before."

Chris knew he had no defense. He could see the pain in David's eyes. He knew how his friend felt because he'd been in his shoes only a few weeks ago, watching the woman he cared about with David. He hated himself for being the one to cause this situation because he'd been too afraid of his future to see what was in front of him all along.

ALICIA CIRCLED HER buckskin gelding, Boogie, around the warm up pen. He'd been incredible this past week in practice but she knew riding him instead of Beast was taking a chance. He wasn't as experienced, but when he was having a good week he was unstoppable—until his week turned sour. But she was trying to turn over a new leaf and, so far, taking chances was turning out well for her. She'd taken a chance on partnering with Chris, putting in their offer on the property, telling Chris she loved him. Why not take a chance on Boogie, too?

Just the thought of Chris had her looking around the arena for him. She'd witnessed part of the argument between him and David and it broke her heart. She couldn't help the guilt that wormed its way through her at being a part of the reason for contention between them. She should've let David down easier, or sooner. She shook her head, trying to keep her focus on Boogie, when a sorrel horse charged past her.

"'Scuse me!"

Alicia took a deep breath, recognizing Delilah's crazy horse, Dingo. As usual, she was barely hanging on, running the horse into the ground. Like too many people who had everything given to them, she disregarded the welfare of the animal, intent only on winning at any cost. She saw Delilah sawing at the animal's mouth with the bit and cringed at the pain she knew it caused the mare.

"Alicia," she called in her falsetto voice. "I didn't see you." She waited for Alicia to slow her horse and walked next to her. "I heard about the new rodeo school. Do you really think you're going to get clients based on your reputation? I mean, who wants to learn to come in second."

Alicia remained silent, arching a brow at the insult that was meant to sting. After years of listening to Delilah try to break her confidence, this was pretty tame and she was waiting for the next barb.

Delilah giggled. "Besides, everyone knows you're just whoring it up with Chris and David to try to get out of that hovel you call home."

Alicia wished for a moment they were on the ground so she could snatch Delilah's extensions from her head. "Even if I were, who are *you* to talk about anyone sleeping around? You've slept with every cowboy who's come within a ten foot radius."

"Ooh," Delilah cooed, "look who's getting defensive now." She shrugged. "I was just going to congratulate you for finally getting ahead. It's too bad Chris is already getting bored with you."

Alicia rolled her eyes. "As if Chris would ever give you the time of day."

"If that's what you want to believe but you can ask anyone. He was over by my trailer as soon as you guys got here. He didn't waste any time leaving you to do the work while he stopped by to see me. We do have a history, you know." She nudged her horse and bolted to the other end of the arena.

Alicia tried to think back to when they arrived. Chris had left right away but he said it was to find David. This had to be Delilah playing her usual game, trying to stir up as much trouble as she could in an effort to destroy Alicia's confidence before a run. She had to keep her mind on the task at hand—winning this run. The sooner she could pay Chris back, the sooner she could clarify their relationship without this debt hanging over her head.

She walked Boogie back to the trailer and saw Chris tossing a rope over a dummy steer, barely paying any attention to what he was doing. "There you are." He wound up the rope and hung it from the dummy's horns, hurrying to take Boogie's reins. "How's he doing?"

"I don't want to jinx it but he's doing really well." She debated asking him about Delilah but decided the conversation could wait until tonight. She didn't want to risk either of them getting worked up and losing. "Have you talked with David since this morning?"

He shook his head. "He's been pretty scarce and, even then, he's saying only what he absolutely has to." He clipped Boogie to the side of the trailer and held up the bucket for him to get a drink of water. "He's pissed and feels betrayed. I should've called him as soon as I realized."

She laid her hand on his forearm. "Maybe. But Chris, I didn't know who owned the property and, either way, I was putting an offer on the place. Even if it meant quitting rodeo," she reminded him. "He's going to realize you weren't trying to betray him eventually."

"But I'm not sure he'll realize in time for us to still make the Finals."

She could see the worry clouding his eyes as he set the bucket on the ground. Chris stood, reaching out and grabbing her by the waist, pulling her against him.

The worry was quickly replaced by yearning. He leaned toward her ear, nibbling on the edge. "You have no idea how sexy you look on this horse."

She relaxed into his embrace. This didn't seem like he was tiring of her. Her fingers slid up his arm, wanting nothing more than to forget this entire rodeo and drag him into the trailer. When his lips trailed down her neck, she felt the heat circle in her belly, spreading to her limbs.

"I'm supposed to be focusing on my ride," she reminded him. He sighed against her neck so dramatically she laughed. "Later, I promise."

Chris captured her lips, scorching her with desire, leaving her wanting more. It took every ounce of control to step away from his arms.

"You," she said, pointing at him, "are dangerous to my ride."

He laughed. "Go grab something to drink. They're just starting so you don't have long."

CHRIS SAT IN the header's box, trying to get his head on straight as he watched the steer enter the chute. David still wasn't speaking to him other than one word phrases about their run. It certainly wasn't for lack of trying on his part. Ali had won her qualifying race, in spite of the turmoil around them, and now he needed to do the same. If for no other reason than to put this purse into their business. They could figure out the logistics once he convinced David to join them, and he would convince him. He couldn't imagine trying to run the school without him. But right now, he had one thing to focus on—the two horns nudging the chute gate.

Gathering the reins, sliding them through the fingers of his left hand, Chris settled the loop on his rope and inhaled, letting it out slowly. He felt his gelding shift his weight against the back of the box and looked at David. As his chin jerked, Chris nodded and the chute opened, releasing the steer. His horse paused for a second until the barrier released and they shot out, like a bullet from a gun. He'd barely circled the rope twice when he let it fly over the steer's horns, pulling his hand backward, tightening the rope and dallying quickly. With a sharp turn to the left, he watched David over his shoulder as he circled his loop over his head once before taking a blind throw.

David dallied his rope and Chris's gelding spun, pulling the ropes taut on the steer and stopping the clock. Both of their heads turned toward the announcer's booth, waiting for their time.

"Well, shut my mouth. We're setting records all over the place tonight. That's an arena record tonight with a 5.2 second run."

The crowd erupted as David urged his horse forward, loosening the rope, and Chris led the steer to the back gate. They needed this to be a great run in order to put them in the average for the purse and higher into the standings for the National Finals. Not to mention that Chris was hoping this would remind David of how well they worked together.

"That was amazing, David," Chris said, riding up beside him as he headed for his trailer.

"Not now, Chris."

The wall was back up already. Couldn't he just get past this? "Damn it, I didn't know, David. We just made a great run. Can you forget about it for this weekend and just enjoy the win?"

"Life is not about having fun all of the time, Chris."

"And it's not about living up to your father's unattainable expectations, either."

David's jaw clenched as the muscle in his cheekbone tightened. "Leave him out of this." He dismounted at the trailer and slipped the gelding's halter around his neck. "You don't know anything."

"I know he expects you to bail him out of his messes. I know he guilt trips you until you feel responsible for him but unworthy of him. I know he's using you and your brother to support his gambling habits while you work your ass off trying to save the family name he's destroying."

"I'm going to give you three seconds to get the hell out of here before I yank you off that horse and beat the crap out of you."

Chris saw a crowd starting to form around the trailer. How the hell did they go from working perfectly in unison five minutes ago to creating a scene? He saw Ali heading their direction, the worry creasing her forehead. This was the worst way to advertise their business or to prove their professionalism, or lack of.

"You need to grow up and face reality, David. When you do, Ali and I will be waiting to add you as a partner. Until then, you're welcome to stay in the guest house."

"You think I want your charity?" David spit out the word like it was poison. "I wouldn't stay there if my life depended on it."

Enough was enough. Chris understood David feeling betrayed that he'd purchased his father's ranch. He understood the hurt of losing Ali. But did he want Chris to give up both as well? The thread holding back his temper snapped.

"Fine. Then be out when we close escrow in three weeks."

"Chris." Ali's voice was pained and he knew he'd gone too far but he was tired of feeling like no matter what choice he made, it was the wrong one.

David took a step backward and scowled at him. He turned and looked at Ali before shaking his head sadly. "You know what? I think you need to find another roping partner. It might take a while to find one but I'm sure there's at least one person around here you haven't stabbed in the back yet."

Chapter Twenty

UNLIKE BEAST WHO pranced and reared when he was excited, Boogie waited at the gate patiently for their turn. She was one of the final racers and the only thing that gave away his excitement for the event was the twitch he got in his shoulder. Alicia ran a hand over his neck and spoke to him softly. When the cowboy walked toward the gate, she gathered her reins into her hand, second-guessing whether she should have ridden Beast. He wasn't always the fastest but he was consistent. It was too late to do anything but let Boogie run now.

As the gate opened she heard the announcer call her name and bumped Boogie's side with her heels. He immediately responded, bursting through the gate at near full speed, his head already turned, looking for the first barrel. He ate the short distance with long strides, heading directly for the barrel until the last second when he slid around the turn, wrapping his muscular body around the barrel. She felt it barely brush her leg as his rear bunched under him before charging forward toward the next turn.

In her mind, everything was happening slowly. She could feel him change leads, shifting his weight to the outside before wrapping his body around the barrel and pressing on toward the final turn. The audience went wild and she thought she could hear Chris's voice among the others but tried to tune out everything but Boogie.

"Come on, boy. You've got this. Go!"

As they rounded the final turn, she bumped his sides, yelling to spur him on but Boogie didn't need any encouragement as he stretched his body out, laying his ears flat against his head. She was merely here for the ride. He was showing off for the crowd and she found herself laughing as they crossed the finish line. She couldn't see her time but listened for the announcer.

"Ladies and gentlemen, we have another new arena record! That ride is going to be tough to beat."

She leaned forward, slapping Boogie's shoulder. "What a good boy!" she gushed as he slowed to a jog, prancing proudly with his head held high. She laughed at his antics as she headed for the warm up arena to cool him down.

"Nice run."

She spun her head and saw David smiling at her, leaning against one of the metal panels where the steers were relaxing in the shade. She jumped off the saddle without thinking and threw her arms around his neck. Alicia realized her mistake as soon as he stiffened.

"I'm sorry, I—"

David shook his head. "It's okay, Ali. I know about you and Chris." He gave a sad chuckle. "I probably should have seen it all along but I should have known the day we had coffee. My loss, I guess." He shrugged. "Heading for the arena? I'll walk with you if you want."

He was trying to take the first steps to accepting the situation, to renew at least some semblance of a friendship, at least with her. Maybe she could help smooth things over between him and Chris. She smiled at him. "I'd love that."

They walked down the dusty path toward the smaller arena in silence for a few moments, with only the soft clop of Boogie's hooves in the packed dirt and the sound of the heavy metal music in the arena. David jammed his hands into his pockets before he broke the silence.

"Congratulations on getting the ranch." He sounded defeated. "And the rodeo school."

"David, I'm so sorry. I didn't know it was your home." She wasn't sure what else she could say.

He gave her a sideways glance. "I know you didn't." He looked straight ahead. "But Chris did. I bet it was his idea for the rodeo school, too, wasn't it?"

She eyed him. "Sort of. I was going to put an offer in but didn't have enough for the down payment. He offered to buy in half. He didn't know at the time it was your place I was putting an offer on."

"It wouldn't have mattered if he did." He shot a sidelong glance at her. "Chris always gets his way."

She could hear the disgust in his voice and stopped. "David, he's torn up about this."

"Sure he is. Let's look at the facts, Ali." He ticked the items off on his fingers. "He got the business, the ranch, and the girl. All three things I was trying to get." He arched a brow at her. "So forgive me if I don't feel much like congratulating him on his success."

"You're partners," she pointed out. "Yes, he should have told me it was your dad's place but he made a mistake."

"No, I made the mistake. I trusted him." She could read the pain in his eyes and see how much this hurt him. "I should have listened to my dad. I lost focus on the job that needed to be done."

"I don't see our friendship as a mistake."

David's mouth twisted to the side and he raised a hand like he was going reach for her but dropped it. She could read the hollow sadness in his eyes. "That's because you ended up with everything you've always wanted. I ended up with nothing."

"How could you say that to him? In front of everyone?"

It was the first chance Ali had to talk to Chris after his fight with David. David was hurting and said several things he shouldn't have but she couldn't comprehend Chris kicking him off his own property. Technically, it was their property but he and David been friends for years. She couldn't understand either man letting this come between them.

"Me?" He threw his rope on the ground beside the trailer and went around to the side of his horse, tugging at the cinch strap. "I was just trying to talk to him. He's the one who started this."

She put her hands on her hips and stared at him, incredulous. "Are you listening to yourself? You sound like a two-year-old." She reached for his arm. "You started this when you didn't tell him about the property."

He looked down at her hand on his arm and back at her face. "This isn't about the property, Ali. It's about you."

"Me?"

"If this were about the property, he would have taken me up on the offer to buy into the school as a partner. It's about the fact that I got you and he didn't."

She let go of his arm. "I'm not a horse for the two of you to fight over."

"That's not what I meant. I just mean that this wouldn't have happened if not for our relationship."

"So, this is my fault?" she asked. "This happened because you couldn't decide what you wanted and you kept secrets, Chris. This is about you throwing away a five year friendship that you can never replace. You need to apologize to him, Chris."

"I'm not saying *anything*." He pulled the saddle and blankets from Jaeger's back, setting them into the tack compartment. "I'm done talking to him."

"You're going to talk to him." She climbed into the living quarters of the trailer. "And don't come back until you have." She slammed the door shut, flipping the lock.

"Ali," he warned outside the door. "You better unlock that door."

"Go talk to him, Chris," she said through the closed door. "Or don't come back tonight."

CHRIS HADN'T EXPECTED her to lock him out but Ali had been good to her threat and left him to feed the horses and fend for himself to find a meal.

"This is ridiculous," he muttered at the locked door. She was humiliating him in front of everyone who'd seen his fight with David. This wasn't his first fight with David, but it was his first fight with Ali and he wasn't sure how to best handle it.

He knocked on the door, jumping back in surprise when she opened the door and leaned toward him. "Did you talk to David or have you been moping out here all day?"

"No, I haven't, and I told you, I'm not going to." She might be stubborn but he could be just as obstinate as she was.

"Then you can sleep out there." She started to close the door when he reached for it.

"This is my trailer, Ali."

She smiled at him and he was taken aback by the feisty grin. "Actually, it says 'AC Rodeo School' so, according to our business agreement, it's a business asset. That makes it just as much mine as yours. Now, go apologize." She pushed him back from the doorway and slammed the door in his face.

Chris opened his mouth to argue and realized she'd beaten him, at least for tonight. He was regretting his suggestion to combine assets. "Son-of-a-bitch!" Chris slapped his hand against the trailer door.

"It's pretty easy, Chris. It's just two simple little words," she yelled through the door.

"Not going to happen, Ali."

"Suit yourself." He heard her shuffling around inside and wondered what she was doing now. The door opened and he hurried toward it. "Here," she said, thrusting the blanket he kept on the bed into his arms. "So you don't get cold tonight sleeping outside." The door slammed in his face for the second time in as many minutes.

CHRIS COULDN'T SEE straight. The entire world seemed to be spinning sideways. Luckily, several ropers took pity on him and invited him to join them at their fire pits for dinner, but a six-pack and several whiskey shots later, he was feeling frustrated and just wanted to go to bed. It didn't come as any surprise to see several parties start up around the trailers but they didn't usually get this rowdy and loud, nor did he drink this much, but with nowhere to go and no bed now that Ali locked him out, he was at a loss. Chris heard his name called and turned to see two fellow ropers making their way toward him.

"That run today was awesome. I'm Jeff Roberts and this is my partner Devlin." The young cowboy slapped Chris's shoulder, grasping his hand in greeting. "You've got to have a beer with us."

They dragged him toward their trailer, putting a bottle in his hand and introducing him to several of their friends. He couldn't keep track of the compliments he received from his peers but tried to thank them all. At least someone appreciated him.

Ali still wasn't taking pity on him and David was no place to be seen, not that he could see anyone clearly at this point. He tried to convince himself he wasn't looking for David but he knew he'd apologize if given the chance. He and David had been friends too long to let anything come between them. Not a business, not property, and not a woman, no matter how tempting and delicious she might be. He needed to dig himself out of this hole.

"There you are. I need your help, Chris."

Chris turned, his head spinning from the abundance of alcohol and he dropped into a nearby lawn chair, trying to place the female voice since he couldn't see her face clearly.

"Don't pass out on me now, Chris. I need you. He keeps following me."

Chris squinted, trying to make out the face of the familiar voice in the flickering light from the portable fire pit. "Delilah?"

"Yes, now get up, please." She tugged at his arm, trying to drag him from the chair. "Shit, there he is."

"Who?" Chris could hear that he was slurring his words but pushed himself to standing as a cowboy approached. He reacted without thinking and moved Delilah behind him.

"You need to leave me alone," she yelled as the cowboy walked closer. Her hands held onto Chris's waist and he wondered if it was to help him stop swaying on his feet.

"Honey, you promised to show me a good time. It's time to make good on the offer."

Chris didn't recognize the man but right now, that didn't surprise him in the slightest. He probably wouldn't recognize his own sister.

"The lady asked you to leave her alone. You should probably move on, cowboy." Chris slid his hand to Delilah's back and moved her toward the direction of her trailer. He wasn't sure what was going on and he couldn't stand Delilah but he wasn't leaving her at the mercy of this guy.

The cowboy pushed the back of Chris's shoulders, knocking his forward, stumbling into Delilah who caught him and pushed him upright. She grasped the front of his shirt. "Please, Chris. Just pretend that we're together. Tell him you're my boyfriend or something. I'm really afraid of what he'll do."

Chris wasn't sure if she was really scared or just wanted the guy to go away. But, even drunk as he was, he knew he had to get her to her trailer and away from this man. He just prayed her trailer wasn't as far away as it felt like it was. He squinted, looking for the garishly elaborate rig.

"Go," he ordered, forcing her ahead of him. "Get into the trailer and lock the door."

"What about you?"

"I'll be fine," he slurred. "Go!"

Delilah stumbled into the trailer, slamming the door shut behind her and he barely heard the click of a lock when he was shoved against the aluminum side.

Did this asshole really just put his hands on him? Chris ducked faster than he'd realized he could in his state and heard the cowboy's howl of pain as he slammed his fist into the side of her trailer. With a well-placed jab that somehow managed to land in the cowboy's abdomen, Chris spit blood from his mouth onto the ground.

"Find someone else to show you a good time," he warned. "This lady is off-limits."

"Says who?" Chris saw the bull of a man take a step backward, hunching over and he wondered if the man was giving up or just had the wind knocked out of him momentarily.

"Her boyfriend." The words tumbled out without him thinking. He just wanted to get rid of this guy and go back to his trailer.

"You're such an idiot, Chris Thomas," the cowboy muttered, pushing his hands against his knees to stand. He turned from Chris and started to walk away. Maybe he realized this woman wasn't worth him getting into a fight for.

Chris took a step away from the side of the trailer. Delilah was safe in her trailer. Enough was enough. He was going to find David, apologize, and curl with Ali in the trailer to sleep this off. He heard the trailer door open as Delilah burst from inside and Chris felt something solid fly just past his nose. He barely took a step backward, turning to warn Delilah to get back into the trailer when he felt the impact against the back of his skull. Just before everything went black.

ALI WOKE THE next morning to find herself alone. She'd felt a bit conscious-stricken to think of Chris sleeping in his truck and unlocked the trailer door, knowing he would be in for coffee. She should have let him in last night instead of trying to force him to remedy the argument. As disappointed as she was at the way he handled David, she loved Chris. He wasn't perfect but neither was she. They would work on their flaws together. She looked through the window as she filled the coffee pot wondering if he was up yet.

Filling the percolator with coffee grounds, she set it onto the stove and she turned it on. Poking her head out the door, she half-expected to see him shivering in one of the lawn chairs but was greeted by only the quiet whinny of the horses. She grabbed one of his sweatshirts from the closet, pausing long enough to inhale the musky male scent of him still clinging to the material, and headed out to feed the animals. She looked around the grounds while the animals milled quietly but didn't see any sign of Chris. He wasn't inside the truck and she wondered where he could be. He wouldn't have gotten up and taken off without feeding the animals. She went back inside and grabbed a mug of coffee when she heard a quiet knock on the door.

"Finally," she grumbled as she opened the door. "Oh!"

David stood in front of her, looking sheepish. "I don't suppose you could spare a cup of that for me?" He gave her a lopsided grin.

She grinned at him, hoping he planned on staying long enough to talk with Chris. "I think I can manage to find another mug. Come on in." She held the door open for him. "Chris isn't here right now."

"Yeah, I know. I wouldn't be here if he were."

She heard the bitterness in his voice and turned, tipping her head to the side. "David, you guys need to talk. Chris didn't exactly go about things the right way but he was trying to help us both out. His heart was in the right place."

"You'd forgive him just about anything, wouldn't you?" She could read a melancholy in his eyes. He seemed ready to say more then changed his mind and she wondered what he wasn't saying.

"I'd have thought you would, too. Are you willing to throw away everything you've both accomplished, together? What you could still accomplish? You're on your way to the Finals, David."

She slid a mug of steaming coffee into his hand and David let his fingers linger over hers longer than necessary. Alicia decided it was better to get things into the open. David needed to hear the truth, not some sugar-coated version of it. "You realize it wouldn't have worked between us, don't you?"

She saw the flicker of pain in his eyes followed quickly by defeat. "Yeah," he agreed, nodding. "I do. But then there are times I wonder if we'd met under different circumstances, or if we'd had more time to get to know one another." His eyes met hers. "If Chris wasn't in the picture."

She wasn't sure how to respond. Would time have made a difference? Would she have fallen in love with David? They had so much in common but there wasn't the spark between them, no matter how much either of them might have wanted it to be. Then there was also the situation with his father. She wasn't sure any woman would ever meet that man's standards.

"But he is in the picture, David."

"And how long do you think this *partnership* will last?" He followed her outside and sat down in a lawn chair as she checked the horse's water bucket. "What happens when you two don't work out? It's not like he's known for having lasting relationships. How are you going to run a business together?"

She sat in the chair across from him and sipped the coffee, buying time to figure out what to say, or not to say. "I'm planning on buying him out next year."

"Does he know that?" She nodded. "I'll bet that went over like a lead balloon," David muttered as he sipped the brew.

"I don't think he believes me," she confessed.

"Probably not. If he did, he wouldn't have offered for me to join you both." She looked up from her cup, surprised Chris had gone ahead and made the offer without her involvement. "You didn't know?"

"He mentioned he wanted to, but I told him I didn't think it would work."

David chuckled as he ran a hand through his dark hair. "You might have done better to partner with me. At least you know I'd stick around and share the workload.

With Chris, who knows what you're going to get." He shook his head. "You don't want me as a partner?"

His criticism of Chris was beginning to bother her but she couldn't deny the truth in his words. This was a difficult situation and letting David buy into the business could cause more friction between all three of them. It would be practically impossible for her to buy both of them out, even if she was able to win at the Finals.

"Don't worry, Ali," he chuckled into his mug. "Your eyes pretty much say it all."

"It's not that I don't want you to but it will change everything."

"Yeah," he agreed, sarcastically. "It does make things a bit more complicated when your boyfriend and ex-boyfriend are living on the same property."

"Well, that doesn't make me sound like a whore or anything. Thanks."

"That's not what I meant." He rose and dumped the cold coffee onto the ground. "I just meant . . ."

Ali saw him pause and turned to see what caught his attention. Chris was exiting Delilah's fancy white horse trailer and rubbed his eyes, slapping his cowboy hat onto his head, shielding his eyes from the sun. He didn't see either of them and Ali turned away from the sight, unable to catch her breath as her heart dropped to her toes. She felt her entire chest constrict, as if a fist was squeezing her heart. Her stomach rolled and she wondered if she was going to throw up. She hurried for the trailer.

"Son-of-a-bitch," she heard David whisper. David followed her but she slammed the door on him. "Ali, wait."

She couldn't face David because he'd been right and she didn't want to see Chris because he'd just shattered her heart. It wasn't even seven AM yet and her day had gone to shit. She didn't want to see anyone right now.

Chapter Twenty-One

CHRIS STUMBLED DOWN the steps, pulling his t-shirt on over his head and slapping his hat on. He squinted at the sunlight glaring in his eyes and tried to get his bearings. There weren't many people up at this hour and he had no idea whose trailer this was until he saw David striding toward him, shaking his head in disgust.

"You just couldn't do it, could you? I knew you would do this." He turned and started to walk away.

"Do what?" Chris groaned as he rubbed at the ache throbbing between his eyes with his thumb.

David spun, his hands shooting out and shoving Chris back against the metal trailer, holding him up by the front of his shirt. "What the hell are you doing in Delilah's trailer? Don't you realize that Ali just saw you coming out of here?"

It took him several moments to register what David was saying. "Delilah?" He struggled to recall what happened as he shoved David's hands away from him.

Memories of last night came in pieces, unconnected and illogical. Sitting near a fire, Delilah begging him for help, a big cowbow ... after that, nothing.

"I've bailed you out of a lot of situations like this, Chris. I *told* you that you were going to do this to her." He shook his head. "You had it all and you couldn't just keep it in your pants, could you? You slept with Delilah?"

"No," Chris denied, trying to think through the painful crashing of blood through his temples. "I wouldn't do that to Ali."

David rolled his eyes. "Please. Like always, Chris, you're the only person you think about."

Chris reached for David's shoulder as he turned to leave. "I'm telling you, I didn't sleep with Delilah. Where is she?"

"Who, Ali? She's in the trailer. Hopefully packing up her gear and getting the hell away from your cheating ass."

"Delilah. Ask her. I know I didn't sleep with her. I was so drunk last night I could barely walk."

"And, yet, you end up in her trailer. You were pulling your shirt on when you came out, Chris," he reminded him.

"Wait, I woke up with my pants on." His head hurt but he tried to force the cobwebs away. "And my buckle." He shook his finger. "As a matter of fact, I had my boots on, too. I know I didn't sleep with her."

David crossed his arms. "You really didn't?" He eyed Chris speculatively.

"No!" Chris shook his head, feeling the throbbing worsen. "I wouldn't do anything to screw this up with Ali. *You* were the reason I wasn't in the trailer to begin with. She kicked me out until I apologized to you."

David snorted. "That's why you were wandering from trailer to trailer last night? If I didn't like Ali before, I would now." David wiped a hand over his jaw, his expression going serious. "She's not going to believe you. I can't believe I'm even considering that you might be telling the truth."

"David, you've got to help me."

"Are you kidding? After everything you've done to me?" David spun on his heel to leave.

"I'm sorry." Chris followed after him. "I'm sorry about Ali. I didn't realize how I felt and I should have backed off. I should have told you before anything happened." Chris rubbed his face. "Damn it, I should have told you about the ranch as soon as I found out. There' are a lot of things I should have done differently. But you're not innocent in this, either."

David turned and looked at Chris like he'd just grown horns. "Nice apology, Chris. How is any of this my fault? I tried to get you to admit how you felt about Ali, remember?"

"You didn't explain the situation with your dad. I would have offered the money to you instead. We could have bought the ranch, just the two of us, and started the school."

"You know this isn't just about the ranch, Chris. This is about you not wanting something until it's mine."

"She was never yours." Chris didn't want to hurt his friend any more than he already had but Ali had never been in love with David, any more than Chris had ever been in love with any other woman. Sydney was right. Since they were young, there had never been anyone else. "Or is that the problem? That she chose me over you?"

David shook his head, looking back at the trailer where Ali had disappeared. "And where did that get her? A broken heart and a boyfriend waking up in someone else's trailer. You're on your own for this one. I'm done rescuing you, Chris."

ALICIA HAD SWORN to herself she wasn't going to cry so the burning in her eyes had to be from the horse hair as she groomed Beast. She saw Chris hurry away from Delilah's trailer and head her way, looking furious. She tossed the blanket onto Beast's back, following it with the saddle and reaching for the cinch under his belly, ignoring the irate man in front of her.

"Ali, look at me." She wanted to ignore the demanding tone of his voice but found herself flicking her eyes toward him. "I didn't do anything."

Laughter burst from her throat. "Do you really expect me to believe that?" She reached for Beast's hoof and started to pick it out. "It's not a big deal," she lied. "We're business partners for the next year. Nothing more."

"Ali, you know me."

She stood up and moved to Beast's rump, laying her arm against him. "You're right. I *do* know you and I should have known that you were full of it when you told me your reputation was rumor. And when you told me you . . . you know what, it doesn't matter."

Alicia wanted to let her anger spill over but doing that would release the tears, the ache building in her heart at his betrayal, but she couldn't allow herself to do that. Not here. It was better to pretend he didn't hurt her, that she didn't care, and let the tears fall later, while she was alone. She bent down and lifted the gelding's hoof against her thigh.

"I have two horses to warm up and a go-round to win today. You can tell Bimbo Barbie and her twin, they are more than welcome to have you join them again tonight."

She set Beast's foot down and looked up in time to see his face cloud over. "I'm not staying in there tonight. I'm staying in *my* trailer. That's what got us into this mess."

"No, your lying got us into this mess. The fact that you're a cheating bastard got us into this. My being stupid enough to trust you got us into this." She shrugged as if she couldn't care less. "If you won't go, then I'll find another place to stay tonight. I'm sure I can find one of the other barrel racers to room with for the weekend." She bent and took the hoof in her hand.

"Damn it, Ali." Chris ran a hand through his hair, pain shooting through his skull as his fingers hit his nape, and he took a deep breath. "Why won't you just believe me?"

She shook her head. "Why would I? You've done nothing but play games with me since the first time you introduced me to David." She finished cleaning Beast's feet and checked the cinch before slipping his bridle over his head. "You may not know what you want in life but some of us do. Right now, that means I have to win this go-round and the average and I'm not going to let you or that floozy distract me from doing it."

She stepped into the stirrup and swung her leg over. "By the way, the next time you want to invite someone into the business, we should probably agree on it before you make the offer. Unless you plan on buying me out, no one else is coming into this deal." She started to walk Beast toward the practice arena and looked back at him over her shoulder. "You're only here short term. I *am* buying you out before the end of next year and that will be the end of this partnership."

ALICIA ALREADY WALKED and groomed Boogie after another amazing run. He was on a hot streak and she prayed it would hold out for another couple of days to win her the average purse as well as the go-round money. Two go-rounds down with two left to go. So far, the horses and the barrel runs weren't her problem. Her problem was the man getting ready to head into the box right now.

She sat in the stands, watching him as they made their run, awed by the way he and David worked together as a team. It was incredible to watch how they seemed to speak without words, almost as if they instinctively knew what the other was going to do. How was it possible for them to be so in sync when they weren't even speaking right now? How did they get so out of sync in the first place?

She felt guilt and shame wash over her like a spring shower. If she was honest with herself, she was a big part of the problem. She should have told Chris a long time ago how she felt, or explained to David from the beginning that her heart belonged to someone else. How could she have let this go this far, cause this much turmoil?

Chris spun to face David as they pulled the rope taut and the flag dropped, signaling the timer to stop. Their run was incredible, close to setting another arena record. It was great for the business and she'd already had several people come talk to her about setting up training and lessons but the way things were going, she wasn't sure they would even have a business by the time they got back to California.

"Oh, my goodness, he was *amazing* last night."

Ali cringed when she heard the voice coming from the end of the stands. She glanced over to see Delilah and several of her friends shooting daggers her way but was bound to ignore them. She wasn't about to let the witch know how much it hurt to think of Chris with her last night. If only she hadn't tried to force him to apologize to David and had let him come into the trailer.

If not Delilah, it would've been someone else. The cynical voice scratched at her self-confidence. *Of all the women he could choose, you thought you were the one he'd pick? The poor little wannabe from the trailer?*

Her doubts crowded out the trust she'd once had in Chris. She wasn't sure what to believe anymore. She'd trusted Chris with more than just her body and his betrayal had shredded her heart, leaving the bleeding remains in tatters. She didn't have a clue how to begin trying to put it back together. It wasn't just that he'd lied about loving her. He slept with the one woman who had gone out of her way to hurt Alicia. And the fact that he'd seen the way Delilah treated her made it seem like a slap in the face. Just another reminder that neither thought she was worthy of their respect.

"And those hands," Delilah spoke in a loud whisper, determined to making sure Alicia heard every sordid detail of her escapade. "Trust me, he knows how to use those. Now I see why he's in the top ten because those hands are magic."

Tears began to well in her eyes. She had to get away before they saw. The last thing she wanted was for Delilah to see her comments hit their mark. Alicia stood up and brushed past the group. "Excuse me."

"Oh, and there is nothing sexier than a guy with tattoos. He has this one . . . Oh, hello Alicia." Delilah acted surprised to see her but grabbed her wrist, demanding her attention. "There's nothing like a man in bed who knows what he's doing, is there?"

Alicia could see the hatred in Delilah's eyes, the intent to inflict as much pain as possible. She was like a lioness stalking prey and was watching for any weakness in her victim. Alicia wasn't about to give her the satisfaction.

"You ought to know, you've had enough of them there." She jerked her wrist away and Delilah laughed.

"Aw, don't be such a bad loser. You've had enough practice coming second to me that you should be used to it by now. Did you really think he'd pick you over someone like me?" She adjusted her shirt to show off her ample, medically enhanced cleavage. She looked Alicia up and down. "I mean, come on. What man in his right mind would pick you . . ." She waved her hand at Alicia dramatically before turning it toward herself and snickered. "Over this? I certainly don't know any."

"Well, congratulations, Delilah. I hope the two of you are very happy together. Maybe he can help you celebrate your twelfth place run today." She turned to leave the group of catty women on the stands.

"Just because you won today doesn't mean you're anything special."

"No," Alicia called, praying luck would be kind and remain on her side in spite of what she was about to say. "But yesterday's win and last weekend's win does. Maybe you should concentrate more on riding your horse than you do riding cowboys."

She heard the gasp of surprise from several of Delilah's friends and couldn't help squaring her shoulders with satisfaction. She was tired of being bullied and she wasn't going to let Delilah or her friends do it anymore. She was done being nice, letting their comments roll off her back, pretending she didn't care, trying to prove her worth so they would stop. No matter how hard she tried, it would never be enough for Delilah to accept her.

She was sick of rolling over and letting people take advantage of her. That included the man tying his horse to their trailer. She stormed over, ready to make sure he knew she'd had her fill of being abused.

"How could you do that to me?" The anger she'd been so determined to hide from him earlier erupted with full force. "How could you want to be with someone like me and someone like her?"

"Ali, I didn't—"

She didn't give him a chance to say anything. She didn't want to hear any more words, because that's all they were to him. Words, excuses, justifications, and apologies. It was a merry-go-round of tolerance and it was breaking her down. She was losing herself in weakness and refused to give into it any longer.

"I don't want to hear anything, Chris. I've heard enough and it means nothing anymore because I can't trust you."

She saw his jaw clench and knew he was barely restraining his own temper. "You've always been able to trust me, Ali. I promised not to hurt you and—"

"And yet you did." She could see the defeat in his eyes. She wanted him to fight back, to prove he hadn't slept with Delilah, to make her believe she was the only woman he wanted. But he said nothing and that said it all. "You don't love me, Chris. You don't love anyone but yourself. I don't even think you know how."

She moved toward the trailer door. "I'm getting my things and staying somewhere else. Anywhere else."

Chris followed her inside, shutting the door behind him. "What can I say, Ali? Nothing is going to change your mind since you won't believe the truth."

She looked back at him as she threw her clothes into her duffel bag. "I saw you leaving her trailer, with no shirt on, before six-thirty in the morning. What other reason could you possibly come up with?"

Chris reached for her hand and dragged her against him. Her softness cradled him as he buried his hands into her hair and his mouth covered hers, cutting off any protest she might offer. His tongue swept into her mouth, stealing her breath and her resistance. She wanted to hate him, fight him, push him away, but her heart couldn't deny this last kiss, one last touch.

Her hands slipped around the back of his neck, drawing him closer, begging for more of him. If she couldn't have his heart, she would take what he was willing to give and hate herself for her weakness later. Her fingers clutched at him, desperate to touch him and be touched by him. He slid a hand to her low back and pressed her against him, his fingers sliding up the back of her shirt and releasing the clasp of her bra. Her shirt disappeared over her head, followed by his, and his hands were at the waistband of her pants.

Clothing was shed quickly while his lips seemed to be everywhere at once. She was on fire with need, his mouth and hands burning a path over her flesh until she felt like she was going to explode. Chris laid her on the bed. The weight of his body over her, his skin scorching every inch of her, was sensual, making her tremble in anticipation.

With him poised at the core of her desire, inching himself forward, the love she felt for him, the need, the aching torment—all of it outweighed the pain he caused and she couldn't turn him away. She couldn't stop herself from loving him any more than she could stop the sun from rising. If she was going to give in to this weakness, she was going to do it on her terms.

Alicia rolled so that she was straddling Chris, her hands against his chest, holding him down. "Say it," she whispered.

Chris circled his hands at her waist and stared up at her. "You said it didn't matter."

She bent and kissed him, taking his lower lip between her teeth. "I lied," she whispered against his mouth. "Tell me, even if you don't mean it." She slid down the length of him slowly, wrapping him with the sheath of her heat, and he groaned against her mouth.

It was torture, sweet and painful, but she stilled. "Chris?"

He cupped his hands around her face, forcing her to look into his smoldering blue eyes. "I love you, Ali. I promise you can trust me. This is the real thing." He pressed himself farther into her, sending her over the edge, no longer able to hold back as she dropped her head backward, crying out his name.

It was primal, raw desire, needy, demanding an answering passion from him. Her nails dug into his sides as his hands cupped her breasts, driving into her as she held on. His thumbs stroked over the tight buds and her body quaked against him, clutching him as she rode the waves of ecstasy. Unable to wait for his release, she arched her back, her body exploding into thousands of points of light.

It was the only encouragement he needed and he thrust into her. Alicia realized he'd been holding back his own release, waiting for her, and felt herself cresting the wave again as he took her breast into his mouth, drawing every ounce of passion from her. She shook against him, unable to control her body's response to him, feeling her body contract around him. He nibbled and sucked at the flesh as she trembled against him.

Chris swirled his tongue around the nipple and she fell over the edge, her body convulsing as she felt herself lose control. He groaned against her and gave himself over to his release. Alicia knew she'd regret this moment soon enough but for right now, she was going to savor the moment of ignorant bliss. She would allow herself this one respite to pretend they were happy and that they could move forward. Even if it was only for tonight.

Chapter Twenty-Two

CHRIS WOKE UP the next morning and reached his arms out to circle the soft woman in the small bed with him but his hands found nothing but cold sheets. He opened his eyes but knew exactly what he'd find. The trailer had no trace of Alicia left other than her scent left clinging to his skin and the pillow.

"Damn it." He rolled onto his back and covered his eyes with his arm. He'd prayed after last night, she believed him.

He swung his legs over the edge of the bed. She couldn't have gotten far. He knew she wouldn't leave this close to winning the overall average purse. He still had twenty-four hours to convince her. Pulling on his jeans and slipping his arms into a t-shirt, he headed out to feed the horses, only to find his horses already munching on alfalfa and her animals nowhere in sight. That wasn't a good sign.

He opened the tack compartment and saw only his tack and dread balled in his stomach. Maybe this wasn't going to be as easy as he thought. She wasn't just planning on staying somewhere else tonight. It looked like she was trying to avoid him completely.

"What's wrong, cowboy? You look like you just lost your best friend."

Chris turned and saw the last woman he ever wanted to set eyes on again. "You're going to clear up this mess right now." He reached for her arm but she jerked it away from his fingers.

"I don't know what you're talking about." She clutched at her arm as if afraid of him. "I can't help it if you didn't tell your girlfriend about us." She deliberately raised her voice, looking around for an audience.

"There is no *us*, Delilah. You know damn well nothing happened and you're going to tell Ali." Memories began to piece together in his mind. "I helped you last night. That cowboy . . ."

Delilah took a step closer, forgetting the pretense of lying, and sneered at him. "Was a friend of mine. I'm not clearing anything up for you. You and that tramp deserve this." She turned to leave and stopped, throwing him a glance over her shoulder. "You know, I might be persuaded to tell her the truth if you convince her to stop competing."

"Why? Because you can't beat her on your own?" Chris narrowed his eyes. Ali wouldn't quit this close to winning, and he wouldn't ask. "You're so far behind her right now, she's got this average in the bag."

Delilah laughed bitterly. "You're really are an idiot," she scoffed. "Or did we just hit you in the head too hard last night. I mean she quit altogether. No more rodeos. At all."

That explained the headache that wouldn't go away.

Ali had never been closer to competing in the National Finals. He couldn't ask her to give that up. There had to be another way to prove himself to Ali. Delilah wasn't that clever so it shouldn't be too difficult.

"Sorry, Delilah, but it's going to be far too much fun watching Ali leave you in the dust. I wouldn't miss that for anything." He wasn't about to bow to her conniving ways.

She arched a perfectly waxed brow at him. "Suit yourself. It's too bad, though. You two made a cute couple." She pouted at him. "It's kinda funny that you were the one who introduced her to David. I guess it's sort of fitting that he gets the girl in the end."

"What are you talking about?"

She pointed to David's trailer where Boogie was tied. "If I didn't know better, I'd think she was playing you two against each other." She pressed one hand against her ample bosom in mock outrage. "What a slut!"

Chris had never hit a woman but, if he ever did, this would be the one he'd make the exception for. "You ever mention her name again and I promise you'll be sorry, Delilah," he growled through clenched teeth.

"Don't you get pissy when you don't get your way?" She laughed as if she didn't care what he threatened. She looked around make sure she had witnesses. "Too bad you didn't just keep it in your pants the other night. You weren't that great anyway."

"Well, thanks for the warning, Delilah," he countered. "I'll be sure to get myself checked out now that I know which STD you're passing around." It wasn't going to make his case to Ali look any better but he wasn't sure anything was going to make him look worse than he already did.

She narrowed her eyes as the girls began whispering behind their hands and one pointed at Delilah. "You'll be sorry for that, you bastard," she hissed.

"Trust me. I've never been sorrier than I am that I tried to help you last night."

He turned on a heel, leaving her staring after him, and headed for David's trailer. He wasn't going to cave to Delilah's threats. He would get the truth about this situation and his best friend was just the person to help. Even if they were barely speaking right now.

DAVID CLEANED HIS gelding's hoof out again but he could see the horse was coming up lame on his front foot. He could ride his mare, it was the reason he brought two horses to every rodeo, but this gelding was the better of the two—far better. This rodeo was leaving him more frustrated every hour. First the fight with Chris, then Ali moving into his trailer, now this? What was next? Chris wasn't going to be happy about him changing horses but he couldn't figure out what caused the gelding to go lame for no apparent reason.

"Need help?"

David glanced up in time to see a pretty blond with a rhinestone crown on her hat looking down at him expectantly. Her rhinestone-studded, red Western shirt made him close one eye as the sun glinted off it, blinding him. The crown and sash were dead giveaways and he knew who he was looking at—the rodeo queen.

"You think *you* can help me?"

She cocked her head at him, her long, curled hair tipping to one side. "Yes. Does that seem so unheard of? Or are you usually rude enough to make people not want to help you?"

Setting his gelding's hoof on the ground, David dusted off his hands on his pants and eyed her. "You're kinda feisty for a queen, aren't you?"

"And you're awfully cocky for a roper with a lame horse."

He swung his hand toward the horse, not bothering to hide his sarcasm. "I'm so sorry. Please, be my guest."

She bent over and picked up the foot, pressing with her thumb against several areas of the inside, watching for the animal's reaction. The gelding twitched as she pushed on the middle. "Looks like he bruised the frog." She showed him a tender area and pressed against it, pointing out when the horse tried to draw his foot from her. "You'll need to get your farrier to put some pads on him until it heals. I wouldn't ride him today though."

David eyed her speculatively as she carefully released the hoof and patted his horse's shoulder. "He'll be fine in a week or so."

He breathed a sigh of relief and leaned against the trailer. At least it wasn't a major injury. "Not bad for a rodeo queen."

"Yeah? Maybe that's because I'm a vet first." She gave him a dazzling smile. "Well, almost a vet. I still have another year to finish."

"That explains it. So, what do I owe you, Doc?" He wasn't sure why he was antagonizing this woman when she'd helped him but she seemed to take it in stride. Her pretty blue eyes were mischievous and filled with humor, making him relax a bit.

"I guess I can let you off with a freebie this time, especially since I don't have my license yet."

She started to leave and he found himself looking for a reason to keep her lingering. "You gonna be around later, Doc? Just in case he needs you to check up on him again?"

She turned around and flashed him that brilliant smile again. "Are you asking for your horse or yourself?"

"Does it matter?" The door to his trailer opened.

"Hey, David, I hope you don't mind but I . . . oh! Sorry, I was just—"

David saw the pretty vet narrow her eyes before they clouded over with guarded irritation. "Alicia Kanani, this is . . ." David paused, realizing he didn't even know her name.

"Summer Williams," she finished for him, holding her hand out to Alicia. "I was just checking out his gelding's hoof."

Alicia looked between the two of them, obviously sensing the tension, and a broad smile spread over her lips. "Miss West Hills Rodeo, right?"

Summer nodded and wiggled the white sash over her chest. "Only until the weekend's over. I decided to do one last queen's run. It was nice to meet you, Alicia." She glanced at David. "You too, David."

David frowned as she turned to leave. He hadn't introduced himself.

"Wait a second," he called after her, jogging to catch up. "How'd you know who I was?"

"I'm the rodeo queen and it's part of the gig that I stay up on rodeo standings. You and your partner are back up to number four right now."

If she knew who he was, then she certainly knew Chris. Just the thought of her falling for Chris's charms soured him.

Why do you even care?

The question took him by surprise and he pushed it aside, not wanting to open that can of worms right now. He had enough trouble at this rodeo for one man to handle.

She glanced back at Alicia. "You'd better get back. I don't want to make your girlfriend mad and I'm not into flirting with another girl's cowboy."

His brows dropped and David shook his head. "Ali's not my girlfriend. I mean, at one time she was," he clarified. "But we're just friends now."

Summer shook her head, doubtful and laughed. "I've heard that one before. I'll see you around."

David watched her walk away, feeling disappointed and irritated with himself but unsure as to why, which only frustrated him more. He didn't like feeling off-balance.

"David, I'm sorry. I didn't mean to—"

"Don't worry, Ali. It was nothing. She was just taking a look at his foot for me."

She cocked a brow and eyed him. "It didn't look like nothing."

He didn't want to argue with her, or think about the situation too closely. He didn't need any more female complications in his life right now. Between losing the family ranch, dealing with Ali and Chris, and trying to stay in the top standings, he didn't have a second to waste on any sort of relationship. Especially with someone as high maintenance as a rodeo queen.

She gave him a half-hearted shrug and her eyes grew serious. "David, I need you to do something for me."

"Anything." It was an open invitation and he meant it but found his thoughts straying back to the woman who'd just walked away from his trailer.

"I want you to buy out Chris in the rodeo school." The words spilled from her lips, as if she might take them back if she didn't say them quickly. "Be my only partner. I can't do this with him," she said, her voice catching. She took a deep breath, getting her emotions under control again. "Especially now."

The sadness in her eyes ate at him. He wanted to do something to alleviate her heartbreak but knew he was the wrong man. The realization stung a bit but he had to be honest with himself. She didn't love him, she never had. And he hadn't loved her, at least, not yet, although he was sure they could have headed that direction. David looked away, unable to face the need haunting her eyes.

His gaze fell on Summer as she bent over and laughed with a child, tapping the front of his miniature cowboy hat, and his heart lurched at the tender moment. Could he find a way to move on while working with Ali every day?

"I don't know if I can, Ali." His eyes flitted back to hers before they sought out the pretty blond rodeo queen again.

She followed his gaze, placing her hands on his shoulder. "We're friends, right?"

His brow scrunched together in confusion. "Yeah, why?"

"Please, don't take this the wrong way, and I know you care about me, but we were never more than friends. Even when we both wanted there to be more." She jerked her chin in Summer's direction. "And, honestly, I'm happy to see you getting back into that saddle. You're too great a guy to not have someone to care about you the way you deserve."

He looked at Summer then back at Ali. He cared about Ali but she was right, they were friends and nothing more. It wouldn't help either of them to try to force something that wasn't there. She wasn't ready to love anyone but Chris and, he knew she was right, he did deserve someone to love him completely. The realization seemed to lift a dark cloud from him, giving him perspective.

"What if I just buy into the rodeo school? Chris already made the offer."

She shook her head. "I can't work with him, David," she whispered. "If you buy him out, you still have your ranch, or at least half of it." She looked up at him and he could see the unshed tears shimmering in her eyes. "I can try to buy you out at the end of next year like I was going to do with Chris."

He knew his surprise registered on his face. "Then why did he ask me to join you guys?"

"He doesn't really believe I'll buy him out."

David cocked a brow at her and shook his head in disbelief. "What's wrong with you two? How do you expect to have any sort of lasting relationship when neither of you believes the other?" His words broke the dam of her tears. "Come here."

David pulled her into his arms and held her, pretending not to notice the warmth of her tears on his t-shirt or the way she leaned into him for strength. He looked toward the arena in time to see Summer's questioning blue eyes meet his, curious and slightly accusing.

GREAT, HE THOUGHT. *There went any chance with her.* Chris watched David with Ali and the knot of jealousy in his chest tightened, threatening to choke him when she hugged him before taking Boogie to the practice arena. He'd stood by once and almost let David steal her. He wasn't doing it again. He'd waited too long to lose Ali now.

"I need your help."

David turned and saw him coming. He crossed his arms and leaned back against the side of the truck. "Good morning to you, too."

"Is Ali staying with you?"

A smirk slid over David's face and it took every bit of self-control Chris had not to punch him in the mouth. "I don't have to answer that. If she wanted you to know, she'd have told you. She's in the arena right now if you want to talk to her."

Chris shook his head. "She won't listen to me anyway. I need you to help me prove I'm telling the truth about Delilah."

David snorted a laugh. "Why in the world would I do anything for you?"

"Because if you do, you can have my share of the ranch. I just want Ali. If I have my way, we'll all end up partners anyway."

David arched a brow. "Are you saying what I think you are?"

"I love her, David. I'm not going to let her go."

A slow smile spread over David's face. "Well, it's about damn time. I wondered if there was anything more than a player under that skin of yours."

Chris was tired of this reputation and was going to clear it up once and for all. "I was never a player. I dropped most of those women home and slept in my truck."

David nodded and rolled his eyes. "Yeah, because that makes total sense." He studied Chris. "You're serious?"

"Is this really that hard for people to believe?"

David's laughter grated on Chris's last nerve. "I guess you play the horny hound dog too well." He caught Chris's glare and sighed, growing serious. "You really love her?"

"I do." He shook his head, throwing his hands up. "I don't know why I didn't realize it sooner. I can't believe the mess I made of all of this."

"I can," David muttered, pushing himself off the truck. "You really didn't sleep with Delilah?"

"I was angry because Ali wanted me to apologize."

"And you should," David interrupted.

Chris glared at him. "I drunk but then Delilah came up begging me to help her, that some guy was following her. I got her back into her trailer but I never went inside it."

"You don't remember anything after that?" David pointed out.

"The next thing I knew, I was waking up. With my boots and pants on," he pointed out. "I've had a headache all day but I thought it was a hangover until Delilah said something about hitting me too hard. I think they knocked me out. Plus she just tried to get me to convince Ali to quit barrel racing. Said she'd tell her the truth."

"When you dig a pit for yourself, you make it deep, don't you?"

"David? Come on," Chris wasn't used to asking for help but he'd beg David if he had to. He couldn't lose Ali.

"Fine, I'll see what I can do to help but I'm not sure what you expect me to do."

"Talk to Ali."

David laughed in disbelief. "What am I supposed to say to her? She's not going to believe me either. Didn't your mom ever tell you that actions speak louder than words? Show her. I'll work on getting Delilah to admit it's a lie."

ALI WISHED SHE could celebrate her final go-round win with Chris but she had to stay away. She couldn't trust herself; last night proved that. She couldn't be near him without wanting his hands on her, without putting her hands on him, without her heart feeling like it was slowly tearing in half. David didn't seem inclined to buy him out either. How in the world was she going to be able to work with him on the ranch daily? There was no way she could live in the same house with him. Chris was going to have to move in with David. If the two of them ever started speaking again.

She should be celebrating right now. Alicia was sitting at the top of the average and was taking home three first place wins. She was supposed to be ecstatic. Instead she was dwelling on this situation with Chris that should have never happened in the first place. She'd known to stay away. His reputation had always preceded him. She'd been naive to think Chris could change or feel more than lust for anyone. There was no happily ever after and she'd been gullible to believe they could be partners, in business or love. There was no partnership. It was all about Chris getting what he wanted without consequences.

She'd been foolish to think their past meant anything to him, that their friendship was anything more than a means to an end. Sydney couldn't possibly know what her brother had turned into. Alicia's shoulders slumped forward as she rode Boogie back to the trailer. It was going to be a long year. Maybe she should just let David buy her out, give up on this dream, and get as far away as she could.

She hooked Boogie's halter around his neck and unsaddled him. She was just about to pull his saddle from him when two hands pulled it off from the other side. She jumped back in surprise when she saw Colt put her saddle into the trailer.

"I hear congratulations are in order." He leaned over the back of her horse and handed her a curry comb. "I see you're still playing my son for a fool."

She jerked the rubber tool from his hand and began to groom the horse, attempting to ignore him.

"Oh, don't get all quiet now. You're a ranch owner and you're going to have to give lessons. Maybe you can give me a few and I can find out what sort of spell you're putting on these boys. You seem to have several of the cowboys around here enamored."

"I doubt barrel racing is in your wheelhouse. You should talk to Chris."

"I hear he's giving you *private* lessons." He gave her an insinuating grin, his eyes skimming her frame. She held his gaze, refusing to let him intimidate her, even as he disgusted her.

"You're a pig."

"So, when David wouldn't let you worm your way into his wallet you decided to work on Chris? I wouldn't have thought a bunny like you would have the funds to buy a ranch like mine."

"I wasn't worming my way into anyone's wallet. I can earn my own."

"Sure you can." He smiled at her but it didn't reach his eyes. "You're one conniving bitch, I'll give you that." He moved around Boogie to stand behind her, dwarfing her tiny frame. "And now it looks like you're sleeping with

David again. Tsk, tsk," he scolded. "It won't work, you know."

"I don't know what you're talking about. David and I are friends." Alicia continued to groom the horse, refusing to look at him.

"Hmm," Colt murmured, "sure you are. Either way, you're too late. I already saw him cozying up to some blond by the stands." He took a step closer, pressing up against her back, forcing her to take a step closer to the horse as he leaned over her. She could feel his heated breath against the back of her head and smelled the yeasty scent of too much beer.

"And he's got too much to lose to dump your *partner*. They will pair up and run you out of this rodeo school. And when they do, I'll be back in my house so fast your head will spin. A few wins doesn't make you good enough to live on *my* ranch."

Colt Greenly didn't like her and he might be a bully but she didn't think he was stupid enough to hurt her, at least, not in front of this many witnesses. She wasn't about to take a chance. Alicia turned to push him away.

"Back off, Colt. You're drunk." Chris grabbed the bigger man's shoulders and jerked him away from Alicia. "As usual, you have no clue what you're talking about."

"You don't need another whore for your harem, Chris," Colt ground through clenched teeth.

Without warning, Chris swung his fist, knocking the older man to the ground. He grabbed him by the front of his shirt. "You ever talk to her again and I'll beat you until neither of your sons can recognize you." He looked back at Alicia, making sure she was unharmed. "David and I might end up in business together but it will never include you. When that house closes escrow, you are no longer welcome on the property, Colt. Not ever."

He let the man fall back to the ground and turned to Alicia, cupping her cheeks in his hands. "Are you all right?"

She reached for his wrists. "I'm fine." She saw David hurrying toward them. "I can't stay here."

"I'll take you home," he offered.

"No!" She spit the word out and moved away from him. She hadn't meant to yell but she couldn't be around him right now. She looked at the crowd beginning to gather around them.

"Ali? Dad?" David bent and helped his father from the ground "What's going on?" He looked to Chris.

"Your father decided to harass Ali."

David spun on his father. "Again?"

Colt rose from the ground and dusted off his jeans. "You're gonna take this whore's side after she snatched the ranch out from under—"

Colt hit the ground again. He didn't even see Chris take a swing. "I warned you, you son-of-a-bitch!"

"Chris!" Ali cried, reaching for his arm and pulling him back. Boogie shifted sideways at the commotion and several cowboys hurried in to pull Chris away, holding him back from attacking Colt again.

"Take her to Sydney's like you planned and I'll meet you both at the ranch tomorrow night," David ordered. "I'll take care of him but she doesn't need to be subjected to any more of this."

She didn't want to go anywhere, especially with Chris. She wasn't about to turn tail and run like she was afraid of Colt Greenly.

"Ali," David looked her in the eye as if reading her thoughts. "Go. I'll meet you tomorrow. I promise."

Trust me, his eyes pleaded.

Knowing she had little choice, she let Chris pull her toward his trailer.

Chapter Twenty-Three

CHRIS SAT, BROODING silently, while Ali ran a cloth under water. "Where's your first aid kit?"

Her voice was quiet, soft but hesitant. It wasn't like her and he wondered at her inconsistent behavior. "Under the sink."

She pulled a chair in front of him, reaching for his hand. "You split your knuckle," she pointed out, dabbing at it with the cloth. She popped open the kit and, unable to find any antiseptic ointment, took out an alcohol swab. "This is going to hurt."

"Not as much as other things have." He hadn't meant to say the words out loud.

Her eyes leapt up to meet his, staring into the depths as if she was trying to read his thoughts. Unless Delilah confessed, it was her word against his. He clenched his jaw, refusing to say anything further. She should know him well enough to believe him.

She drew her lower lip into her mouth as she ripped the top off the package. "Chris," she began then stopped, shaking her head, and dabbed at his knuckles.

He sucked in a quick breath at the sting on his hand but it faded before she could finish bandaging it. He was having enough difficulty breathing with her leaning forward over him. Her scent filled his nostrils, surrounding him. He could feel the tension emanating from her, like a current between them as her fingers moved over his hand.

"Thank you," she said, smoothing down the edges of the bandage against the back of his hand. Her eyes flicked to his and back to his hand.

"For what, Ali?" He hardly recognized the pained huskiness of his voice. He wanted to give up on her, forget her and move on, but she was like a lingering dream, clinging to the edges of his reality but just out of reach.

She set his hand down, ignoring his question. "Are you going to be able to rope with your hand like this?"

He could see her retreating within herself, putting her protective walls back up and he wasn't sure he had the ability to scale them again. Chris flexed his hand a few times, testing the mobility.

"It'll be fine in a day or so." He saw fresh blood seeping through the bandage from the movement. It felt like his heart. Just when he thought he'd stopped the bleeding, she did something to break it open again. He sighed. "Let's get the horses loaded and I'll take you home."

Her head jerked up. "I thought we were staying with Sydney for a few days."

Chris shook his head in frustration and rose. "I don't know what we're doing. Every time I think I figure it out, you knock me off balance." He opened the door and hung his head, his words laced with double meaning. "Just let me know where we're going, Ali, because I'll take you wherever you want to go."

SHE WATCHED CHRIS walk out the door, wondering if she dared tell him what she really wanted to say. Did she dare confess she wanted him to take her to Sydney's, to hear him profess his feelings even if she wasn't sure she'd believe him? She wanted to believe him, especially when he looked as defeated as he did leaving the trailer just now. The desperation she saw in his eyes had nothing to do with lust. He looked devastated when she continued to doubt him and it made her second-guess her instincts.

Instinct told her not to trust him, he was lying, his reputation was well deserved. But her heart said something different. It ached to see him hurt. But one thought continuously circled through her mind—one night with him wasn't enough. A lifetime with him wouldn't be enough, she realized. She wanted him, every part of him. If she couldn't have his heart, and she wasn't sure he would ever give his heart to anyone, she had to forget him. Her heart pounded painfully against her ribs. Moving on would be impossible. There would never be anyone else who she would give herself to completely. There never had been until Chris.

She walked outside to see him loading her horses into

the trailer. He barely cast her a glance as she loaded their gear. She noticed her bag along the wheel well.

"David brought that over when he brought the horses."

His voice was cold, matter-of-fact, and emotionless. What she wouldn't give to return to the fun-loving tease she'd known forever. Would they ever be able to have a simple friendship again or had her weakness complicated things forever?

Her phone vibrated in her pocket and she pulled it out. Sydney. It was as if her friend had ESP and could sense her emotions. She opened the text message.

How'd you do? Can't wait to see you today! Syd

Would it be so bad to spend a few days at the ranch with Sydney like they'd originally planned? Chris would be with Scott and Derek most of the time and maybe it would give her some time to sort out what she was feeling. She had to make a decision because she couldn't operate a business with him as long as things remained like this between them, but she wasn't sure she could walk away from him either.

DAVID WATCHED CHRIS and Alicia pull away. He'd made arrangements with Chris to meet them at Findley Brothers' ranch tomorrow for a barbecue. He wasn't sure how Chris managed to convince Ali to go there instead of going home but he had to give the guy credit. His plan to reveal Delilah's lies might be genius, even if the execution might turn his stomach a bit. Now, David just had to convince her to open up to him.

She made her way past his trailer with several of her plastic friends, giggling as she waved at him. It gave him a perfect opportunity to put Chris's plan into action. He winked at her and jerked his chin in greeting. She smiled as he crooked a finger, indicating she should come over. He saw her lean toward her friends before breaking away from their pack and turning toward him.

"What's up, sexy?" she asked as she reached the trailer, her lips turning into a pout. "I shouldn't even talk to you. You've ignored me ever since that night at the bar."

David barely kept his face impassive, wanting to cringe, and took a step closer. "I've been sort of busy." He shrugged and gave her a lopsided grin, wondering how Chris managed to do this all the time. He felt awkward trying to flirt, especially with someone he couldn't stand. "Doesn't mean I wasn't thinking about you," he lied.

She looked up at him though hooded eyes and heavily mascaraed lashes. "You never called. I'm beginning to wonder if you're not still hung up on Alicia."

She was so transparent. He slid his hand to her waist. "No," he said, shaking his head. "That was a mutual thing. I have my eye on someone else."

An image of a beautiful rodeo queen with sky blue eyes flitted through his mind and he felt his body immediately react. He took a step back in surprise but not before Delilah wound her arms around his waist, assuming his reaction was for her. She eyed his jeans and gave him a catty grin.

"Do you now?"

David was finding it hard to continue this ruse. He wanted to laugh at Delilah's assumption but knew Chris was depending on him pulling off this pretense. "I was hoping you'd go to a barbecue with me tomorrow."

"David Greenly, are you asking me out on an official date?" She ran her fingers along the center of his chest.

"It's at Findley Brothers' though. Are you going to be all over Chris if I take you?" He pasted a worried frown on his brow.

She eyed him. "I thought the two of you weren't speaking."

He shrugged. "He's my roping partner and if we want to make the Finals, what choice do I have? Doesn't mean I'm happy about it, or that I wouldn't mind letting him see me with his woman."

He pulled her against him as she giggled. "I am *not* his woman." She wound her arms around his neck, playing with the hair at his nape.

"After last night, I thought—"

"Don't think," she whispered, pressing her lips against his jaw before drawing her lips together in a disappointed pout. "But I can't make it. Maybe we can have some fun tonight instead?"

Damn, he cursed his luck. Chris wanted Ali to hear her confession. Maybe he could still make that happen.

"Hang on." David casually slipped his hand into his pocket and found his cell phone and, glancing at the screen, pretended to get a text. He punched a few buttons while she took a step backward, coyly glancing his way as she played with his rope, twirling the loop awkwardly.

"Sorry." He tucked the phone back into his pocket. "My dad is in the medic tent and wanted to make sure I was taking him home tomorrow."

"Where were we?" She scooted closer, slapping the end of the rope against her leg. "Oh, that's right." She lifted his arm to her waist and curled hers behind him. "Tonight, my trailer."

David sighed. "I don't know, Delilah. I don't like sleeping with a woman after Chris has. Makes me feel second best." He cocked his head at her, sliding his hand down her spine to pause at the curve of her waist. "It's not a good feeling."

"Oh, honey," she purred. "You're not second best."

He started to take a step back and she curled her fingers into his belt loops, not allowing him to move far. "I don't know. Maybe after things die down with us. Or after the Finals."

A look of panic slid across her face. She curled her hand around the back of his neck and dragged his mouth down to hers, sweeping her tongue inside his mouth. "Tonight," she whispered against his lips. "I promise you won't regret it."

"Hmm," David pretended to consider her offer. "I'm sure it would be a night I wouldn't forget but . . . he's my partner."

"It didn't seem to bother him that you were with Alicia first," she pointed out, her fingers tripping over his biceps.

David sighed and ran his hands over her arms, setting

her back a step and trying to look injured. "Yeah, but I'm not like Chris. This is one of the reasons I don't do it. It makes things . . . messy." He turned on his heel to walk away from her.

"I didn't sleep with him."

He turned back toward her, twisting his mouth to the side. "Everyone knows you did, Delilah."

"No, I didn't. I just let people think that to get back at him. He . . . passed out and snored all night. I didn't get any sleep at all." Her fingers tucked into his front pockets and pulled him toward her. "So, what do you say?" Delilah rubbed herself against the front of him like a cat in heat and he arched a brow, smiling down at her.

"Not many women would lie and say they slept with a guy they didn't." He chuckled conspiratorially. "And, I've never known Chris to just pass out, no matter how much he drinks."

She shrugged. "I know you still trust Alicia but I can't stand her. And Chris has always been mean to me so I might have given him a little help," she hinted. "So I got even with both of them at once."

"Help?"

She pressed her lips against his neck, her tongue snaking out over his skin. "Let's just say he's not as hard-headed as everyone thinks."

David looked up in time to see Summer glance his way and raise her brows.

So much for asking Summer out. He wanted to follow her and explain that this wasn't him, he wasn't a player, but how in the world would he ever explain this? His stomach turned as Delilah sucked at his neck like a leech. Chris had better appreciate this.

ALICIA STARED OUT the window silently as the miles passed. Chris didn't even try to engage her in any conversation. Instead he ignored her completely and turned on the radio. She pulled out her phone and texted Sydney, warning her of the storm coming her way. She didn't want her friend unprepared.

She took a deep breath and rested her chin in her hand as the trees blurred by. Chris had begged her to give their partnership a test run at this rodeo and they proved they couldn't make it. Her stomach flipped as anxiety twisted in her belly, making her nauseous. This wasn't the way their weekend was supposed to go. Sure, she was coming back with a big win but she felt like the biggest loser of all.

She glanced at Chris as they turned off the highway and pulled onto the gravel road that led through the gates to Sydney and Scott's house. She opened her mouth to say something, anything to break the silence echoing in the truck, beating against her chest painfully. Every second that ticked by with nothing said between them drove more of a wedge between them. She licked her lips, unsure of what to say when nothing seemed appropriate.

Shifting his eyes toward her, Chris leaned on the center console. *That has to be a good sign, doesn't it?* He reached forward and changed the radio station, turning up the song, effectively making sure she didn't speak. *Guess not.*

Frustration blossomed in her chest. Why was he mad at her? Shouldn't it be the other way around? He'd been the one to set her up with his friend only to get jealous. He'd been the one who professed love and then slept with someone else a few hours later. She glared at him.

"Do you plan on giving me the silent treatment the entire time we're here?"

"I'm not giving you the silent treatment." He shrugged his broad shoulder, his fingers tapping against the steering wheel in time with the radio.

His blasé attitude infuriated her and she reached forward, turning off the radio with a quick jerk of her hand. "Yes, you are."

He looked at her and sighed. "Ali, I'm just trying to give you some space. I messed up, I get it."

"Space? You think I need space?" She laughed in disbelief. "You break up the only relationship I've had in years because you convince me that you love me and then turn around and sleep with the one person who's made my life a living hell. And you think space is going to make it better? Pull over."

"Why?" He slowed the truck and pulled to the side of the long driveway, stopping the truck and dropping it into gear. She opened the door and started walking down the driveway. "Wait! What are you doing?" Chris scrambled from the driver's seat and ran after her.

"Go away, Chris. I don't want to spend one more second with you in that truck. How's that for some space."

"You . . . what?" He threw his hands up and looked back at the truck and trailer. "You know what? Fine!"

He walked back toward the truck, infuriating her further as she watched him go. She set her shoulders and looked back down the empty driveway. They were only about halfway to the house but she figured the half-mile walk might give her some time to think, away from the scent of him that sent her spiraling into a puddle of yearning this entire trip. How could she want him after what he'd done to her? How weak was she? She felt like she was trying to hold the pieces of her heart together with cheap glue with nothing but a mess to show for it.

She heard the tires turn on the gravel and waited for the dust as the trailer passed her. Instead, he pulled alongside her, the truck barely moving as he kept pace beside her.

"Are you really planning to walk the entire way down to the house? I'm sure these horses would like to eat tonight." His mouth turned up in that damn sexy grin of his, irritating her.

"So go. Don't worry about me. I know the way."

"Ali, get in the truck."

"No."

"Damn, if you aren't *the* most stubborn woman I've ever met. If I tell you to walk, will you still do the opposite and get in the truck?"

She fought the grin she knew he was trying to worm out of her. Humor wasn't going to get them out of this mess. The fact that he couldn't seem to take anything seriously, including their relationship, was what caused this trouble in the first place. She stopped and looked at him through the passenger window.

"Maybe I do need space. But I need space *away* from you, Chris. You say you want one thing and then you do something completely opposite. Actions speak louder than words, Chris."

His brow furrowed, creasing between his eyes. "You're the second person to tell me that," he muttered.

"Then, maybe, you should take note. Now, please just leave me alone." She pushed herself away from the truck and started walking again, waiting for the truck to pass her.

He braked gradually and she could hear the horses shuffling nervously in the trailer, unaccustomed to traveling more than short distances this slowly. She looked back at him over her shoulder, irritated to see him settling in the driver's seat and cruising slowly behind her. She sighed again. Why couldn't he just listen to her for a change?

"I said, go." She waved him to pass her and looked to her left as he edged the truck at her side.

"You're right, actions do speak louder. So I'm not leaving you, Ali. Not ever. You can either walk the whole way with me driving alongside or you can get in the truck but I'm not going anywhere."

She stopped, knowing full well he wasn't talking about only this moment. Alicia could read the stubborn set of his jaw, in spite of his relaxed stance with one arm hanging over the steering wheel. The corners of his mouth tipped up and his eyes were alight with mirth but there was something more. She could see the hope he was trying to keep buried in the blue depths.

"Come on," he said, pushing the button to unlock the door. "Give the horses a break, they want to eat."

"Fine," she sighed, giving in to him yet again and hating herself for it. "But this doesn't mean anything."

A smile played on his lips. "Of course not." She didn't appreciate his sarcasm and glared at him as he picked up speed.

SYDNEY AND JEN were both waiting on the wide wraparound porch when they finally pulled up. His sister hurried down the steps and wrapped Chris in a bear hug as soon as he exited the truck. Her excitement was palpable but he didn't want to set Ali off any more than he'd already done. He needed to find a way to prove his innocence to her and quickly.

"Don't ask," he whispered quickly as he hugged her back.

"What? Oh," her voice dropped as Ali got out of the truck and immediately headed to the back of the trailer, not even looking their way. "What did you do?"

It annoyed him that she immediately blamed him but he couldn't deny fault. "Long story but I'll explain later," he promised.

Sydney glared at him and went to the back of the trailer as Ali backed both of her horses out and led them toward the corral. "Come on in the house, Ali. Jen and I were just about to have some lunch. Chris can finish out here." She cast him a warning look. "Won't you?"

"Yes, ma'am." He gave his sister a mock salute and sighed as he went after his animals.

"At least it's not me this time."

Chris looked up in time to see Derek, Scott's younger brother, coming out of the barn. He'd always felt an easy familiarity with the man. They were about the same age but he felt like Derek got him, and they had similar personalities. In Sydney's terms, neither one took life too seriously and it got them both into trouble.

Chris rolled his eyes. "You have no idea how much I wish it were you instead of me." Derek slapped him on the shoulder, knocking him forward in spite of his stature. "Damn, you been lifting those weights again because pretty soon you're going to outweigh those bulls out there," Chris teased.

"Physical therapy after the accident."

Chris sobered at the mention of the accident that nearly killed Derek when a bull charged his horse in the arena, pinning him against a gate and puncturing a lung. "How is everything?"

Derek shrugged it off. "I'm fine, finally back to work and going to be a father soon."

"Congratulations," Chris laughed at him. "I think I'm better off avoiding the water here. You guys must be putting something in it to get these women pregnant."

"According to your sister, that's not too far off for you." Derek cocked a brow at Chris.

Wonderful. His sister had been talking about him and Ali. He let the horses loose in the corral and tossed several flakes of alfalfa into the pen. "Not after this weekend."

Derek chuckled. "Did you apologize for whatever you did? That usually seems to get me out of trouble." Chris was grateful he didn't ask about the situation but nodded. "And she's still that mad. You must've screwed up big." He shrugged and patted Chris's shoulder again. "She'll get over it. They always do."

"The way I did?"

Both men spun to see Derek's wife Angela behind them, a sly grin curving her full lips, her red hair shimmering over her shoulders like fire.

"Yes," Derek teased as he walked to his wife's side, his hand gently covering the swell of her very pregnant belly. "You know I have you eating out of the palm of my hand." He pressed a kiss to her forehead.

"Sure you do." She rolled her eyes. "Your sister sent me out to let you know it was safe to come inside. Alicia is upstairs taking a shower." Her green eyes shimmered with amusement. "And if I were you, I'd do the opposite of whatever this guy has been suggesting."

"I got you, didn't I?"

"Tell her I'll be there in a second." Chris laughed at the pair as they headed for the house. He and Derek had a lot in common so why was he working so much harder than him or Scott to convince Ali to believe in him.

Because neither of them were players. Neither of them got caught in a mess like this one.

Well, Scott had but that was because of his manipulative ex-girlfriend, and it had taken a grand gesture on Scott's part to convince Sydney of his love afterward. Chris stared at the horses in the corral, suddenly realizing what he needed to do. He was going to give Ali proof she'd never forget.

Chapter Twenty-Four

"WHAT THE HELL, Chris?" Sydney screeched.

"Shh! If you don't stop squealing, she's going to hear you." He pulled his cell phone from his pocket and texted David. He needed him here for this, preferably with the proof to back up his claim of innocence.

"Derek's going to head into town with you?"

"No, I'm going alone, but I need you to arrange things here. Get her to talk to you because she's not talking to me right now. If this doesn't work . . ." Chris let his words fade. This had to work, it was his last hope. His next move was to give up.

His phone vibrated with a return message from David. "What the hell?" Sydney looked at him expectantly. "Ali told David she wants him to buy me out of the business." He threw his phone onto the kitchen table and pinched the bridge of his nose. "Am I making a mistake? Is it supposed to be this hard or is this just the universe telling me to let her go?"

Sydney laughed quietly. "No. She's scared and you haven't done anything to make her believe she doesn't need to be. Everything is going to work out. After tonight, none of these little details will matter."

Chris took a deep breath. "I sure hope you're right because if this doesn't work—"

"It will," she promised.

His phone vibrated on the table and he lifted it enough to glance at the screen. "At least he got the proof from Delilah. I'm not sure I even want to know how he managed that."

ALI SAT ON a chaise on the back patio watching the couples surrounding her. Derek and Angela were on one side of the fire pit in a loveseat with her head on his shoulder and his hand absently rubbing her belly. Scott sat on a chaise with Sydney between his thighs and his hands resting on her baby bump while Scott's sister Jen sat on the far side of the fire with her husband's hands resting on her shoulders as she held their son. She hated feeling like a seventh wheel and looked around the yard, wondering where Chris had gone after they arrived. Sydney said he was running some errands but she hadn't seen him all afternoon. She missed him.

She hated to admit it but she missed the teasing note of his voice, the companionable silence, and the heated looks he gave her when he thought she wasn't paying attention. She wanted to slip her hand into his and curl against his side by the fire. In spite of everything, regardless of the pain in her heart, she still loved him. She knew she always would.

The sounds of tires crunching over gravel turned several heads and Sydney rose awkwardly from the chair. "Sounds like Chris is back."

Alicia wasn't sure whether she should follow Sydney as Derek and Scott did or stay with the other two women. Every part of her body wanted to be near him, to touch him, but her mind warred with her physical need, reminding her of the painful ache of his betrayal. She should have just stayed away from him, never given in, but regrets and what-ifs would get her nowhere now. They were like wishes made on stars—worthless.

She barely listened as Angela and Jen talked over her. They both lived on the property, sharing daily events of their married lives and she was nothing more than an outsider, eavesdropping. It was the same thing she'd been through all her life—never fitting in, never being good enough, never measuring up. She turned as Sydney and Scott returned.

"Look who the cat dragged in!" Sydney announced.

Behind her, Alicia saw David. A broad smile curved her lips at the sight of his friendly face. A wave of relief washed over her, filling her eyes with tears, and she wondered why she was being so emotional. Maybe she just needed to get home and move to the ranch, get the new chapter of her life started. As long as David was able to convince Chris to sell.

"Hey, Ali." His voice was soft as he bent and gave her a warm hug. "I got here as soon as I could." His eyes were sympathetic when they met hers. "Do you need to go talk?"

He kept his voice low enough that she was the only one who heard him but she shook her head and patted the end of the chaise for him to take a seat.

He took the beer Scott held out to him and sat at the foot of the chair, laying his hand on her knee. Alicia latched onto his support and comfort, feeling his quiet strength pour into her. When they heard another vehicle driving up, Sydney rose again.

"Finally, I'm starving."

"Nothing new there," Scott teased his wife and was met with hoots from the other men.

"Feeling feisty with your boys around, huh?" Sydney pushed his shoulder playfully. "Why don't you go fire up the grill, O brave one?"

As the other men headed for the grill, David turned to Alicia. "Dad is off the property. I know escrow doesn't close for a little longer but if you want, you can start moving things in when we get back."

"Have you talked to Chris yet?"

His eyes clouded over. "He won't sell. I tried but he's refusing."

She knew it had been a long shot. He had no intent on selling to her at the end of the year and this proved it. He'd lied about so many things and she'd been too naive to see through any of it. Why would the ranch be any different?

"At least the two of you are speaking again." She gave him a sad smile.

She would just have to sell her share to David. It was the only solution she had. It would mean letting go of her dream and staying with her parents. She might as well give up any hope of barrel racing in the Finals because she'd be starting over from square one again—no ranch, no clients and, now, no hope for anything more than a position at the Diamond Bar because her father didn't want to leave. Her shoulders sagged in defeat.

"Ali," David broke into her thoughts. "I ran into Delilah before I left. She lied."

Alicia looked up at him through her lashes. "What else is new? She lies about everything, David."

"Chris didn't sleep with her."

Her heart stopped in her chest, lurching against her ribs, and she wondered if it had just burst. "What?" Her voice was barely a whisper of sound.

"I don't even want to talk about how I got her to confess but she did. It was all to hurt you, to shake your confidence and get you off your game. She wanted Chris to get you to quit and she wanted to punish him."

She wanted to believe David but a nagging doubt ate at the edges of her thoughts. He was Chris's best friend. Sure, they might argue but what if David was lying for Chris? But what could either of them hope to gain from lying to her? Chris already had everything she had to offer.

"David, don't do this." Tears burned her eyes, threatening to fall and shatter the wall of indifference she was trying to keep around her heart. "Please."

David pulled his phone out of his pocket. "Ali, you know I wouldn't hurt you." He punched a button and she heard Delilah's voice.

"I didn't sleep with him."

Followed by David's voice. *"Everyone knows you did, Delilah."*

"No, I didn't. I just let people think that to get back at him. He . . . passed out and snored all night. I didn't get any sleep at all. So what do you say?"

There was rustling in the background, like the phone was being moved or bumped.

"Not many women would lie and say they slept with a guy they didn't. And, I've never known Chris to just pass out, no matter how much he drinks." She heard David laugh quietly before Delilah's voice whined.

"I know you still trust Alicia but I can't stand her. And Chris has always been mean to me so I might have given him a little help. So I got even with both of them at once."

Her eyes shot up to meet David's. "Chris wasn't lying to you."

"Hey, Ali, you might want to come here." She looked at the group of men gathering at the gate where Sydney waited.

Alicia rose and hurried to her friend, fear spiraling down her spine. "Are you okay?"

"I'm fine."

She opened the gate as Alicia walked up to reveal Chris standing in the driveway looking incredibly sexy, wearing a tuxedo shirt and jacket, black hat, and boots, holding a lead rope attached to a gorgeous gray colt.

Around the animal's neck was a circle of pink carnations, Alicia's favorite flower. Sydney pushed her forward while the group of their friends crowded behind her.

Chris walked toward her as her trembling hand covered her mouth.

"Ali, please hear me out." He took her shaking hand and pulled her toward him. "I want you to know that I never lied to you but I *did* lie to myself. I convinced myself that I never wanted to be in love, that it was settling for half a life. But seeing you with anyone else is killing me. I want you, Ali."

She could only stare at him in dumbfounded shock. He was beyond magnificent; he was every woman's dream. The earnest appeal she saw in his eyes chipped at her resolve to keep her distance from him.

"Ali, I don't want you for a day, or a week, or a month. I want you forever. I told you I love you and I've never said those words to anyone else, ever. I don't deserve you. I'm irresponsible, brash, and unreliable."

"Don't forget self-indulgent," David called from behind her, laughing.

"And reckless," Derek joined in the ribbing.

Chris's eyes flicked toward the group at the fence. "Not helping." He looked back at Alicia, his eyes growing tender. "I want to prove to you that, for the first time in my life, I mean it when I say forever. This stud is one of Valentino's. He's going to be a great foundation for our plans for the ranch and the rodeo school. He's my commitment to you in our business partnership. And this," he reached into his pocket, "is my commitment to you."

Chris dropped to a knee as he opened the small box in his hand. "Marry me, Ali. I've spent far too long trying not to see what was in front of me all along. I need you, the way I need air."

She looked down at the diamond solitaire glinting against the velvet, the dying light of the sun reflecting from it but not nearly as brightly as the love she could see in Chris's eyes. She wanted to melt into the blue depths.

"Please, Ali," he whispered. "I know you deserve so much better than me. I've hurt you."

The agony she heard in his choked voice shot straight to her heart. She was nothing more than a poor kid whose father cleaned stalls for a living. He was a rancher's son, a rodeo celebrity. How could he think he wasn't enough for her?

A nervous grin touched the corners of his mouth. "Say something, Ali, because my knee is starting to get sore."

She looked back at the group crowded around the fence, waiting expectantly for her answer. She could read the excitement in their eyes and the pressure weighed on her shoulders. The young stallion pawed at the ground, as if he wanted to escape. She understood the feeling.

"I can't," she whispered, her heart breaking as his face fell in defeat. She closed her eyes to the pain she saw in his blue eyes, swiping at the tears that hung on her lashes.

Suddenly, his arm was around her waist, his mouth slanted over hers, drawing her yearning for him to the surface with a touch. She leaned into him, her body craving his. He drew back only until his lips feathered over hers.

"Why?"

Her brain couldn't function enough to think of a lie and the truth spilled out. "I'm not enough for you. You'll get bored and want someone new, someone who isn't a poor imitation. I can't piece my heart back together after that."

He smiled against her lips. "Oh, Ali. It's always been you. Every other woman has been me trying to find my way back to you. I once told you I could only be with a woman who could outride and out rope me. Honey, you're the only woman who's ever done that," he teased.

She shook her head, denying them both. The colt jerked his head up and down with impatience and Chris laughed. "See, he's even trying to tell you to say yes."

She couldn't help the laughter that tumbled past her lips and dropped her forehead against his shoulder. He put his finger under her chin and forced her to look into his eyes, to see every emotion there—need, desire, love, hope, and fear.

"I can't lose you, Ali. I want to marry you and start our family on our ranch. You are my forever. Marry me?"

"Are you sure this is what you want?"

He chuckled and quirked a brow. "Do I need to get a preacher out here right now to prove it?" The stallion nipped at his jacket sleeve and he tugged his arm away. "If you don't hurry up and say yes, this boy is going to climb into our laps."

"Yes," she whispered.

"Yes?"

She nodded, joy flooding her, making her feel like she'd just grown wings. "Yes," she repeated.

"She said 'Yes!'" He wrapped his arm around her waist and lifted her against him, causing the colt to jump backward.

"Finally," Derek teased, coming forward to take the colt back to the barn.

"Wait a second," Alicia said, taking the lead rope from his hands. "I want to check this boy out myself."

Derek shrugged and handed it over as Chris laughed. "That's my Ali. It's all about the horseflesh."

She ran a hand over the neck of the stallion, admiring his sleek lines and well-muscled frame. "I was hoping you might walk him back to the barn with me." She couldn't help but think of the times they'd been in other barns alone together. Warmth spread through her limbs, coiling in her core, waiting to be ignited by his touch.

Chris's eyes sparked with raw desire and she knew he'd caught her innuendo. "Don't bother waiting dinner on us," he warned Derek. "But first . . ." Chris pulled the ring out of the box and slipped it on her finger. "I want this official." He cupped his hand at the back of her neck and pulled her forward for a kiss when the colt nipped at him again. "Damn, horse!" he yelped, jumping backward.

"Don't listen to him," Alicia cooed at the massive beast. "He'll love you more when you've given him lots of babies that make him money." She started walking toward the barn as their friends headed back to the patio as if this was an everyday occurrence.

"Oh, Ali," Sydney called. "Welcome to the family."

Epilogue

ALI POURED THREE cups of coffee and waited on the porch for David and Chris to return from feeding the animals. The ranch was coming together nicely after the hard work they'd put in since January. In the distance, she could see the small cabins that would have the first inhabitants arriving later today. She glanced at the clouds in the sky and prayed that the rain would hold off for another week. It was their first camp and they were completely booked with several groups of team ropers wanting one-on-one lessons from NFR champion team ropers. She even had six upcoming barrel racers vying for her mentorship. She'd known winning the titles would help their business but she hadn't expected it to boom the way it had since December. It was a good thing David and Chris had insisted on putting in the covered arena, allowing them to give lessons year-round.

She saw the pair walking toward her from the barn, laughing as Chris slapped David on the shoulder. It was surprising how quickly they'd fallen back into an easy friendship, especially considering how David's father had practically disowned him for joining their partnership and refusing to allow him back onto the ranch. She could still see a loneliness in David's eyes and felt a twinge of guilt when he watched her and Chris together. She'd catch him at times but she knew it wasn't jealousy. There was something else in his eyes, something sad and troubled. She knew he didn't still carry a torch for her but she couldn't get him to open up about it.

Chris sauntered up the stairs and curled an arm around her waist, welcoming her with a kiss that practically melted the silver buckle at her waist. She couldn't help but cling to him, wishing they had time to head inside before their guests arrived. When he pulled away, Chris pressed his forehead against hers and sighed.

"I've missed you."

She laughed. "In the thirty minutes it took you to feed?"

"Trust me, all I hear is Ali this and Ali that. It's kinda sickening," David joked, taking the coffee from the railing and heading toward his house. "I'll be back in a bit. I want to shower before our first group gets here."

"Don't be too long," Ali called after him. "I'll make you both breakfast." He waved back, letting her know he'd heard.

Chris circled his arms around her waist and pulled her against him, nuzzling the hollow behind her ear, brushing her long sable hair back. "What if breakfast isn't what's on my mind? I'm hungry for something else."

Alicia slid her hands into the back pockets of his jeans. "I don't think we have time for that, cowboy."

"I need a shower, too." His eyes glittered with desire. "Don't you?"

She tried to hold back her grin. "Maybe." The sound of a truck coming up the driveway drew her attention. "Mom and Dad are here."

Chris growled at the interruption and slid his thumb over her breast, causing a shiver to break over her. "That was so you'll remember what you're missing while you're visiting," he teased, turning to greet her parents.

"Cristobel," her mother called, hurrying forward to give both of them a hug. "Baby." She turned to Ali. "We need to get these wedding invitations addressed today and mailed out or no one will be at the wedding next month. I still think you're rushing things."

"Mom, rodeo season is starting. If we wait any longer, no one will be here but us," she reminded her.

"And you still want to do it here?"

Alicia smiled at her mother. "This is our home. It's the perfect place."

"Ali'i," her father stepped forward and gave her a hug. "Thank you."

"For what, Daddy?"

"For making me realize this really is my dream. I was afraid to take the first step but between you and this guy," he reached out and squeezed Chris's shoulder. "You made me see it was more important to go after what I wanted."

She saw his eyes well up. "I'd better get some horses saddled before your guests arrive." He hurried toward the barn as her mother headed into the house.

Chris moved behind her, circling his arms around her waist, leaning his chin on the top of her head. She felt herself relax against him. Nothing made her happier than the day Chris had asked her father to be their head trainer and convinced him to build a house on the property. A proper, wood frame house built to her mother's specifications. It allowed her father to head up their training and breeding program and freed them up for clinics and lessons. She leaned her head back against his shoulder, watching her father head toward the barn.

"He's pretty happy, isn't he?"

"Yes," she agreed, looking up at his jaw. "Thank you."

"For what?"

"Everything. Being there when I needed a friend, helping me get this place." She laughed quietly. "Refusing to let me buy you out."

Chris laughed. "I still can't believe you thought I'd take your NFR winnings."

"I didn't think you would." She gave him a saucy grin. "It was a test, cowboy."

"Good thing I passed." He brushed his lips against her temple and desire curled around her heart, swirling ribbons of need through her veins. "I'd hate to think you might have left me."

"Never," she whispered, turning in his arms. She cupped his jaw, noticing he needed a shave before everyone arrived, even though she preferred him a little scruffy. "Thank you for helping Dad to see what he really wanted. That he could do so much more than he thought he could."

"Now I see where you got it from." He smiled down at her.

"What's that?"

"You're so much more than you give yourself credit for. Ali, you're such an amazing woman, so much more than I deserve. Do you have any idea how much I love you, how lucky I am that you picked me?"

Tears welled in her eyes. "I love you." She knew there was so much more she wanted to tell him but as her heart swelled, emotion choked out any other words. She pressed her lips against his knowing she would count herself blessed each day that this was the cowboy she kissed goodnight, the man whose blue eyes stared into hers each morning, and the roper who'd lassoed her stubborn heart and tied it to his forever.

Acknowledgments

To MY GIRL, Kassidy, without your eyes on this book first, I don't know what would happen and how much more work I'd be in for. You always push me to reach new limits, even if you drive me nuts at times.

To Tessa, my editor extraordinaire, for being the first to give me a chance and the one who never lets me be lazy. Because of you I have reached new heights I never thought possible (and can't wait to see how far we go!).

To my writer besties and mentors: Leanne, Codi, Candis, and Cynthia. You have gotten me through the messes I make for myself and celebrated with me every step of the way. You are my go-to girls and I love you for the laughter, the advice, and even the necessary kicks in the rear when I need them.

To my husband, Bryun. I know this roller coaster ride isn't the one we signed up for but I have loved every moment of the last seventeen years and I'm looking forward to the rest of our lifetime.

Want more rodeo?
Check out T. J. Kline's first book in the rodeo series,

RODEO QUEEN,

to see Sydney and Scott fall in love.

An Excerpt from

RODEO QUEEN

THE DRAWLING VOICE of the rodeo announcer boomed over the loudspeakers. "Ladies and gentleman, we'd like to welcome you to the Fifty-first Annual West Hills Roundup Rodeo! But first, let's have one last look at the ladies vying for the title of your rodeo queen!"

The array of glitter, sequins, and beads was dazzling in the April sunlight, nearly blinding her. She patted her dapple gray stallion to calm him as he shifted eagerly at the end of the line, kicking up dust in the newly tilled rodeo arena. Sydney looked down the line of young women on horseback, spotted her friend Alicia first in line, and gave her a reassuring smile.

"First, let's welcome Alicia Kanani!" Sydney watched as her best friend coaxed her gelding from the line, taking off into a slow lope along the fence. Alicia cocked a two-fingered salute to the crowd, her black tuxedo shirt glittering with silver and gold sequins, before filing back into the line of contestants. The next seven contestants duplicated Alicia's queen run. "And, last but not least, Sydney Thomas!"

Pressing her heels into Valentino's sides, Sydney made a kissing sound to the stallion as he took off from the line like a bullet from a gun. Leaning over his neck, Sydney snapped a sharp military salute while facing the audience. The sequins of her vest were a blinding flash of red light as Valentino stretched his body into a full run, his ears pinned against his head. Sydney reveled in the moment of flight as she and the horse became one, his hooves seeming to float over the tilled earth. As they rounded the last corner, Valentino slowed to a lope and Sydney sat up in the saddle. Reaching the end of the line, Sydney sat deep into her saddle, cueing the horse to bury his hocks in the soft dirt and slide to a dramatic stop. As the blood pounding in her ears subsided to a mild roar, she could still hear the audience cheering.

"There you have it, ladies and gentlemen, your contestants for West Hills Roundup Queen," the announcer repeated. "May I have the envelope, please?"

Glancing at the fence line, Sydney caught her brother's gaze as he winked and gave her a thumbs-up. She smiled, appreciating that he had come to cheer her on when he had his own event to prepare for. The "crowd" was sparse in the morning hours before the rodeo actually began. It was mostly family and friends of the queen contestants and a few rodeo competitors who performed before the rodeo due to too many entrants in their events.

"Without any further fanfare," the announcer paused

for effect as the meager crowd immediately quieted to a hush. "Your princess this year is . . . Alicia Kanani!" Cheers erupted from the grassy hillside where Alicia's family was seated with Sydney's. She cheered from the line, excited for her friend. "And now, the moment we've all been waiting for . . ."

Sydney's heart raced. She felt it in her throat and in her toes at the same time as she waited for the name of the new queen to be called. Only her brother, Chris, knew how many hours of training and preparation had gone into this competition, all in hopes of having her name come to be associated with the best horse trainers in rodeo. As queen, she would be attending rodeos all over California, meeting and networking with stock contractors and other rodeo participants. She hoped that it would all lead to more exposure for her mounts, which meant more horses to train.

"The new West Hills Roundup Queen is . . . drum roll please . . . Sydney Thomas!" The applause rose to a roar on the hillside again as Sydney's family rose, laughing, cheering, and hugging one another. Sydney edged Valentino forward as the previous year's rodeo queen placed the silver-and-rhinestone crown on her red cowboy hat. She was soon encircled by the other contestants, who offered congratulations as they exited the arena and headed for the horse trailers.

They'd barely dismounted at Sydney's trailer when Alicia tackled her with an enthusiastic hug. "I can't believe we did it! You won!"

Sydney opened her mouth to respond but was cut off

by the massive arms that lifted her from behind and spun her around. "Congratulations, Queenie."

"Chris, put me down," she squealed. As her boots touched the ground she slapped him on the shoulder. Her brother might be a year younger than she was, but he'd inherited their father's tall, lanky frame.

"Ow!" He rubbed his arm. "You'll never find a king acting like that," he teased.

"Please. That is the last thing I'm looking for." Sydney rolled her eyes and turned to tie Valentino to the trailer.

"What about you, Alicia? Want to be my princess?" Chris asked as he snuck his arm around her shoulders.

Chris was a hopeless flirt. At nineteen, he was striking with his jet-black hair, aqua eyes, and broad shoulders—everything a girl would imagine from a cowboy, including the drawling charm. The fact that he and his roping partner were consistently ranked in the top of the national standings for team roping made him a pretty hot ticket around the rodeo circuit. But he'd never shown any indication that he would ever settle down with one girl.

"Why don't you go find yourself one of those 'buckle bunnies' that hangs out behind the chutes?" Alicia asked, shaking his arm off.

One of the drawbacks of rodeo were the women fans, young and old alike, who wanted to snag a cowboy. Too often Sydney found the cowboys around the circuit expected all of the other women to do the same.

"No thanks." Chris laughed. "When I find the right girl, she's going to outride and out-rope me."

"Good luck with that." Sydney laughed.

Alicia pulled her cowboy hat off, exposing her long dark hair, and set the hat on the back of the truck. Sydney didn't miss the look of appreciation Chris shot her best friend. "You never can tell, sis." He tapped the red line her hat had left on her forehead before stepping back. "I'll never understand why you girls wear hats that tight."

Sydney slipped her sequined vest over her arms and unbuttoned the tuxedo shirt, grateful for the tank-top underneath, and hung her shirt in the tack compartment of her horse trailer so she could wear it again once the pre-rodeo events finished. "You guys should try doing a queen run sometime. If that hat hits the ground with a crown on it, my head better be in it. Rule number one."

She flipped the front of her brother's cowboy hat, knocking it to the ground. "Unlike you ropers, no one picks up our hats when they come off in the arena," she teased as she pulled a light cotton Western shirt from the trailer, wishing again that short sleeves were allowed. "Okay, I'm going to head back to find the stock contractor and see what they'll allow us to do during the rodeo."

It was typical for the stock contractor to allow the rodeo queen and her court to carry the sponsor flags for the events, but Sydney was hoping to network a bit and charm her way into being allowed to clear the cattle from the arena in the roping events. It was good exposure to show off Valentino and her accomplishments as a trainer. She exchanged her red cowboy hat for a baseball cap, pulling her russet curls through the opening in the back.

"Can you keep an eye on Valentino for me?" Sydney spotted their families heading toward the trailer. "Here comes the crew," she said, jerking her chin in their direction. "Let them know I'll be right back."

"Talk with Mike Findley," Chris instructed. "He's in charge. He should be pretty receptive to you."

"Thanks. I'll be right back."

Chris glanced toward Alicia, who was being hugged by both of her parents. "No hurry." Sydney smiled, wondering if the dance tonight wouldn't be the perfect opportunity to give Chris and Alicia a little nudge to take their friendship to the next level.

Sydney rolled up the sleeves of her shirt to her elbows and pulled the shirt from her chest in an attempt to cool herself. It was only April, but her shirt was already sticking to her skin at nine in the morning. She couldn't help but smile and take in the smell of alfalfa, dust, and leather as she made her way through the jumbled maze of trucks and trailers, most with horses tied in the shade, dozing before their events. She knew how lucky she was; most people couldn't honestly say that they loved their life, but she loved every minute she'd spent growing up in rodeo.

Sydney heard the unmistakable pounding of horse hooves on the packed ground behind her and moved closer to the vehicle on her right. Usually there was more than enough room for riders and their rigs in the walkway, but with the unexpected turnout at the rodeo today, there was barely room to maneuver. The horse was jogging pretty quickly and she didn't have anywhere else to go, especially since another truck and trailer had chosen that moment to pull out of the gate ahead of her. The driver of the truck spotted her and waved her on. She tried to hurry through the opening he'd left her at the gate, but the rider behind her chose to slip between them, his mount's shoulder knocking her into the gatepost on her right.

Sydney reached up to massage her shoulder before registering the surprise on the face of the driver of the truck.

"Are you okay, Sydney?" It was Bobby Blake, a friend of her father's who must have been delivering some panels in the back of the arena.

"Yeah, I'm fine," she assured him before raising her voice. "I guess chivalry really is dead," she yelled at the cowboy's back.

She saw him jerk his mount to a stop before glancing back over his shoulder at her. "Look, honey, I don't have time for you girls who don't belong back here. This area is for contestants, not their groupies."

"Want me to set him straight?" Bobby asked.

Sydney smiled her appreciation. "No, but thanks Bobby. I've got this."

"Go get him, honey," he teased. "He doesn't know who he's dealing with. By the way, congratulations."

"Thanks, Bobby." Sydney made her way toward the obnoxious cowboy seated on the sorrel. "Look, I don't know who you think you are, but around here we tend to have a sort of unspoken code. When that walkway is packed with cars and horses like that, you slow down and you certainly do not push your way between a truck and someone walking. I don't really appreciate hoofmarks across my back."

She looked up at him as she came closer, refusing to let him intimidate her from his seat on the horse. "And as for being a groupie, I could probably outride you any day of the week," she challenged.

The cowboy arched his right brow and a slow smile spread across his face. "Maybe we'll have to see about that later." With a tap of his heels, the horse jogged forward a few steps toward one of the stock pens.

Sydney narrowed her eyes as he left. What a jerk, she thought. Shaking her head, she rubbed her shoulder again and searched the back of the arena for the stock contractor's trailers, noticing a lanky cowboy setting up folding chairs beside a Findley Brothers stock trailer.

"Excuse me," Sydney began, making her way across the short grass. "Can you tell me where I might find Mike Findley?"

A weathered face returned her smile and Sydney realized he was much older than she had first assumed. "What's that?"

Sydney realized that he probably couldn't hear her over the clattering of stock panels as the cattle moved into the pens. "Mike Findley? Do you know where I can find him?"

"Oh, no, I'm not Mike. I'm Jake," the man hollered.

"Hi Jake, I'm Sydney Thomas." She raised her voice as well. "I was just crowned rodeo queen and I'm looking for Mike to see if we might carry the sponsor flags or run cattle for him today."

Jake turned and faced her, crossing his arms. The cattle had quieted so he toned down his voice as well.

"Well, Mike's up with the announcer right now working out of a few details. But he's not who you'd want to talk to about that." He leaned back against the trailer, crossing his ankles as if getting relaxed for a long conversation.

Sydney raised her brows in expectation. When Jake didn't say anything, she pressed. "So, who should I talk to instead?"

"That'd be Scott Chandler."

Sydney sighed, finding it difficult to restrain herself from punching something. First she'd been shoved into a fence post and now a cryptic cowboy was obviously enjoying a joke at her expense.

"And where would I find Mr. Chandler?"

The Cheshire-cat grin on Jake's face made her heart sink. No, life couldn't possibly be that cruel. Her gaze followed the direction of his finger as he pointed to the cowboy atop the sorrel at the stock pen, obviously eavesdropping on their conversation. Swallowing the dry lump that had suddenly materialized in her throat, Sydney squared her shoulders and raised her golden eyes to meet the black eyes of her foe.

"Well, I think you just finished telling him off." Jake grinned, anticipating the showdown to come.

Sydney had a few choice words that might have suited this moment if her mother hadn't ingrained in her how unladylike it was to curse. A blush crept up her cheeks as Scott Chandler dismounted his horse and bowed deeply before her.

"Your Majesty," he mocked. "I am at your disposal."

She realized that the noise from the stock pen hadn't

kept him from overhearing her conversation with Jake. "I'm sorry. I didn't know who you were."

Sarcasm colored his chuckle. "Somehow I don't think it would have mattered if you had. Now, I am busy, so what did you need, Miss Thomas?"

Sydney took a deep breath and ignored the warmth flooding her cheeks. "I came to see about carrying the sponsor flags and returning the cattle during the rodeo."

"Experience?"

"Well, I've worked for Marks' Rodeo Company for the last four years doing both, as well as training for the last eight years, five of those professionally." Sydney's chin rose indignantly as she felt his gaze weighing heavily on her. She felt suddenly self-conscious in her red jeans and red-and-white plaid Western shirt. Did she look like an immature girl?

Scott gave her a rakish, lopsided grin. "Oh, that's right. You can outride me." His brow arched as he articulated her words back to her. "Any day of the week."

It took everything in her to try to ignore how good-looking this infuriating man was. He towered over her, well over six feet tall, and the black cowboy hat that topped a mop of dark brown hair, barely curling at his collar, gave him a devilish appearance. With sensuous lips and a square jaw, his deeply tanned skin reflected raw male sexuality. She wasn't sure if he was actually as muscular as his broad shoulders seemed to indicate due to his unruly Western shirt, but his jeans left no imagining necessary to notice the muscular thighs. However, his jet-black eyes almost unnerved her. Those eyes were so dark that Sydney felt she would drown if she continued to meet his gaze.

So much for ignoring his good looks, she chided herself. "Give me a chance out there today to prove it."

"I don't see why she can't run them, Scott." Jake must have decided that it was time to break up the showdown with his two cents. "She is certainly experienced enough, more than most of the girls you let run flags."

Scott glared at Jake before turning back to Sydney. She caught Jake's conspiratorial wink and decided that she liked this old cowboy. Scott would be hard-pressed to find a reason to deny her request now that Jake had sold him out.

"Fine, you can do both. But if anything goes wrong, if a steer so much as takes too long in the arena, you're finished. Got it, Miss Thomas?" The warning note in his voice was unmistakable.

Sydney flashed a dazzling smile. "Call me Sydney, and it's no problem." She clutched her shoulder. "Unless I'm unable to hold the flags since someone ran me into the fence post."

His look told her he didn't appreciate her sense of humor. "I mean it. Rodeo starts at ten sharp. Be down here at nine thirty, ready to go."

As the sassy cowgirl walked away, Scott shook his head. "What in the world possessed you to open your mouth, Jake?"

"Aw, Scott, she'll do fine. Besides, you did run her down with Wiley at the gate. You kinda owed her one."

Scott watched Sydney head for the gate, taking in her

small waist and the spread of her hips in her red pants and down her lean, denim-encased legs. That woman was all curves, moving with the grace of a jungle cat. With her full, pouting lips and those golden eyes, it certainly wouldn't be painful to look at her all day. "I guess."

Scott mounted Wiley and headed to change into his clean shirt and show chaps, but he couldn't seem to shake the image of Sydney Thomas from his mind. He knew that she'd been attracted to him—he'd seen it in her blush—but he'd had enough run-ins with ostentatious rodeo queens over the years, including his ex-fiancée, to know that they simply wanted to tame a cowboy. It was doubtful that this one was any different, although she did have a much shorter temper. He chuckled as he recalled how the gold in her eyes seemed to flame when she was irritated. He wondered if her eyes flamed up whenever she was passionate. Scott shook his head to clear it of visions of the sexy spitfire. No time for that, he had a rodeo to get started.

About the Author

T. J. Kline was raised competing in rodeos and rodeo queen competitions from the age of fourteen and has thorough knowledge of the sport as well as the culture involved. She has written several articles about rodeo for small periodicals, as well as a more recent how-to article for *RevWriter*, and has written a nonfiction health book and two inspirational fiction titles under the name Tina Klinesmith. She is also an avid reader and book reviewer for both Tyndale and Multnomah. In her spare time, she can be found laughing hysterically with her husband, children, and their menagerie of pets in Northern California.

Discover great authors, exclusive offers, and more at hc.com.

Give in to your impulses . . .
Read on for a sneak peek at eight brand-new
e-book original tales of romance
from Avon Books.
Available now wherever e-books are sold.

THE COWBOY AND THE ANGEL
By T. J. Kline

FINDING MISS McFARLAND
THE WALLFLOWER WEDDING SERIES
By Vivienne Lorret

TAKE THE KEY AND LOCK HER UP
By Lena Diaz

DYLAN'S REDEMPTION
BOOK THREE: THE McBRIDES
By Jennifer Ryan

SINFUL REWARDS 1
A BILLIONAIRES AND BIKERS NOVELLA
By Cynthia Sax

WHATEVER IT TAKES
A TRUST NO ONE NOVEL
By Dixie Lee Brown

HARD TO HOLD ON TO
A HARD INK NOVELLA
By Laura Kaye

KISS ME, CAPTAIN
A FRENCH KISS NOVEL
By Gwen Jones

An Excerpt from

THE COWBOY AND THE ANGEL

By T. J. Kline

From author T. J. Kline comes the stunning
follow-up to *Rodeo Queen*. Reporter
Angela McCallister needs the scoop of her career
in order to save her father from the bad decisions
that have depleted their savings. When the
opportunity to spend a week at the
Findley Brothers ranch arises, she sees a chance
to get a behind-the-scenes scoop on rodeo. That
certainly doesn't include kissing the devastatingly
handsome and charming cowboy Derek Chandler,
who insists on calling her "Angel."

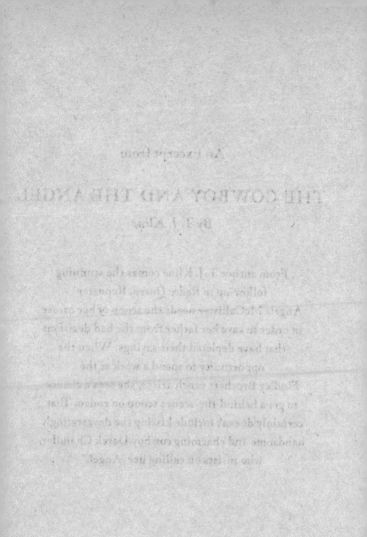

An Excerpt from

THE COWBOY AND THE ANGEL

by J. J. Kline

From author J. J. Kline comes the stunning
follow-up to *Right Guess, Reporter*.

Angeli McCallister needs the money or her career
in order to save her father from the bad decisions
that have depleted their savings. When the
opportunity to spend a week at the
Bradley Brothers ranch arises, she sees a chance
to get a behind-the-scenes scoop on rodeo. That
certainly doesn't include kissing the devastatingly
handsome—and charming cowboy Derek Chandler
who insists on calling her Angel.

"Angela, call on line three."

"Can't you just handle it, Joe? I don't have time for this B.S." It was probably just another stupid mom calling, hoping Angela would feature her daughter's viral video in some feel-good news story. When was she ever going to get her break and find some hard-hitting news?

"They asked for you."

Angela sighed. Maybe if she left them listening to that horrible elevator music long enough, they'd hang up. Joe edged closer to her desk.

"Just pick up the damn phone and see what they want."

"Fine." She glared at him as she punched the button. The look she gave him belied the sweet tone of her voice. "Angela McCallister, how can I help you?"

Joe leaned against her cubical wall, listening to her part of the conversation. She waved at him irritably. It wasn't always easy when your boss was your oldest friend, and ex-boyfriend. He quirked a brow at her.

Go away, she mouthed.

"Are you really looking for new stories?"

She assumed the male voice on the line was talking about the calls the station ran at the ends of several news programs asking for stories of interest. Most of them wound up in her mental "ignore" file, but once in a while she'd found one worth pursuing.

"We're always looking for events and stories of interest to our local viewers." She rolled her eyes, reciting the words Joe had taught her early on in her career as a reporter. She was tired of pretending any of this sucking up was getting her anywhere. Viewers only saw her as a pretty face.

"I have a lead that might interest you." She didn't answer, waiting for the caller to elaborate. "There's a rodeo coming to town, and they are full of animal cruelty and abuse."

This didn't sound like a feel-good piece. The caller had her attention now. "Do you have proof?"

The voice gave a bitter laugh, sounding vaguely familiar. "Have you ever seen a rodeo? Electric prods, cinches wrapped around genitals, sharp objects placed under saddles to get horses to buck . . . it's all there."

She listened as the caller detailed several incidents at nearby rodeos where animals had to be euthanized due to injuries. Angela arched a brow, taking notes as the man gave her several websites she could research that backed the accusations.

"Can I contact you for more information?" She heard him hemming. "You don't have to give me your name. Maybe just a phone number or an email address where I can reach you?" The caller gave her both. "Do you mind if I ask one more question—why me?"

"Because you seem like you care about animal rights. That story you did about the stray kittens and the way you found them a home, it really showed who you were inside."

Angela barely remembered the story other than that Joe had forced it on her when she'd asked for one about a local politician sleeping with his secretary, reminding her that viewers saw her as their small-town sweetheart. She'd found herself reporting about a litter of stray kittens, smiling at the animal shelter as families adopted their favorites, and Jennifer Michaels had broken the infidelity story and was now anchoring at a station in Los Angeles. She was tired of this innocent, girl-next-door act.

"I'll see what I can do," she promised, deciding how to best pitch this story to Joe and whether it would be worth it at all.

An Excerpt from

FINDING MISS McFARLAND
The Wallflower Wedding Series

by Vivienne Lorret

Delany McFarland is on the hunt for a husband—
preferably one who needs her embarrassingly large
dowry more than a dutiful wife. Griffin Croft
hasn't been able to get Miss McFarland out of his
mind, but now that she's determined to hand over
her fortune to a rake, Griffin knows he must step
in. Yet when his noble intentions flee in a moment
of unexpected passion, his true course becomes
clear: tame Delaney's wild heart and save her from
a fate worse than death . . . a life without love.

She *had* been purposely avoiding him.

Griffin clasped his hands behind his back and began to pace around her in a circle. "Do you have spies informing you on my whereabouts at all times, or only for social gatherings?"

Miss McFarland watched his movements for a moment, but then she pursed those pink lips and smoothed the front of her cream gown. "I do what I must to avoid being seen at the same function with you. Until recently, I imagined we shared this unspoken agreement."

"Rumormongers rarely remember innocent bystanders."

She scoffed. "How nice for you."

"Yes, and until recently, I was under the impression that I came and went of my own accord. That my decisions were mine alone. Instead, I learn that every choice I make falls under your scrutiny." He was more agitated than angered. Not to mention intrigued and unaccountably aroused by her admission. During a season packed full of social engagements, she must require daily reports of his activities. Which begged the question, how often did she think of him? "Shall I quiz you on how I take my tea? Or if my valet prefers to tie my cravat into a barrel knot or horse collar?"

"I do not know, nor do I care, how you take your tea, Mr.

Croft," she said, and he clenched his teeth to keep from asking her to say it once more. "However, since I am something of an expert on fashion, I'd say that the elegant fall of the mail coach knot you're wearing this evening suits the structure of your face. The sapphire pin could make one imagine that your eyes are blue—"

"But you know differently."

Her cheeks went pink before she drew in a breath and settled her hand over her middle. Before he could stop the thought, he wondered whether she was experiencing the *fluttering* his sister had mentioned.

"You are determined to be disagreeable. I have made my attempts at civility, but now I am quite through with you. If you'll excuse me . . ." She started forward to leave.

He blocked her path, unable to forget what he'd heard when he first arrived. "I cannot let you go without a dire warning for your own benefit."

"If this is in regard to what you overheard—when you were eavesdropping on a *private matter*—I won't hear it."

He doubted she would listen to him if he meant to warn her about a great hole in the earth directly in her path either, but his conscience demanded he speak the words nonetheless. "Montwood is a desperate man, and you have put yourself in his power."

Her eyes flashed. "*That* is where you are wrong. I am the one with the fortune, ergo the one with the power."

How little she knew of men. "And what of your reputation?"

Her laugh did nothing to amuse him. "What I have left of my reputation will remain unscathed. He is not interested in my person. He only needs my fortune. In addition, as a second son, he does not require an heir; therefore, our living apart should not cause a problem with his family. And should he need *companionship*, he is free to find it elsewhere, so long as he's discreet."

"You sell yourself so easily, believing your worth is nothing more than your father's account ledger," he growled, his temper getting the better of him. He'd never lost control of it before, but for some reason this tested his limits. If *he* could see she was more than a sum of wealth, then *she* should damn well put a higher value on herself. "If you were my sister, I'd lock you in a convent for the rest of your days."

Miss McFarland stepped forward and pressed the tip of her manicured finger in between the buttons of his waistcoat. "I am *not* your sister, Mr. Croft. And thank the heavens for that gift, too. I can barely stand to be in the same room with you. You make it impossible to breathe, let alone think. Neither my lungs nor my stomach recalls how to function. Not only that, but you cause this terrible crackling sensation beneath my skin, and it feels like I'm about to catch fire." Her lips parted, and her small bosom rose and fell with each breath. "I do believe I loathe you to the very core of your being, Mr. Croft."

Somewhere between the first *Mis-ter-Croft* and the last, he'd lost all sense.

Because in the very next moment, he gripped her shoulders, hauled her against him, and crushed his mouth to hers.

An Excerpt from

TAKE THE KEY AND LOCK HER UP

by Lena Diaz

As a trained assassin for EXIT Inc—a top-secret mercenary group—Devlin "Devil" Buchanan isn't afraid to take justice into his own hands. But with EXIT Inc closing in and several women's lives on the line, Detective Emily O'Malley and Devlin must work together to find the missing women and clear both their names before time runs out . . . and their key to freedom is thrown away.

"I want to talk to you about what you do at EXIT."

"No."

She blinked. "No?" Her cell phone beeped. She grabbed it impatiently and took the call. A few seconds later she shoved the phone back in her pocket. "Tuck's outside. The SWAT team is set up and ready to cover us in case those two yokels decide to start shooting again. The area is secure. Let's go." She headed toward the door.

"Wait."

She turned, her brows raised in question.

He braced his legs in a wide stance and crossed his arms. "If I'm not under arrest, there's no reason for me to go to the police station."

Her mouth firmed into a tight line. "You're not under arrest only if you agree to the deal I offered. The man who killed Shannon Garrett and the unidentified victims in that basement is holding at least two other women right now, doing God only knows what to them. All I'm asking is that you answer some questions to help me find them, so I can save their lives. Doesn't that mean anything to you?"

Of course it did. But he also knew Kelly Parker, and anyone with her, couldn't be saved by Emily and her fellow cops. It was becoming increasingly clear that Kelly was the bait in a trap to catch *him*. The killer would keep her alive, maybe even provide proof of life at some point, to lure Devlin to wherever she was being held. Did he care about her suffering? Absolutely. Which meant he had to come up with a plan to save her without charging full steam ahead and getting himself killed. Because once the killer eliminated his main prey—Devlin—he'd have no reason to keep either of the women alive.

He braced himself for his next lie. If Emily thought he was bad to supposedly get a woman pregnant and abandon her, she was going to despise him after this next one.

"Finding and saving those women is your job," he said. "I have other things to do that are a lot more fun than sitting in an interrogation room."

The shocked, disgusted look that crossed her face was no worse than the way he felt inside. Like a jerk, and a damn coward. But if sacrificing his pride kept her safe, so be it. He had to get outside and offer himself as bait to lead his enemies away from the diner before she went out the front. He strode past her to the bathroom door.

"Stop, Devlin, or I'll shoot."

He slowly turned around. Seeing his sexy little detective pointing a gun at him again seemed every kind of wrong, especially when his blood was still raging from the hot kiss they'd just shared.

"Seriously?" he said, faking shock. "You're drawing on an unarmed man? *Again?* What will Drier say about that? Or Alex? I smell a lawsuit."

She stomped her foot in frustration.

The urge to laugh at her childish action had him clenching his teeth. She was the perfect blend of innocence, naiveté, and just plain stubbornness. Before he did something they'd both regret—like kissing her again—he slipped out of the bathroom.

A quick side trip through the kitchen too quickly for anyone to even question his presence, and he was down the back hallway, standing at the rear exit. Now all he had to do was make it to some kind of cover—without getting shot—and lead Cougar and his handler away from Emily, all without a weapon of his own to return fire.

Simple. No problem. He shook his head and cursed his decision to go to the police station this morning. Then again, if he hadn't, he wouldn't have gotten to kiss Emily. If he were killed in the next few minutes, at least he'd die with that intoxicating memory still lingering on his lips.

He cracked the door open and scanned the nearby buildings. Then he flung the door wide and took off running.

An Excerpt from

DYLAN'S REDEMPTION
Book Three: The McBrides
by Jennifer Ryan

From *New York Times* bestselling author Jennifer
Ryan, the McBrides of Fallbrook return with
Dylan McBride, the new sheriff. Jessie Thompson
had one hell of a week. Dylan McBride, the boy
she loved, skipped town without a word. Then her
drunk of a father tried to kill her, and she fled
Fallbrook, vowing never to return. Eight years
later, her father is dead, and Jessie reluctantly
goes home—only to come face-to-face with
the man who shattered her heart. A man who,
for nearly a decade, believed she was dead.

Standing over her sleeping brother, she held the pitcher in one hand and the cup of coffee in the other. She poured the cold water over her brother's face and chest. He sat bolt upright and yelled, "What the hell!"

Brian held a hand to his dripping head and one to his stomach. He probably had a splitting headache to go with his rotten gut. As far as Jessie was concerned, he deserved both.

"Good morning, brother. Nice of you to rise and shine."

Brian wiped a hand over his wet face and turned to sit on the sodden couch. His blurry eyes found Jessie standing over him. His mouth dropped open, and his eyes went round before he gained his voice.

"You're dead. I've hit that bottom people talk about. I'm dreaming, hallucinating after a night of drinking. It can't be you. You're gone and it's all my fault." He covered his face with his hands. Tears filled his voice, his pain and sorrow sharp and piercing. She refused to let it get to her, despite her guilt for making him believe she'd died. Brian needed a good ass-kicking, not a sympathetic ear.

"You're going to wish I died when I get through with you, you miserable drunk. What the hell happened to you?" She handed over the mug of coffee and shoved it up to his mouth to make him take a sip. Reality setting in, he needed the coffee and a shower before he'd concentrate and focus on her and what she had in store for him.

"Don't yell, my head is killing me." He pressed the heel of his hand to his eye, probably hoping his brain wouldn't explode.

Jessie sat on the coffee table in front of her brother, between his knees, and leaned forward with her elbows braced on her thighs.

"Listen to me, brother dear. It's past time you cleaned up your act. Starting today, you are going to quit drinking yourself into a stupor. You're going to take care of your wife and child. You're going to show up for work on Monday morning clear eyed and ready to earn an honest day's pay."

"Work? I don't have any job lined up for Monday."

"Yes, you do. I gave Marilee the information. You report to James on Monday at the new housing development going up on the outskirts of town. You'll earn a decent paycheck and have medical benefits for your family.

"The old man left you the house. I'll go over tomorrow after the funeral to see what needs to be done to make it livable for you and Marilee. I, big brother, am going to make you be the man you used to be, because I can't stand to see you turn into the next Buddy Thompson. You got that?" She'd yelled it at him to get his attention and to reinforce the fact that he'd created his condition. His eyes rolled back in his head, and he groaned in pain, all the reward she needed.

"If you don't show up for work on Monday, I'm coming after you. And I'll keep coming until you get it through that thick head of yours: you are not him. You're better than that. So get your ass up, take a shower, mow the lawn, kiss your wife, tell her you love her and you aren't going to be this ass-hole you've turned into anymore. You hear me?"

"Your voice is ringing in my head." He stared into his coffee cup, but glanced up to say, "You look good. Life's apparently turned out all right for you."

Jessie shrugged that off, focused more on the lost look in Brian's round, sad eyes.

"I thought you died that night. I left and he killed you. Where have you been?"

"Around. Mostly Solomon. I have a house about twenty miles outside of Fallbrook."

"You do?" The surprise lit his face.

"I started my life over. It's time you did the same."

An Excerpt from

SINFUL REWARDS 1
A Billionaires and Bikers Novella
by Cynthia Sax

Belinda "Bee" Carter is a good girl; at least, that's
what she tells herself. And a good girl deserves
a nice guy—just like the gorgeous and moody
billionaire Nicolas Rainer. Or so she thinks,
until she takes a look through her telescope
and sees a naked, tattooed man on the balcony
across the courtyard. He has been watching
her, and that makes him all the more enticing.
But when a mysterious and anonymous text
message dares her to do something bad, she
must decide if she is really the good girl she has
always claimed to be, or if she's willing to risk
everything for her secret fantasy of being watched.

An Avon Red Novella

I'd told Cyndi I'd never use it, that it was an instrument purchased by perverts to spy on their neighbors. She'd laughed and called me a prude, not knowing that I was one of those perverts, that I secretly yearned to watch and be watched, to care and be cared for.

If I'm cautious, and I'm always cautious, she'll never realize I used her telescope this morning. I swing the tube toward the bench and adjust the knob, bringing the mysterious object into focus.

It's a phone. Nicolas's phone. I bounce on the balls of my feet. This is a sign, another declaration from fate that we belong together. I'll return Nicolas's much-needed device to him. As a thank you, he'll invite me to dinner. We'll talk. He'll realize how perfect I am for him, fall in love with me, marry me.

Cyndi will find a fiancé also—everyone loves her—and we'll have a double wedding, as sisters of the heart often do. It'll be the first wedding my family has had in generations.

Everyone will watch us as we walk down the aisle. I'll wear a strapless white Vera Wang mermaid gown with organza and lace details, crystal and pearl embroidery accents, the bodice fitted, and the skirt hemmed for my shorter height. My hair will be swept up. My shoes—

Voices murmur outside the condo's door, the sound piercing my delightful daydream. I swing the telescope upward, not wanting to be caught using it. The snippets of conversation drift away.

I don't relax. If the telescope isn't positioned in the same way as it was last night, Cyndi will realize I've been using it. She'll tease me about being a fellow pervert, sharing the story, embellished for dramatic effect, with her stern, serious dad—or, worse, with Angel, that snobby friend of hers.

I'll die. It'll be worse than being the butt of jokes in high school because that ridicule was about my clothes and this will center on the part of my soul I've always kept hidden. It'll also be the truth, and I won't be able to deny it. I am a pervert.

I have to return the telescope to its original position. This is the only acceptable solution. I tap the metal tube.

Last night, my man-crazy roommate was giggling over the new guy in three-eleven north. The previous occupant was a gray-haired, bowtie-wearing tax auditor, his luxurious accommodations supplied by Nicolas. The most exciting thing he ever did was drink his tea on the balcony.

According to Cyndi, the new occupant is a delicious piece of man candy—tattooed, buff, and head-to-toe lickable. He was completing armcurls outside, and she enthusiastically counted his reps, oohing and aahing over his bulging biceps, calling to me to take a look.

I resisted that temptation, focusing on making macaroni and cheese for the two of us, the recipe snagged from the diner my mom works in. After we scarfed down dinner, Cyndi licking her plate clean, she left for the club and hasn't returned.

Three-eleven north is the mirror condo to ours. I

straighten the telescope. That position looks about right, but then, the imitation UGGs I bought in my second year of college looked about right also. The first time I wore the boots in the rain, the sheepskin fell apart, leaving me barefoot in Economics 201.

Unwilling to risk Cyndi's friendship on "about right," I gaze through the eyepiece. The view consists of rippling golden planes, almost like . . .

Tanned skin pulled over defined abs.

I blink. It can't be. I take another look. A perfect pearl of perspiration clings to a puckered scar. The drop elongates more and more, stretching, snapping. It trickles downward, navigating the swells and valleys of a man's honed torso.

No. I straighten. This is wrong. I shouldn't watch our sexy neighbor as he stands on his balcony. If anyone catches me . . .

Parts 1 and 2 available now!

An Excerpt from

WHATEVER IT TAKES
A Trust No One Novel
by Dixie Lee Brown

Assassin Alex Morgan will do anything to save
an innocent life—especially if it means rescuing
a child from a hell like the one she endured. But
going undercover as husband and wife, with
none other than the disarmingly sexy Detective
Nate Sanders, may be a little more togetherness
than she can handle. Nate's willing to face
anything if it means protecting Alex. She may
have been on her own once, but Nate has one
more mission: to stay by her side—forever.

What was Alex doing in that bar? She had to be following him. It was too much of a coincidence any other way. Nate nearly flinched when he replayed the image of her dropping Daniels and then turning on those goons getting ready to shoot up the bar. Shit! Was she suicidal along with everything else? Anger, tinged with dread, did a slow burn under his collar. He needed to know what motivated Alex Morgan . . . and he needed to know now.

He clenched his teeth, whipped his bike into an alley, and cut the engine. If she was bent on getting herself killed, there was no fucking way it was happening on his turf.

She dismounted, uncertainty in her expression. As soon as she stepped out of the way, he swung his leg over and got in her face. "Take it off." He pointed to the helmet.

Not waiting for her to remove it all the way, he started in. "What in the name of all that's holy were you thinking back there? You could have gotten yourself killed."

A sad smile swept her face and something in her eyes—a momentary hardening—gave him a clue to the answer he was fairly certain she'd never speak aloud. Ty had told him the highlights of her story. Joe had freed Alex from a life of slavery in a dark, dismal hole in Hong Kong. From the haunted look in her eyes, however, Nate would bet she hadn't completely dealt with the aftermath. His first impression had been more right than he wanted to admit. It was quite likely that she nursed a dangerous little death wish, and that's what had prompted her actions at the bar.

His anger receded, and a wave of protectiveness rolled over him, but he was powerless to take away the pain staring back at him. He could make a stab at shielding her from the world, but how could he stop the hell that raged inside this woman? Why did she matter so much to him? Hell, logic flew out the window a long time ago. He didn't know why—only that she *did*. With frustration driving him, he stepped closer, pushing her against the bike. Her moist lips drew his gaze, and an overwhelming desire to kiss her set fire to his blood.

She stiffened and wariness flooded her eyes.

He should have stopped there, but another step put him in contact with her, and he was burning with need. He pulled her closer and gently slid his fingers through her hair, then stroked his thumb across her bottom lip.

Her breath escaped in uneven gasps and a tiny bit of tongue appeared, sliding quickly over the lip he'd just touched. Fear, trepidation, longing paraded across her face. Ty's warning sounded in his ears again—she was dangerous, maybe even disturbed—but even if that was true, Nate wasn't sure it made any difference to him.

"Don't be afraid." *Shit!* Immediately, he regretted his words. This woman wasn't afraid of anything. Distrustful . . . yes. Afraid? He didn't even want to know what could scare her.

Her eyes softened and warmed, and she stepped into him, pressing her firm body against his. He caught her around the waist and aligned his hips to hers. Ignoring the words of caution in his head, he bent ever so slowly and covered her mouth with his. Softly caressing her lips and tasting her sweetness, he forgot for a moment that they stood in an alley in a questionable area of Portland, that he barely knew this woman, and that they'd just left the scene of a real-life nightmare.

He'd longed to kiss her since the first time they'd met. She'd insulted his car that day, and not even that had been enough to get his mind off her lips. Good timing or bad—kissing her and holding her in his arms was long overdue.

An Excerpt from

HARD TO HOLD ON TO
A Hard Ink Novella
by Laura Kaye

From *New York Times* and *USA Today* bestselling author Laura Kaye comes a hot, sexy novella to tie in with her Hard Ink series. When "Easy" meets Jenna, he has finally found someone to care for, and he will do anything to keep her safe.

As the black F150 truck shot through the night-darkened streets of one of Baltimore's grittiest neighborhoods, Edward Cantrell cradled the unconscious woman in his arms like she was the only thing tethering him to life. And right at this moment, she was.

Jenna Dean was bloodied and bruised after having been kidnapped by the worst sort of trash the day before, but she was still an incredibly beautiful woman. And saving her from the clutches of a known drug dealer and human trafficker was without question the most important thing he'd done in more than a year.

He should have felt happy—or at least happier—but those feelings were foreign countries for Easy. Had been for a long time.

Easy, for his initials: E.C. The nickname had been the brainchild years before of Shane McCallan, one of his Army Special Forces teammates, who now sat at the other end of the big back seat, wrapped so far around Jenna's older sister, Sara, that they might need the Jaws of Life to pull them apart. Not that Easy blamed them. When you walked through fire and somehow came out the other side in one piece, you gave thanks and held tight to the things that mattered.

Because too often, when shit got critical, the ones you loved didn't make it out the other side. And then you wished you'd given more thanks and held on harder before the fires ever started raging around you in the first place.

Easy would fucking know.

The pickup paused as a gate *whirr*ed out of the way, then the tires crunched over gravel and came to a rough stop. Easy lifted his gaze from Jenna's fire-red hair and too-pale face to find that they were home—or, at least, where he was calling home right now. Out his window, the redbrick industrial building housing Hard Ink Tattoo loomed in the darkness, punctuated here and there by the headlights of some of the Raven Riders bikers who'd helped Easy and his teammates rescue Jenna and take down the gangbangers who'd grabbed her.

Talk about strange bedfellows.

Five former Green Berets and twenty-odd members of an outlaw motorcycle club. Then again, maybe not so strange. Easy and his buddies had been drummed out of the Army under suspicious, other-than-honorable circumstances. Disgraced, dishonored, disowned. Didn't matter that his team had been seriously set up for a big fall. In the eyes of the US government and the world, the five of them weren't any better than the bikers they'd allied themselves with so that they'd have a fighting chance against the much bigger and better-armed Church gang. And, when you cut right down to it, maybe his guys weren't any better. After all, they'd gone total vigilante in their effort to clear their names, identify and take down their enemies, and clean up the collateral damage that occurred along the way.

Like Jenna.

"Easy? *Easy?* Hey, *E?*"

An Excerpt from

KISS ME, CAPTAIN
A French Kiss Novel
by *Gwen Jones*

In the fun and sexy follow-up to *Wanted: Wife,*
French billionaire and CEO of Mercier Shipping
Marcel Mercier puts his playboy lifestyle
on hold to handle a PR nightmare in the
US, but sparks fly when he meets the
passionate captain of his newest ship . . .

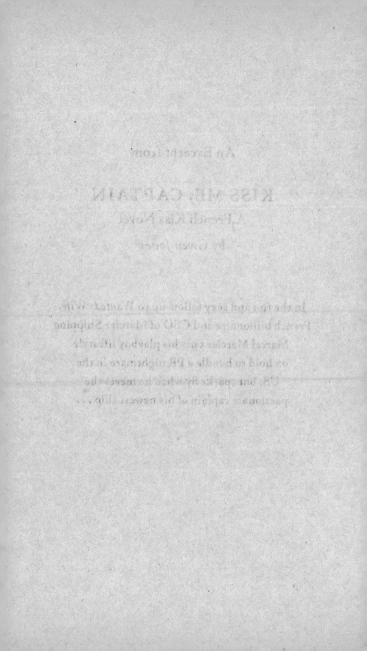

Penn's Landing Pier
Philadelphia
Independence Day, 5:32 AM

"Of course I realize he's your brother-in-law," Dani said, grinning most maliciously as she dragged the chains across the deck to the mainmast. "In fact I'm counting on it as my express delivery system." She wrapped a double length of chain around her waist. "My apologies for shamelessly exploiting you."

"Seriously?" Julie laughed. "Trust me, I'll try not to feel compromised."

"Like me," Dani said, her hair as red as the bloody blister of a sun rising over the Delaware. She yanked another length of chain around the mast. "But what can *I* do. I'm just a *woman*."

"And I'm just a media whore," Julie said. "And a bastard is a bastard is a bastard." She nodded to her cameraman, flexing her shoulders as she leveled her gaze into the lens. "How far would you go to save *your* job?"

Two days later
L'hôtel Croisette Beach
Cannes

P*ineapple*, Marcel Mercier deduced, drifting awake under the noonday sun. A woman's scent was always the first thing he noticed, as in the subtle fragrance of her soap, her perfumed pulse points, the lingering vestiges of her shampoo.

Mon Dieu. How he loved women.

"Marcel," he heard, feeling a silky leg slide against his own.

He opened his eyes to his *objet d'affection* for the past three days. "*Bébé . . .*" he growled, brushing his lips across hers as she curled into him.

"Marcel, *mon amour*," she cooed, fairly beaming with joy. "*Tu m'as fait tellement heureuse.*"

"What?" he said, nuzzling her neck. Her pineapple scent was driving him insane.

She slid her hand between his legs. "I *said* you've made me very happy." Then she smiled. No—*beamed*.

He froze, mid-nibble. Oh no. Oh *no*.

She kissed him, her eyes bright. "I don't care what Paris says—I'm wearing my *grand-mère's* Brussels lace to our wedding. You wouldn't mind, would you?"

He stared at her. Had he really gone and done what he swore he'd never do again? He really needed to lay off the absinthe cocktails. "Mirabel, I didn't mean to—"

"Why did you leave me last night?" she said, falling back against the chaise, her bare breasts heaving above the tiny triangle of her string bikini bottom. "You left so fast the maids are still scrubbing scorch marks from the carpet."

Merde. He really ought to get his *dard* registered as a lethal weapon. He affected an immediate blitheness. "I had to take a call," he said—his standard alibi—raking his gaze over her. She really was quite the babe. "I didn't want to wake you."

All at once she went to full-blown *en garde*, shoving her face into his. "*Really.* More like you couldn't wait to get away from me. And after last night? After what you asked me?" Her enormous breasts rose, fell, her gaze slicing into his. "You said . . . You. *Loved. Me.*"

Had he? *Christ.* He needed to diffuse this. So he switched gears, summoning all his powers of seduction. "Mirabel. *Chère.*" He smiled—lethally, he knew—cradling her chin as he nipped the corner of her mouth. "But that call turned into another, then three, and before you knew it . . ." He traced his finger over the bloom of her breasts and down into the sweet, sweet cavern between them, his tongue edging her lip until she shivered like an ingénue. "You know damn well there's only one way to wake a gorgeous girl like you."

"You should've come back," she said softly, a bit disarmed, though the edge still lingered in her voice. "You just should have." She barely breathed it.

"How, *bébé?*" He licked the hollow behind her ear, and when she jolted, Marcel nearly snickered in triumph. Watching women falling *for* him nearly outranked falling *into* them. "Should I have slipped under the door?" he said, feathering kisses across her jawline. "Or maybe climbed up the balcony, calling 'Juliet? Juliet?' "

She arched her neck and sighed, a deep blush staining her overripe breasts. Marcel fought a rush of disappointment.

Truly, they were all so predictable. A bit of adulatory stroking and it was like they performed on cue. She pressed against his chest as he tugged the bikini string at her hip, her mouth opening in a tiny gasp.

"Mar-*cel* . . ." she purred.

He sighed inwardly. It was almost *too* easy. And that was the scary part.